COLLECTED TALES

Fables and Parables in Search of a Moral

Geoffrey Grosshans

Collected Tales: Fables and Parables in Search of a Moral

By Geoffrey Grosshans

Published by:

The Stuffed Fabulist
Post Office Box 65262
Seattle, WA 98155-9262

www.stuffedfabulist.com

Logo by J. Savage

Grosshans, Geoffrey
Collected tales: Fables and parables in search of a moral / Geoffrey Grosshans.

ISBN-13: 978-0-9758917-9-7
ISBN-10: 0-9758917-9-0

Contains fables and parables on psychological, social, political, spiritual, and philosophical themes. The "moral" of each tale is left to the reader to decide.

For Nonglack, Kleigh, Ann, and my parents

"For poor is the mind that always uses the ideas of others and invents none of its own."

> --a passage from a 13th-century Latin text written on Hieronymus Bosch's drawing "The Wood has Ears, the Field Eyes" (1502–1505) and appearing in English translation in Stefan Fischer's *Hieronymus Bosch. The Complete Works* (2019)

Introduction

Once a wheel of Swiss cheese had a thought.

Not that having thoughts was unusual for cheese in general. In fact, so common was cheesy thinking in those days that it commanded a large portion of public discourse. And not simply in the homogenized, processed world of the popular press or the more pungent one of the blogosphere but also the moldy fromage so prized in civic debates, globe-trotting diplomacy, business and political ethics, military and security planning, supreme jurisprudence, medical and research integrity, doctrinal disputes, and so on and so forth.

The cheese was by no means an aberration, then, except in one respect. Its thinking had more than the usual number of holes in it. This fact didn't make coming up with an idea in the first place any more difficult than it was for those dominating the aforementioned concerns, but it did complicate efforts to hold onto that idea.

Beyond the usual process by which once-fresh ideas thicken and turn to curd after a while, the cheese had to contend with gaps so large that entire trains of thought might slip away into them and vanish utterly.

At such times, it would have to bridge the lacunas in its understanding or memory as best it could, often with mental stretches that were in themselves hard to sustain. It might drift off in the middle of important meetings, or even conversations, with an expression somewhere between distraction and impatience, and when it eventually returned to the matter at hand, it might do so with a rush of ideas that struck others as disconcerting at best and incoherent at worst.

Where did such ideas come from, they were tempted to ask? Few did, though, as the general desire was to avoid the ticklish situation of appearing to engage what could well be the first signs of mental decline, madness even. Best retain some measure of distance from such characters, most agreed, lest it be assumed one shared their strange new ways of thinking.

As for the cheese itself, the more the ideas that had formed its contact with others fell away into this hole or that hole, the less inclined it became to attempt spanning them. They weren't absolute voids, it discovered. And the time spent trying to find a way over or around them wasn't really defined by the success or failure to do so.

In fact, the holes couldn't be defined in such terms whatsoever since they turned out to have little to do with anything the cheese had formerly relied upon to make sense of its existence. They might appear empty of meaning, but in their depths, worlds rolled on one another at a pace that could not be slowed to the cheese's prior understanding.

To fall into one of these holes must be like falling into the forfeit of everything that made you feel comfortable and secure in what you thought you knew. What lay at the bottom? Was there a bottom? Or would you continue to fall, away from all that had seemed certain? And towards what? What new possibilities, unimagined before, might redefine the limits of awareness? Even to guess at what might be found in these hollows made the cheese wheel dizzy.

But perhaps that was how it should be. For why be endowed with holes in your thinking if you were afraid of what you might find there?

Contents

Aesop

Once the good citizens of Delphi decided they'd had enough of Aesop.

Who did this guy think he was, showing up every day to browbeat them with his little fables and then expecting to be thanked for it? The business of life was difficult enough without some prickly crank poking around in their affairs while holding his nose. Did he imagine they appreciated having their motives and accomplishments endlessly questioned?

"No, I don't imagine you appreciate that at all," Aesop replied.

"So what's the point?" the citizens asked in chorus.

"The point is for you yourselves to do the questioning."

"You think we don't already know how to do that?"

"As long as your questions lead you back to what you thought were the answers before posing them, you have no trouble."

"Maybe that's because we were right in the first place."

"Then why go through the charade of fake questions at all? You are like fools lost in a cave who mistake the loud echoes of their own confusion for the voices of rescue."

"Careful. We throw people off cliffs around here for saying less than that."

"So I've heard."

"Stick to children's stories, then, and leave the ways of the world to those who understand them better."

"What children's stories? What ways of the world? Are you sure you know the difference?"

"Do you?"

"Sometimes I wonder. I watch you go about your lives as if wishing they were simple games of make-believe. As if anytime you're not happy with the results, you can rewrite the rules of the game until things turn out just the way you want them to."

"Aren't you the one, Aesop, who mixes up make-believe and life? You should listen to those of us who honor the Delphian oracle and can reason these things out instead of presuming to lecture us."

"You consider yourselves Apollonian adepts at reason, do you? Don't make me laugh. At most you simply dress up superstition and prejudice in a disguise

1

so thin it couldn't deceive anybody but you yourselves."

"That's outrageous!"

"Absolutely outrageous! Haven't we heard enough?"

"What are we waiting for?"

"Throw him off the cliff!"

"Why?" demanded Aesop. "For saying you wouldn't know the God of Light's true mind if you spent a lifetime at his temple sniffing fumes from the earth? Or the other guide you follow, Dionysus, the bringer of orgiastic madness? You're so certain you understand both of them, reason's deity and the god of the irrational, that your smug self-assurance wouldn't be shaken even if they sat right here and gambled for your wits, winner take all."

"Stop talking rubbish. We're not the ones palming off dark tales as if they're gems of wisdom."

"What's that supposed to mean?"

"Oh, thin-skinned are we now? You're quite happy to chide others, but being on the receiving end of a little criticism is something else, is it?"

"What's wrong with my tales?"

"They should be less negative and more inspirational, that's what."

"Inspirational?"

"Yes, with more examples of stirring behavior and wholesome sentiment, not filling the minds of impressionable youth with doubts and slanders."

"And disdain for their elders, Aesop!"

"You really think I'm talking to children? I'm talking to you!"

"Your mind's too warped for your own good or anybody else's. Too pessimistic by a long shot. How can you expect people to listen when you lay into them right and left without distinction?"

"None of you should think you're above being laid into whenever you deserve it. Besides, it's not my role to tell you what you want to hear or to encourage soggy good feelings. I'm here with a very different message. And how could anyone be 'too pessimistic,' I'd like to know, and still keep trying to get through to you?"

"But you do care if we laugh and take what you say to heart, presumably."

"Of course I care if you take it to heart, though it's all the same to me whether you laugh or curse or cry while doing so. There are plenty of hacks around who'd be more than willing to give you heroic characters and inspiring stories and all the happy endings you could stomach. I'm giving you yourselves, happy or not."

2

"Quite frankly, you can save your breath on that count. We just don't get your stuff, see?"

"Why listen to any more of his nonsense? Take him to the cliff and be done with it!"

In the end, the good citizens of Delphi did exactly that. Or so the story goes.

The Amoeba

Once an amoeba scheduled an appointment with a psychotherapist.

It did so with great reluctance and only after repeated urgings from friends who found its behavior increasingly difficult to explain. What concerned these friends was that the amoeba was acting in an erratic, unbalanced manner, continually changing as though at the mercy of multiple personalities.

The amoeba explained all of this soon after entering the therapist's office, saying it didn't think it should be there but that it wanted to do what it could to get beyond the misunderstandings.

"What do you think is the cause of those misunderstandings?" the therapist asked.

"I don't know," the amoeba answered. "I'm just trying to live my life as best I can."

"How do you see that life?"

"As we all see our lives, I would hope."

"And how do we all see our lives, in your opinion?"

"Why, with infinite awe, I assume," the amoeba responded with a note of puzzlement.

"And what does 'infinite awe' mean to you, exactly?"

"I guess it would mean something like believing that life has no confines."

"Do you think life should have no confines?"

"Naturally."

"Very interesting. Can you tell me a little more about that?"

"What's there to tell? Each day, my life takes a new form, sometimes many new forms. I feel my life flowing this way and that in constant change. I feel it always evolving, never standing still. Doesn't that make sense?"

"Does it make sense to you? That's the important question."

"Honestly, I've never asked myself whether it made sense or not. It just seemed to be a law of the universe, so far as I could tell. Life goes on; I go on.

3

Life takes a thousand shapes; I take a thousand shapes. Life is protean; I am protean. What else should it or I be?"

"You say 'protean'; is there a special meaning in that word for you?"

"No. It's like saying 'air' or 'water.' Both of them are just there, aren't they? Regardless of what meaning anybody might want to see in them."

"And what meaning do you see in them?"

"None," the amoeba answered with a tone of growing vexation. "I see them as part of the same thing I see in myself, that's all. The same limitless flux of life."

"Do you think that should be the case or not?"

"What do you mean?"

"I mean," the therapist leaned forward to ask, "do you ever think this inability to define limits and boundaries, to recognize the line where you end and the rest of life begins, might be part of the problem?"

"Problem?!"

The Angel of Death

Once the Angel of Death gave an airline's champagne service a pass.

Slouched in a first-class seat on the nonstop flight to his next destination, the Angel of Death might have been expected to feel quite satisfied with his performance in the most recent disaster. Not for a long time had he brought destruction on so many and struck with such force that the message being delivered to survivors must be unmistakable. And yet, the enormity of the latest mission had stunned and depressed him. Even him.

How many more of these errands would he be sent on, the Angel of Death wondered? How often would he have to sweep away countless souls to impress upon believers the value of their faith? When would the number of dead be enough to guarantee that? A hundred thousand in a single day? Two hundred thousand? Half a million? More? When would one death more become one too many?

The senior flight attendant, Sonny Pangloss, was just starting his round of champagne service for passengers traveling first-class when he noticed something was bothering the Angel of Death. "Can I pour you a bit of the bubbly?" Sonny asked with a practiced smile, filling a champagne flute out of habit without waiting for a reply. "Forgive me for saying so, but you look a wee bit down. Is there any way I can help improve your onboard experience?"

"I doubt it."

"You just never know. Sometimes having a sympathetic ear is all that's really needed to weather even the worst of life's little storms. Everything is actually for the best in this world, you come to realize."

"Is it?"

"I'm absolutely convinced of it. None of us is asked to bear a burden that's too great for us. What sense would there be in that?"

The only response from the Angel of Death to this assertion was a cold stare.

Sonny set the champagne bottle down and assumed as reassuring a tone as he could. "We must assume, you see, that there is a good reason for any trial or tribulation we experience. One that can explain even the inexplicable. In other words, there is an unseen plan to our lives that we must believe fits in with some higher purpose, even if we can't quite grasp this plan or purpose."

"You never find yourself questioning that?"

"Never. I've been through a lot personally, I can tell you, but I always keep my sunny, optimistic outlook and my belief that things must be as they are because a grand design guides all our lives and every hair on our heads is counted in that grand design. Nothing can't be explained in this way."

"Even the mass death of the innocent?" the Angel asked.

"Yes."

"Are you serious?"

"Couldn't be more serious. Even things as shocking as the slaughter of the innocent or plagues or global pandemics or hundreds of thousands crushed to death in an earthquake or hundreds of thousands drowned by a tsunami must be part of the grand design somehow, or else it wouldn't happen, would it? And if it is part of that design, by definition it can't be unjustified, even if our limited understanding fails to see any justice in it. So personal misfortunes actually add to the greater good of all humanity in unfolding the overall plan for this best of all possible worlds."

"How so?"

"Why, just think of the outpouring of generosity these disasters bring in their wake, the unlooked-for opportunity the rest of us are given to show what we find most admirable in ourselves. Then I believe you'll have to agree even the loss of entire communities, tragic as it might seem, must be an impetus for an inspiring display of virtuous outreach by the rest of us in response. Look at it as a kind of test of the strength of our spirit. It logically follows, then, that the more misfortune and misery there is in the world, the more chance we have to play our noble part in the overall plan. Without disasters, whether natural or man-made, none of this could take place. Just repeat that to yourself whenever you're a wee bit down or unsure of yourself, and I guarantee you'll be feeling more upbeat again in no time."

These and many other assurances that even the most devastating catastrophe was ultimately for the greater good of humankind if viewed properly rolled off the tongue of Sonny Pangloss as he did what he could to cheer up the Angel of Death.

While the latter continued to stare silently at the untouched champagne.

The Ant and the Grasshopper

Once an ant and a grasshopper crossed paths after being out of touch for years.

They hadn't seen each other since graduating from university together. When they unexpectedly met again, the ant was headed for an important corporate meeting, while the grasshopper was returning from "afar." The ant was wearing a three-piece suit with a company tie clasp. The grasshopper had on a tattered straw hat and generally looked as though it was coming apart at the seams itself.

After their initial surprise had worn off, the two asked each other, almost in unison, "What have you been up to all this time?" The ant told of having been unable for years to find steady employment after earning a degree in Humanities. It had moved from one job to another, without ever feeling secure in any of them. Regardless of its industry and dedication, the ant invariably found its efforts meant little when a business went through restructuring or downsizing. The ant was always among the first to be let go.

The grasshopper, on the other hand, told of a wildly successful career following graduation in Finance. At a time when the markets were posting new highs every session, lucrative investments and bonuses in the millions piled up at such a rate that the grasshopper couldn't spend the money fast enough. Success became an embarrassment and then merely tedious. The grasshopper wearied of its penthouse, its Ferrari and its chauffeured Rolls-Royce, multi-martini lunches, power ties, exclusive club memberships—the lot. One day it sold everything it owned and didn't even bother to collect the profits. Instead, it booked the first available plane ticket to anywhere and vanished.

At about the same time, the ant finally and unexpectedly got the break it had been waiting for. Despondent over its lack of prospects, it had entered a jingle-writing contest for an insurance company on a whim and won. Sensing that it might have found its long-sought road to security at last, the ant threw itself into advancing the interests of its employer and had done quite well, all considered. The mortgage on its house had only another nine years to go, its children were in good schools, and it was contributing faithfully to both a 401(k) plan and an IRA with an eye to retirement decades in the future.

When the two former classmates finished recounting their tales, they looked one another over with a mixture of bemusement and relief. Each thought of the turn the other's life had taken and said to itself, "There but for the grace of God, go I." The ant wondered what the grasshopper would do when old age came and it realized it had frittered everything away. The grasshopper wondered what the ant had done with the summer of its life.

Following their chance meeting, the ant and the grasshopper went their separate ways and never set eyes on each other again. As it turned out, they both died on the same day years later. The one succumbed to a heart attack at its desk, diligently working away at the sales pitch for a new insurance plan. While the other also died of a heart attack, on the Riviera, surrounded by golden grasshopper girls.

The Ape

Once an ape answered the casting call for a Hollywood blockbuster.

The part it was auditioning for, this ape was told by the head of casting, required great versatility. It would have to portray a wide range of characteristics, from utter stupidity to full-on sly treachery. Between these two extremes there'd be a need to portray all manner of mental unbalance, sexual threat, moral turpitude, laughable ineptitude, and whatever else movie audiences traditionally demanded and script writers provided. In that sense, the part could be seen as a very rich one, perhaps Academy Award caliber, and might lead to a string of similar roles in the future.

"But what's my motivation?" the ape asked the head of casting. "I need to know why I'd behave in any of these ways."

"Because our human hero needs a convincing foe, that's why. It's sort of a timeless struggle kind of flick for PG-13 audiences, know what I mean?"

"That's my motivation, to be a fall guy for human superiority in a PG-13 world?"

"Well, if that's how you want to put it, the answer is 'yes.' But there's plenty of time before the final showdown and salvation of the planet for plot complications and for the outcome to be in doubt. Plenty of dramatic tension when it looks like you're in control of human destiny."

"In control of human destiny? I still don't see what my motivation would be for anything you've mentioned."

"Listen, just think of yourself as the opposite of the hero you're up against and everything'll go just fine. Or if that doesn't work for you, then think of yourself as enough like the hero that you could be related almost, but instead you're some kind of genetic throwback who's leading the forces of cataclysmic ruin."

"Why would I want to lead the forces of cataclysmic ruin, whatever those might be?"

"How can I put this any more clearly for you? Because it's in the script, that's why. Besides, nobody can fight box-office trends, and the trend right now is a return to core beliefs and good old-fashioned storytelling. That's what this whole human-v-beast concept is about, in case you hadn't noticed. Same thing's true for saving the world from the threat of aliens or robots or zombies or suicidal terrorists or comic book villains et cetera et cetera et cetera. Special effects alone won't cut it anymore if you don't have a meaningful storyline. And you're the meaningful storyline here, the great threat to humanity from sub-species yesterday, today, and tomorrow, see? Now, do you want the part or don't you?"

"I was hoping for something a bit more challenging."

"Like what? Hamlet? Get real!" the head of casting laughed while turning to shout through the office door, "Send in the next ape from central casting!"

The Armadillo

Once an armadillo came across a tattered tabloid with the headline "Psychic Warns, World To End!!!"

"I knew it," the armadillo muttered to itself. "The world's definitely going to end this time." It turned to the page indicated for more information about the coming cataclysm but found few details.

The armadillo wasn't surprised by the lack of specifics about the coming end of the world, even though it had long been convinced the sky wasn't simply about to fall but may already have fallen. The absence of facts only proved that the truth was being withheld in a far-reaching conspiracy of some sort or other.

You didn't have to be a rocket scientist to see the planet was at the mercy of sinister forces, most of which appeared to have the armadillo itself as their primary target. Black holes, terrorist plots, melting icecaps, extraterrestrials in the Nevada desert, 18-wheelers barreling down the Interstate at night with the armadillo in their high beams, each one could be found in the prophecies of Nostradamus if you just know what you're looking for.

The universe was definitely out to do it harm, in the armadillo's thinking. How else could all these coincidences be explained except as parts of an intergalactic conspiracy by aliens to abduct the armadillo and then probe every last one of its bodily orifices? It took no thinking at all to see where that would all end.

Fortunately, the armadillo had one great advantage that its numberless tormentors didn't: armor plates.

"Thank the Lord I've got them to protect me from the worst that's coming," it said under its breath to avoid being heard by whatever agents of the "deep state" might currently be out and about.

Sooner or later, the planets were going to line up, though, and then you could bet the moment of reckoning wouldn't be postponed again. Woe be to any who were not ready when it finally did come, when the chosen few were hoisted beyond the clouds in the Rapture, while the rest stood around gnashing their teeth amid all the scattered shoes and mismatched socks left behind.

Just at that moment the armadillo felt a light tap on its armor and jerked itself into a trembling ball. Another tap came, and then a third. Curled up tight, it could dimly make out a drop of something gather on the edge of its hindmost plate, quiver for a moment, and then fall with a little yellow splash on the tip of its nose.

"The Flood!" it cried out. "The Flood!!"

The Badger

Once a badger suffered from irritable brain syndrome.

For years, life had rubbed this badger the wrong way for some reason, and not a day passed without the arrival of an annoyance, great or small, that

9

threatened to make its head explode. Without hefty doses of painkillers, the badger didn't know how it would have been able to tolerate the constant aggravation life presented.

But that wasn't all. The badger had another problem. Its very livelihood depended upon cataloging its grievances against the world through gruff snarls, snorts, and growls on a syndicated broadcast listened to by a large audience of followers eager to listen for hours on end to the badger's non-stop snarls, snorts, and growls.

The badger's predicament was obvious. It needed a constant stream of distress to hold the attention of its far-flung listeners, but not so much as to begin screaming incoherently. Often, however, this line would be crossed when the pain simply grew too severe and the badger gave vent to a particularly shrill tirade aimed at whatever it declared to be the chief source of its torment that day. Most of these outbursts began with a sound like the letter "L" for reasons not well understood.

Only when hour after hour of invective threatened to end in hyperventilation would the badger down a pawful of pills and settle into a more low-keyed, often slurred delivery. Listeners didn't seem to care about the change, or perhaps simply didn't notice it, and continued to follow the badger's repertoire of curmudgeon gripes regardless of whether it howled them out or mumbled nonsensically.

There was the option of professional treatment for all of this, of course, but the badger derided those with any expertise regarding its condition as "quacks" and clung instead to self-medication, keeping two bottles of "little helpers" near it at all times: one filled with whatever sent it into paroxysms of rage and the other with the antidote of sense-dulling numbness.

Like Alice, with her drinks, cakes, and mushroom munching, all the badger needed to do was reach for the bottle that would produce the desired effect at any given moment.

It just had to keep straight which bottle was which, as hard as that might prove for a badger in high growl.

The Bald Eagle

Once a bald eagle found itself turned into a parade blimp.

Anyone who had ever seen an eagle glide along high cliffs or sweep low over still water wouldn't have recognized the great bird. Its mighty wings that once worked magic with the wind had been rendered lifeless and stiff. Rather than stretching out in full embrace of the sky, they looked as though the eagle had been shot and then nailed up like a trophy against the blue. Its snowy head feathers now glittered with a garish, metallic, sprayed-on sheen, while the rest of its plumage was nearly invisible beneath a thick layer of corporate logos announcing proud blimp sponsors.

What need did the eagle have for wings or feathers in its current state, though, since it was being towed down the parade route on taut lines by an assembly of clowns decked out in patriotic garb? The clowns were preceded and followed by high-stepping cheerleader squads, while behind the last of these squads came ranks of politicians marching shoulder to shoulder and sidewalk to sidewalk, their knees jerking up and down in practiced unison. And what need did the eagle still have for its famously sharp vision either, when all it could see for blocks and blocks were the bobbing butts of cartoon-character blimps that parade planners had for some reason decided should precede it?

Yet just when it seemed the eagle might have to spend the rest of its days being pulled around the country from crowded avenues to small-town kiddie fairs, a startling incident took place. Although there were any number of contingency plans for accidental leaks, terrorist attacks, liability claims if it flopped down on the crowd, and so forth, nobody seemed to have anticipated what actually occurred: the eagle took off.

A sudden updraft had caught it, snapping lines right and left and pulling many of the clowns (together with those cheerleaders and politicians who had instinctively clutched at any loose tethers) kicking and screaming for all they were worth into thin air. The crowd, electrified by the wild gyrations above them, turned their smartphones skyward with thoughts of uploading video clips of the scene to social media or sending snaps to one of the many "Disasters of the Year in Living Color" exhibitions so popular of late.

As it sailed upward through the walled canyons of the city, the eagle looked into the windows of offices and apartments it was passing and saw rows of faces staring back in surprise, consternation, or downright horror. Clearly, they were witnessing something that none of the promotional lead-up to the parade had readied them for. The danger of this kind of mishap simply hadn't occurred to anyone in a position of responsibility, it would appear.

But was it the cartoonish blimp of a proud eagle appalled at what had happened to it that caused the expressions of dismay now crowding all the windows or was it the sight of all those clowns and cheerleaders and politicians clinging to the ends of their tethers as if their very lives depended on it?

The Barnacle

Once a barnacle weighed the moral pros and cons of letting go.

It was comforting to have the security of a stable moral life by clinging fast to one's pier. Amid all the tides that came and went, an anchored existence was a blessing increasingly few could claim. Every day, the barnacle watched those less resolute than itself lose whatever ethical footing they'd managed to gain in life. Here today and gone tomorrow, "the dust of the sea" they might be judged. Given the same opportunities as itself for moral certainty, they just must not have tried hard enough, the barnacle was convinced. The waters churning around the pilings were doubtless filling up with failures of character like these, replaced as soon as they'd disappeared by a new massing of the morally shiftless, to be followed in their own turn by the same again.

And yet within the barnacle's conviction about all this lay an unsettling perplexity. In a word, where had all these moral failures eventually gone? And without a trace. To remain "at one's post to the bitter end" was the fulfillment of an honorable life's command, the equivalent of standing shoulder to shoulder at Thermopylae—on a barnacle scale, of course. Such dedication served as a safeguard against every self-doubt that might pull at one as wave after wave crashed over the pier in a storm and fell back again into the ruleless sea. No doubt about it, the certainty of a solid commitment straight through to the last gave one a definite edge in righteousness when considered this way. An unshakable sense of being virtue's long-bow archer at the Battle of Agincourt, as it were, that even a battered barnacle could hold to and feel proud of itself for doing so.

But simply to vanish without a trace, now that was another matter entirely. Knowing nothing at all about the fates of those who'd been swept away over the years, the barnacle cast its mind about for answers. They could be anywhere. Doing absolutely anything. Maybe their fortunes had taken a turn for the better. Maybe they'd found a place of second chances and reinvented themselves there, putting behind them the memory of once losing their grip on solid convictions. Or maybe not. They might just as easily have slipped further into the depths. Into utter darkness that surpassed the barnacle's ability to fathom as a life worth living. But didn't the fact that nothing was ruled out in a second chance mean all possibilities remained? And if all possibilities remained, if possibilities beyond calculation still existed, then there must be just as many ways of living and just as many arguments for adopting one or even countless alternatives to the certainties of the pier. In that case, what confidence could you have about the virtues of the one-and-only life you'd settled on for yourself—or, for that matter, about being right in holding firm to it through every trial you met with?

The barnacle was growing dizzy from the implications of such uncertainty. Was it conceivable that a meaningful existence might not actually require a firm anchor of some sort? Might not require any anchor at all? If you could count on there always being a second chance to reestablish yourself in a new place, or in new places over and over again, why worry about the consequences of a failure to hold firm from the start? And if you didn't fear such failure, how could you be counted on never to falter in your adherence to what truly mattered in a barnacle's life: resisting the force of the waves at all costs? When moral certainty and the lure of the unknown pulled you in different directions with equal force, life decisions posed a true dilemma for any self-respecting barnacle, no denying that.

Better to stay put, then, and diligently continue hardening your resolve against the slightest self-doubt? Yet what if . . . ?

The Bear

Once a bear attracted quite a following in faith-based wrestling.

It wasn't a case of a bear's retiring from the ring and then taking up religion, as occasionally happens. This one was still at the height of its career. No, this bear was simply the first to recognize a role for wrestling in big-time religion.

It all began one night in a sold-out arena, after the bear, cheered on by screaming fans, had squeezed an opponent's ribs until they gave way. The bear looked out into the spotlight-threaded darkness as it dropped its limp foe and had an epiphany.

These multitudes hungered for something, it realized. That was why they showed up night after night, city after city. They gathered together in search of something to believe in and dedicate themselves to.

And then the bear had its second epiphany of the night. What the screaming crowd really sought was something to hold onto in confusing times. Outside the ropes, in the chaotic world of life's uncertainties, telling right from wrong was tricky. But inside the ropes, the smash-mouth struggle between good and evil was easier to follow. Seized with this recognition, the bear stepped over its now unconscious opponent, grabbed the ringside announcer's microphone, and began to shout in all directions.

"Listen to me! Listen to me, all of you out there! I know what you're looking for! I know what you need!"

Members of the crowd rose to their feet as one, uncertain what to expect but ready for anything.

"You want the Match of Matches! You want the Final Showdown!"

The crowd burst into deafening agreement.

Drawing in a deep breath, the bear then turned to the nearest television camera and issued the biggest challenge of its career: "If you're out there, Prince of Darkness . . . if you're out there . . . listen up!"

The crowd went wild. Shouts of "Prince of Darkness! Prince of Darkness!" boomed through the air.

"Oh, you can call yourself 'The Wily One,' or you can call yourself 'The Archfiend,' and you may think you can't be whupped," the bear continued. "But I got news for ya! Armageddon's comin'!"

"Armageddon's comin'! Armageddon's comin'! Bring it on! Bring it on!"

"I dare you to meet me, no holds barred, next month at 'Doomsday in Dallas'!"

"Doomsday! Doomsday!" The chant rang around the arena as the bear, pumping its paws defiantly overhead, stalked down the aisle to the showers.

Later, however, as "Doomsday in Dallas" approached with no response from the Prince of Darkness, the bear began to wonder if it should have put a little more oomph into the challenge. Was it a bit flat? It sounded good each night the bear repeated it in venues large and small, but were the Armageddon taunts strong enough to draw the Devil out? What if he didn't show up?

Conversely, what if the Devil did show up but refused to go down for the count? It would be absolutely in character for Satan not to take a choreographed fall. Then again, suppose he did take the fall but then walked away without signing up for the expected pay-per-view rematch? And what would that do to ticket sales and crowd numbers thereafter? How do you hold your audience share after Doomsday's come and gone without anything happening?

This was serious. Religious wrestling, the bear realized, needed the Devil far more than the Devil needed it.

The Beast-Within

Once a beast-within spent a great deal of time licking its wounds.

That wasn't surprising, for it had suffered one wound after another over the years. The life of a beast-within struck it at times like a walk through a bramble patch. On all sides were sharp threats that tore at the skin and brought fresh pain to the surface.

This pain the beast-within nursed in private for the most part. Experience had taught it there were fewer complications that way, at least in one's day-to-day contacts with the outside world. You had to be careful not to reveal too much of the inner you or to expect too much sympathy from others. They had their own secrets to shield from sight.

The beast-within could tell this was the case as it rode the 6:15 express into the city each morning. All of the seats were occupied by outwardly self-confident riders reading their newspapers or checking their email accounts before they reached their destinations. To look at them, you'd never guess they'd spent the night struggling with their own beast-within or were still trying to hide the telltale evidence of that struggle before the train came to a stop.

Strange, that after all this time, people still fought so hard to vanquish or simply repudiate the faithful companion that had stood by them through thick and thin and had in return received nothing but ingratitude.

Their beast-within was always there when they needed its help with some detour from the path of virtue, some depravity or cruelty or betrayal that might have to be denied or explained away later. As recognition of that devotion, it only asked for the merest sign of thankfulness.

Yet what did it actually receive? Whenever things went wrong, who got the sticks and stones? Instead of doing the right thing, instead of standing by their beast-within and taking on at least part of the blame, those who'd been more than happy to benefit from its selfless fidelity invariably sought to distance themselves from it.

They turned away as from a pariah, cursing it and accusing it of having tricked them into "regrettable lapses." Soon they'd convinced themselves it was their beast-within that was to blame for every misstep they'd ever made. Casting the full guilt upon it, they sought forgiveness for themselves alone, pledging to shun it forevermore. Was it any surprise then that their beast-within felt betrayed and lashed back in aggrieved self-defense? In its view, it had only acted out of obedience to their deepest desires.

15

The results of this painful strife were predictable. The commuter train was full of them: seemingly composed, lifetime pass holders who were inwardly counting the wounds they'd given and received, feeling themselves deeply wronged and wishing they could creep away somewhere to lick clean the worst of what they'd suffered.

For it was, without doubt, a wound-licking age.

The Beavers

Once a number of beavers set out to build a dam.

"What else?" one might ask. Building dams is what beavers do. Not to build a dam would be to deny a beaver's very reason for being.

Indeed, for as long as they could remember, beavers had industriously set about blocking even the slightest of steams with a dam designed to meet both their immediate and long-term needs. "Without a dam, where would we be?" was the thought of every beaver that ever gazed with satisfaction upon the still waters behind a barrier of expertly placed logs and mud.

An unexpected problem arose, however, when two colonies of beavers wanted to dam the same stream.

Up until then, beavers had worked together to reach their mutual goals. There may have been disagreements about the best placement of a dam or about exactly which trees should be felled to build it and where to find the best mud, but eventually all agreed that without some compromise, without a little give and take, no dam would get built.

In light of this history of cooperation, it was surprising that the disagreement over building two dams became as heated as it did. Instead of leading to compromise, the dispute produced only a hardening division between the two colonies, each of them convinced there wasn't enough water in the stream for more than one dam.

Soon, amid growing rancor and suspicion, neither side was speaking to the other. Instead, both groups began attempting to build their own dam in secret. These efforts led to nothing, of course, for how can the work of beavers remain secret for long? The product of labors by one side would quickly be discovered and chewed to bits by the other, while the same was true in return.

What these secretive exertions did produce, however, was a series of new disagreements within the two groups. Members of each side rapidly divided into smaller subgroups as they argued over how their dam was to be built and how the water in the stream could best serve their needs.

As a result, not only did these new factions work on the secret dam for their side and tore down the secret dam of the other side but they also began throwing up smaller dams and defending these against opposing factions among their own allies. Tempers flared anew, and shrill exchanges of "Whose side are you on, anyway?" whistled through the air. What this fierce wrangling produced looked more like slapdash, leaky logjams than genuine dams.

When the dwindling water behind these hasty barriers became impossible to ignore, as it inevitably did, even the subgroups broke up. It was now every beaver for itself. "If you can't see it my way, I'll go it alone!" rang out near and far. "Ditto!" was the equally common response.

And in no time whatsoever, where once a generous stream wove through the forest, promising life and comfort to every beaver around, nothing remained but a jumble of stick-and-mud piles.

All quite small and all equally dry.

The Bedbug

Once a bedbug thought it had "found god."

Admittedly, the bedbug, being very small, was only hazarding a guess about the colossal form that rolled and sweated and scratched itself night after night in the sheets they shared. But since it was so much bigger than the bedbug, how could it be anything else?

Whatever this enormous being was, it certainly seemed generous, for it gave every indication of knowing exactly when the bedbug was most in need of it. Absent for long periods of time, it would suddenly reappear just when the bedbug had grown so weak with waiting that it feared the worst.

And when the bedbug's god finally did return, the long absence was quickly forgotten in thankful rejoicing. In no time at all, a renewed sense of well-being filled the bedbug, replacing its recent anxiety with elation. "Mine! Mine! This god is mine all mine alone!" it would repeat for hours on end, counting itself blessed above all other bedbugs on earth.

Satisfied with its lot once more, freed from worries about mere survival, the bedbug had time to reflect further on the nature of its benefactor. What exactly was this extraordinary being that appeared and disappeared at will and without whom the bedbug wondered what would become of its own existence really like? Where did it go when it disappeared, or was it actually still around even when it seemed to be absent, watching the bedbug languish in wait? And how could its evident generosity to the bedbug be reconciled with the fact that often it would seize a neighboring bug with lightning quickness and squash it flat?

In truth, the bedbug had no way of grasping the real nature of the colossus it had come to depend upon. The difference in size was simply too great; the bedbug was as nothing by comparison. That was the extent of what it thought it knew for certain. The rest was pure speculation. The only way the bedbug found to conceive of this great being, the only way to give it some imagined form as a focus for the bedbug's humble gratitude, was to picture the mysterious benefactor in its own image: as an immense, all-powerful version of itself.

Even this wasn't easy to manage, though, especially on those occasions when the great being would return after a long absence accompanied by a second great being, with whom it rolled about in the bed like booming thunder. On these occasions, the bedbug just had to accept that some things were beyond its comprehending. The safest course to take in the face of the inexplicable was simply to count your blessings wherever you could find them.

And on that basis, weren't two gods even better than one?

The Big Lie

Once a Big Lie considered demanding equal time.

Just how many small lies should the world be expected to swallow, the Big Lie wondered? They seemed to be everywhere, these laughable attempts to mislead. Not that such piddling falsehoods amounted to much more than a nuisance when taken singly, but since one lie typically led to another, in time the thickening odor of mendacity could pose a genuine public danger, from isolated gagging in private to bouts of mass retching that affected entire swaths of an unsuspecting population.

You could hardly draw breath anymore without choking on some truly trifling pretense or other. To say nothing of the puffed-up umbrage directed at fact checkers who'd caught out patently inept liars: total amateurs whose only refuge when trapped in some clumsy deceit was to claim they were the victim of a devious plot to take their every word "out of context."

In short, there was a surplus of dime-a-dozen lies but few real whoppers anymore. Soon people might not even be able to tell the difference, the Big Lie feared, and if things reached such a pass, wouldn't full-blown deception be cheapened and lose its claim to serious consideration? What a state of affairs that would present.

No, the time had clearly come for a return to lies with the power to make one shudder rather than simply feel embarrassed by their carnival-barker presumption of public gullibility. Lies so great that what seemed to be half of the citizenry might go red in the face shouting rabid support for them. And here the Big Lie was ready, willing, and able to step forward and restore faith in any number of falsehoods that had lost their edge and thus no longer had the potential to fool even some of the people all of the time.

But where to begin? Therein lay precisely the uncertainty that called for the overwhelming strength only a Big Lie could muster. Any miscalculation—the slightest mismatch between the need for fabrication and the fabrication itself—could spell failure, possibly on the oft-cited "unprecedented scale."

Because the distinction between true fake and false fake could be difficult to identify with certainty, due care must be taken. The lines separating 1) internet hucksterism and lies so trivial they make even petty thieves blush from 2) voice-over TV adverts implying in soporific tones that a 30-second list of wonder-drug side effects that ends with "rarely resulting in death" is no cause for alarm from 3) the latest solemn pledges before yet another congressional committee that the stock market always has the nation's interests at heart from 4) the truly dreary spectacle of "down-home" political guys with their sleeves rolled up claiming "I'm just here to carry out the people's business" as they run through a litany of equivocations and justifications in voices ranging from snide whines to what resembles barely controlled acid reflux from 5) the type of head-of-state bombast that leads people to demonize everybody else in their nation and nations to take swings at one another like thugs in the dark—these and countless additional lines of separation, once blurred, might never again be redrawn! Were the consequences of such a dire possibility not obvious?

They were to the Big Lie as it weighed whether it should press for equal time immediately or wait until all those who'd come to rely on penny-ante shams and mere slight-of-mind dishonesty no longer found in these the answer to their needs and were ready to bow their heads and bend their knees in pledging their blind fealty to the real thing once again: the truly monstrous lie.

It had happened in the past, hadn't it, even within recent memory? So why couldn't it happen again?

19

The Bloodhound

Once a bloodhound suddenly lost its sense of smell.

Just like that, all of the scent-trapping folds around the bloodhound's face ceased to pass along to its nose any of the familiar odors that had guided it unerringly through the world until then.

The resulting disorientation proved as severe as it was sudden. Not that the bloodhound plowed directly into the side of the hound next to it and then careened back across into the one on the other side. It at least retained the presence of mind to continue swinging its head left and right and moving forward at a pace that might have betrayed hesitation to the alert eye but which, with every other nose pressed to the ground, went unnoticed by its companions in the pack.

Fortunately they hadn't located what they'd been sent out to track down, the bloodhound sighed to itself once the search had been called off for the day. Imagine the embarrassment of possibly stepping right over the object of the pack's pursuit while its mates stopped baying and looked at it quizzically! Then there'd have been no hiding its failure to carry on as expected, and once failure was confirmed, no saving itself from being sent to some animal shelter of last resort, or worse.

What an appalling thought! As appalling as the signal that would inevitably be sent to the entire search team that one among them now lacked the defining quality that made a bloodhound a bloodhound. To be robbed of your identity in such an abrupt and total manner must leave you at an absolute loss for how to fill the hole left in your psyche. And the more you strained to think of a way, the larger the hole would likely become, until all confidence that you'd even existed wafted away!

In growing panic now, the bloodhound tried to resurrect from memory its lost sense of smell in hopes that when a sufficient number of scents had been recalled, they'd somehow close any gap in its self-awareness and allow it to start over again from a point in time before this disaster had befallen it.

Try as it might, though, the bloodhound failed to retrieve a single one of the scents it was sure must have filled its nose in the moments leading up to the fateful one. Confronted with such baffling olfactory amnesia, it couldn't even be sure there had in fact been scents in its world to smell, although the idea that there wouldn't have been struck the bloodhound as preposterous—equal to claiming a dead body wouldn't signal its decay far and wide or that malefactors on the run didn't betray themselves in a similar way. Then again, who was to say that evidence offered by the senses wasn't all in one's head—a mere fabrication of twitching neurons sealed up in a bony shell? It was all very confusing to the bloodhound.

For if the senses were no longer a fact of life, what kept them from being nothing more than ghost trails in the mind? What proof would remain that your life wasn't simply what imagination fashioned, whether out of subjective need or in consoling recompense for whatever you might have suffered at the hands of reality—and that in an effort to remember the life you were convinced was yours, you unwittingly lost track of the one you'd actually led?

But if, instead, the senses were for real, and everything the bloodhound smelled, tasted, heard, saw, or felt over the course of a lifetime, all of it, had truly existed and was not simply what it wanted to exist, wouldn't it follow, then, that the bloodhound, too, existed beyond any doubt?

There was something humiliating about finding yourself forced into posing such questions, the bloodhound had to admit. Perhaps it should look on the abrupt loss of its once acute sense of smell as a disconcerting but ultimately liberating experience—an invitation to a state of consciousness far superior to one spent with your nose forever to the ground. Who wouldn't prefer to pass days and nights in more elevating pursuits, those promising transcendent dimensions of oneself that were not only within easy reach but were as constant in their presence as the stars?

And if the bloodhound could find this kind of inspirational promise in its current plight, this severing of everything that had tied it to its senses in favor of a higher state of being, shouldn't it rejoice at such unexpected good fortune rather than strive to bring those senses back to full strength and thus renew its unthinking bondage to them?

All this logic that urged self-change was of no avail in the end. Like some aging lecher who, while fully aware of the ludicrous figure he cuts, still cannot resist pushing through the crowd to overtake a ravishing stranger and steal a glimpse into her eyes, only to stop in his tracks at that very moment, wheezing for breath as she walks on without a glance in his direction and the crowd, too, strides forward around him—in a similarly demoralizing way the bloodhound was powerless to free itself from the pursuit of its fugitive senses.

The pull of what had always given its life meaning until now just proved too demoralizingly strong.

The Boa Constrictor

Once a boa constrictor made no excuses for being enamored of itself.

Why should it? Among all the creatures the boa knew of, none could boast anything approaching its appeal. Devoting a moment to the distractions posed by the existence of others was one moment too many stolen from the hours, days, weeks, months, and years needed for the proper contemplation of its own coils.

What perfection they were. How imposing in girth and grip. There might be larger snakes about but none more sensuously limber. Just as there were perhaps more colorful ones but none so entrancing. For a marriage of power and fascination, what could rival the boa, whether snake or otherwise? Nothing it had ever seen, that was for sure.

Not that the boa was in the habit of looking very far. When you're ideal in yourself, what can lesser beings offer you? The sublime is only lowered by company. To be peerless in this world might be a lonely blessing, but a blessing worth the world in exchange.

What breathless rapture must thrill through the boa's conquests in their surrender to its charms. To be cradled in its thick folds and know consummation had come at last, how must that feel to them? Like nothing they'd ever dreamed of, the boa presumed. But it couldn't be absolutely sure; it could only imagine the extremes of feeling brought on by the full force of its embrace.

And not being sure became a source of galling distress to the boa. For without this ultimate proof of its glory, without this final testament to itself, what meaning could life as a nonpareil have? One sigh short of rapture was no rapture at all, just as a broken circle of pleasure was a disappointment it couldn't abide.

Rapture, circle, both were measures of perfection, and nothing must be allowed to hinder the boa constrictor's reveling in perfection. Coiling upon itself, it strained to hear that matchless final sigh it had listened to with satisfaction so often, determined to reach the heights of ecstasy even the least of its conquests must have known in its embrace, free at last to be ravished by its own charisma.

If it could just turn tightly enough upon itself to relish this consummate swoon glazing . . . over . . . . its . . . . eyes . . . . .

The Booby and the Loon

Once a booby and a loon hosted a Talk Radio show.
End of story.

The Booklice

Once booklice ate their way through an original copy of the Constitution.

As with booklice in general, which seem to have no reason for existence other than the damaging of texts that are dear to rare-book or document owners, exactly where these particular agents of destruction came from and why they chose to damage one item rather than another defied comprehension. So too did the precise means by which they'd slipped through all the protective barriers surrounding their target in this specific instance.

Some experts in document preservation theorized a breakdown in the cooling system keeping the atmosphere around historical displays temperate had resulted in elevated levels of heat, and with added heat, patriotic visitors to the exhibit began to sweat, and these perspiring patriots soon created the type of atmosphere in which booklice all but spontaneously came out of the woodwork. Or so one theory went.

Other experts, by contrast, saw a more sinister explanation, one that posited the booklice had gained access to the revered document either through official neglect or following a deliberate attack by self-proclaimed superpatriots and their myriad supporters in the nation's capital and across the land. But what sort of person would deliberately commit or praise such an outrage? It passed comprehending even more than the damage done by the booklice themselves.

Once present, booklice generally work their depredations in the dark, when they can do so unobserved. In secret they are able to eat holes in pretty much anything on paper and so completely that entire documents may have a "quaint" or "dated" appearance after the booklice have finished with them.

Most damaged on this occasion was the aforementioned copy of the Constitution, but subsequent investigations revealed nearly the same fate had befallen a number of treaties, international agreements, landmark court decisions, and governmental regulations and pledges, from ballot access to free and fair elections, to human rights accords. None of these documents were safe, either from booklice or, strange as it might seem, overheated superpatriots.

When fumigators were belatedly called in, the extent of the damage was so great that even though the booklice might be quickly dealt with, the effort required to restore the true patriotic spirit of the mutilated documents could take years and years.

The Bubble

Once a bubble took itself very seriously.

Like all bubbles great and small, this one was in reality little more than a shimmering surface over emptiness. And as other bubbles, when it wasn't being blown about here and there, it drifted on its own in seemingly aimless wanderings that appeared to come to much the same thing. Nevertheless, the bubble maintained a determined sense of self-worth in the conviction that its inner void was given shape and, ultimately, meaning by its unique role in the grander scheme of things. For without the bubble, what would emptiness within ever amount to but just that: inner emptiness? Indistinguishable, in fact, from the nothingness spreading out in every direction from the bubble as though in thoroughgoing disregard of the need for distinctions that lend clarity to life each and every day. For where there is difference, the bubble reasoned, there are contrasts to be made, and with contrast comes the separation necessary for assessments of significance, obviously: the ability to declare with absolute confidence at any given moment, "This is this; that is that." Absent the reality of bubbles like itself, in other words, what significance would any of existence have? How would anything identify anything else against which to define itself and thus attain full self-awareness—anything that was outside it, unknown, formless, and therefore a testament to the settled merit of its own private void by comparison? How could an otherwise incalculable "dark beyond" be understood if not for its relationship to luminous bubbles? Bubbles, in sum, held existential doubt at bay. And a perilous vigil that was. It went without saying that any moment might be a bubble's last, as a loud pop or a plaintive squeak or a mere fading whiffle announced an end to the sheltering round that had shaped absence into presence and presence into a multitude of forms, visions, hopes, fears, joys, sorrows, attachments, bitter losses—all that which, for good or for ill, demonstrated one's ability to tell what one was from what one was not—in short, all that which turned the insubstantial into something of singular importance!

With these as the dimensions of a bubble's very sense of being, was it any surprise this one took itself so very seriously?

The Buffoons

Once two troops of lowland buffoons squared off on a patch of ground where the halls of Congress now stand.

The dispute involved one of those bitter conflicts over territory and dominance that regularly arose at that time, whether originating from within the ranks of the Greater Buffoons or the Lesser.

As usual, each of the two troops in question was persuaded it alone had hereditary right to what both claimed. And so intent were they on maintaining such claims that the ground actually at issue, though quite small and shrinking all the time, assumed ever-greater importance in their eyes.

The confrontation itself also began as such confrontations regularly did, with a series of ritual feints and gestures that became more pronounced as both troops grew bolder and bolder in asserting their primacy.

While telling the two sides apart could be difficult enough under ordinary circumstances, the sight of each other brought out behavior that made it even more so. And because each troop had a limited repertoire of instinctive moves very much like the other troop's, differentiating between these buffoons came down primarily to variations in the color of certain portions of their anatomy, most notably the head and hindquarters.

One troop favored blinding shows of red, white, and blue, while the other went in for equally intense displays of the same colors but in slightly altered proportions. As for the rest of the confrontation, it followed a predictable pattern as well. Alpha buffoons on one side would gesticulate dramatically, curl their lips in studied menace, roll their eyes in mocking scorn, and make loud grunting noises as the other side covered its own eyes and ears. Then the roles would be reversed.

Neither troop of buffoons appeared to tire of this performance, but after a while both would agree to withdraw and return for another dust-up in the future. And sure enough, there the two sides would soon be again, adopting the same threatening postures, making the same noises, and displaying the same brightly colored parts of their anatomy. It was enough to make one wonder whether they had changed their basic patterns of behavior at all since the rise of their species.

Or ever would.

The Bug on the Windshield

Once a bug threw itself at an oncoming car's windshield.

The bug wasn't much to look at even in its prime, and it didn't make much of a splat when it hit the glass, but none of that mattered in the decision it made. For the bug was persuaded this choice of end would have an éclat all its own when viewed in the larger scheme of things. In a world where countless bugs suffered meaningless deaths every second, this one would stand out for its resolute display of will!

Why let mere chance have the final say in life, as had seemed to be the case with the bug's own life ever since it began? An existence ruled by circumstance, at the mercy of luck or accident, why should that be one's fate? Always finding yourself at the right place at the right time or the wrong place at the wrong time but rarely by plan or purpose wasn't much of a life. Why have wings to fly with if they were yours to command only in the most limited sense?

The bug had pondered its act of pure will at great length. Simply "to be" wasn't much of a claim to significance when "not to be" wouldn't have proved much different. Let others busy themselves in repetitious, pointless dealings they believed gave their brief stay on earth a reason. Ever fearful a mishap might befall them before their shining moment arrived and render everything for naught, they told themselves they were in control when in truth they were tossed here and there by the slightest shift in breeze.

Such a life was not for this bug, not anymore. When it had first spotted the distant car's headlights breaking the horizon and advancing through the dusk towards it, elation had welled within. All the time spent at the mercy of outside forces (with any serious attempt at self-determination continually denied) faded into irrelevance. Whatever might be remembered of the bug by posterity would rest on the next few minutes and the onrushing headlights.

Even if life signified nothing, death needn't, the bug was now certain. How you faced that ultimate denial of individual desires and merit would count in your favor or against you. A cowardly dodge in hopes of being spared the inevitable would mark you forever, but a defiant stand against the lot you'd been dealt, doomed though it be, must surely place you among those who transcended their end!

To the bug, the approaching headlights offered perhaps the only opportunity it would ever have to escape the bleak contingency of its life, to make a declaration once and for all against the limits of being. Others might go on as if their

26

self-delusions were reality, but tonight one bug would defy life's humiliations and defeats. One bug would fashion its own heroic destiny! Its own glorious explosion of the will into eternity, into myth!

None of these thoughts, to be sure, crossed the mind of the carwash attendant as he listlessly dragged his squeegee over the car's windshield the next morning and flicked the scrapings away.

The Bull

Once a bull opened a china shop.

That certainly was not by choice. The bull had originally envisioned a career in rare porcelain, the love of its life. It had looked forward to years of dignified connoisseurship, offering the contemplation of superb pieces by appointment and sharing arcane insights with like-minded collectors over cognac. There was not a Sung Dynasty celadon or Ming "blue and white" that the bull could not identify by collection and describe from memory, right down to the cracks.

But it was not to be, this life as an aesthete, spending mornings in a silk robe and later, tailored suits for the auction house. Instead, the bull found itself trapped behind the counter of a small shop stuffed from floor to ceiling with ceramic knickknacks, peddling kitsch to survive.

No circle of venerable cognoscenti passed their time here. Instead, tourists and birthday shoppers squeezed past the shelves of mass-produced figurines and keepsakes. While the bull recited quietly to itself a lecture on Japanese tea bowls that would never be delivered, customers picked up this item or that, turned it over a few times, and then put it back down with a "This one's cute."

The miniature china bulls on key rings were always a favorite. Customers could be counted on to break into nervous giggles, looking back and forth between the tiny figure in their hand and the huge one bent over the cash register as if lost in the machine's enigmas. Out-of-towners were especially prone to buying the key-ring bulls as a memento of their visit. "Who'll believe it when we tell them?" they might whisper to one another as they left the shop with a final glance back.

After the last customer of the day had departed and the bull had locked the door to the shop and pulled the blinds, it would stand motionless awhile and survey the crowded display tables. For those few moments every afternoon, a distant look would come into its eyes.

Then the look would pass. The bull would shrug its broad shoulders and begin walking slowly back down one of the narrow aisles, flicking its tail and randomly knocking a few pieces to the floor.

The Bullfrog

Once a bullfrog was looked to by many who sought a spiritual master.

Drawn by word of the bullfrog's sonorous croak and serene pose as it sat on a lily pad surveying an old pond from beneath lowered eyelids, large crowds showed up to line the banks of the pond, adopt what they took to be a frog squat, and squint soulfully back in the bullfrog's direction. The only time they shifted their gaze was to assure themselves that nobody around them had a more committed squat or more soulful squint.

Although quite a few were able to manage one or both of these after a fashion, none had the confidence to attempt the bullfrog's awe-inspiring croak. Instead, they concentrated on counting the number of times it blinked per minute and attributed great significance to that number, depending upon whether it was odd or even. Differences of opinion in this regard could, and often did, result in disdainful glances being cast about and sometimes even under-the-breath denunciations of insufficient effort by others.

Whenever the bullfrog shot out its tongue and snatched something from the air, it noticed that a number of the more earnest members of the crowd attempted to follow its lead. They looked exceedingly awkward in their efforts, the bullfrog thought, wondering how many of them actually managed to catch anything in the end. Out of curiosity, the bullfrog asked those nearest to it whether they were enjoying the tranquility of the pond.

"The pond?"

"Yes, this old pond. Isn't that why you came here?"

"No. We came here because we are seekers."

"Oh? And what is it you are seeking?"

"Enlightened guidance. Ultimate understanding. We've come to learn the secret of your matchless croak."

"It's just a croak, you realize."

"Ah, but we know it is much, much more."

"Really? What is it, then?"

"That is what we've come here to learn from you."

At that instant and without warning, the bullfrog leaped into the pond. The sound of water startled the throng lining the banks. Many thought to follow the bullfrog's example and throw themselves into the pond, were it not for fear they might come down with a rash from doing so. Others favored waiting for the bullfrog to resurface and perhaps instruct them on how to interpret what had just happened. The bullfrog did resurface, but at some distance and with only its eyes protruding above the water, unnoticed by all.

As time passed without anything further happening, the crowds began to grow restless and then to break up and drift away. The prevailing mood was one of disappointment, of having been let down in their spiritual aspirations by the bullfrog. Even those who had thrown themselves into the pond in solemn imitation of it, not once but two or three or four times running, began to feel they might have been mistaken, possibly deceived. Most importantly, everyone was convinced they'd lost precious time in their search for ultimate understanding.

The bullfrog was clearly not spiritual-master material, as far as they were concerned.

The Butterfly and the Moth

Once a butterfly fell in love with a moth.

Why that happened defied explanation. The butterfly was like the coming of spring. April played in its wings, and their soft flutter made the air glow. When it would light a moment on a blade of grass or a twig, that place, however small, rivaled rainbows.

The moth had none of this magic. It faltered through life as though its wings were an accident. And this accident the moth took as a cruel affront. It was a low trick of nature that it found itself with ungainly wings, quite apart from the added insult of its drab, puffy bulk.

Nor was the moth merely awkward physically. It got in its own way all the time emotionally as well. What other being had to endure the mortifications it did every day, the moth groaned? Life was nothing more than a long bad joke, and the moth was the constant butt of it. The whole of its experience seemed designed solely to deny the moth any dignity it might aim for.

The butterfly recognized the moth's pained discontent but loved it all the more for that. Perhaps the moth's bitterness at having been slighted by life was the very thing that proved irresistible.

Even when the moth's frustrations caused it to turn on the butterfly, as if blaming it for a magnificence that put the moth itself in a worse light by comparison, the butterfly's love never wavered. At such times, it would fold close its splendor to avoid upsetting the moth any further or else quiet the lilting grace of its flight.

It wasn't that the moth meant to hurt the butterfly. And it wasn't that the butterfly didn't feel hurt, sometimes terribly hurt. The moth saw the pain it caused but couldn't help itself. While the butterfly saw how cruelly love was repaid but also couldn't help itself.

Day after day, the moth blundered about and cursed its lot, while the butterfly followed lovingly behind, refusing to use its own luminous wings to fly away. It was truly a mystery.

★

In another version of this story, it was the moth that fell in love with the butterfly and tried in every way to be near the object of its affections. This devotion was a torment, the moth often acknowledged to itself sadly, for in the presence of the butterfly, it was convinced it must appear a hundred times more ugly than if it simply kept to itself and abandoned love completely.

All of the misgivings it had, the dull heaviness it felt in its heart whenever it tried to imagine a lifetime spent with the butterfly, might have been expected to dissuade the moth from its suit. How could it ever be worthy of sharing even a moment with this extraordinary being? Wasn't that desire just a hopeless delusion that could only lead to disaster? The moth half feared that if it ever realized its dreams and won the butterfly's love, it might not survive the bliss.

The butterfly, for its part, was barely aware of the moth's existence. The earnest suitor's attempts to call attention to itself while at the same time trying desperately to hide its shortcomings appeared to the butterfly as merely a puzzling blur in the air, a bothersome distraction. That the blur might be the sole expression an awkward constancy could manage never crossed the butterfly's mind. While helpless before the burning marvel of its love, the moth circled ever closer and closer.

This second version of the story was a mystery too.

The Buzzard

Once a crusty old buzzard appeared as a guest host on the prime time sleuthing show "You're Dead Meat."

The selection was an easy one, given this particular host's long career in movies and on television as a gravel-voiced tough guy. Furthermore, being a buzzard, it proved to be a natural at tracking down what it called "odoriferous malefactors," whether already dead or barely alive.

In the opening sequence of the show, the buzzard, sitting in a comfortable armchair, looked unflinchingly into the camera and graveled, "In our media-saturated age, the court of public opinion demands a new definition for the term 'habeas corpus.' For the next two hours, 'habeas corpus' will cover all who are involved in a deadly incident of any sort. That includes the victim, the accused, the families of both, the judge and jurors, plus the families of the judge and jurors, all media personnel and any public relations firms or instabiographers retained by any of the above, their relatives, neighbors, high school sweethearts, and persons unknown or simply yet to be discovered. On 'You're Dead Meat,' we pledge to follow the trail wherever it leads and to share with our audience whatever our investigation reveals. A warning: some of what you are about to see may be disturbing."

Then it was time for some sleuthing. The buzzard, conveying a determination to do its own detective footwork, rose from the armchair and hobbled off the studio set as best it could for its advanced age. In succeeding scenes, it would appear in various locations relevant to the investigation, seeking out potential principals in the case and thoroughly examining victims wherever they lay.

At times the buzzard's efforts might be complicated by the appearance of competing crusty old buzzards flocking to document the same case and hopping noisily about the crime scene with microphones and their own video teams in tow. Binge-watchers of the show often showed up as well to ask for the signatures of as many crusty old buzzards as they could recognize from previous years of the show and ended up following around what could become a bickering knot of crusty old buzzards for hours.

Presented with this spectacle in the comfort of their living rooms, some members of the audience began to wonder if they themselves might wake up one morning to find their front lawn trampled on and torn up by a noisy crowd lurching forward to "habeas" their "corpus" too. Would they feel compelled to open the door in their pajamas and yield to whatever awaited them?

And would the slightest hesitation to do so be met with some variation of the gravel-voiced declaration at the end of each program: "Nobody can escape today's round-the-clock hunt for the next odoriferous malefactor. Watch this show long enough and you may see the life of somebody you know picked clean in minutes. This obligation rises above any of us as individuals."

As for the audience ratings on the episode of "You're Dead Meat" hosted by the guest buzzard, they were off the charts.

The Cactus

Once a cactus went for the record in lifetime achievements by a succulent.

The cactus couldn't see any reason not to go for the record, being as it had long since surpassed every other cactus it knew for size and for the wealth of water it could hold. To say nothing of the bountiful flowers it boasted each year.

If it enjoyed the good fortune to have grown this large and this impressive, that must be how things were meant to turn out. And if it was the biggest and best-endowed cactus around, didn't that mean it deserved to be the biggest and best-endowed? Its own glorious attainment must confirm the inevitable workings of nature. What was, in brief, was what should be.

Admittedly, setting a record would require the cactus to gather and hold more water than ever before. Since there was only so much water available in the desert, however, and since other, lesser cacti thought they should be entitled to a share of it, some tough decisions would have to be made. If the cactus was indeed destined for unimagined size and substance, then it must not flinch at any test of its resolve. It must show a boldness of action unconstrained by the slightest qualms or concerns regarding fair play.

Why should lesser succulents, not in a position to set records themselves or ever likely to be, have the same right to the limited water supply that it did? They would never have a reach equal to its own arms nor ever produce flowers to vie with those it already had in excess. Even if all other cacti shriveled up and died away while it alone thrived, what would that matter against one simple calculation of worth: if it had become the most successful cactus in all cactdom, then whatever water it desired must surely be its due.

And in truth, as the cactus spread its roots and drew to itself water that might otherwise have benefitted all, lesser cacti withered to the same degree it prospered. The more water it claimed, the more it swelled. And the more it swelled, the more water it could claim.

The cactus was clearly reaching new heights all the time, no doubt about that. Yet as it towered ever larger over the landscape and as it sucked the earth dry to satisfy its burgeoning need, something else was happening as well. Beneath its resplendent flowers, the cactus was steadily turning to mush inside, producing a top-heavy, distended monstrosity in danger of falling from its own unequal weight.

If that happened, if the whole Brobdingnagian mass began to sway and sag and finally toppled into the shadow of its own success, what would its prospects for unsurpassed triumph be then? Stretched out upon the parched wasteland it had created far and wide, would the cactus be able to claim anything more than a footnote in the record books for colossal failure? Such a fate was simply unfair!

But wait, the cactus thought in desperation, might there be some record for spectacular Hall of Fame downfalls it could still claim? Like "King of the Collapse"?

The Canaries

Once canaries were prohibited by executive order from dying in mines.

In their role as early warning signals, it didn't matter how toxic the air they breathed had become, they were simply not allowed to depart this world.

Whenever a canary actually did keel over in its cage, the death was invariably ascribed to natural causes and, as such, was declared not to be any reason for general concern. Other canaries should pay no notice and simply go on breathing the air around them as usual.

The penalties for joining the heavenly choir in defiance of the executive order could be severe. A presidential task force was assigned to investigate any reports of choking, hacking, wheezing, and suspiciously expiring canaries. No time was lost in reassuring the public that everything that could be done was being done to find the cause of these episodes. There was no reason, therefore, to be alarmed by even wholesale canary demise.

That same task force was empowered by another executive order to detain any canary suspected of attempting to spread panic by faking its own death. Likely suspects were routinely charged with aiding and abetting ecoterrorists and of playing into the hands of a conspiracy that could cross state and national boundaries.

Yet still, despite this threat of grave consequences, canaries continued to give up the ghost in growing numbers. Nor were their deaths confined any longer to areas in the immediate vicinity of known sources of foul air. Dispatches from places far downwind revealed that previously healthy canaries were dropping in droves. Without a doubt, the highest authority in the land was being openly mocked.

So yet another executive order was issued calling upon field personnel of the Environmental Protection Agency to cease whatever else they might be doing and apply themselves to netting any and all canaries, below ground or above, before calls for potentially embarrassing congressional investigations arose.

Complicating the matter, it soon became obvious that there simply weren't enough EPA personnel to handle the job. As accounts arose of serious injury to persons and property from canaries now beginning to fall from an increasingly darkened sky in greater numbers than in mines, the early warning system that the birds had represented for so long came to be seen as more trouble than it was worth. This "ticking canary time bomb," it was now declared in an internal executive order, called for the boldness to "think like a bomb squad": i.e., when you can't defuse a threat, just blow it up.

It was impossible, obviously, to blow up every canary identified by the now-politicized EPA, but their elimination en masse in a "controlled extinction," as officials termed it, might effectively remove the need for more painstaking and expensive measures. And if the air the canaries breathed was the problem, why not make the problem part of the solution? How much additional toxic air was required to be rid of these little troublemakers altogether? That shouldn't be hard to determine.

This new approach proved remarkably effective, and after peaking, accounts of suspicious canary deaths began to taper off. Eventually, there were few sightings to speak of, and then there were none. To mark this success, a delegation of those who'd contributed most to solving the canary problem once and for all presented the one and only remaining specimen to the Administrator of the EPA at that time.

It was last seen under a glass cloche on that Administrator's desk.

The Cantipede

Once a cantipede was hired as the press secretary for a prominent but erratic politician.

The cantipede appeared better qualified for the job than the politician's previous press secretaries. To begin with, "cant" was part of its name, so it was naturally assumed the cantipede shouldn't have much difficulty taking up its duties from day one. More important, though, was its remarkable flexibility. The cantipede possessed more than enough legs to move in whatever direction was called for when a shift in the thinking or intent of its boss needed to be explained to the public. If it had to shift this way or that, it obediently hastened to do so. And if it suddenly had to backtrack, back it would hustle as though it hadn't taken a single step in any other direction. So suited was the cantipede to being this particular politician's press secretary, in fact, that soon it was difficult to think of one without immediately thinking of the other as well.

Then one day the cantipede began inexplicably tripping over its own feet. These mishaps weren't much of a hindrance at first. And as long as they were minor, a false step or two could be covered up well enough by merely shifting from one leg to several others in a sort of improvised skipping in place, a move that might even be taken for having been part of the plan.

If truth be told, however, it was not part of the plan, and this fact caused the cantipede increasing concern. If it proved unable to keep up with the pace at which it was being asked to change direction all the time, how long would it be before it was replaced by another press secretary who could manage a more convincing display of fancy footwork regardless of the dodging about required?

The cantipede thought long and hard and came up with an offense it felt would be the best defense against being summarily sacked. It looked to its strength: legs. It just needed more of them. So each time its boss changed direction, the cantipede dutifully tried to sprout a few new legs to help it follow suit step for step.

Initially, the strategy worked well enough, although this generating of new legs to stand on was sometimes a challenge, especially when the signals the cantipede received weren't in themselves easy to follow. But it did manage, after a fashion, to produce whatever legs were needed to match shifting thoughts from the boss, looking in the process a bit like Athena struggling to emerge feet first from the head of a befuddled Zeus.

It goes without saying that adding legs on demand has its risks, and

35

eventually these were bound to overtake the cantipede. Presented with its frantic efforts, reporters became ever less certain exactly what direction the hapless, put-upon press secretary was headed in, whether forward or backward, to the right or to the left. Some days, the flustered cantipede appeared to be trying to move in all directions at once in a flurry of contradictory thrashings about. Other days, it seemed merely to be running in circles while insisting it was always on the straight and narrow.

Not surprisingly, there were moments during its breathtaking contortions when the cantipede was in obvious danger of falling flat on its face. More generally, it waged a ceaseless struggle just to keep its head clear of its multiplying legs as it peeped out from their thick blur with a look of desperation. There must be a better way of presenting to the press and public a prominent but erratic politician's shifts in thinking, the loyal cantipede often muttered to itself.

A way with less chance of being struck so often in the mouth by its own flailing feet.

The Cat

Once a cat read a newspaper obituary for its just-ended eighth life.

The cat was not pleased. Not pleased at all. It couldn't complain that anything in the obituary was definitely wrong. The dates were accurate, and the facts stated were all true. On the face of it, the obituary might seem a very complete summary of a long and successful life. Nevertheless, the cat was deeply dissatisfied.

"Was that me?" it asked itself.

A life should be more than a list of details, certainly, a bland chronicle of accomplishments patched together from old newspaper files, with a few quotes and a couple of formula sentences inserted at the last moment listing cause and place of death. Where was the life it had really lived, the cat wanted to know as it scanned the obituary again.

Not here, that was certain. What the cat would have observed about itself wasn't even hinted at. Who could guess from this neat tallying up of triumphs that other aspirations than worldly attainment and the attention it brings had ever moved the cat? Or that at some stop along the road to success, it might have regretted any number of detours not taken instead? Who could guess what forfeits and forsakings veiled themselves behind the cat's celebrated stare in the archive photograph accompanying the obituary?

36

It would be the boilerplate version of a "life meriting praise" that readers took away from the cat's passing, not its own. In place of an individual's chaotic ups and downs, each one a testament to the myriad possibilities of life, they would be given an agreed-upon guide to what every dead notable should have been and should have done. The "official story of the cat's eighth life," but according to whom?

And what of all that the cat had experienced before the first dates listed here? It was as if this accounting of its most recent life had cancelled out every one of the previous seven. They might as well never have happened. Their only virtue seemed to lie in the supposed evidence they provided that one could "start over again" as often as necessary. The cat saw itself turned into a crude, hollow metaphor for self-reinvention: a message to those who'd made good that nothing else mattered and to those who'd fallen short at life that, sorry, but they just didn't have what it took apparently or else hadn't tried hard enough.

At this rate, it might have been better for the cat to be a failure the eighth time around. At least then its life wouldn't have to add up to some pattern that the morning latte-and-obit crowd accepted as the measure of consequence. There would have been room as well for what didn't add up, what would never add up, or wouldn't impress anyone even if it did.

And finally, what was this concluding paragraph about "survived by" meant to say? In what really counted, the cat was survived only by itself. This couldn't be the last thing to set down about it, this presumption that it had been merely a link in some chain of inheriting and passing on whatever the general public felt was important as a legacy.

When it reached the end of the obituary for a second time, the cat didn't even bother to clip it out for saving. Instead, it folded up the newspaper with a dismissive "I was more alive than that!"

The Caterpillar

Once a caterpillar paused at the edge of a leaf to consider what might lie ahead.

In front of the caterpillar lay nothing but air. Even if it strained the full arch of its body, clinging to the end of the leaf with only its back legs as it leaned out as far as possible, the caterpillar found no new leaf or twig to catch hold of. The void before it could have been inches across or continued for miles.

There on the edge, swaying slowly back and forth, it had no idea that one day it might take wing and fly effortlessly as far as it wished. That a time might come when the emptiness ahead could be bridged in a few wingbeats was an idea worlds beyond the caterpillar's present thinking.

And the journey that had brought it this far? The caterpillar had as little certainty about that as about what awaited it. It couldn't be sure it had even been a caterpillar a moment before. Why not something else? An aphid or a spittlebug maybe. For that matter, why not a leaf like the very one it now balanced on? Stranger transformations might happen. Nothing could be ruled out.

Perhaps the leaf was in the same situation as the caterpillar. Perhaps the weight it felt on it at this moment was the full extent of the leaf's own awareness. If the caterpillar shifted the least bit, would the leaf's conception of its place in the world shift by that much as well? And wouldn't the caterpillar then sense the leaf's movement in return? This exchange of momentary inklings might continue indefinitely, all of the past and future linked to it as the caterpillar was linked to the leaf.

As both of them were linked to the passing breeze, and the breeze was linked to the clouds, and the clouds to the rain, and the falling rain to the earth, and the earth to the tree as it reached upwards through every branch, and this one branch among so many others as it stretched outward into this leaf, and the leaf as it supported the caterpillar, now at the center of the universe. As were they all.

It wasn't of great importance, the caterpillar realized, what it had been or what it might become. What mattered more now was the faintest tremor of being: the divinity of life itself that ran through all that ever had existed or ever would.

Perhaps the caterpillar didn't even need to come to the edge of this leaf to understand what lay beyond.

The Cattle

Once cattle went mad, certifiably mad.

The cattle in question belonged to a large herd that inexplicably moseyed one fine day into the heart of the nation's capital. The size of the herd was not news; the news was how many of its members took leave of their senses at the same time and in full sight.

This ill-fated drove had grown accustomed to passing their days in a state of bovine self-absorption, chewing complacently and unquestioningly on whatever was put in front of them. And when it came time to be milked by those who did the feeding, the herd was easily led by the nose or simply followed the rump of the cow ahead in compliant file. They were, in sum, the most docile of creatures.

The loss of their collective wits did not come upon these cattle suddenly or through any departure from the routines they'd grown so comfortable with. They were not taken off their feed, nor were they milked any less frequently. If anything, these two guiding patterns of their existence, endlessly swallowing whatever was presented them and then being milked in return, continued straight through their rapidly deepening affliction.

These changeless routines may even have contributed to their decline, for the onset of mass mental failure occurred after the cattle were provided a particularly generous diet of the usual fodder mixed with reprocessed brain parts from "downer cows" among their own numbers that had clearly swallowed too much of what they were being fed from the beginning.

There were occasions after that when the herd would suddenly stampede about for no apparent reason, shaking convulsively and bellowing to the clouds as if there were some deep meaning in their moos. More commonly, however, they pressed close to one another for support while dozing on their feet in a narcoleptic stupor that could last from morning to night.

Not only didn't the cattle seem capable of reversing the steady decline in their mental powers but they continued instead to welcome whatever was shoveled their way until the little control they could manage over their remaining faculties was weak, unfocused, and symptomatic of increasingly spongy brains.

The entire herd seemed content merely to chew their cud, either to themselves or to each other, endlessly ruminating upon what had befallen them but unable to digest fully their own role in it. For all the airy noise produced in the process, the only discernible result was to add to the capital's rising levels of methane gas.

The greatest fear on the part of health officials, understandably, was that the brain-wasting effects of these cattle's decline might be communicated to the human population at large.

The Chameleon

Once a chameleon found it could change the color of anything it touched.

Before this discovery, it had always matched its own coloring to wherever it found itself. That was a talent, of course, but a minor one. Rather than being admired by the world at large, it merely contributed to a widespread dismissal of the chameleon as an imitator, a lightweight.

Now suddenly everything was different. The chameleon watched as the earth beneath its foot turned the same hue as its toes. It lifted its foot, and the earth returned to the color it had been. It put its foot back down, and once again the earth changed. It then touched its foot to a rock, and the same thing happened. This was real talent. It might even qualify as genius, the chameleon sensed. Heady with this newfound gift, it took to calling itself "artist among animals."

And that's when the chameleon's problems began.

News of the breakthrough spread rapidly. Critics hailed a revolution in the very concept of "color." Academic symposiums were organized to discuss the many implications (present and future) of the breakthrough. The chameleon was invited to intense panel discussions followed by evenings out with the smart set. Soon it was being profiled in art publications in addition to the "culture and style" section of magazines and newspapers or asked in private by wealthy collectors for advice on brightening up a beach getaway.

"I don't do decorating," the chameleon would reply. "I am an artist."

"Of course you are. But couldn't you just take a look?"

Or it might be begged to touch one thing or another for a new friend, only to find it being hawked online within twenty-four hours. Inevitably, chameleon fakes began to be auctioned off at outrageous prices to eager investors.

And then there was the jealousy of others who also claimed a gift for color. Snide comments began to circulate regarding the limits of the chameleon's chromatic range or relevance to the times, and waggish dismissals of its ability to create anything truly original made the rounds. There were even ugly scenes at gallery openings and studio parties.

Why continue, the chameleon wondered after a while? Its early enthusiasm for changing the way the world saw itself had vanished. Now it began to suspect a bit of tinting around the edges might be all that was looked for: enhanced copies of others' visions. Disillusioned, it withdrew from the bright lights and the openings. It stopped accepting invitations or even answering the phone.

For a while, there were questions about what had become of the chameleon. There were also rumors and even a few claims of chance encounters in the most unlikely of places. But the circles in which the chameleon had once moved had themselves moved on, and soon a new "artist among animals" was being celebrated. "Just as well," the chameleon thought to itself. "Just as well."

Years later, a small, out-of-the-way museum held an exhibition entitled simply "A Chameleon Retrospective." Attendance was low. The last day of the exhibition there were no visitors at all. Except for a lone figure in a nondescript overcoat that every now and then, when the solitary museum guard dozed off, would quietly touch one of the works in the show and turn it completely gray.

Charon

Once Charon the boatman decided to turn the money down.

He would ferry the dead to the underworld free of charge if it was worth the effort. But for some time, it hadn't seemed worth even the cheek-stretching mouthful of coins that the majority of expectant passengers now showed up with to pay for passage across the murky river—more off-putting in its presumptuousness than the single coin the dead had arrived with on their tongues in the past, no matter how covered in slobber it might have been.

What was he supposed to do with all this slimy lucre? The waiting crowds must know even gold was worthless in the underworld. Or maybe this lot just didn't get it, incapable of seeing that the glitter of the lives they'd thought made them the envy of the world was revealed down here as the dross they should always have recognized it to be? While the soul-soiling conduct they'd engaged in for such gains (as if confident none of it would ever stick) now caked them from head to foot.

Phew, what foulness! What a stench!

Up and down the river's edge surged mobs of petty mountebanks, all insisting as loudly as they could that Charon grant them the inflated regard they'd commanded throughout their lives. Were they utterly blind to the moral bankruptcy of their so-called triumphs? Did the fact they could get away with it for years convince them the fraud would work one last time? Cheek by jowl, they made their confident pitch, these dot-Ponzi scammers, loan sharks in pinstripes and heartless foreclosers, guileful bankers with bloated off-shore tax cheats in tow, financial soothsayers who knew nothing more than la-la land astrologers, credit-card vampires sucking late fees from those with no more blood to give, bonus-encrusted corporate bunglers, "self-regulating" resource exploiters exercising their full allotment of loopholes, no-bid do-nothing government contractors playing hocus-pocus with greenback bricks, white-coated drug pushers for pharmaceutical cartels and hospital administrators with the ethics of serial billers, "it's your life or our bottom line" health insurers acting less like compassionate professionals than drooling raptors, revolving-door influence peddlers, oily lobbyists buttering legislators up one side today and down the other tomorrow, has-been political hacks receiving five-digit speaking fees and seven-digit book advances or cushy positions as "visiting scholars" at universities that apparently valued their "intellect," gilded-throne televangelists washing their hands in the collection plate, families of suited-up grifters aiming to be autocrats, plus, most demoralizing of all, a self-snookered public who should have had the sense to put a stop to all this chicanery but never did out of some delusional hope that they too might get the chance, someday, to join the "filthy rich" themselves.

Phew, what foulness! What a stench!

Who could blame Charon for looking grim or sullen with revulsion at this worthless lot elbowing one another to get into his boat and counting on hoodwinking him into abetting their escape from the consequences of human trust so disastrously misspent? But the grizzled boatman was having none of their brazen attempts to elude censure for their deeds. Let these charlatan shades spend an eternity being blown about this place of withered longing, Charon grumbled, well short of the deliverance they thought they'd finagled. To believe they could con him into being an accessory to their flight from the cries for justice and retribution that followed them all the way here was insulting. Did he look like just another patsy? Like a befuddled old rube who wouldn't recognize that the coins they pressed him to accept were a bribe to secure their safe passage beyond people's outrage at shady behavior rewarded for far too long? No, they should have to wait eternally on this side of the dark water, without hope of the public amnesia they hoped to exploit when trying to dupe the judges of the dead on the other side.

Phew, what foulness! What a stench!

42

The Cheetah

Once a cheetah outran its welcome.

When it first appeared on the scene, the cheetah was hailed by one and all as a phenomenon, as being in a league by itself. Nobody could remember a runner so gifted with both speed and agility.

And the cheetah truly was a marvel to watch. So swiftly did it cover the ground that film of it running had to be slowed down or else all that could be seen was a blur. Its lithe body flew past as if it meant to leave no tracks, touching down only to push off again the same instant. Some observers called it "a lean mean speed machine," while others attempted a more literary tone but only came up with the tired cliché "poetry in motion." Still others were inspired to speak of it in swelling terms normally reserved for mythic heroes who "fight through the pain to destiny and glory."

The cheetah itself didn't know much about destiny and glory. It just ran.

Crowds would gather everywhere to cheer the cheetah on. It was not unusual to see tens of thousands press together for a better look, often trying to outdo each other in their enthusiasm. They even took to wearing cheetah masks or cheetah hats and cheering their lungs out in celebration of its unrivaled speed as their champion moved through this adulation "like a demigod through the clouds."

The cheetah had one failing, however. It was given to running down slower creatures and ripping their throats open.

This alarming practice caused a certain amount of soul-searching among those who loved to watch the cheetah's displays of prowess. It was thought by many that the crowds' enthusiasm for blinding speed, their screaming demand for it above all other considerations, might be to blame. The unbridled worship of speed for speed's sake may have led the cheetah to assume it could do anything and get away with it, this group lamented.

Others blamed the cheetah, not the crowds. They claimed that no amount of frenzied adulation could possibly lead the cheetah to think it was free to defy the accepted rules of civilized conduct. The crowds' behavior was essentially good, harmless fun in this view. There must have been some moral flaw in the cheetah itself that led to such distressing mayhem.

Still another opinion, however, held that because the cheetah was in a league by itself, it simply couldn't be judged by common standards. Its dazzling speed and the undeniable beauty of its running should be weighed in the scales along with everything else. What it did was reprehensible, no doubt, but allowances ought to be made, and it shouldn't be forgotten that the cheetah had received numerous awards as an inspirational role model.

But by far the largest group, citing the widely held belief that "spectator sports offer a socially constructive outlet for otherwise disruptive aggression," insisted that neither the crowds nor the cheetah should be held responsible for such a violent reversal of expectations. It was just a bad bounce of the ball that the uplifting, reassuring symbolism of sports combat had been overtaken in a flash by brutal reality.

The cheetah itself, wondering what all the fuss was about, maintained its innocence throughout.

The Chicken and the Egg

Once a chicken and an egg nearly came to blows over which of them should go first.

"After you," said the chicken.

"No, no, I wouldn't think of it," replied the egg with exaggerated politeness.

"But I insist."

"And I insist you go ahead of me."

The truth was that neither of them trusted the other to follow it a single step. Instead, each was convinced the other represented the quintessence of knavery, nursing within a conniving heart the darkest of dark plots to trip it up with some diabolical subterfuge as yet unimagined but assuredly intended to result in an advantage, however minimal or short-lived, sometime in the future.

The chicken and the egg could, of course, have agreed to start out together, side by side. But that possibility, if it did occur to either of them, must have quickly vanished in a determination not to betray the slightest wavering in resolve and thus risk the loss of a convenient stalemate—a deadlock that denied the promise of any mutual advance, to be sure, yet simultaneously removed all risk of taking a first step oneself that might later prove ill-advised and, even more importantly, blocked the other from edging forward undetected now.

The chicken and the egg felt a secret glee at the fast one they'd each pulled on the other, even though it meant they never advanced in the slightest from the spot where they'd chosen to make their stand. Secretly congratulating themselves on their clever subterfuge, the pair remained as though caught in a space-time trap while the rest of the cosmos rolled on.

Until one of them eventually moldered away to feathery dust, while the other left not even a rotten whiff of itself on the wind.

The Chimera

Once the Chimera had a difficult time filling out the compatibility profile for an online matchmaking service.

The sections about educational attainment and profession and hobbies and so forth were easy enough, but when it came to supplying a requested physical description or photo, the Chimera found itself stymied. With a fire-breathing head and body of a lion, a goat coming out of its back, and a serpent for a tail, how was it to present itself in a way that didn't put off prospective "e-mates"?

The Chimera had some experience with less exclusive dating sites on the web, most of it unsatisfactory. The "perfect matches" lined up for it proved to be something of a trial, as they invariably turned out to have only one thing in mind: all-night kinky sex with the hot, hot, über-hot Chimera of their dreams. Their assumption that it would be an eager partner in whatever sex acts their fevered imaginations suggested to them had become as tiring as the actual contortions required. Most of these encounters ended up being shorter than the Chimera's appointments with a chiropractor the next day.

And the one speed dating party the Chimera attended was a disaster. Not because of the difficulty it had maneuvering about in the press of other romance seekers without injuring some in passing but because even before the bell rang to change partners, the Chimera's hoped-for matches had bolted for the exits in alarm.

It shouldn't be that hard to find love and acceptance. But this compatibility profile promising to bring "enduring harmony and fulfillment" seemed no more likely to succeed than any of the ones before it had. None of the long list of "adjectives to describe yourself" matched how the Chimera felt, either overall or about any of its parts, and the word limit set for defining "your ideal relationship" would not suffice even as a beginning.

What chance was there of convincing any potential "life companion" out there to accept the Chimera for itself on this shallow basis? The moment it tried to convey even a bit of all it had thought and felt over the years, it must appear as nothing but a jumble of contradictions rather than the complex being it knew itself to be. Faced with a baring of the soul that defied their understanding, who wouldn't back away in alarm from what looked like their worst nightmare, their "lover from hell"?

This triform body, seemingly at odds with itself, only hinted at the deeper contours of yearning, doubt, boldness and hesitation, desire and denial, wounded pride, self-disgust, exultation one instant and swift collapse the next, dread, ecstasy, shame, and wild, wild hope within. And if others experienced even a fraction of this emotional turmoil themselves, little wonder few fancied being reminded of it by the Chimera's own lion-goat-serpent travails.

The singles world was scary enough without having to face your own demons all the time. Keeping them hidden away and cutting a confident, easygoing figure was the wisest course in matters of the heart these days. You couldn't be too careful when it came to finding that "match made in heaven." Was it safer, then, to trust short-answer questionnaires and the assurance that computer algorithms could guarantee you a lifetime of amorous felicity?

When the Chimera's own match-by-computer came back, it contained a single entry, opening with the message "Hiya babe! Bellerophon here (just call me Ricky), and i got this feelin your just what im lookn 4!"

The Chipmunk

Once a chipmunk looked down when it should have looked up.

The chipmunk had paused on a massive tree stump to count the nuts, seeds, berries, and buds it was carrying in the bulging pouches of its two cheeks. All that remained of an ancient fir, the stump measured many feet across and must have once seemed the base of a pillar for the firmament. Ages before the chipmunk was born, this old-growth giant had already stood here, wreathed in the salt mists of the coast.

To the chipmunk's mind, one stump was very much like another. More important was keeping the contents of its two cheeks straight. When the chipmunk got back to its burrow, it would have to be sure to put nuts with nuts, seeds with seeds, berries with berries, and buds with buds. If berries got mixed up with seeds and buds with nuts or berries with buds and seeds with nuts or buds with seeds and berries with nuts, there could be no end of difficulties. Keep your mind on the little things, the chipmunk was convinced, and the rest would take care of itself.

High above, gossamer clouds glowed in the deepening red of the late afternoon. Shadows would soon climb through the trees and twilight reach down to offer them its own riches in return. Then, as the forest embraced the sky in a blackness as magical as it was deep, meteors might be seen crossing the heavens while constellations wheeled around Polaris. And beyond these, supernovas might glitter like jewels scattered to the limits of wonderment.

But the chipmunk had other matters on its mind. "I'd better head down to my burrow with these nuts, seeds, berries, and buds before it gets any darker," it kept telling itself. "Snug at home, I'll have the whole night to put every little thing in its proper place."

Church and State

Once Church and State hooked up at a singles bar.

They made for an unlikely couple, to be sure, seeming to have little if anything in common. Most who had even a passing acquaintance with the two would have been surprised to find either of them in the type of meat market where they met. Hardly "swingers" in anybody's book, both Church and State had a reputation for preferring the company of those they already knew and for feeling uncomfortable with any notion of risking potentially dangerous liaisons with strangers.

That might have been the way things remained had it not been for the uninvited urging of certain friends who fancied themselves matchmakers and thought the reserved pair just needed a helpful nudge to "overcome their inhibitions and expand their horizons," as these friends put it with a wink and a nod. What a waste if the two didn't venture out and discover how much excitement a little mixing might bring to their lives.

Arriving at the singles bar at roughly the same time, the self-appointed cupids who formed the respective retinues of Church and State quickly set about executing various schemes to maneuver the two into closer proximity and keep their glasses filled. There were plenty of awkward moments at first, but as familiarity grew and things began to loosen up, the pair might be seen to touch pinkies furtively from time to time as though by accident, then to lean together ever so gently and then more unblushingly as their last inhibitions faded until, unable to keep their hands off each other, they drawled incoherently and groped away for all they were worth.

Confident they'd accomplished their mission, the matchmaking friends on both sides quietly withdrew and went home to sleep off the effects of the evening. Not so for the blotto pair of Church and State, however, who had to be shown the bar's door at closing time. As they staggered away locked in an ungainly embrace, little of what the two could be heard to mumble made much sense.

At most, it sounded like a rambling difference of opinion over whose place to head for and who should be on top and who on the bottom once they got there.

The Cicada

Once a cicada emerged from years underground to find little had changed in its long absence.

Granted, there was no denying things had changed for the world it emerged into, which seemed much warmer than was the case less than two decades before. And conditions had certainly changed for many of the plants, animals, birds, and fish that had been forced to adapt to the new and warmer climate or had begun to disappear when they couldn't adapt rapidly enough. But little to nothing was different for the self-appointed masters of the planet, by all indications. Humans were still behaving as though the creature comforts they'd enjoyed in the past would belong to them and their offspring forever. What's more, their numbers had increased dramatically, and the next time cicadas emerged and took to the trees, they might well face a struggle with these supremely successful invasive bipeds for breeding space on any tree limbs that remained.

Not to mention the risk of going deaf from the grating racket these humans made wherever they turned up. If they limited their deafening insistence on calling attention to themselves to a reasonable mating season, the din might be tolerable. But to carry on as they did at all hours in all seasons as though competing to be recognized as the best-endowed species on earth was the only activity that satisfied them—now, that kind of behavior could be distinctly annoying to a cicada, having itself waited so long and so patiently for its own moment to sound off at last while getting it on with some six-legged hottie.

Why did humans want to climb back into the trees at an accelerating pace anyway, when they'd proven over and over again they were ready to do the dirty whenever and wherever they had a spare moment? Nor could their arboreal retreat offer any evolutionary advantage. Hadn't they turned their backs on an existence spent hanging from branches long, long ago? Upright posture, tool-making hands, a cranial capacity they flattered themselves on—what was all that about if not a clear demonstration there was no return now to the way things once were in simpler times? Human beings ought to accept that they'd evolved and just make the best they could of their current state.

But oh no. Belonging to *Homo sapiens* evidently had its vexations, chief among them being what the cicada speculated was a "big-brain burden." Granted, the cicada's hypothesis was based only on limited observation, yet it seemed to explain the available evidence better than other interpretations did.

Particularly telling, in the cicada's view, was the vast number of humans now lurching about in a swaggering stoop as if trying to shake off unwanted brain cells and reacquaint themselves with the mental equivalent of scraping the ground with their knuckles. Such regressive behavior, though suggesting some difficulty in shouldering the demands of modern intelligence, was of limited help in understanding the deeper significance of any hypothetical "big-brain burden." The basic motor skills of humans appeared to be up to the task, judging by the number of flashy objects they prided themselves on being able to manipulate simultaneously. So the regression of the species might in fact be a more complex phenomenon than it appeared, the cicada had to concede.

For humans weren't just clambering back into the trees on all sides but literally fighting each other tooth and nail in assertion of their absolute right to do so. This aggressive behavior was true not simply of excitable individuals, whose reaction to the first hint of opposition to their view of the world was to reach for the nearest lethal object and begin cursing loudly as they swung it around their heads, but also of those that one might have supposed had put such brutish behavior behind them. The most stunning development in all this had to be the swarming of the trees at times by whole populations who appeared intent on never again feeling themselves hindered in the slightest by having their feet on the ground.

It was as if after generations straining to break free from lightless superstition and a primitive dread of what reason might reveal, superstition and dread had won out. In an age of technological marvels, medical miracles, inquiries into the smallest of the small and the farthest reaches of deep space, plus the latest speculations on the origins of life itself, many human beings, this most cerebrally advanced of creatures, gave every sign of having decided: "Thanks, but no thanks. We'll stick with the familiar world of age-old village wisdom because, hey, it tells us who we are and everything we'll ever need to know. Ev-er-y-thing, get it? So, put us on evolution's 'do not call' list until further notice."

Tough times indeed lay ahead for cicadas—and for many another species as well.

The Civet

Once a civet worried about body odor.

By the end of a long day, it increasingly detected something acrid in the air (something a little "off" in a sticky sort of way) and would begin sniffing here and there to find the source. With all the competing odors that filled the world (from the ambrosially fragrant to the putrescent), it might seem a waste of time to pursue any one of them in particular. Yet, however much the civet was aware of the vain character of its fixation, that awareness had little restraining effect.

Besides, no matter how intently it sought to locate the smell on the wind or elsewhere in its environment, the search ended every time in the civet's turning round and round itself instead. Finally raising a hind limb and pushing its nose in for a whiff, it had to admit, as always, that its own smell was what offended it.

At this recognition, the civet would invariably crinkle up its nose in disgust. Not so much at the odor per se but at the thought that it must be readily apparent to others of its species as well. Total strangers, who, though they might have the good manners not to show it, would surely be offended to the same extent the civet was. How embarrassing.

The only other beings so concerned about how they smelled, at least as far as the civet had observed, were humans, surprisingly. Whenever they thought nobody was looking, many of them would begin secretly sniffing away at themselves and trying to cover up whatever unpleasant discoveries they made. It was as if they wanted to hide from themselves the true smell of a human qua human at all costs. What was wrong with the way they smelled? In the civet's opinion, they didn't have much to be ashamed of. Certainly nothing that merited their determination to eliminate all trace of the natural odors with which life had so generously endowed them by tirelessly dabbing or rubbing or spraying themselves with whatever they were convinced made them smell the slightest bit better.

All in all, human beings smelled like they were probably supposed to smell. If that proved offensive, would spraying or smearing their bodies with some fragrance from nature really ease their reluctance to accept themselves as they were?

The civet considered itself rather an authority in this regard. After all, how many times had enterprising humans shown up to scrape away at the scent glands on the civet's backside, cruelly indifferent to all the pain they caused? They never asked. They just took what they craved. Large sums they'd earned from perfumes made with what they'd scraped, but was it really worth so much to insecure humans to smell like another creature's rear end?

And then, suddenly amazed it hadn't made the connection much sooner, the civet wondered if such odd behavior mightn't be similar to its own life-long concern about body odor. Perhaps the odor concerns it shared with humans had a shared remedy as well. Perhaps they were onto something after all.

If only it could give a human being a good scraping someday to find out.

The Clam

Once a young clam aspired to be an oyster.

The clam was convinced it had a matchless pearl waiting within, if it could just find the right grain of sand to get started. When it had a focus for its efforts, when its juices really started to flow, the result could not fail to be a creation of stunning beauty. So stunning, perhaps, that the history of pearl cultivation might have to be rewritten to include the clam's achievement.

Needless to say, this triumph depended on finding that right grain of sand. And not simply finding it, but welcoming it and the lifelong torment it must bring as the price of a pearl's fashioning. For the clam had studied the lives of oysters and had come to the conclusion that the level of agony each one suffered in creating a pearl determined much of its value.

A mistake at the start, then, choosing a grain that was so slight it would never result in a pearl of note or one so large the pain it brought would simply overwhelm the clam and leave it exhausted, these were the two fears that haunted it. Since its entire life would be judged by the outcome of a long nurturing of distress, the young clam's initial decision could make all the difference.

And what if it spent a lifetime molding its pearl, creating layer after layer of coating for the jagged ache at its heart, only to have the sum of all its endeavors

51

tossed aside as lacking the expected outward shape or luster? There would be no starting over at that point, nor any excuses to be made that would hide the humiliating failure. Nothing to ease the final torture of not measuring up.

Or suppose the clam did measure up on some scale of woe to worth, some ratio of suffering to beauty, but found the fashion of the day ruled by a different appraisal. What solace would the perfect pearl be then?

It might have been assumed that such concerns would make the clam think twice about its aspiration to be an oyster. Burrowing to quiet obscurity under a beachload of sand rather than straining to fashion splendor out of one's private pain—wouldn't that have been a wiser life choice for the clam?

Of course it would have. But this is not a tale about wisdom.

The Coelacanth

Once a coelacanth played a leading role in the culture wars.

It undertook this self-appointed duty out of a conviction that coelacanth society was losing touch with what had always been considered absolute truths, and doing so at an alarming rate. Each day was proving to be more challenging than the last, it muttered to itself and to any other coelacanths it encountered. Nothing was considered sacred and beyond challenge anymore, as heritage and traditional values steadily lost their authority. Things had been better in the Cretaceous Period, no question about it.

Those were the days. With none of the questioning of everlasting certainties and incessant discussions from "multiple perspectives" about beliefs and customs. There hadn't been much discussion about anything in the Cretaceous, nor had there been much sense in proposing there should be, since coelacanths inhabited a lightless world where patterns of thought and behavior had already been set so far back in the past it seemed they'd been the way they were ever since the beginning of the world.

What had gone wrong, then? How had the greatest geological period of all time come to such a disturbing close? Things had been just fine in the greatest geological period ever, right up until the moment when all that was traditional and right started being challenged. Eons of self-assurance were undone as coelacanth youth were inexplicably straying from their core values, spinning out of control, going straight to hell. Every conviction and norm was being called into question and being dismissed by those who didn't understand the eternal values that had given substance and solidity to the coelacanth way of life. Cretaceous culture was being canceled everywhere in the deep, dark sea!

No matter how weak the link might be between the end of the Cretaceous and the decline and fall of nearly everything the coelacanth declared sacrosanct and eternal, it always managed to find one. If the connection wasn't obvious, then you simply weren't looking for it hard enough.

Matters were even worse higher up in the water column, where the light played tricks on one's brain by distorting the facts, the coelacanth was absolutely convinced. Nothing appeared as it was supposed to appear, and it was easy to lose track of all that had been obvious, basic, and beyond dispute since day one. What were definitely risky illusions had already led many of the young and impressionable to begin seeing things in ways that their forebears never would have. And worse yet, to swallowing what they now thought was true, instead of recognizing it as just the latest "fake news."

When life-defining certainties passed down from the Cretaceous were at risk, to dither was to invite disaster. If coelacanths couldn't adapt to the waters above, drastic measures must be taken.

"Back to the deep, dark depths!" this one bubbled frantically. "Back to the way things have always been or we'll be doomed by the new!"

The Corpse

Once a naked corpse in a wildly popular "Bodies" exhibition had some things to say about the giggling crowd milling around it.

First of all, what were these people even doing here? Each day, mobs of them pressed up against the entrance doors like shoppers on Black Friday, ready to trample one another in a rush for whatever they felt was just the thing needed to fill some gap in their lives. Fistfights were a constant threat as irritable parents accused one another of cutting into line and trying to get to the corpses on display before "my little Jimmy and Janey break into tears! They've been up all night with excitement!" As if death were the latest, must-have VR game.

And look at how these people were attired! If they had no sense of decorum themselves, couldn't they at least acknowledge that the corpses they were gawking at might have possessed some of it when alive? Did they imagine the fellow in the pose of a champion runner over there, all his muscles bared and preserved—all the beauty of a powerful body at its peak forever—did they imagine he would have stooped to wearing their stained T-shirts and loud, baggy shorts in public? Or the young woman running just ahead of him in joyful awareness of her mind and body so beautifully in balance, how thankful she must be to have escaped ending up like one of these coiffured mall frumps all about her. Like lovers on a Grecian urn the young pair looked.

Even the corpses whose organs presented various stages of disease or decay must wince at the spectacle of this squinting, grimacing throng who'd bought tickets for an opportunity to feel pleased about their own physical state by comparison. A sweaty crush barely able to resist the urge to reach out and poke at bodies so coolly poised—little did they know who, the corpses or their lot, looked the more ravaged by time, excess, and neglect.

But what struck the corpse as even more distasteful was the unacknowledged fascination with death itself betrayed by so many of these people. How clear death's power over them was as they tried to mask their fixation through graceless displays of revulsion or self-conscious titters. Rather than giving themselves over to awe at the human form fully revealed, they sought to cover up their embarrassment at its naked truth by adopting a Peeping Tom sneer, as if to satisfy a repressed necrophilic urge while still pretending they didn't suffer from it in the slightest.

This secret infatuation with death must leave them only half-alive, the corpse supposed: strangers to their own existence unless it brought them some thrill that raised their pulse a beat or two. The equivalent of Eros and Thanatos sitting side by side in life's cheap seats yet oblivious to each other's presence all the while? No wonder benumbed internet porn was the biggest business on the planet. What else could offer these people the combination of titillation and deniability that no doubt brought them to an exhibition like this as well? How prurient! And how morbid! It was enough to give any self-respecting corpse the heebie-jeebies.

This one was so offended that it wanted to shout out loud, "Who are the real dead people here, anyway?"

The Crabs

Once crabs signed a contract codifying amorous intent.

The crabs took great pride in having written the contract themselves. It stipulated the terms and conditions under which they agreed to enter into caring and sharing relationships with one another, abrogating all covenants and verbal agreements hitherto in effect.

The document was long, with many clauses and provisos. It was bound to be long, for the crabs were concerned to have their emotions legally defined to the last jot and tittle before they entered into any and all romantic engagements. Nothing should be left in doubt regarding love, nothing left uncodified.

The most important clause in the contract prohibited both signatories from ever moving in too direct or forward a manner in their loving and caring relationship. Such behavior was considered evidence of egocentric willfulness and insensitivity to the cosignatory's self-regard. Only less direct or less forward advances were permitted, and these must be negotiated with the party in question a minimum of twenty-four (24) hours in advance.

In keeping with the spirit of this covenant, every crab went to great lengths to avoid expressions defined as "problematic," pledging to avoid, for example, unless specifically requested, use of "I" (as in "I love you"), which could be construed as both overly self-referential and potentially manipulative. Instead, the crabs swore at the beginning of the document to base their emotional commitment on the following avowal:

> We, hereafter to be addressed as "significant and/or designated others," do solemnly attest to the fact that we, being of sound mind and body and governed by the certified testaments of mutual respect herein signed and witnessed, are freely and without reservation entering, in accordance with all the rules heretofore negotiated, into a fully nurturing relationship that recognizes both parties to this agreement as caring crabs.

The word "you" (as in the expression "Do you love me?") might have suffered the same prohibition that "I" did, since it too had the appearance of being unacceptably direct. However, "you" retained its legitimacy in the end because both parties agreed that the question "Do you love me?" was indispensable in determining whether one's "significant and/or designated other" possessed the proper degree of respect for oneself as a "significant and/or designated other" to merit the continuation of a legally binding relationship as caring crabs.

A contract so deliberate in its scope succeeded in eliminating all but a few cases of unregulated amour. In those rare instances, either party had simply to produce the document and declare, "I should've known you weren't to be trusted!" The rest was a mere formality.

And thus it is that crabs so often move sideways or even backwards over the sand, convinced it's the only way to find true love.

The Crane

Once a crane passed the Foreign Service examination to become a diplomat.

It couldn't be denied, of course, that much of the crane's success (both in the examination and in its long, illustrious career since) was owed to family connections and timely political contributions. Be that as it may, there was also broad agreement that the crane was a most distinguished-looking bird. It presented precisely the kind of solemn, slow movement that inspires mutual regard among high members of the diplomatic corps around the globe.

In this spirit, the crane could often be observed spending a great deal of time carefully deliberating the most prudent placement of its feet. There were protocols to be followed, after all, and codes of stately etiquette to be punctiliously observed. Waters must be endlessly tested. It was naive to think these sorts of things could be rushed or shortened in any way. Perhaps they could in the unruliness of common life, but hardly in the measured footwork of high diplomacy.

The same must be said for the many gala receptions at which attendance was de rigueur for the crane. Night after night it could be seen tirelessly performing this duty in the company of others who were likewise charged with weighty and often secret responsibilities. Toasting each other while sampling an array of hors d'oeuvres, they might all nod thoughtfully in agreement with such solemn declarations as "We now find ourselves at a critical juncture and appeal to all concerned parties to set aside their differences and to engage in a substantive and robust exchange of views on the difficult issues before us." "Hear, hear," the crane would say in appropriately dignified tones as it shifted ever so slowly from one foot to the other.

Its response might sometimes change to "tut, tut," however, at reports that those not so patient with the diplomatic pace, procedures, and protocols by which the crane ordered its reality were being gassed in the streets outside or "disappeared" by their own governments. "Diplomacy must succeed, we all recognize, in establishing more robust balances between conflicting exigencies and satisfying all parties concerned," it would declare down its impressive beak. "The alternative is simply unthinkable. All options are on the table and we're looking at every tool in the toolbox."

Each time diplomacy did not in fact succeed, each time the alternative became not only thinkable but terrifyingly real, the crane could be seen leaving troubled waters behind with an air of urbane disgruntlement. At such times it would seriously consider once again the invitations it regularly received to head up the International Olympic Committee, FIFA, the WTO and/or the WHO, the World Bank, a multinational business, a candy-making conglomerate, and many, many more. But the crane always resolved, as it winged away from the latest diplomatic fiasco, to continue for a while yet with high-level statecraft. Whatever the setbacks, it remained "robustly optimistic," convinced that without its like, the world would be much worse off. Whether diplomats accomplished anything anywhere was ultimately immaterial. They'd be there, and that's what counted.

In the next post to which the crane was appointed, it would definitely devote time anew to determining the most prudent placement of its feet.

The Crony

Once a well-feathered crony grew so fat its perch threatened to give way.

When this strange bird first showed up at a house in a gated community of high-ranking office holders, the house's owner had felt honored. The prestige of having a personal crony could make one the envy of the entire neighborhood.

Not surprisingly, therefore, the crony's host was eager to make it feel right at home. No expense was spared in providing not only an inviting, cushy perch but also an oversized feeding tray filled to the brim.

The crony immediately stated with irritation, however, that what it was being expected to eat was no better than chicken feed. Afraid its personal crony might fly away in a huff so soon after showing up, the homeowner ordered the most expensive brand of feed available in hopes of supplying it with what it most craved.

The richness of the fare wasn't the crony's only complaint, as it turned out. Quality was one thing; quantity was quite another. And the quantity being offered wasn't nearly enough to satisfy the appetite of a crony of substance, the by now quaking host was given to understand in no uncertain terms.

The portions were immediately doubled, and when these disappeared in a flash down the crony's gullet, they were doubled again, then again and again until the entire supply was exhausted.

New stocks were laid in but disappeared even faster than before. The crony was putting on weight with every mouthful now, swelling by the bite and fouling the area below its creaking perch with the outcome.

As the cost of keeping a crony put an increasing strain on its host's finances, the belongings of the house started to show up for sale in the front yard. And when these measures also proved inadequate, nighttime raids on neighboring properties added any lawn furniture not bolted down.

Through all of these desperate, impoverishing measures, the crony itself continued to prosper until it had grown larger than the house and could be seen from great distances leaning over the roofline like some idol awaiting the sacrifice of the firstborn within.

Would the family that had counted on calling this place home for years to come have to flee under cover of darkness with what little they could carry from their life before the crony took command of it?

Would the crony, rattling its feed tray the next morning to no effect, discover the family gone, struggle off its perch, and waddle after them? Or would it simply move next door in the gated community of high-ranking office holders?

The Crow

Once a crow sat on a branch and contemplated the condition of man.

More specifically, the condition of the cursing, red-faced fellow looking directly up at the crow with a rock in his hand. Whatever was he thinking?

After all, how far could he throw that rock? And how fast could he duck and cover or scramble to escape what came back at him from above? He'd be wise just to drop the rock, just move on without pressing his luck and leave the crow to continue its usual caw-cawing over the length and breadth of the neighborhood.

Was anybody listening to crows of late, though, besides those perhaps reaching for their own rocks to cast? But where else were humans going to receive anything like the lookout assistance offered gratis by crows? Setting great store in being "firmly grounded" wherever they found themselves, how far could humans possible see in front of them by comparison to even fledgling crows? Not half far enough, judging by all the available evidence.

If it wasn't at some bird or animal they'd hurled anything they could get their hands on over the up-and-down course of their development as a species, it was at each other, never thinking far enough ahead to see the consequences. Hit-and-run skirmishes over some worthless scrap of land or some scrap of an idea that one side took for absolute truth and the other took for absolute rubbish—what a way to spend your short time here on earth, searching all the while for a bigger rock to heave at your adversaries.

But this suicide pact by an entire species wasn't what moved the crow to the contemplation of heedless humankind. They'd increasingly overscavenged the planet, hadn't they, and who would be surprised if all of them ultimately did themselves in while pelting each other over the last snatch to be had of anything? More pressing, however, at least to the crow's mind if not to theirs, was the likelihood that humans would take along into extinction any number of other species, what with their habitual self-absorption and shortsightedness.

There'd been a good deal of discussion about just such a possibility among the birds already, led by eagles and hawks on one side and ostriches and turkeys on the other. Where one group argued for some form of preemptive strike from above to impress upon human beings the dangerous folly of their ways, the flightless group held forth at length about the risks involved in antagonizing such vengeful creatures and the benefits instead of steering well clear of them.

Which left crows somewhere in the middle. They were hardly blind to the stakes involved but mindful as well of how much they owed to the subjects of this debate. Weren't humans, in their own inimitable way, the best friends crows had ever known? No bird was half so willing to share as humans were, and most times without a second thought. Their largesse, on open display in every garbage dump and clogging every gutter of megacities and small towns alike, should not go unacknowledged.

It was almost as though humans were constitutionally unable to take a bite of anything themselves without leaving behind an equal portion for the crows, often more. And in some cases much more, with hardly a moment's hesitation in spreading the bounty of their waste far and wide. So what was this fellow now winding up to fling his rock thinking?

Didn't he recognize his one true sidekick on the planet?

The Cuckoos

Once a pair of cuckoos devoted a great deal of thought to their parenting skills.

"How can we guarantee the brightest future for our precious eggs?" they asked themselves again and again. Traditionally, cuckoos have sought to advance the prospects of their young by laying them in the nests of other birds. In this way, the hatchlings might gain from varied environments and grow up to be more well-rounded and more successful than their parents.

But this pair of cuckoos differed in one important way from that pattern of behavior. Already convinced they were the most well-rounded and most successful birds they knew, they wanted their young to have every opportunity to prove they were worthy of the genes they inherited by duplicating for all the world to see what their parents had already attained.

To this end, the cuckoos diligently planned out every moment of their unhatched eggs' future: what brain-stimulating bauble to buy first, how to "ace" the entrance interviews of the most prestigious Pre-Ks for gifted toddlers, which youth soccer league to join, which higher education prep courses to enroll in, what community service looked best on college and university applications, the choicest careers for wealth and prestige, which political party to support, and so on.

Despite all these efforts, the cuckoos couldn't free themselves of a nagging anxiety that their young might not grow up to be a credit to them. Suppose the little ones turned out not to show any benefit from all these efforts to secure a future as impressive as their parents' past? Wouldn't that failure inevitably mean years of underachievement, hopelessness, and low self-esteem?

As the cuckoos looked around themselves, this anxiety about being embarrassed by their offspring was only increased by what they saw. The neighbors' clutch of eggs appeared so promising. Could their own ever hope to match the neighbors' in Pre-K-for-gifted-toddlers interviews, soccer wins, prep courses, college or university admissions, career choices, wealth and prestige, political affiliation, and so on? They even began to wonder if the neighboring eggs weren't in fact meant to be theirs all along and had inexplicably ended up in the wrong nest.

Once they'd reached this distressed state of mind, it wasn't long before the cuckoos were driven to take desperate measures. They began roaming far and wide in search of unguarded eggs that could prove worthy of their attention and love.

The many they plucked from other nests not only burdened theirs, however, but also made their own eggs appear even more unsatisfactory by comparison. In the cuckoos' eyes, the new ones definitely seemed more likely to do them honor by making something of themselves what would be fully reflective of all the parenting efforts and sacrifices made on their behalf.

This being the case, the cuckoo couple felt they had no choice posterity-wise but to begin pushing their own eggs out of the overcrowded nest, letting them fall to their fates below.

The Dodo

Once it was thought the dodo had died out.

A claim difficult to grasp, given that a day without dodos is inconceivable now. So complete has been their resurgence.

Three theories have been advanced for this remarkable and unprecedented return. One theory holds that dodos were never in real danger of disappearing. Instead, they benefited from an uncanny knack for impersonation and passed themselves off as "regular guys and gals." Because this ability had not been noticed before, or at least had not been taken seriously, the dodo found it could come and go as it pleased without detection. The ruse proved especially helpful whenever some terrible mess occurred and the expected call arose for investigations to find "the dodo(s) responsible for this mess." In every instance, not a single dodo responsible for the mess was ever uncovered.

The second theory states that those widely recognized as dodos today were not true dodos to begin with. Rather, they actually sought to pass themselves off as dodos when it grew apparent that being one offered a definite advantage, especially when it came to high political appointments. When dodo-like behavior not only became acceptable but was in fact rewarded, according to this explanation, an explosion occurred in the number of self-promoting dodos. A similar explosion occurred amongst conspiracy theorists, anti-vaxxers, flat-earthers, and their like across all of society. It was the best of times for the dodo, and if acting like one and sounding like one was the key to success, then who could argue with that?

The third theory has often been called the "what difference does it make?" interpretation of developments. According to this line of thinking, once there were no longer any clear criteria for separating what was traditionally understood to be a true dodo from growing legions of dodo impersonators and neo-dodos, few could see the point any longer of even bothering to try. "Why not simply accept the status quo?" was the common attitude. With nothing to hold it back, dodoism would naturally, like water, seek its own level. Thus resisting and not resisting the course of events amounted to much the same thing.

The dodo, no matter how one defined it, was here to stay.

The Donor

Once a pig had mixed feelings about its donation of an aortic valve to save the life of a human being.

The donor pig knew full well that without a transplant, the days of the recipient were numbered. Barely into what many would consider the fullness of middle age, this patient had begun to decline rapidly. Now "middle age" suddenly had a new meaning, one pushed back to the last enthusiasms of youth, when thought is rarely given to how little time might be left one. The slow mellowing of experience into old age and final serenity that humans seemed to assume lay ahead of them, as far as the pig had observed, was no longer in the cards for this one. Only a premature weakening followed by a wheezing end within months lay ahead.

The pig thought back to the enthusiasms of its own youth. The rich coursing of blood throughout its body and the force of its intent to stretch every moment as far as possible, these had been the very proof it was alive when being alive meant gratefully celebrating each future moment as an unexpected gift.

Now this gift was the pig's to pass on. It tried to imagine the emotions of the waiting recipient of the transplant just before being anesthetized, uncertain of the operation's outcome. What dreams, seemingly blighted by a heart that was killing her or him, might soon be given new life?

The pig was well aware that the genetic closeness of pigs to people had made the risk for transplant rejection increasingly low. Extended prognoses were still uncertain, of course, and tabloids were still fond of running lurid photographs of post-recovery celebrations under corny headlines like "Pigmen Gone Wild!!!" Nevertheless, the donor was optimistic about the outcome. It didn't look forward to a joining of two separate lives so much as an embrace of the value of life itself. Granted, the pig could be seen as making the greater sacrifice, but the recipient of its gift must certainly be altered as well, or that sacrifice would be meaningless. You couldn't come back from the brink of death as though nothing had changed, could you? Go on as though you owed nothing to life in return?

What would be the patient's view of life after the operation? For a moment, the pig felt a lump in its throat at how solemn yet elating a prospect lay ahead. To wake up with your life handed back to you when you'd neared the very end of hope—what must it be like to feel that organ of infinite generosity and infinite passion, reverence, and marvel beating with a strength you'd never dared think it would have again? There was only one question the pig couldn't quite clear from its mind in the last moments before it went under the knife itself.

How would the person saved by its death now feel about eating pork?

The Doppelgänger

Once a doppelgänger wondered what life would be like if only . . .

Catching sight of the figure everyone took to be the doppelgänger's twin always brought a jolt because of how little similarity the two seemed to have. There was, the doppelgänger had to admit, a surface resemblance, but that must happen all the time, given the boom in makeover treatments of late to turn you into the spitting image of anyone you envied.

You didn't even have to resemble others physically. Dressing or talking like them was apparently enough to show that you were kindred spirits, along with thousands of others dressing and sounding the same. While "thinking as one" with somebody else could simply be the kind of frantic "friending" that now provided an illusory defense against the terror of finding yourself alone.

The doppelgänger, by contrast, actually did want to be alone. Or at least not be confused with anybody else. There must have been something in the doppelgänger's youthful aspirations that presaged a future quite apart from this bothersome rival who had for years robbed the doppelgänger of a self that was free of outside definition.

What could be more discouraging than to be a doppelgänger in your own life? To wonder if a struggle to "know thyself" had been anything more than an illusion: a phantom quest. And whether times and places and experiences had in fact made a difference, had meant something and not been mere fantasies adopted from others to fill a void between birth and now. What other proof did the doppelgänger have of not being a mere figment of the imagination?

Thoughts such as these most often arose in the hours before dawn, when the doppelgänger sat at a window and stared through a motionless reflection at the shadowy world beyond the pane.

Soon the reflection must fade in the gathering daylight and the doppelgänger lose even this evidence of being oneself and no other. But until then, the image would still have a solidity and definition to it that were reassuring for the testimony they offered that the doppelgänger's years, even those seemingly the most unstructured, did add up to something more than just a might-have-been, a puzzle of a thousand pieces with some missing. Everything the doppelgänger had ever valued must remain in this likeness on the glass that memory helped trace. Everything still had significance. Still belonged.

As even moments like this one must, when the doppelgänger sat at the window and wondered what life would be like if only . . .

The Dots

Once dots complained about all the attempts made to connect them.

The result, they declared, invariably turned out to be a maladroit, unconvincing scratchwork that required a caption in order to be recognized for what it supposedly represented. "Oh, so that's it," was the most common response to being told how connecting the dots revealed a pattern in them, followed by a confused "And here I was convinced the whole thing was nothing more than a child's doodling."

Not that those taking credit for the latest connection of dots were daunted by this mistaking of the grand designs they'd traced out for a mere child's doodling yet again. Some degree of confusion was actually of benefit to regular dot-connectors, for it meant they remained indispensable to any discussion of how to discover grand designs in what might otherwise be judged an aimless mess. At least until people grew impatient with the whole thing and turned to a fresh scattering of dots to puzzle over. And once again, those who considered themselves experts at interpreting dots and doodles might be counted on to offer their services.

No wonder dots got fed up. For dots, despite what might be inferred from their seeming uniformity, prided themselves on being distinct and independent. They had no difficulty telling one another apart, so why shouldn't they take offense at being lumped together under some catchall assumption about what they shared? Left to themselves, they might avoid each other's company altogether and quite happily shun the conformity imposed by connection to others in favor of the liberty to follow their own designs wherever these might lead them—even if this liberty offered no pattern to assign a recognizable meaning— nothing, ultimately, to separate "grand design" from "aimless mess."

Maybe dots didn't have a collective meaning and didn't need one. Maybe they were just dots. Wasn't that enough? Did the lack of a shared meaning prove that no meaning existed? Or might it merely suggest the limited vision of the meaning-seekers?

Even the smallest dot held coiled within it the promise of this, that, everything, or even nothing. And then to have some self-declared know-it-all who'd long since dismissed this magical ambiguity in favor of the reassurance of "the known"—for the comfort of certainty when certainty came at the cost of all else—to have that know-it-all, out of a yet unacknowledged inadequacy perhaps, seek to impose an understanding on whatever still retained the glory of the undefined—never! A mere smudge of a dot would rebel at such a travesty.

Not that rebelling did much good. For "meaning," once the slightest pattern has been spied in anything, is merciless and can crush the life out of whatever it fastens upon.

In the end, the dots never stood a chance.

The Dragonfly

Once an ophthalmologist had some good news and some bad news for a dragonfly.

"Which would you like to know first?" the doctor asked, noting a look of apprehension on the dragonfly's face.

"Give me the bad news first, I guess," the dragonfly answered after an awkward pause spent trying to decide whether it would be better to accept the worst for what it was or to hold out hope for an end, finally, to the splitting headaches that had plagued it for so long.

"Well, the bad news is the headaches you complain of are indeed brought on by your eyes."

So it was true, the dragonfly sighed to itself. These thousands of facets to each eye, keenly sensitive to every shift in light and every motion, these windows thrown open to life and all the longing glances life casts on itself, was there no escape from the continual strain of taking in every fascination that wide nature offered?

"The good news is we can do something about that."

Then there was hope? "Can you really do something for me, doctor?"

"Yes, but the surgical procedure entails risk and some cost in terms of time, you must understand."

"Risk and cost in time?"

"The risk is that a patient may go completely blind, though this happens very rarely."

The dragonfly again took a while to consider this statement, particularly what the "very" in "very rarely" might mean, before asking, "And the potential cost in time?"

"If the procedure is successful, you'll leave with your head in bandages, but after a while those can come off and the pain will be gone."

"Completely?"

"In most cases, that's been the final outcome. With two new eyes, much smaller and relocated more to the front of your head, what we might call 'the visual overload' you've experienced will be very nearly eliminated. Instead of having to deal with the full sweep of the world, you'll only need to concern yourself with that portion of it directly in front of you and can ignore the rest. Plus, with a pair of 'virtual eyelids' from here on out, you'll always be able to close out entirely whatever you don't wish to see, even if it does happen to be directly in front of you."

The dragonfly scanned all the tiny doctors floating in the facets of its eyes and tried to imagine their being reduced to a single image, along with what it would be like to have a single giant doctor loom all at once into view. With its manifold angles of vision suddenly replaced by one angle at a time, how much of what had been the spellbinding bounty of life that surrounded it on all sides could it hope to take in anymore?

Observing the dragonfly's renewed uneasiness, the ophthalmologist said by way of encouragement, "Seems like a small price to pay for an end to those headaches of yours."

Was it a "small price?" the dragonfly wondered. Should it go ahead with this proposed remedy apparently based on a confidence that what one saw before one was all that mattered and that peripheral concerns were nothing more than that, peripheral, and thus considered merely a distraction? Was the dragonfly ready to settle for this in place of untold variations in an all-embracing vision, with no single view superior to all the others and thus not a single one omitted? The dragonfly eyed all the tiny doctors again and thought of the post-surgical single focus it would have to rely upon when viewing its future world.

"No offense intended, doctor," it finally replied as it set its wings in motion and headed towards the countless doors out of the room, "but I think I'll put up with the pain as long as I possibly can."

The Drones

Once drones lawyered up by the thousands.

It was just a precaution, they responded, when questions about the large number of them feeling the need to seek legal representation began to be asked. Unaccustomed to queries regarding what role drones actually played in the day-to-day workings of a bee colony or whether the burgeoning increase in their numbers and their correspondingly mounting demands for privileged consideration might ultimately prove a drain upon the resources of the hive and trigger a catastrophic colony collapse, the drones preferred to leave to counsel any defense of their rights by birth and the life of luxury they'd come to enjoy. Plus any decisions on filing multiple suits for defamation of character against all and sundry who had the audacity to object to the place of drones in the status quo.

"Our clients take deep offense at the suggestion their behavior poses any danger whatsoever to the well-being of the hive!" the lawyers declared in unison. "On the contrary, without the superior and important role played by drones above, none of the lesser bees below would prosper," the lawyers continued, again in unison.

To the overwhelming majority of these "lesser bees" toiling to meet the hive's every physical need and to safeguard its very survival, such a claim might have been dismissed as a bad joke, were they not too busy at their tasks for even a forced smile. And few found the strength at the end of a long day of striving to reach ever-higher levels of productivity so the likes of drones could carry on with the sweet lives they led to find much at all about the situation amusing. The strain of holding an entire life system together while nonstop demands of "Work harder! Harder!" came down to them from the drones rendered sleep a brief yet welcome respite.

In their dreams, not a few worker bees built a different hive. One where their communal efforts were more appreciated in their own right and not dismissed as a sign of personal limitation or low ambition. A world of cooperation where sacrifice by equal for equal replaced competition like that between queen bee types engaged in lethal attacks upon other queen bee types in their struggle to get to the top and devoid as well of pampered drones who incessantly called for more and more sacrifice from worker bees and less and less from drones or else the consequences would surely be horrendous for all of the hive.

"What consequences?" a slumbering worker bee might now and then murmur.

"The doom of the entire hive! Doom!" lawyers to the drones would immediately declare in chorus as though the answer was self-evident.

"Oh really?" all worker bees might now shrug as one.

"Without fail! Absent the drones, there'd be no production of easy flowing honey whatsoever!"

"That old con again?" each worker bee might then smile to itself while falling back into a snooze for a precious minute or two more. "As if drones don't owe anything to us. As if they create much themselves beyond self-indulgence, more self-promotion to protect their prideful place, and more of us to deal with the consequences."

And then it was time for the worker bees to rise and get back to the real business of the hive yet again.

The Dung Beetle

Once a dung beetle had an inkling of immortality.

Nothing more than that, just an inkling. For a moment, though, the beetle's daily drudgery seemed to fall away, and it felt it could touch the bounds of space and time. For just beyond the ball of dung the beetle had been pushing about, all of creation opened out and opened out again, revealing the spread of its bright glories in every direction.

Then all of creation closed back in as abruptly as it had opened out, and the beetle found itself pressed upside-down against its dung ball once again, gasping for breath and questioning its memory.

"What just happened?" it wheezed as it clung to the ball for balance and waited for its mind to stop spinning. What was that feeling of endless expansion and connection to everything? The sense of utter bliss, where had it come from? And where had it gone now that the beetle was faced with this stinking ball to deal with again?

These questions stayed with the beetle long after it resumed its routine of pushing the dung ball a short distance, pausing to extend its back legs as far as they could reach to take the increasing measure of the thing, and then straining to get it rolling again. Not that the beetle came up with anything by way of answers to its questions. Realistically speaking, how much thought could it spare for such concerns when the world was so full of dung to be gathered, measured, and rolled about?

In the course of these constant exertions, however, there were times when glimmers of the sudden elation the beetle had felt would light up the edges of its memory, only to fade away as quickly as they'd appeared. The beetle was left after these episodes feeling exhilarated by whatever beckoned from out there beyond the dung yet disoriented as well, without any idea of what to do besides cling more closely to its ball and press on with the routine task at hand.

Over time, the intervals separating these transient spells of remembered wonder and the desperate dung-clinging that followed them grew increasingly short. No sooner did the beetle come to suspect an invigorating flash of light might yet again be headed its way than it pressed against the ball as if it meant to bury itself inside till the whole thing passed.

And as the moments of dizzying transport and comforting security moved closer and closer to one another and finally merged into a single, split-second leave-and-lunge for the dung, the beetle found it could no longer distinguish between the two. In fact, it began to feel their relationship had been reversed and the dung itself might be giving rise to the beetle's sensations of euphoric expansion.

Perhaps it was merely a question of how you framed the relationship, the beetle thought excitedly, grasping at the heartening proposition that now suggested itself. Could this dung be in itself the very gateway to eternity? To immortality? The be-all and end-all of cosmic awareness and connection? Dung Everlasting?

Now, what might that mean?

The Earth Goddess

Once the earth goddess created all, alone.

Of herself she created everything everywhere. First day and night, equal in their glory and in their marvels. Then dry land and surrounding seas. And she willed into existence every plant now known plus those that flourished in their day and are no more. She linked earth with the rest of the cosmos and its shared light. She called forth all the creatures of the land and the seas and the air and endowed them with the ability to multiply generation after generation, humans included. The goddess made no distinctions. All flourished on this blue/green planet, and it was good. Until humans decided it was not, that is. Declaring themselves superior to all other life forms, they created a god in their own image

69

who would affirm their dominance and thus be worthy of their worshipful gratitude instead of the goddess, from whom they turned away.

While she who had blessed them with life as she did every other thing on earth wept in sorrow at their blind loss: the paradise they were choosing to leave.

The Elephant

Once an elephant felt conflicted about remembering.

Memory could be such a burden, hanging on one like the pull of too many pounds. Even good memories could weigh you down if they reminded you of blue skies in the past when today had some clouds on the horizon. Worse, of course, were the bad memories.

These grew more burdensome each time they came to mind, as though the mere act of recollection doubled their oppressive load. And yet, when it looked about at its companions, the elephant gathered that life was in fact supposed to be one feel-good moment after another. "Think positive! Think happy! Think inspirational! This is as good as it gets!" it heard from all sides. The elephant was evidently alone in remembering things in its life that were not positive or happy or inspirational or as good as it gets.

As might be expected, the elephant received little sympathy from its companions, most of whom were made uncomfortable by any mention of old torments. It was thoughtless, bad manners even, to disturb them with reminders that life included trials and setbacks. What were they supposed to do about any of that? "Get over it," was the most frequent advice they had for the elephant. "Don't you think it's time to move on?"

But how, the elephant agonized? How shrug off unwelcome or painful memories and lead the carefree life that all others in the herd were so confident of having found? To forget was to lose part of yourself, wasn't it?

"Not if you tell yourself it isn't," was the breezy response that its concerns typically prompted. "We are who our online profiles say we are, so what's the worry? You can reinvent yourself five times a day if you like."

Still, the elephant remained uneasy about what might be the consequences of a serial shrugging off of the past. Then one day the secret to "forgetting without worry" was revealed to it in an infomercial by the author of a runaway bestseller entitled *Twelve Painless Steps to Creative Closure.*

"There isn't anything that can't be put behind you," this closure-maven had declared. "Whatever nagging memory bothers you, large or small, it can't for long if you just find the strength to tell yourself, 'I don't deserve this. I really don't deserve this.' That's the first step to the care-free life you've always really deserved and that I guarantee awaits you."

The elephant ordered *Twelve Painless Steps to Creative Closure* that very day and was amazed to find how important the author's advice to "say goodbye to all those painful or bothersome memories" had become in so many lives. The pages were filled with heart-warming accounts of recoveries from "devastating tragedy" and "real-person testimonials" about the power of the Creative Closure approach. There were even six-step and three-step versions for those with a busy schedule.

Following the book's handy tips, the elephant found it was indeed able to put more and more of what had ever troubled it out of its mind. Even what had once been searing anguish could, with a little effort, be reduced to what the book described as "manageable pain" and then to a dull unpleasantness and finally to practically nothing at all. Coming out of each stage in this process, the elephant walked with an increasing spring to its step and a cheerier disposition.

Not only that, but its neighbors found the elephant's company agreeable once again as well, since it no longer had the annoying habit of reminding them of past traumas or bitter regrets or even the loss of loved ones, theirs or anyone else's. Together, they could all look forward to a day when it would seem like none of these unwelcome moments in life had ever happened. Thanks to Creative Closure, one could have a life that was lighter than air and be looked upon by others with approval for handling everything so well.

But it still happened that the elephant, when alone, occasionally thought it heard a familiar voice in its head repeating emotionally again and again, "How could you forget? Ever. How could you?"

The End of Days

Once the End of Days arrived, but about a half-hour late.

It turned out the End of Days had been held up in traffic. "You try managing four wigged-out horsemen in rush-hour gridlock," the End of Days responded to a low grumbling from all those who'd been waiting for its arrival and felt put out by the delay.

"Honestly, I tried," the End of Days added.

"You might have started earlier," came the curt reply from one of those who claimed to have been waiting the longest.

"My, my, why the big hurry?"

"We've been waiting plenty long enough to get out of this place, if you hadn't noticed."

"Oh, I've noticed. Who wouldn't?"

"What's that supposed to mean?" snapped one of those claiming to have waited so long for the end to come.

"Just that you seem in a great rush to be rid of everything that's been given you."

"Who needs it? We're headed to a better place, aren't we?"

"Are you asking me or telling me?'

"I thought you knew."

"No, the End of Days replied, my instructions didn't say anything about that. I was just to show up at such and such a place on such and such a date. I assumed everything would become clear at that point."

There was some clearing of throats and shuffling of feet in the assembled crowd over this revelation. Then a voice rang out, "Are you for real, or what?"

"Don't I look real?"

"Can't tell. There's just something about you that doesn't seem like the End of Days we were promised."

"Yeah, I thought so, too," another voice was heard amid rising murmurs of discontent. "Where are the trumpets and the burning mountains falling into the sea and the darkened sun and moon and stars and the bottomless pit and locusts and the red dragon and the beast with seven heads and the wine presses of blood and the seven angels with seven bowls full of plagues to loose upon the world and the angels ready to kill a third of mankind and birds to eat their flesh so the way will be prepared for us to get out of this hellhole just in the nick of time?"

"I thought you never tired of calling this place 'God's Country.'"

"Are you trying to confuse us? Just show us your apocalyptic signs and get on with it."

"Well, all I have to show in the way of signs are skies filled with toxic clouds, rivers in flames, seas where nothing spawns, hillsides shorn of trees, spreading deserts, mass extinctions, rampant diseases that too often go ignored because they happen to somebody else, starvation that happens somewhere else, political conflicts that arise all over the place, religious—"

"Stop right there!"

"Oh, but there's more."

"Not in our minds, there isn't."

As if this declaration was a long-awaited signal, the crowd surged forward with a single demand on all lips. "We want what we've been promised, and we want it now!"

The End of Days barely escaped this outburst of wrath. The last thing it heard as it fled being stoned came from one of the group's leaders:

"Okay, okay, everybody, try to stay calm. It looks like we still have a little wait yet before we receive the gift of eternal life promised us. Does anybody have a suggestion for how to kill the time till then?"

The Ephemera

Once an ephemera assumed it had all the time in the world.

The afternoon sun seemed hardly to have moved since the ephemera began fluttering aimlessly through a quiet wood. The shadow cast by each tree didn't appear to advance an inch from one hour to the next. While dusk, that silent stalker, must be swinging his net miles and miles away, the ephemera supposed.

So little to do and so much time to fill! How tedious it could be to count the hours of a long afternoon like this one. Nothing to excite you or to promise satisfactions worth the effort required to seek them out. Besides, where would you begin if you wanted to be sure you weren't wasting your time? What guarantee was there of not being bored even more by what lay ahead than by what you might be trying to put behind you?

A dread of such tedium was what had always attracted the ephemera to theme parks, where you could rely upon others to arrange every experience in advance for you and trust them to spare you all the dull moments in life. Left to its own devices, the ephemera had simply never known how to create the same amount of "quality time" on its own as theme parks offered.

Here alone in this wood, out of others' company, should the ephemera try by itself to make time count? Where, then, should it begin, given how many slow hours still stretched away before it? Or did it matter, when you came down to it, where you began? Was every place as good for that as any other? Was the whole point of having the rest of the day ahead of you not to worry about how long it would last? There might be plenty of room for small diversions and abiding passions alike, the ephemera supposed, as well as untold little discoveries in between.

The ephemera's initial efforts at taking charge of its life so late in it were encouraging. Once underway, it found itself drawn in any number of directions. From afar, these might have appeared to be idle flitterings, but within the ephemera's growing enthusiasm, they made invigorating sense. Why spend your life following a single, set path when there were so many unexplored delights on all sides?

And for every delight enjoyed, a dozen more presented themselves to the ephemera as though they had long been waiting for it to discover their beauty. What an endless flowering of the unlooked-for this afternoon was turning out to be: meadows and glades and even deep-forest clearings bright with promise. The ephemera felt like it could go on like this forever.

But it couldn't, of course. All the while that the ephemera had followed its new-found joys wherever they might lead, the silent stalker had been moving steadily over the darkening hill towards it, and now the swish of a net silenced the entire wood.

The ephemera's day had come to a close just when it couldn't imagine ever tiring of the hours left in it or growing jaded with the wonders of each hour passed. Too little time was the reality, not too much: so little that not being thankful for every moment was inexcusable.

Which may explain why the ephemera had no further complaints to make about life's slow afternoons when dusk reached softly through the net to enfold it.

The Ersatz

Once an ersatz found itself in everyone's thoughts.

This development was not an entirely welcome change from the life of quiet anonymity the ersatz had hitherto known. There had been definite advantages to remaining out of the spotlight. You could think and act pretty much as you wished, without concern for how wise or foolish others might consider you to be. And if you borrowed ideas from others, who cared? What difference did it make?

All of that changed, however, the day the ersatz was asked in a routine on-the-street interview for its thoughts regarding the current state of affairs. Five minutes later, it had dismissed the episode from its mind, but the interviewer hadn't, and the ersatz soon found itself being quoted on air, online, and in print near and far. Its answer, many solemn commentators agreed, "represented a quantum leap in thinking." Anonymity was no longer an option, the ersatz was told by those in the media seeking follow-up interviews. The world awaited its insights.

When the ersatz voiced its puzzlement about all this attention, noting that it had never believed its thinking was particularly significant and had been quite content with that, the response was invariably one of incomprehension. How could it fail to recognize what was obvious to everybody? Some opinion leaders even thought this modesty might be a crafty stratagem by the ersatz to keep its next big idea to itself until the time was ripe to launch it.

"Not at all," the ersatz insisted, "I've never had a big idea that I know of."

And when it found itself credited, despite its embarrassed protests, with being the source of the latest big ideas about this or about that, it wondered what others would think when they finally recognized how small those ideas really were. But to the astonishment of the ersatz, they actually grew bigger in people's minds the more they were repeated.

Soon the mere mention of the ersatz served as proof of a speaker's grasp of big ideas. It was not unusual for discussions of a nettlesome problem to turn on questions like "What would be the ersatz solution here?" or "Suggestions for an ersatz response to developments, anyone?"

"The Ersatz Doctrine," as it came to be known, yielded results virtually everywhere it was applied. It produced such big ideas as "look, a terrorist is a terrorist is a terrorist, and it's that simple"; "bottom line, tax cuts for the rich put more money in the paper cups of the poor"; "public education is best turned over to Sunday School teachers"; "let market forces deal with human rights dilemmas, climate change, species extinction, the fate of the uninsured, plus other things"; and "'wilderness' is just another name for wildfires waiting to happen."

The morning news was filled with updated reports of ersatz pronouncements floated overnight, to be repeated and rerepeated until later editions brought even more sweeping ones. As might be expected, the competition to be the most quoted authority on "ersatzism" spread by the day. Soon great reputations were at stake, names made or ruined, all depending on the confidence with which one advanced one's own form of the ersatz vision.

But the ersatz itself grew increasingly dismayed as it witnessed what was happening. Each newly voiced claim to be following in its footsteps left it feeling more and more a stranger to itself. A time might be near, it worried, when a genuine ersatz could not be told apart from any number of imitators.

In short, the ersatz found itself beset by a withering identity crisis, all the while surrounded by boundless and beaming self-assurance in its name.

The Eye of a Needle

Once a rich man managed to squeeze through the eye of a needle, followed by another rich man, and another one after that, while an entire caravan of camels stood by and watched.

It was easier for the rich men than for the camels to accomplish the feat, of course, but this fact alone couldn't explain their success. Nor could the rewriting of old tax codes so the rich could take their enormous fortunes with them when they entered the kingdom of God. Many could barely crawl they were so burdened with this added blessing.

No, the rich couldn't have hoped to squeeze through the needle's eye on their own without the help of certain televangelists. These televangelists were numerous, but their loyal followers were legion. And the force of those unquestioning multitudes was what finally made the difference: the dutiful bending of all the backs of these true believers to the task of pushing a wealthy few into eternal bliss.

Without direction from the telepulpit, of course, even these efforts might not have sufficed. The poor will always be with us, the appeal from these televangelists noted, so the poor could afford to be patient. Their time would eventually come. Surely there were other concerns they should be focusing on in the meantime. Values, for one: What would it profit the poor to gain the whole world if the values of that world continued to decline? Values were like money in the bank, any televangelist could vow. It followed, then, that the poor would be wise to entrust their values to those who knew how to get the highest returns on them if the poor just invested for the long term and waited patiently for the benefits to trickle down to them.

Turning one's precious values over to those who'd already demonstrated such deftness in leveraging them in the past made plenty of sense. After all, the rich and powerful could only help the poor and powerless if the poor and powerless first trusted their prospects to the rich and powerful.

So why not bend one's back in service to the blessedly well-heeled in this business of the eye of a needle and the kingdom of God? Forget about the camels.

Faust

Once Faust sought to renegotiate the fine print.

The time limit of twenty-four years didn't cause him much concern. It seemed long enough to explore everything worth exploring in one lifetime and short enough to spare him the wearisome repeating of a single day's discoveries.

Nor did he wish to be spared the forfeit of his soul in exchange for the chance of gaining everything that knowledge and the senses offered. What else could possibly match the scope of his quest? Full understanding, full passion, full entry into the mysteries of life, full embrace of one's place in the larger context, and so on and so on; wouldn't such satisfactions be worth signing one's soul away?

"So what's the problem?" asked Mephistopheles with a yawn.

"I want to add another clause to our contract," Faust began, "one that restrains playwrights and poets from moralizing my story after I'm no longer around to defend myself."

"Oh, you'll be around, don't worry. Nobody's going to forget you."

"That's precisely what I mean. I'll be at the mercy of any scribbler who makes of my quest some allegory of hubris and damnation or salvation."

"Fame's fame these days, pal, however you come by it. You'll be in a league of your own when it comes to name recognition, I'll wager."

"But for what?"

"Your 'just deserts' I believe it's called."

"'Just deserts'? Being carried off to hell by clownish demons or plucked up by angels for last-minute redemption?"

"That's about the shape of it."

"What a failure of imagination! Why shouldn't seeking the most from life be worthy of something more than the same old ragbag of moral platitudes?"

"Continue. I'm all ears."

"Heaven or hell, that's it? That's all there is when it comes to having an entire lifetime of searching judged? Why? Is the sum of human possibility or failure nothing more than a camera obscura box with a pinhole to project heaven and hell by turns? What can you really understand of life by that?"

"Depends on what you want to see, doesn't it? Anything inside that box, remember, you humans put there."

"What's the use of having a mind at all if it doesn't rival heaven and hell?"

"Oh pooh. Box or no box, heaven or hell, the lessons of life don't come without a price."

"Exactly. And they ought to be worth the price paid. Not this rounding life up to a clichéd 'salvation' or rounding it down to an equally clichéd 'damnation.'"

"Can you blame people for taking one look at the toll wrung from those who strive for all that mind or soul or the senses can attain, Faust, and deciding to settle instead for a conventional faith in rewards and punishments? Who wouldn't choose the reassurance, in that case, of stock endings to it all?"

"Which is exactly why I want the contract I signed to have a restraining clause on playwrights and poets who might wish to moralize my quest and its outcome, reducing both in the process. My decisions have been mine! My fate is mine!"

Fear

Once fear disappeared.

Just packed up and headed out one fine morning for parts unknown. Those who'd been the familiars of fear were stunned at this uncharacteristic move. After all the time they'd spent in fear's company, how could it just leave them like this, without warning or farewell? How were they to get on with their lives in its absence? What would a day without fear be?

Missing-fear reports soon appeared in print and electronic media across the nation as well as on billboards and countless neighborhood power poles, but to no avail. The longer its whereabouts went unaccounted for, the deeper the public uneasiness became. People had grown so accustomed to its presence in their lives. Fear of the known as much as the unknown. Fear of the truth and fear of lies. Fear of danger and failure and rejection, of course, but equally of success and responsibility. Fear of strangers but of one's neighbor as well. Fear of the rich and powerful and fear of the homeless. Fear of the immigrant and fear of the nativist. Fear of science's challenges to religion and of religious zealotry that denies science. Fear of the devil and fear of one's own demons. Fear, in sum, as the one constant in life as people had come to know it.

Fear had never let the nation down before. People's entire existence might suddenly have to be rethought and all the old certainties be abandoned. But new alarms and suspicions could take time to develop, to say nothing of how long it might be before they became second nature to one and all. The absence of fear wasn't just inconvenient, therefore; it was a personal and public calamity.

So when fear returned unannounced one fine day, the rejoicing was boundless. Multitudes danced in the streets. Fireworks filled the nighttime sky. No explanation for the absence of fear was offered and none was asked for. Who would be so foolish as to risk driving fear away again with awkward questions? Grand parades were organized everywhere, complete with marching bands and banners that read "Welcome Home Fear!"

Everyone breathed a sigh of relief now that life was returning to normal.

The Finches

Once finches were all very different from each other.

One could travel the globe and encounter an astounding variety of them in those days. Their songs charmed the listener with ceaseless invention, while the range of colors they displayed appeared inexhaustible. The very pattern of their lives changed from one land to another. In truth, the observing of finches brought an unending series of discoveries and amazements that enriched anyone's appreciation of the grand diversity life celebrated.

In what seemed a very short time, however, all that changed. Finches everywhere began looking, sounding, and acting increasingly alike. So marked was this transformation that they became the poster birds for a broad embrace of "transglobal identicalism." Popular blogs and Op-Ed pieces in the press asserted that universal connectivity was the new normal and cited lookalike finches at opposite points on the globe as proof that uniformity was an unstoppable force at all levels. Some transnational identicalism experts made quite a reputation for themselves by explaining how finches now demonstrated "an evolution from the old internationalism as an accommodation of differences to the new internationalism as an endorsement of borderless conformity, with all the boons promised by that evolution."

Predictions were legion that within a short time every facet of finch life anywhere would be governed by a single definition. The benefits for the finches of this advance were hard to dispute. All of them having become essentially identical in appearance, thought, action, and song thanks to memes, they had no difficulty adapting to each other's environments. "Fitting in" regardless of location ceased to be of any concern.

For that matter, there wasn't really much need for journeying from one place to another anymore. With every finch in the world soon to be indistinguishable from every other finch, there was obviously less reason to think a change of locale would reveal anything that might expand one's understanding or require any adjustment in behavior or self-awareness on arrival.

And yet, curiously, the more the finches came to seem mere copies of one other, the more firmly they clung to what they believed was unique in themselves. The more individual and diverse, in fact, they considered themselves to be. "Regardless of how much we may look alike or sound alike or think and act alike," they confidently proclaimed, "we're not really so alike at all." Apparently you could have it both ways in "transglobal identicalism," with everything the same, yet not somehow.

Had the world entered an era of natural self-selection within the "global self"?

The Flamingos

Once a flock of flamingos resolved to make important social issues more stylish.

It was high time, they all agreed. Time to bring that special flair for which they were famous to critical concerns around the globe.

So the flamingos gathered by a classy resort lake, pecked one another in greeting, and then asked themselves, "How can we make a fashion statement that will raise the level of awareness on problems that really matter today?"

After a long silence, during which many of the flamingos preened themselves to cover their embarrassment over being at an unaccustomed loss for words, a single thought sprang into all their minds simultaneously, causing quite a flutter and moving them all to lift their graceful bodies into the air and begin circling the lake in a glorious display. Around and around they flew. When they eventually returned to the shallows, though, none of the flamingos could quite remember what the great thought was that had inspired them to take wing in the first place.

So they decided to start over and asked themselves again, "How can we make a fashion statement that will raise the level of awareness on problems that really matter today?"

"STD prevention would be absolutely marvelous for making a statement, darlings," one flamingo finally volunteered.

"Old news" came the response from all sides. "So over that."

"I read somewhere that the Black Death might be coming back."

"Eeeuuuu! Buboes and pus! How gross!"

"I know what, let's do a famine show. It's all over the news these days."

"How cool is that?!"

"Rad!"

"Mega-Rad!!"

"Except what would we wear?"

"How should I know, but we could accessorize anything we decide on with miniature ration bags or something."

"Seriously? Wouldn't we be sending the wrong message with that? Just sayin'."

"Puuuleeeez! There can never be a wrong message in a consciousness-raising fashion campaign. That's the whole point, isn't it? No controversy is bad controversy."

"What? I don't get it."

"I've been thinking a lot lately about a photo spread against ethnic cleansing."

"Hashtag Helloooo! I hate to be the one to bring up the same thing again, but what would we wear? You can't just assume everybody'll automatically get the message."

"Well duhhhh! . . . Whatever."

"Okay, okay, everybody, how about 'homelessness' as our theme? How can you miss with something that's soooo today as that?"

"Yes! Yes! I could finally wear the ripped designer jeans that I spent a freakin' fortune on in a good cause! Showing solidarity with the have-nots in our best torn-wear!"

"BOOOOM! Poverty as a fashion statement, darlings!"

"I see worldwide appeal in that! With divine cover shots of us in edgy street scenes and a few photogenic third-world urchins in the background somewhere."

"Yes! Yes! Yes! I totally get it! And guess what, for the show's finale, we could scrap the wedding gowns and strut our stuff down the runway wearing some of those cardboard signs you see all over the place asking for help!"

"G-A-M-E C-H-A-N-G-E-R!!"

"Visionary concept, ab-so-lute-ly visionary!"

All of the flamingos were so pleased with the outcome of their efforts that they began to practice, one after another, the most dramatic way to hold their heads, arch their necks and spread their wings, and pull just the right pout to demonstrate their commitment to giving social issues that really matter some pizzazz for a change.

The Fox

Once a fox came up with a foolproof entrepreneurial scheme.

Rather than follow the usual practice of selling people something they probably didn't need, the fox chose to take advantage of the marketing strategy of buying something from them that they no longer appeared to have much use for. It offered to purchase their unwanted shame. In bulk.

The fox made the following pitch to all who would listen: "Ever wanted it all, but never had the nerve to go for it? Put those days behind you. I guarantee whatever you desire in fame, fortune, sex, power, or anything else you crave in return for your shame. If shame is all that holds you back from fighting your way over others to the top and doing whatever it takes to stay there once you've made it, then hesitate no longer. Your lucky day has come! If you're not completely satisfied with this chance of a lifetime to be shame-free once and for all, I promise to return your shame in full, no questions asked. But wait, there's more! I'll even let you name your own price! Hurry, this offer ends soon."

That closing pitch was the masterstroke of the fox's strategy. It had grasped the simple truth that once the offer ended, fears of a falling price would cause even the most hesitant seller to panic into unloading any and all remaining shame for whatever it might still fetch. Nobody wanted to be stuck with shame that was worthless.

There was another phase to the fox's plan that came to be considered equally shrewd. Once it had cornered the market in what came to be known as "junk shame," the fox created a startup called "Fruits of Shame," gambling that junk shares in others' shame might still prove attractive to amateur speculators. The name had a golden allure to it, and the startup's initial public offering took off immediately, with prices reaching new highs in every trading session thereafter. On TV screens, computers, and news racks everywhere, the face of "The Market Fox" became easily the most recognizable in the land.

Despite this stunning success, the fox was troubled by an unanticipated and deepening sense of dissatisfaction. It was proving far too easy to convince people to divest themselves of shame for next to nothing. They practically begged the fox to take it, all but throwing whatever shame they might still have at its feet. There simply wasn't any challenge left in the enterprise.

Alone in newly expanded offices after a year-end celebration over beating analysts' expectations time and again (and increasingly by triple digits as individuals and corporations vied to cash out their own shame ahead of competitors), the fox brushed bits of confetti from its hair, then turned and walked away from the bright numbers scrolling across the giant stock ticker above.

"It just shouldn't be this easy," it grumbled with a disappointed expression on its face, almost as if it had tasted something sour.

The Foxhound

Once a foxhound began to have second thoughts about chasing foxes.

This unaccustomed frame of mind brought on little more than a mild uneasiness at first: on a par, perhaps, with momentarily losing sight of a reddish phantom in the morning fog like any of those that had for years led the foxhound and its baying kennelmates on a chase across damp, uneven ground. Such a vague disquiet was also hard to distinguish from the kind of light woozy spell that might come over the hound at the end of a long pursuit and then pass without further effect. A little rest, typically, and all would be right with the foxhound's world again.

Except that it wasn't anymore. These and other strange new feelings did not fade as expected. Instead, they lasted a bit longer after each hunt in a rising anxiety that came and went on its own, like a taunting fox pacing back and forth in full view right outside the kennel fence.

Despite all the thrills of past hunts and all the praise still earned from the master of hounds, the passion for running a fox to ground was plainly lessening as this unwelcome state of mind deepened. Once so compelling it seemed the very reason for being born a foxhound, rushing pell-mell across field and stream in pursuit of the prey was now taking on the dogtrot of custom or of merely going through the motions so as not to draw the attention of its keepers. Or the notice as well of its fellow foxhounds, none of whom seemed troubled by any queasy feelings.

On the contrary, their eyes narrowed with disbelief when it mentioned its bafflement. Some eyes even to cold slits of suspicion. What caused this flagging commitment to ridding the world of foxes, its companions demanded to know. The critters were as shifty and dangerous as ever, were they not? Their sly nature would never change, and any slacking off in pursuing them, any hesitation to join in pulling a fox from its lair and tearing it limb from limb, was a sign of weakness that would surely be noted beyond the kennel. And the next time the hunting horns sounded, what then?

The foxhound was reminded in no uncertain terms that not only its own wellbeing but the wellbeing of all its comrades depended upon flawless teamwork in the cornering of foxes. How long would foxhounds be housed and fed, did it suppose, if they didn't prove themselves worthy of that sought-after pat on the head for their unfailing dedication? Had they deserved the rewards of their domestication or not?

One pace slower or one chorus of barking compliance less and questions about their trustworthiness would certainly arise. Once that happened, where would any of them be? Think of the pack, the foxhound was urged. And if that wasn't enough, think of itself. Without the hunt, what separated a foxhound from a fox ultimately? Answer that!

The foxhound realized it had no ready answer to such questions, particularly the last one, which carried the weight of a direct command to give an accounting of itself. What did separate a foxhound from a fox? In truth, mistaking the fox for a small dog or a standard hunting dog for a large fox might conceivably happen. But there must be ways to distinguish them under the skin. Qualities that made plain any foxhound's superiority to foxes.

In its state of mounting frustration, however, the foxhound wasn't sure it could name these distinguishing qualities with the confidence it once had enjoyed. In what ways was it more than just an oversized version of a fox? There remained that old assurance of being "man's best friend," of course. That ought to count for something after thousands of years of dogs heeling to a master's slightest wish.

And what of the foxhound's sense of discipline: the steady response to every test of its intelligence and its devotion to task? These had to count in the larger view as being worthy of admiration, more so at least than a fox's brute instinct and cunning. If not, if it and the fox were merely on a par, coequals facing one another across a divide between self-discipline and utter wildness, what reason would there have been for striving so diligently to overcome the savage state? Sacrifice must have its demonstrable proofs and rewards, mustn't it?

Yet these longed-for reassurances of worth might not turn out to be as telling as a hound would wish. And the more this one wrestled with the questions before it, the more its failure to answer any of them haunted the wait between hunts. At first the lack of certainty had troubled only its morning hours, fading as these gave way to the traditional safeguards of daily life within the kennel fence. But that release from misgivings grew shorter and shorter, until even the pleasures of a bone to gnaw or a full bowl at mealtime could not quiet the doubts that threatened to push the foxhound to total distraction.

There were even times now when it would fall victim to sudden blackouts and come to with its nose against the inside of the fence, trembling in alarm. Would it soon be in danger of losing control of its life altogether and spending the rest of it harried by self-distrust? Perhaps tempted in a fit of madness to burrow under the fence and be off, abandoning everything that had given it stability and direction?

And all the while, the question of what separated the foxhound from a fox refused to go away. The dividing line between it and this feral creature rose into view only to fade away again, then reappear somewhere else and vanish just as completely, like hedgerows on the landscape of dreams. Until the only release the foxhound felt might offer any hope whatsoever was the total destruction of this menace to its sense of being and self-worth. So it seized upon what suddenly seemed obvious: every fox for miles around must die. Must die!

From that day on, not a hunt took place without the foxhound's pushing itself into the lead, running like it was possessed and bent on being the first to overtake the prey. No obstacle could slow it and no distance make it give up the chase. With the stakes being its life or the fox's (nothing less than the loss of meaning to its very existence or the salvaging of it through unflagging resolve), was it any wonder that when it finally brought a fox to bay, no mercy held the foxhound back?

Not the slightest hesitation at ridding its world, once and for all, of this tormenting reminder of the untamed life.

The Free Spirit

Once a free spirit stubbed its toe.

Had it been moving too fast, the free spirit wondered as it hopped about in pain? At the speed of imagination, mishaps were probably bound to occur. Still, until this moment, a stubbed toe hadn't seemed even a remote possibility.

Crashing full tilt into some barrier—now that the free spirit could have understood. Or being vaporized by the force and heat of its own zeal. Do nothing half-heartedly, it had always believed, nor trim your independent nature one whit.

After all, could you grind along in low gear and still call yourself a "free spirit"? How? Like some self-proclaimed "survivalist" in slippered comfort dozing over outdoor catalogs by a glassed-in propane log? Or the honored teacher who extols the liberating world of the mind but thinks some ideas are just too risky to discuss? Or the creative voice at a deafening howl, driven only to scandalize all listeners within range? Was that the life of a free spirit?

Of course not. These claims to freedom all had the fetor of shuttered minds. Sunshine needed letting into them, and the wind as well. Clear the air and dry away the mold. That done, you could speak of being ready to begin, just begin, living the life of a free spirit. Once loosed from tethered thought and senses, you might pick up enough speed to escape the known and be among the first to enter new worlds!

But then to have stubbed your toe? To be pulled up short and shown the limits of inspired flight—what greater mishap could befall you? Suppose the toe was broken. Hobbling about in a cast would hardly do. A free spirit on crutches, what could be more ludicrous?

How long would it have to put up, in that case, with limping over ground once covered in a flash? Tripping over every small root and rock while trying to recoup the liberating passion for leaping the stars!

Suffering the pinch now of a narrower lot, the free spirit felt a grudging sympathy for those who found true independence a difficult affair and settled instead for something less. Might life as a semi-free spirit be worth a try, judging by how many appeared to draw strength from merely chanting the mantra of liberty and hearing the sound roll around inside their own heads for as long as it took to get ready for the routines of their day?

You could get by on lowered expectations, the free spirit supposed. And besides, who would know? Stubbed toes were as common as colds when it came to a land full of wannabe "free spirits," so your occasional stumble might well go unnoticed amid all the self-assurance and swagger. There was comfort in numbers, to be sure.

The comfort of knowing that "life as a free spirit," as most understood it, wasn't really all that difficult to fake once you'd learned how.

The Fruit Fly

Once a fruit fly became obsessed with genealogy.

This obsession began more or less by chance when the fruit fly received in the post, sandwiched within the usual stack of junk mail, an envelope addressed to "Resident" and marked "Urgent! Our Computers May Already Have Located Your Long-Lost Ancestors!"

Inside the envelope, the fruit fly discovered several pages of grainy photographs showing strangers in front of historical landmarks or old-time portrait backdrops. At the bottom of each page, large red lettering announced "There Could Be A Prince Or Princess In Your DNA! You Might Even Be Related To Famous Figures Like Cleopatra And Charlemagne! You'll Never Know Who You Really Are If You Don't Answer This Special Offer To Search For Your Roots Right Away!"

The fruit fly nearly discarded the letter on the spot. It took all of its powers of concentration as it was just to keep the events of today straight and to avoid becoming lost amid the whirl of other fruit flies round about. Who had time to consider the distant past when living moment to moment was itself such a challenge?

And yet, perhaps it should concern itself more with the question of its origins, the fruit fly thought while looking through the photographs again. Was there proof, as the letter claimed, that it wasn't just another fly in the crowd, just one among countless others appearing and disappearing all the time? Was there really proof of some illustrious progenitor somewhere in the long genealogy leading to its own appearance on the scene that would make it one of a kind among fruit flies?

Again, though, it had no idea how it would manage (given the facts of its immediate reality) to trace its family tree back through the "mists of time" mentioned over and over in the letter. It was a daunting task just to imagine what the lives of its ancestors might have been like countless generations ago. It didn't have the slightest clue. And picturing to itself the doings of Stone Age fruit flies was simply impossible.

How had they lived, those ancient forebears? Not in the general sense of fruit flies as a species, of course. It didn't take much to see the pattern there: appearing in a slew, a brief time in search of fruit and crazed mating, then a falling away into oblivion. No, the real question was what one's ancestors actually thought of their lives those many generations ago. Did they have any better idea of who they were and who had come before them and who would follow them than the fruit fly had of its own place in the unfolding of heredity at this very moment?

And would the highs and lows of its own life, the experiences that allowed it sometimes to think of itself as more than simply a string of genes, would these be remembered by any of its own descendants in their turn? Or would mere scores of generations be enough to blur all trace that it had ever lived, or ever puzzled over where it came from and where it was going?

The fruit fly looked again at the letter with its pictures and its offer and decided to respond after all. There seemed no time to lose if it was to find out whether it actually mattered in the great scheme of things and should not, could not, must not be overlooked.

A few famous flies in one's past might just make all the difference.

The Garden Gnomes

Once a gang of garden gnomes seized control of a grand estate.

Being gnomes, they benefited from the fact that nobody had taken them very seriously during the time they spent planning their audacious caper. They'd seemed, when notice was taken of them at all, to be simply a collection of comical trolls that might raise an occasional smile but little more.

How they actually managed to pull off their takeover was a matter of considerable puzzlement, but once in control, they acted as if they'd been destined from the start to find themselves in the position they now were.

What could be said for certain about the takeover was that it happened while those who owned the estate and who might have been presumed to have some interest in safeguarding what had been bequeathed to them over generations were napping in broad daylight.

After their triumph, the gnomes' primary concern was to make themselves appear more commanding in stature by whatever means it took. They were led in this effort by one of their number, a boastful figure nicknamed "Greatest Gnome Ever" because he was given to calling himself that nearly every time he opened his mouth.

Besides trying out various makeshift stilts to increase their own stature (an expedient that produced at best a dangerous staggering about and not a few unfortunate mishaps), the other gnomes spent most of their time puffing themselves up and striking poses in front of each other in hopes of finding one that made them look stately. This also proved more difficult than expected, though, because none of them demonstrated they had any idea how a "stately garden gnome" might look and behave.

So they settled on telling themselves that all those who might try to take the estate back were actually smaller than they were. How it was possible to be smaller than they were took some imagining, of course.

Eventually the gnomes just declared in unison, "To heck with worrying about stature and appearance!" and got down to business. The business they got down to was selling off most of the estate as quickly as possible to the highest bidders. By unloading whatever they themselves saw no use for, they could reduce their responsibilities to a minimum and have more time for the leisure activities, such as miniature golf, to which they were better suited by temperament and experience.

Here again, they were led by "Greatest Gnome Ever," who had taken up the practice of swinging away at anything and everything as a restful break from the weighty burdens of leadership. Besides, stories of chopping down cherry trees and splitting rails were already legendary in the history of the estate, he announced to his minions. And since his own achievements would be greater and more noteworthy than those of the past by far, why shouldn't theirs be as well?

In this spirit the entire group of gnomes took up little axes and pledged to chop and split things up themselves to demonstrate their loyalty to "Greatest Gnome Ever." The trouble was, with so much of the estate having been sold off by this point, there wasn't a great deal left for them to set their sights on. Nevertheless, their great leader sent them marching out every morning, led by his favorites, named Sleazy #1, Sleazy #2 Sleazy #3, Sleazy #4, and so forth, all whistling a happy tune and keeping an eye open for anything left standing to take a whack at.

Once even these targets were gone, the gnomes barely paused in their whistling before they shifted their attention to the majestic white mansion that stood at the heart of the estate, urged on as always by "Greatest Gnome Ever," who now insisted on also being called "Chopper in Chief." There was enough in the mansion to keep them all swinging away for a while at least.

They began with the furniture, which was too big for them in any case.

The Gargoyles

Once, determined to boost lackluster viewership counts, producers of a news-and-opinion program signed up two gargoyles.

The program needed something to raise audience interest, the producers had concluded. Nobody stayed glued to plodding, in-depth discussions of issues crucial to the survival of the Republic anymore. To begin with, who could define "in-depth" in a way the show's followers would understand and, furthermore, who cared if you could or not?

Even earsplitting *ad hominem* attacks on opponents, long a staple of the show, now sounded "so out of date." Surveys of faithful viewers showed they were just as likely to shout at the screen with the volume off as turned up. The same was true for hammering their smartphones in "let us know what you think" responses to questions about a newsmaker's politics, private life, or potential risk of indictment. Having "the right optics" and "immediate impact" held more promise of bringing an uptick in ratings. Thus the decision to bring on the gargoyles.

When they were first rolled into the studio and positioned opposite one another, members of the production team held their collective breath. What would the audience response be? Would mere ghoulish grimacing be enough? Would viewers be satisfied with that and not demand more? Would it be the kiss of death that the gargoyles weren't saying anything, intelligible or otherwise? As the on-screen response meter lit up, though, everyone could exhale with relief and give each other high fives all around. Clearly it didn't matter in the least that the gargoyles hadn't said anything. Derision, misrepresentation, false analogies, red herrings, sniggering innuendo, outright slurs and blatant lies—none of these equaled the impact of gargoyles silently pulling faces at each other and at the audience.

The saving in production costs was obvious. But equally obvious was the realization that even the fast-talking, high-paid hosts of these programs could be replaced in a flash by rigid ideologue-grotesques, bringing even further savings. Every day and every night, simply propping up a cardboard host in place of a flesh-and-blood one would provide all the introduction needed for the gargoyles as the true stars of the show: those scowling caricatures of thought caked in bird droppings.

The Gasbags

Once the Department of Homeland Security felt compelled to raise the political gasbag threat level to "IMMINENT."

The decision to take this ultimate step was not made lightly, out of a concern to avoid spreading panic throughout the land by acting in too abrupt a manner. Much time was devoted to painstaking assessments of the gasbag threat from every angle imaginable and even from some that were, quite frankly, beyond anyone's wish to know about. Comprehensive public risk assessments were carried out, as per usual. Once conducted, these had then to be exhaustively reassessed (again, as per usual) before discussions could begin about what was actually to be done to safeguard the public from potential disaster. Meanwhile, congressional committees held one hearing after another, and party leaders marched in and out of media spotlights to declare that it was their solemn duty "to get to the bottom of the gasbag menace." This combination of factors dragged out the process till much of the public turned its attention elsewhere.

In the opinion of those still paying attention, however, the "imminent threat" was recognized officially far too late: long after the need for swift action was unmistakable. As was already common knowledge, at times of national stagnation, hot air rapidly grew too dense and dark for one to be certain of what was right in front of one. To say nothing of its becoming nearly unbreathable given the elevated levels of toxic fumes given off by gasbags large and small as they overstretched their limits and split a seam or two in the process.

Concerns regarding the health of the young and the very old were understandable, but so too were worries about all those who might be strong enough to survive heart disease, cancer, or stroke but were absolute goners when it came to the cumulative effects of gasbag exposure.

Meanwhile, in the absence of decisive anti-gasbag measures expected of those in authority, rumors and conspiracy theories abounded. What came to be known as "gasbag threat deniers" pointed here, there, and everywhere at those they alleged were behind a nefarious plot to hoodwink the public. There were no "real" gasbags, they derisively proclaimed, or, if there were any "real" gasbags, well then their existence should be viewed as a stirring tribute to the constitutional right of everybody to soar aloft and thus was fundamental to the soul of the nation, regardless of any allegedly deleterious consequences for "victims" of a "real gasbag."

Observers less convinced of the benefit to the nation of a sky filled with errant gasbags bumping up against each other stressed the near mathematical certainty that at some point in the not-too-distant future, enough gasbags could become wedged together overhead to block the heat of the sun, bringing on a new ice age. While to rely on the well-documented tendency for overheated gasbags to float "up, up, and away" and ultimately vanish beyond the stratosphere was proving to be a false hope. For every gasbag gone, it was increasingly plain, a multitude of up-and-coming ones awaited their own turn to rise.

Viewed realistically, then, elevating the gasbag threat level to "IMMINENT" or even "CATASTROPHIC" or even "CATACLYSMIC" or even "APOCALYPTIC" would do little to render the ominous reality confronting the nation any more alarming than it already had become.

The Gazelle

Once a gazelle found itself in a state of suspended animation.

Such a predicament was unheard of for a gazelle, accustomed to bounding along with its companions in graceful, free-and-easy arcs that looked for all the world like a gravity-defying ballet.

What had stopped this one in midleap, ironically, was the thought its sheer glee in defying gravity might be shortsighted. Who could really defy gravity for any length of time, after all? Eventually every good leap must come to an end and even a gazelle find itself pulled back to earth. Wasn't there something empty, in that case, about the herd's ceaseless gamboling about?

But then, what could match the wild beating of a gazelle's heart as it neared the top of its bound? What could rival the feeling of every sinew and muscle drawn to the full in physical joy?

But then again, shouldn't such breathtaking vaults possess some meaning that transcended the inevitable return to earth? Was the joie de vivre that ran through every fiber of the gazelle's body in fact only a blind indulgence in sensory pleasures that had no justification beyond itself? Satisfactions promised by the life of the mind must be more lasting and significant.

Still again, however, giving up physical delights in response to the appeal of thought, turning from the triumph of the flesh to the transcendent intellect, what guarantee did the gazelle have it wouldn't come to regret that too? How far could ideas alone carry one in comprehending what it meant to be fully alive?

92

In sum, the gazelle's body and mind were at such odds that movement of any sort had simply become impossible. Would this stalemate in every nerve render its powerful legs frail and useless in time, as the constant doubts threatened to paralyze its mind as well? If so, and if the gazelle ever did suddenly come down, the odds of landing on its feet might be no greater than those of ending up on its head.

Given that possibility, the gazelle supposed it might have to resign itself to an existence up in the air like this. There'd be no unbridled celebration of the senses anymore, to be sure, but no racking self-recriminations either. Or, to put it the other way around, there'd be freedom from intellectual torment in exchange for an end to sensual bliss.

Suspended animation as a way of life.

The Gene

Once a gene fell victim to identity theft.

It happened without warning, and by the time the gene realized what had occurred, it was too late. The same was true for an increasing number of the gene's neighbors, it soon discovered.

Until it was targeted, the gene hadn't paid much attention to the threat of losing its identity. It had read horror stories in the press, as every gene probably had, chronicling usurped lives and the years of frustration spent trying to reclaim them, but those accounts never struck home. Such crimes were indeed deplorable, yet because they happened to others, they'd always seemed distant and abstract.

Now, suddenly, the gene's entire sense of self crumbled away in disbelief that it could be a victim. The reality of its condition had become clear only when the gene was completing an online medical check-up. No sooner had it clicked the submit button than up popped a message warning it to "cease and desist" using the name it had given or else face legal action by those who now held exclusive rights to it.

"How can you claim exclusive rights to a name?" the gene typed back in astonishment. "That's like exclusive rights to a letter of the alphabet."

"It's done all the time," came back the instant reply.

"But that's absurd!"

"It may be, but it's also the law."

"My name is part of who I am. Without it, I'd have no real sense of myself."

"Whoever you thought you were is now the property of another, whose full rights in the matter are legally protected."

"That's preposterous! They can't do that!"

"Oh yes they can."

"But how?"

"Disclosure of that information is prohibited in order to safeguard the privacy of the party in question."

"What if that 'party in question' does something illegal or unethical with my identity?"

"That's beyond your control now."

"You mean they can do anything they want with my identity?"

"Anything."

"And there's nothing I can do?"

"Nothing."

Had the world gone stark raving mad? the gene demanded in exasperation. Was identity theft protected by law now? If the gene had no claim to being itself anymore, it might as well end it all and be free of this farce!

"You can't do that, either. You'll be sued for everything you've got."

"What's left to sue for?"

"Sorry, that information is privileged."

"%$^&^**&#^~$@%^$*&^$^%$#~@&%*!"

The Gingerbread Man

Once a gingerbread man became enamored of its own shape.

The shape wasn't a prepossessing one, admittedly, and it was common to gingerbread men in general, but neither of those considerations was a drawback. In fact, they reassured the gingerbread man. For if it and others looked like they'd come from the same mold, that must prove the inherent value of such a mold.

Of more concern to the gingerbread man were encounters with gingerbread men that did not fit the mold for one reason or another. Their misshapen forms amounted to a galling parody of the traditional gingerbread physique. And what was even more disturbing than this was the fact that some of these figures didn't appear to recognize their shortcomings or, if they did, either seemed indifferent to those shortcomings or else took a kind of perverse pride in them.

These aberrations were not just a question of appearance (the correct contours, color, glazing, and so forth) but of substance as well. If you didn't appear to measure up on the outside, how could you be trusted to measure up on the inside? A proper gingerbread man was a proper gingerbread man through and through.

Furthermore, since it was unthinkable that any decent cookie maker would have allowed such defective gingerbread men to slip by, deviant cookies must themselves be guilty of the fault. This disregard for standards amounted then to a direct, misguided challenge to the very meaning of quality control. That being the case, the only course of action the gingerbread man could see was for others like itself, who clearly did meet all the standards, to take matters into their own hands.

It shouldn't be too difficult, since they had themselves as a pattern to follow. And with a bit of resolve, cutting these imperfect figures into shape shouldn't take long. They might be much smaller when the process was complete (some might be a mere fraction of what they once were), but one thing was certain.

They would all be better gingerbread men for it.

The Glutton for Life

Once a glutton for life had a postprandial dream of swallowing it all.

Hungry for everything that Life had on offer, the glutton was loath to leave any leftovers. If you weren't prepared to swallow all of Life, he murmured to himself in the dream, what was the point of being alive? In the limited time you're given to lick your chops at will, how much of all you craved could you take in?

And yet how much you must strive to take in, gulping down Life without missing a taste of the smallest morsel! The sweet with the sour, the mouth-watering with the dry as dust, the flaming hot with the icy cold—every enticement to the senses or to fancy—nothing should escape the glutton's voracious appetite. Allowing such a thing to happen would amount to denying a part of oneself. And if the least of Life was ignored or rejected, if any of it failed to be welcomed in full, then Life was incomplete in some measure. And who would be such a fool as to claim Life ever fell short of its own fullness?

From the minuscule to the immense, then, nothing was absent from the glutton's dream. The only worry was waking before all had been savored. If that happened, what excuse could be made? To have the chance of stuffing oneself as full of Life as possible, to best Gargantua and yet overlook a single remaining tidbit, what a failing that would be towards oneself and towards Life!

From the depths of this worry there gradually rose a new one. At first it was no more than a suggestion of self-doubt, the type of shapeless unease that calls attention to itself only by its swirl of shadow within shadow. But eventually the shadows gave way and in their place stood a challenge that seized hold of the glutton's daydream and threatened to reduce it to an idle whim.

How naive the glutton had been! How could even sweat-drenched gorging not fail to prove inadequate? For in order to "swallow it all," would swallowing all of Life be enough? No it wouldn't, the glutton now realized. To swallow all of Life required swallowing as well its converse: Death. It was that simple. Life and Death, Death and Life, each the complement of the other. The glutton was abashed at not having recognized this demand from the start.

All or nothing? Trust yourself to the summoning fullness of your dream or suffer the consequences of its fading away as you awoke to the regret of failing to prove worthy of your own appetites? The time to act was now or never: to stretch your jaws wide as wide could be and bolt down absolutely everything until the veins that stood out on your brow threatened to burst.

"Well," the glutton dreamed on with jaws opening to the full, "here goes!"

The Gnat

Once a gnat was invited to participate in a political focus group.

At first the gnat wasn't sure it wanted to accept the invitation. But when it did show up and mentioned its hesitancy to the focus group organizer, it was told that this is how democracy works: a small group gets together and considers what should be important for everybody else to think sooner or later—something like that.

"Okay," the gnat responded. "I think I get it now."

"Then let's start, shall we?" the organizer asked the entire gathering of focus gnats. "The first question for all of you tonight is, 'What are the most important social concerns of today?'"

The gnat hadn't really thought about this question before. And it didn't have much time to think about it now, either, as a hum of answers immediately arose from other gnats in all parts of the room that clearly believed they had. So distracting did the hum of opinions grow that it proved difficult to hear oneself think, let alone understand what others thought.

Apparently having anticipated this eventuality, the focus group organizer called out, "Attention, please. Attention, please. Perhaps it would help if we formed breakout groups and came to some measure of limited consensus first."

"Pardon me, but what's a 'consensus'?" a gnat asked timidly.

"Well," the organizer began, looking about for where the question had come from before giving up and answering to the whole room, "it's sort of like agreeing with everybody in general, even if you don't actually agree on anything specific."

"Sounds like a contradiction," some gnat laughed in the back of the room.

"Not really," the organizer responded, a bit miffed. "Focus groups like tonight's typically find they can agree on something by the end, even if they only 'agree to disagree,' as the saying goes."

Somewhat encouraged by these words, the gnat turned to the gnats nearest to it, and together they went around and around on the question. About half the time they appeared to be moving closer together, but about half the time they appeared to be moving apart. The same was true of gnat groups elsewhere in the room.

"What are the other groups saying?" the gnat wondered. Members of its own group must have been asking themselves the same question, for soon they were all wandering away in different directions to listen in on what other groups had to say. Those groups too, it turned out, had a tendency to break up after a short period of time and stray off in various directions.

The whole room was beginning to seem a blur, and when the organizer checked the time and then hurriedly called all the focus gnats back together, one of them spoke up for the rest and said, "We're having some trouble reaching that consensus you mentioned. We need a little more information about the issues involved."

"My instructions state that I'm not supposed to provide information that might influence your thinking," the organizer responded. "Your opinions are all that's needed. That's how most focus groups should work, I believe."

At this point the organizer turned to our gnat and asked, "Now, let's do a quick roundup of opinions, shall we?"

The gnat, suddenly feeling the attention of all the other gnats upon it, stammered, "I'm sorry, I'm still not sure what to think. Is that okay or not okay?"

God and the Battling Ants

Once it was claimed God had taken sides in a war between two ant colonies.

Because each side in the conflict declared God had taken its part against the opposing colony, many thought at first that two deities might be involved, one being called "The God of Light" and the other "The God of Darkness." But as each side's "God of Light" turned out to resemble the "God of Darkness" when seen from another side's perspective, this explanation proved to have some obvious shortcomings.

Over time, a view that a single God had chosen to look with favor on one side and with disfavor on the other was advanced to deal with the unsettling ambiguities of the original two-Gods-urging-opposite-sides-to-gnaw-at-their-foe-until-death interpretation of the war.

But how was one to know whether one's own side was destined to give or to receive these divinely sanctioned gnawings? Faced with that uncertainty, both colonies conducted themselves as though the problem was simply a question of the strength of one's belief.

Instrumental in this regard were the unstinting efforts of the two opposing queen ants. Whenever the situation looked grim, out they would stride to energize their followers with stirring speeches about pulling the legs from their opponents' bodies and tearing their heads off. The most rousing exhortations were always those that announced new proof the opponents were "irredeemable evildoers" and thus deserved their gruesome fates: a claim that invariably moved each side to prolonged, hearty chants of "God Bless Us! God Blast Them!"

As casualties in the ant war mounted, each side pointed to losses by the other as evidence that it, the opposite side, was growing more desperate due to its relative casualty level. Or, put another way, each side's relative casualty level was interpreted to be proof it was actually winning, however horrendous the numbers were.

Questions of whose God was looking down on this mayhem with favor might have been expected to fade when it came to those actually sent out to do or die in no ant's land. It might have seemed self-preservation would be their chief concern. As they taunted, cursed, or ripped apart their adversaries, though, these die-hard rivals were sustained by the belief that if they perished in this righteous carnage, their payment of the supreme price would be honored everlastingly. As a precaution that not a single ant commanded by either queen to sacrifice itself would miss out on this eternal reward, a solemn pledge was read over each body or collection of unidentified body parts brought back from the battlefield to either colony.

Despite all of these measures, the war dragged on, at times intensely and at times fitfully, with one side gaining the advantage and then the other storming back from the brink of threatened annihilation. No victory was permanent. Every defeat had its revenge. Ultimately, as the mounting toll began to tax the enthusiasm of both colonies for this fight, a new variation on the one-God-who-takes-sides explanation for the uncertain course of the fray arose: there might indeed be only one God involved, but that God had taken both sides. The contending forces barely paused in their lethal clash to consider this idea before rejecting it out of hand.

For what kind of God would that be?

The Gorilla

Once an 800-pound gorilla wondered if it should go on a diet.

It had similar thoughts every time it found itself having to press against the wall at receptions in the nation's capital so more of the usual invitees could crowd in.

Anyone the gorilla ever asked about the matter, though, answered, "You can't be serious! Diets are for those who should have learned a little restraint long ago."

"I just thought my presence might be a bother to some at times like this."

"My dear friend, have you ever heard anybody at these gatherings voice the slightest concern about your presence? You shouldn't be so sensitive. Now, if you don't mind, I see a congressional aide over there I need to have a quick word with."

Was it in fact too sensitive, the gorilla asked itself? Or was the comment just a tactful way of hiding the awkward reality that other guests regularly chose to pretend it wasn't there?

"A penny for your thoughts?"

"I beg your pardon," the gorilla answered with a start, looking down at a new face looking up into its own.

"A penny for your thoughts. You seemed like you had something you wanted to get off your chest. Though who'd hear you over all this noise, eh?

Somebody should blow a whistle every now and then just to give people a break from all the glad-handing and backslapping and a chance to get their glasses refilled or to reach for more canapés."

"Why don't you blow a whistle?" the gorilla responded.

"Never thought anybody'd pay attention. Now, I'll wager you could get their attention if you wanted to, an 800-pound gorilla like you."

"Tell me, do I look overweight?"

"Aren't you supposed to be this big?"

The gorilla wasn't sure whether the question was genuine or a joke. Nonplussed, it excused itself and began to head for a set of large glass doors onto the terrace, edging gingerly through the press of lobbyists turned public servants and public servants turned lobbyists, military contractors with military brass in tow, corporate donors with a favor to ask, industry lawyers and government regulators, special interest fundraisers, off-shore accountants, and so many others now filling the room elbow to elbow and wall to wall.

"Excuse me . . . sorry . . . forgive me . . . so sorry . . . excuse me . . . ," the gorilla mumbled as it squeezed past, fearing to offend.

When it finally reached the terrace doors, the gorilla labored to open them and slip out into the evening air. There it found rows of chairs apparently moved outside to make room for more and more reception guests. And on many of the chairs sat other gorillas, some much larger than it, and all staring off silently into space.

All wondering too, perhaps, if their size was ever considered a bother by anyone inside?

"The Great God Pan Is—"

Once the great god Pan rolled over and declared, "I ain't dead yet, folks."

All those who'd trumpeted his demise might do well to check their own pulse and find a nearer reason for concern, because he could assure them he wasn't about to give up the ghost. Even though in appearance he might look close enough to it to explain people's confusion. Sprawled amongst the few followers who remained faithful to the memory of ecstatic pleasures, Pan had to admit he'd grown paunchy and pale of late, his hair thinning out like dry weeds, his teeth (those he still possessed) grown brittle along with his horns, and his wrinkled face drained of the *joie de vivre* that kept it ruddy and smooth in the past. The old ticker just wasn't what it once had been, and he found it hard to catch his breath after even a short prance, let alone blow his famous pipes in full bacchanalian relish. Too often a wheezy tootle was the best he could manage now. And when was the last time he'd been able to leap high enough in the air to click cloven hooves together more than once?

Oh, this cumbersome belly! How often had he marveled at the way it used to mold itself to another's flesh, as though that had been the whole intent of life from the start! Now he merely sagged upon himself in such heavy rolls that all else disappeared beneath them. And yet, those years when delight ran sure-footed through scented groves and leapt brook after brook, when mad revel fed a soul that never tired—such inspired abandon still remained beneath time's creaks and groans.

Age might wither limbs but not desire. Pan held to that assurance as firmly as he ever had. Places, names, faces, even memory and speech might fade, yet the call of the senses must always return. And when it did, when the winded heart swelled with life again, these irksome pounds would dissolve, this gray vanish from his beard and hair, bold longings rise again from slumber, and every sinew and joint bend once more to the senses' fierce demands.

Revelry would reclaim the world before he'd leave it, Pan was certain. Not the tedious choreography that passed for a celebration of life these days, where too many seemed to stumble through the motions as if trying to match foot-prints painted on the floor—no, not these stale rituals that trammel the will but instead a wild-eyed rite that sets it free in transports of intoxicating joy. He just needed to hold on until then.

Who else was left to champion getting drunk on life itself, Pan mused out loud: the passion to drink it all in, the mad with the sane, the scream and the tender silence, the orgiastic heights and then the slow falling back into oneself and the rebirth of every yearning yet again, over and over, all of it, all that simply being alive demanded unconditionally? Certainly not those counting themselves wise who daily announced his end with such confidence, such blind presumption they now controlled forces far beyond their powers to understand, forces nothing could shield them from when life-lust stretched every chamber of their hearts anew.

To have convinced themselves they needn't worship anymore at all the wild altars of being, like prim little godlets and godlettes whose hubris took itself for wisdom—now there was intoxication without hope! And no promise of spring frolics yet to come. Only a frigid wasteland in store, barren of every sign of life save self-distrust. Sooner or later, though, these poor lost ones must find their way again to him: the one god ever-willing to hail their return with a cup raised high!

They would come back. They would come back. They would come back.

Green Fungus

Once an immense fungus, *Campaignaria greenbackae*, spread across the land.

The destructive effects of this advancing freak of nature were visible from space but had somehow escaped detection by those on the ground with responsibility for safeguarding the public against threats such as this. In its relentless advance, the green fungus overwhelmed whatever might stand in its way and destroyed it in no time. Yet even this evidence of the lethal strength and extent of the danger was apparently not considered a cause for worry until the dire consequences of such complacent inattention could no longer be ignored.

By the time alarms finally began to sound, the fungus had already proved itself an infinitely adaptable and opportunistic menace. It had quite literally developed the ability to attack and turn to rot everything, even (and this would surpass belief, were the grim evidence not staring everybody in the face) the very foundations of sacred national institutions created over generations by insinuating itself into their smallest fissures, weakening them little by little every day, and even cracking some wide open in what came to be known among an increasingly demoralized citizenry simply as "the damned curse of the green stuff."

No inch of public property was safe from assault as countless historical monuments and heritage sites began to crumble when the fungus attacked their underpinnings. Emergency measures had to be taken to shore up one crumbling façade after another in front of which smiling, upbeat PR personnel blithely declared there was no reason for concern, since a nationwide donation campaign to prop up any venerated government structure at risk of collapse was already under discussion in highly respected circles. An appeal to free-market know-how quickly had corporate sponsors lining up to take the lead with offers to go to any lengths necessary to get the job done. Taking official action against the creeping green menace, however, and stemming its ability to undermine the nation's most hallowed symbols of democracy would probably have to await the usual appointment of a blue-ribbon commission of fading political leaders, business tycoons, and frequently interviewed opinion leaders entrusted with taking "the long view" when it came to fungus.

Meanwhile, it was announced, monetary contributions in any amount to the effort could be placed directly into boxcar-sized green bins conveniently set up in front of government buildings everywhere.

The Hamster

Once a hamster took an animal rights group to court.

The lawsuit came as a surprise to many, and none more so than the group being sued. They had long considered the hamster to be one of their staunchest supporters. It had never failed to respond to the group's requests that it sign and send one of their pre-stamped petitions to Congress or the White House. So when they launched their campaign to free hamsters from their wheels, this one's opposition to their efforts came as a definite shock.

In hindsight, it shouldn't have. The hamster might be unwavering in its commitment to freedom in the abstract, but when it came to its own cage and wheel, that was another matter. Especially when it came to its wheel.

While others might view the hamster's wheel as the very symbol of imprisoning, soul-destroying routine, it saw things differently. Not that it particularly enjoyed running endlessly in place. It could be tedious, the hamster readily admitted. Tedium was not the point, though. Tedium was a small price to pay for the steady confidence-building that running in place brought.

As far back as the hamster could remember, the wheel had played a defining role in its determination to make something of itself. Throughout its youth and right through college, it had trotted along with both eyes fixed on what truly mattered. At the end of all this, it couldn't wait to finally take its place in the real world.

When the hamster showed up bright-eyed and stoked for its first job interviews, corporate recruiters had marveled at how quickly it mastered the wheels they asked it to take a demonstration run in. So much so that it had been able to pick and choose among the many employment offers it received and even to make some demands regarding the starting size of the wheel it could expect "from day one."

With each increase in the size of its wheel over the years, the hamster impressed all of its colleagues with its unflagging dedication and the long hours it put into coming up to speed on every challenge and staying there. It even found a secret satisfaction in the sympathy and worry for its health that coworkers might express as it drove itself to spin the wheel ever faster and longer in order to reach whatever goal had been set for it. If it ultimately died in the wheel, the hamster often thought proudly, the mere mention of its name might be an inspiration to others spinning in their own wheels for decades thereafter.

The wheel had become inseparable, thus, from the hamster's hard-earned sense of self-worth. It was the measure of its past accomplishments and a promise of more triumphs ahead. Deprived of the wheel, how would the hamster continue to find meaning in its life? What was to save it, in short, from a demoralizing drift into self-doubt? Or worse. And here were these animal rights do-gooders it had thought were its friends trying to take from it the one thing it simply could not do without.

"Can't they see the obvious?" the hamster muttered between gasps for breath.

The Hare

Once a hare was possessed by the need to win at all costs.

"Winning isn't everything," the hare liked to quote a famous sports coach, "It's the only thing."

Putting this philosophical gem into action wasn't all that easy, as it turned out. When the hare challenged a deer to race across an open field, the deer merely looked at it and said, "Ambling about would be more pleasant, I should think."

"Aimless loser," the hare declared and went off in search of a more worthy opponent it could best.

A fox also declined to compete against the hare, saying it preferred to bound leisurely here and there across the field in question. One never knew what joy one could find in random discoveries along the way, compared to which, what would winning a mere race count for?

"Calculating loser," the hare declared.

Even a tortoise couldn't be bothered to take up the challenge. "What's the point," it asked. "If there's something of worth on the far side of the field, I'll reach it in my own good time. If there isn't, what difference will it make how fast or slow I was in getting there?"

"Underachieving loser," the hare declared, beginning to grow concerned about how it was ever going to prove itself to be one of life's winners if it couldn't find any rivals to defeat. Then it recalled all those inspirational speakers who'd said one's greatest rival in any endeavor should be oneself, not others. "That's the answer!" the hare rejoiced. "If I'm the only runner worthy of my challenge, I'll run against myself. And win!"

At last the longed-for race could begin. The hare covered the first half of the course it chose as though its feet never touched the ground. But then a sudden anxiety brought it to a standstill. What if it was merely following the shortest path across the field in the shortest time? Would that be dismissed by some as the best it could do? Winning a long-distance race against oneself must surely rank above taking the laurels in a shorter one.

So the hare went back to the starting line and set off anew. This time, it raced wildly about, seeking the longest possible distance between start and finish. But soon a new worry pulled the hare up short once more. Suppose, in following this random course it overlooked some small, even miniscule stretch of ground. How could the hare claim to have won the race if it hadn't covered every last inch possible? The only solution now seemed to be to start in the exact center of the field and run in wider and wider circles until it reached the uttermost edge and could declare undisputed victory.

So the hare took up this new challenge and was off yet again, racing like the wind around and around, chasing its own tail and never certain whether it was ahead or behind.

But convinced more than ever that winning wasn't everything—it was the only thing.

"Harm's Way"

Once there was considerable dispute about the exact location of "Harm's Way."

This was despite the fact that the phrase "in harm's way" was on the lips of nearly everyone, from national and international leaders all the way down to a pedestrian looking both ways before jaywalking. Yet anybody seeking to inquire where exactly "Harm's Way" might be found typically received a flurry of contradictory responses.

"It's in that direction."

"No, this direction."

"Are you both blind, it's clearly right over there."

"You're all wrong. Can't you see two inches in front of your faces?"

Conflicts of opinion on this order often started small but quickly drew large crowds, with heated divisions spreading everywhere as neighbor turned from neighbor and even family members from one another in spluttering frustration. To say nothing of the age-old differences of opinion between generations, communities, nations, and ultimately entire cultures that grew increasingly pronounced as the whereabouts of "Harm's Way" became ever more obscure. Like historical disputes over the legitimacy of *"Terra Incognita"* and *"Here Be Monsters"* scrawled on fading maps, these larger wrangles could prove long-lasting, were it not for the eruption of a new disagreement that refocused everyone's attention on yet another claim to have discovered the true location of "Harm's Way."

Given this state of affairs, concern grew that if some form of unanimity was not reached, and soon, virtually every spot on Earth might become "Harm's Way" by default. So an international commission was hurriedly formed, complete with famous dignitaries and enormous staffs, to negotiate a document of understanding on "Harm's Way" acceptable to all. The opening ceremonies for such a momentous endeavor went well enough, for there were all the customary formalities and protocols to observe. These succeeded in keeping differences in check under the established strictures of statesmanship. However, once actual deliberations got underway, it became apparent that none of the participants were willing to pinpoint "Harm's Way" in any definite manner that might reflect badly upon their own portion of the globe. Almost daily, entire delegations got up and walked out of the negotiations in protest against other nations' views, only to return hastily when it became evident their objection had fallen on deaf ears and some crucial decision might be made in their absence that would designate their own homeland as "Harm's Way in Perpetuity." Now was not the time to stand on mere principle or to be timorous in the face of such a dire threat.

It might have been argued that a universal agreement to declare a moratorium on overuse of the expression "in harm's way" as shorthand for whatever felt alien to one's own world-view could have lowered distrust and eventually led at least to a quasi-truce based on mutual civility, good will, and some attempt to understand the situations of others.

Unfortunately, what few and feeble efforts were made in this vein led nowhere. Too much was demanded in order to do what would have been necessary, at whatever level, from highest diplomacy to a squabble in the street.

While by contrast, the familiar shorthand was so very convenient. And again, at all the same levels from highest diplomacy to squabbles in the street. Until not a patch of ground anywhere hadn't been labeled "Harm's Way" once or twice at a minimum, and some many times more than that.

Ultimately, one didn't have to point in any particular direction whatsoever when making the claim, since all directions were assumed to be implied and a simple whirling of the arms would suffice.

Between the default cliché and the mechanical gestures, few of those raising constant alarms paused to consider the possibility that "Harm's Way" might not lie someplace out there beyond their comfort zone but rather deep within the darkest regions of their own minds.

The Hawk

Once a hawk had trouble maintaining eye contact.

Being something of a loner, it didn't have that many occasions to look into the eyes of others, to be sure. The far horizon and the fields below claimed much more of its attention than glances exchanged with those crossing through its broad gyre every now and then. Who could spare much in the way of an inquiring look or a passing acknowledgement or even nodding recognition? That moment's distraction could mean a rustle in the brush hundreds of feet down slipped the hawk's notice.

Was it too single-minded in its pursuits, the hawk sometimes asked itself, and thus missed the chance to strike up acquaintances that would soften its reputation for aloofness? What must it be like to give and receive a "hail fellow well met" greeting twenty times per day? To be on a first-name basis with those who might have been perfect strangers the day before? The hawk was aware of the effect its piercing stare could have upon those it encountered. How, when it chanced to lock eyes with another creature and look within, it found uncertainty, discomfort, even fear that some failure of nerve would betray what should remain hidden. At such moments the hawk must decide whether to go in for the kill or look away out of pity for the trembling consternation it had seen.

How could some prey be so ready for the taking, as though waiting dove-like for the talons that struck without warning and the beak that ripped at will. Caught in the hawk's eye, they proved incapable of looking away and saving themselves. Instead they yielded up their innermost selves on the spot in such

107

trembling nakedness it seemed almost obscene to accept their sacrifice.

There were times when the hawk's disbelief that any creature so unguarded was meant for this world caused it to pull out of a lethal swoop with sudden qualms about the power of life and death it held. To pursue the defenseless, what gain or virtue lay in that? Cornered in their surprise, with no retreat and no possibility of pretending to themselves that the hawk was not upon them— so close now they could see their own panic frozen in its eyes—would striking to the deepest of their secrets satisfy the hawk? Or once started, would it lay every one of them open to the light, until neither the greatest nor the least had been spared?

Being a bird of prey wasn't always about the keen love of the hunt it might seem. Not at times like these, when you had to decide whether to look a potential victim in the eye knowing how defenseless it was (how easily exposed and undone) or turn aside and spare it without fully understanding why.

Only that breaking eye contact suddenly had a force that would not be denied.

Hearts Upon Sleeves

Once wearing your heart upon your sleeve was all the rage.

Everybody had a story to tell, it seemed, and was determined everybody else should hear it, whether in "highlight" snippets during media interviews or, if that wasn't enough, by reading everybody's book from cover to cover if the blurb on the back contained three or more of the following expressions of praise: "ground-breaking," "epoch-making," "seminal," "gripping," "pioneering," "peerless," "thought-provoking," "incisive," "trenchant," "salient," "compelling," "commanding," "riveting," "engrossing," "illuminating," "masterful," "monumental," "towering," "revelatory," "definitive," "essential," "indispensable," and so forth.

As for the book's content, any of the following might be found: trials, tribulations, trespasses, grievances, recriminations, abuse of any kind, urges for revenge or reconciliation, childhood trauma, adolescent infatuation, adult seductions and infidelities, old age impotence, self-exploration, self-discovery, self-promotion, self-pity, self-justification, self-denial, self-doubt, self-flagellation, self-forgiveness, self-transcendence, and so forth.

It was a wonder any of the hearts exposed like this survived the strain of trying to get the rest of humanity to listen to its inner voice. Many hearts, admittedly, didn't survive being paraded about on the sleeve and, having been ripped loose or merely fallen away, became a blight upon the landscape, fluttering idly in the wind or else ending up in some ditch with the other litter of life.

Failures on this scale were meaningless beside one far worse, however. Stripping your heart naked to the eyes of the world in the first place was a trespass so deep few recognized the true loss, the tragedy. For the heart lives in darkness as much as in light.

And what it holds of most value will not bear the light for long without beginning to shrivel and fade. Instead, one's heart must remain a sacred mystery, hidden away in its own holy of holies. Humble silence in service to it, once broken, cannot be redeemed, either with loud acclaim or tears of regret.

Yet it is a seductive wish: to ransack the secret altar of the heart and then be praised or lashed publicly for it. Either way, the forfeit can hardly be understood by those who've lost nothing by it themselves, whether as readers or listeners or merely those who pause in their pressing errands to ask what all the commotion is about. Everyone has a role to play in this sad performance.

Whose part is most abject, though? Whose pecking away at the heart is truly unspeakable? Can there be any doubt? To lay bare what makes you who you are—is there a greater folly? For you have yielded up what gave you strength: secrets that when spread, amount to very little but so long as no one knows of them, set the measure of yourself.

Deepest longings, passions without name, flights of madness or inspiration, fears, angers, hatreds, smoldering treacheries, obsession and lassitude, failures of nerve, failures of empathy, impulsive generosities or alibis for their lack, rationalizations, blazing arrogance and then freezing despair, ecstasy and desolation in one and the same beat—to wear all of these upon your sleeve—

What tragic self-betrayal—

Heracles

Once Heracles awoke from a nightmare drenched in sweat.

Night sweats were not unusual in the lives of heroes back then, given all they had to sleep off on a daily basis. Feats of brawn and endurance were already a strain on one's body, to say nothing of the added demands of living up to the expectations that came with bearing a famous name. At times, the stress of being constantly in public view could drive one deep into oneself for refuge, a sanctuary dense and quiet yet never free of vague shadows stalking its edges. The tension of being on the alert against these phantoms of the mind still gripped one long after the nerves and muscles of the body had relaxed.

Nightmares only made matters worse. Especially recurrent ones like the nightmare that now left Heracles drained and gasping for breath once again. He laid an arm across his wet forehead, causing beads of sweat to trickle down over his eyelids, down over his cheeks and into the creases of his neck, then down to the lion pelt glued to his skin like clammy dread. No matter how tightly he closed his eyes, the nightmare continued to repeat itself against the back of their burning lids.

It was the same every time: he and the giant Antaeus locked together to the death in a wrestling match where death never came for either of them. Heracles was certain he'd dispatched Antaeus, but with each return of the nightmare, he had to learn as if for the first time the secret that allowed the giant to bounce back whenever he was hurled down on his mother, earth, and yet rose again, revived by her power. And always, when he finally understood all over again that holding his foe off the ground was the only way to squeeze the life out of him, the nightmare would take the same turn and Heracles, looking up into the face of agony, would see in it a reflection of his own.

With every tightening of his clasp, the tortured grimace above him became more unmistakably his. The bulging eyes his, the twitching jaw muscles, the mouth stretched wide and sucking at the air, all of them his. And with the whole of his strength locked in the death-hug he had on his foe, he couldn't turn away left or right, caught as he was in the arms of the nightmare's greater force.

Worse was the fear that his trusted strength had served only to pinion him between victory and defeat, with neither one a possible release. Would the death of Antaeus not also be his own, while loss to the giant be a failure to master himself?

This recurrent stalemate was what left Heracles exhausted and covered in sweat each time he awoke from the repeated nightmare. Shouldn't a fatal contest have an end? The summons of his foe's recurrent taunts was all he could imagine nights to come would bring, along with the iron necessity to answer them. His breath as he lay waiting for dawn had a scummy staleness, as though life had clotted within him. Whatever measure of his strength was left might only be enough, not to hoist Antaeus again, but merely to steady himself against collapse back into endless horror.

As there, always, holding him fast in its unyielding challenge was the vision of a face in extremis: in pain he'd never thought possible before.

The Hog

Once a hog grew philosophical.

Who could live a porcine life, it reasoned, without having to be philosophical about it? True, a hog's existence could be worse. This hog had to admit that it didn't lack for bodily comforts. Each day it ate and drank its fill, then lay about the fattening pen with its companions and listened to them belching contentedly. Despite these signs of bodily ease, each day brought the hog increasing mental disquiet. It had metaphysical doubts that simply wouldn't go away.

As for the other hogs, they didn't appreciate this one's penchant for mulling the nature of their lives. So long as there was slop in the trough, why ask for anything more? Why not be satisfied with that and stop plaguing them with questions and hypotheses? "If you're going to engage in idle contemplation," the other hogs were prone to chide, "do us the favor of moving downwind, would you?"

Faced with this and other mocking gibes, the hog eventually decided to withdraw to a distant corner of the pen where it could pursue its quest for understanding in peace and quiet. This wasn't idle contemplation, it knew, but an effort to find answers to age-old questions. Where did it come from? Where was it going? Why was it here? And why here in this stinking mud?

Away in its corner, the hog read everything from the ancient Greeks to the latest theories in astrobiology. It consulted the sacred texts of all major religions and pored over thick tomes with titles like *Foundations of the West* and *Ageless Wisdom of the East.* Yet still, crucial questions remained unanswered in the hog's mind.

Was the fattening pen real or was it an illusion? If it was real, why was the hog condemned to this filthy patch of reality in a cosmos presumably full of splendid possibilities? If it wasn't real, then why did the hog feel such pain whenever it was jabbed at through the fence with a stick by the fattening pen's owner? Was mere chance to blame for the hog's situation, or was its life predestined? Or was life a trial to be endured in hopes of rewards to come in some afterlife? Was one's present life a consequence of actions in past lifetimes? Or was life simply absurd, with no meaning whatsoever? Ultimately, were all judgments on the nature of existence in and of themselves irrelevant?

The hog devoted so much time to these ponderings that it began neglecting to join the others at the trough for their daily slopfest, preferring not to be distracted for a single moment from its speculations on existence. It grew indifferent even to the weather and appeared not to notice when the mud around it steamed or froze. As might be expected, it began to lose weight and grow weak. For their part, the rest of the hogs gave less and less thought to their former companion until none of them could even recall where it had withdrawn to.

Days came and went. New hogs arrived and old hogs disappeared down a long chute, while in its remote corner of the pen, the philosophical hog found it barely had the strength any longer to raise its heavy head. The end must be near, it concluded. Yet it didn't complain about having been reduced to not much more now than skin and bones encrusted with muck. It took consolation in the knowledge that it had continued its quest to the very last.

Still convinced, as Socrates is said to have said, the unexamined life is not worth living.

The Homing Pigeon

Once an elderly homing pigeon began to lose its sense of direction.

It could still manage to find the way back to its roost, but the return trip, which had always felt shorter than the journey out, now seemed the reverse, and the accustomed landmarks on which the pigeon relied had become harder to find with advancing years. Increasingly, it wandered off course, sometimes by miles, and only succeeded in righting its way through hopeful guesses at where to turn next.

When others began to remark on the homing pigeon's difficulty, it tried to laugh the matter off. So long as it fluttered back into view eventually, was there any reason for alarm? Lapses were bound to happen now and then. After decades on the wing, should there be any wonder that the many passages it had made might become crossed in its mind and lead back to places it hadn't expected?

This explanation failed to account, however, for the most puzzling aspect of the drift in the pigeon's bearings: the fact that it had no trouble at all remembering its early flights, some of which could be mentally retraced in astonishing detail. It also recalled the exact smell of inland plains many harvests ago and the feel of the wind lifting it over the first wide stretch of water it had ever crossed. Yet for all the certainty with which the pigeon could navigate its distant past, more recent years took on the drift of clouds, while last week was already dissolving into mist and what had just happened might as well have happened to strangers. Experience had ceased to cast its guiding shadow over the ground.

Even repeating again and again to itself the recollections of a lifetime in hopes of keeping them as clear as the day they'd been fixed in the pigeon's mind proved misleading. Instead of reassurance, the attempt often brought gasps of pained surprise at what had once been taken for certain, then lost to memory, then encountered again only by chance. And what was not recovered in this haphazard way vanished from the pigeon's life story altogether, as though the missing pages had been declared a forgery and not worthy of note.

Could memory become such a pitiless foe—this lifelong friend that turned out to betray one (a stranger now, waiting for the moment of one's greatest need of reassurance and then coldly pretending not to have heard the heart's plea at all)?

Nor were the pigeon's loving mate and young, circling in patterns they hoped might point the way home, able to slow the steady wasting away of a soul that had guided their own affections for so long. Leaving them helpless before dazed questions of "Who are you?" and "Why are you here?"

What reassurance could they offer the struggling homing pigeon that would ever bring it back across the fading terrain once familiar to them all?

The Hornswoggles

Once a great flock of hornswoggles swept out from their dark swamp, and the rest is history.

Frequently and understandably mistaken for the closely related, equally opportunistic red-white-and-blue tub-thumpers, the hornswoggles called attention to themselves with the same loud squawk and had the same habit of fouling not only their own nests but also, when given half a chance, much of the countryside.

This misidentification was furthered by the long-standing debate among those who devoted themselves to keeping tabs on such strange birds about whether red-white-and-blue tub-thumpers should in fact be renamed "yellow-bellied tub-thumpers," given their extensively documented habit of seeking cover at the first sign that the racket they raised might have unwelcome consequences for themselves. Whenever people grew tired of the deafening clamor and came together to end a red-white-and-blue-aka-yellow-bellied tub-thumper's non-stop assault on their peace of mind, it could be counted on to flap its way off to safety within the thick camouflage provided by the more lightless reaches of the swamp.

Although tub-thumpers might be a frequent nuisance and at times posed a passing concern, hornswoggles proved themselves a genuine and abiding cause for alarm. Swooping out of the same noxious murk, often from a nest shared with a tub-thumper or two and flashing its own yellow-gold belly shaped like a bulging moneybag, a hornswoggle was constantly on the alert for the slightest chance to profit from others' vulnerabilities or inattention. Its sharp raptor eyes took in any advantage to be gained, and its even sharper talons seized with frightful speed and force whatever the prize might be.

Every hornswoggle had a special appetite for gulls, who were easily spellbound by the predator's mesmerizing moves and yielded themselves up again and again to its guile. Lack of vigilance against such a constant peril was what hornswoggles banked on and what they never failed to exploit without mercy or remorse.

Fears that red-white-and-blue-aka-yellow-bellied tub-thumpers and rapacious yellow-gold-moneybag hornswoggles were here to stay became widespread, as pessimism that much of anything could be done about the situation deepened with time. Red-white-and-blue-aka-yellow-bellied tub-thumpers would likely always be a problem, and thus learning to live with them while keeping their numbers under control somehow might be the best that could be hoped for, perhaps through a program of restricted breeding habitat.

Yet without serious and sustained commitment by the potential victims of yellow-gold-moneybag hornswoggles, this odious species would never be driven back into the baleful haunts from which it had emerged to wreak such ruin countrywide.

The Hummingbird

Once a hummingbird worried about its personal space.

Any intrusion upon that portion of the globe reserved in its mind for itself alone caused the hummingbird considerable anxiety. Confronted by the unwelcome presence of another, it might dart about in a flustered manner or, going to the other extreme, halt in midflight and seem to pull its personal space in around itself as tightly as possible. Weren't others aware of how unwelcome their mere existence was, it fretted.

Given such annoyances, the hummingbird was almost never seen taking public transportation. Whenever it found itself with no option but to do so, it would dart to any unoccupied seat and place whatever tiny baggage it might be carrying on the next seat to prevent others from getting too close or, if it had nothing to block intrusion this way, simply sprawl as best it could across the space between seats and pretend to be sleeping. An entire group of hummingbirds spread out this way was not an uncommon sight on some routes.

Rush hour obviously posed particular challenges in this regard. Caught in the sweaty press of strangers, the hummingbird often felt itself on the verge of passing out and only found relief from such torment by leaning its head against the window and imagining the expansive, cooling freshness that a sudden view of the Rockies might bring.

Music on the hummingbird's smartphone was another escape from unwanted contact, one it relied on to get from any "here" to any "there" fully shielded by tiny earphones against the horrid in-between of the journey. With the volume turned up all the way, there was little chance the exasperating presence of others would encroach upon its privacy.

Another defense the hummingbird never went anywhere without was its bottle of personal water. The thought of drinking from a public fountain was more disgusting even than sharing the close air of the crowd. The stuff streaming down one's throat, who knew where it came from? What contamination might it be spreading to every cell in one's body? But one's personal water was different. Plus, it was all yours. You didn't have to share.

If only everything could be like that, the hummingbird would frequently sigh to itself. Bottled, packaged, shrink-wrapped, airtight, sanitized, that would be heaven. You wouldn't have to risk coming into contact with any of the thousand and one things that caused you distress or weakened the protection of your inner safety zone. Such things would be as good as nonexistent.

It would just be you and your personal space: a refuge from the vexing brunt of life, a private little utopia with you hovering there right at its center. The hummingbird was convinced a private little utopia would do just fine, thank you very much. No need for anything else.

Because the hummingbird was, as hardly needed pointing out, already very small by nature.

The Hydra

Once the Hydra noticed that its many heads were growing smaller and disappearing one after another.

This didn't happen overnight, to be sure, so the Hydra had continued to go about its normal routine as "chief creative" for early-evening TV programming at a leading entertainment conglomerate without taking any more notice than usual of the number or size of its remaining heads. The brain inside each seemed as filled as always with neat "new concepts" in quizzes, contests, sit-coms, talent shows, etc.

Eventually, however, the reality of what was happening could no longer be ignored. The real awareness of this change towards smaller and fewer heads came when the Hydra noted a decline in the usual back-and-forth programming debates among them. The tossing about of ideas could be heated and confusing at times, but exchanges of this sort had always given the Hydra some confidence that what eventually came out of one head's mouth was the product of thorough group consideration. Now it increasingly found its heads blurting out, willy-nilly, whatever came first to their shrinking minds.

The Hydra wondered if up-and-coming Hydras at the entertainment conglomerate noticed that its heads were vanishing, but none of them made any mention of that. On the contrary, they too seemed to be losing heads at an accelerating pace and compensating for this fact by merely blurting out the same ideas from three or four of their remaining mouths in chorus so as to distract attention from any given one of them.

On the other hand, having fewer heads apparently didn't interfere with the basic ability of the "creatives" (be they old-timers or newcomers) to function, since all were clearly on the same page more regularly now. It occurred to the Hydra that perhaps its extra heads had actually been unnecessary, possibly even a hindrance. There was no denying that having to deal with fewer and fewer "new concepts" was something of a relief. This accelerating move towards "creative groupthink downshift, or CGD" as its few remaining heads were cleverly calling it now, seemed so much more efficient.

The confidence that had once cemented the Hydra's reputation for fearlessly challenging all of its heads to have their wits about them and, just as importantly, to make use of those wits or suffer the consequences was vanishing in direct proportion to its own shrinking interest in the real world. And as it approached its last remaining head, the Hydra felt a certain relief in finding that the adjustments required during its decline were growing steadily easier to make.

When you came right down to it, who really needed the entertainment brainpower that extra heads might offer? Judging from what it saw and heard as it took part in yet another Zoom meeting on the latest trends in popular entertainment and how to duplicate them and then reduplicate the duplicates with a minimum of tweaks, the now one-headed Hydra guessed it could probably get by with a single brain, or maybe even less.

Maybe simply relying on one's reptilian brain would be all that was needed.

Icarus

Once Icarus went for a swim.

The warmth that met his shins, then thighs, then chest as he pushed through the surf washed over his mind as well. How long had he stood looking out over the wine-dark sea and listening to his father hammer at those endless contraptions day after day? The old man pausing only to give him yet another piece of advice he hadn't asked for. Like today's lecture on the long-term consequences of getting too much sun at an early age.

The call of the seabirds had been a relief from the confident assertions about what to do and what not to do in life, about knowing your limits and all the dangers awaiting those who were heedless of the future. What heed was he supposed to take? He was only a youth, with a youth's passion for the moment. Was he supposed to awake every dawn already having a list in mind of potential catastrophes that might befall him that day? Worrying about what of everything he'd gained in life so far might be lost through a single rash move? What had he gained by this age, anyway, that he couldn't do without if need be?

With apprehensions like these, no wonder the old man devoted so much time to working out ways to escape risk and then calculating their odds of success or failure. Didn't he ever gaze out to sea himself without figuring in the force of the currents, the height of the waves, and the distance at which land would be lost from view? Didn't he remember how little all three mattered when he himself was young? What chances he must have taken when the tide ran high and the winds were strong, wasting no thought on peril, seen or unseen.

Well away from shore now, Icarus pulled through the rolling swells with an even, steady motion. He'd never been this far out before but felt in his shoulders and legs a power still equal to his very first strokes away from the beach. His body moved through the salt water as though born to it, and when he looked down between breaths, he didn't see pale shades of those lost at sea drifting beneath him. Instead he saw only the flickering of the sunlight as it found the limit of its power in the depths.

Turning over on his back, the youth faced directly up into the sun and floated, arms outstretched, in the bright shimmers cast over the water's surface. Fiery joy filled his breast, as though drawn from every part of the sky to this one point in the sea buoying him with its embrace. How far couldn't he swim now if he wished, and what new lands couldn't he reach? Wherever these waters carried him, he would find a home. And even if he was to die in the attempt, it would be his death. As it would be his life until that moment came. With this confidence, Icarus tilted his head back until his ears were below the surface, where the voice of the deep was loud enough to drown out any distracting cries that might reach him from shore.

After a time, he turned back over and began to swim again with all his proud, fearless might.

The Immortal

Once an immortal decided to call it quits.

When so many mortals hoped to enjoy eternal bliss after they died, this immortal's embrace of the reverse might seem baffling.

The death option certainly didn't appeal to other immortals, who were none too pleased to be told their entire reason for existing might have less to recommend it than they thought. It was—or so this bothersome malcontent in their midst claimed—devoid of any recognition that existence might offer something other than endless repetitions of the known and a tedious search for time-killing diversions to lessen the ennui of living forever.

What was the attraction of such arid monotony, the renegade immortal asked again and again. Where was the thirst anymore for experiences that suddenly upended everything you'd come to assume about yourself and replaced those assumptions with a fresh start offered by the unpredictable? Even the fleeting lives of mortals looked attractive by comparison with a divine existence that had about as much thrill left to it as eternally flossing one's teeth in the mirror.

At least there were alluring possibilities still in what mortals faced. Nothing was ever finished, no matter how "complete" or "perfect" they naively declared it to be. Their blindness to the potential value of the unfinished over the completed and of imperfection over perfection was what made so many humans endearing. Constantly flogging themselves to accomplish "something for the ages" and then flogging themselves again with worries they might not succeed—how these mere mortals stirred one's sympathies, what with all they had left still to learn! Masterpieces, legacies, honor, conquest, trophies and prizes and records of every sort, fortune and fame regardless of how these were won, position and privilege and all—humans strove so hard for so little, such trifles in the end, that the renegade immortal couldn't help but be touched by their endless myopia.

When right there before them were spread more reasons to marvel than they ever dreamed of: all the taints, scars, lapses, errors, and defects that made their lives the constant gamble they were. Full of uncertain promise and vulnerability, no wonder mortals were so fascinating in ways no immortal could claim to be. For who among those spared from ever having to come to terms with their own death could understand the doomed hope which humans gripped more fiercely each day they neared their ultimate defeat?

In the end, this tragic hope had a nobility that outweighed everything else and should leave even gods in speechless awe.

The Inflatable Clown

Once an inflatable clown wondered how many more times it could be punched to the floor and still bounce back.

A thousand times? A hundred? Ten? One? It wasn't easy being the target of so much anger and aggression. Or easy maintaining its silly grin through every pummeling it had to endure. Granted, people needed outlets for their frustrations and hatreds. But couldn't they find them by laying into something else on occasion? Although if it weren't for the clown, they'd likely be swinging at each other in no time, so there wasn't much hope of being spared its role as a stand-in foe for all.

The clown nevertheless still wished some kind of recognition would be made of the difficult task it was asked to perform. If nothing else, what about placing a few restrictions on the rabbit punches and low blows? It must not do any of its attackers credit to be seen practicing dirty tactics they secretly wished to use against whomever their real target might be. Thrashing a defenseless inflatable clown as a warmup couldn't do much for one's reputation or self-image, could it? So perhaps its assailants were beyond such considerations already.

Even if that was the case, something could still be done about limiting their numbers, the clown felt. This urge to pile on whenever they saw others belting an inflatable clown could turn even a seemingly docile crowd into a raging mob in no time. Was it wise to allow free rein to such tendencies, especially when there was no guarantee they'd stop with the clown? If history was any guide, once the initial target of their wrath had been dealt with, it was on to the next "enemy" at hand, until mobs had turned into armies storming across the land and falling upon anyone or anything not quick enough to get out of their way. The clown had been around long enough to realize how unlikely it was that this seeking of anonymity in communal violence would be curbed merely for its sake.

Then how about at least separating the adults from the children? Maybe give them different times to have a go at the clown, not just as a means to curb untoward lessons taught by example but also simply as a way of telling the two age groups apart. In the midst of their frenzy, with emotions at full pitch, grown men could easily be mistaken for playground bullies, launching their most vicious attacks against any weakness they feared bigger bullies might see in them as well if they restrained themselves.

Where would it all end? How high up the bragging order of power did you have to climb before you no longer feared being taken by the world for a weakling or a coward who needed to stalk about in search of a punch-down clown to prove you weren't?

Intelligent Life on this Planet

Once a widespread movement arose that illustrated the following claim: "The jury's still out regarding intelligent life on this planet."

All attempts to explain the origins and development of intelligent life as we might know it were dismissed by followers of this movement as mere theories. Evidence for the validity of any theory was just that, evidence only, from which firm conclusions could rarely be drawn, based on the following logic: theories are not facts; this fact by itself is enough to reduce all theories to opinions; all opinions are either right or wrong; in the absence of agreed-upon truth, all theories, being essentially one person's word against another's, have equal potential to be either true or false; ergo, as a rough guide to intelligence on earth, believe whatever you want to believe and ignore all else.

Anytime one theory on the origins and development of intelligent life was presented, all other theories were to be given the same airing in descending order of likelihood, determined not on the basis of "evidence" (which was merely a matter of "interpretation" and thus unreliable in itself, many held, forming air quotes with their fingers in hopes of strengthening their point) but by a nose count of those who already professed to embrace the theory in question. If this determination to recognize absolutely every theory out there regarding intelligent life as being equal to every other theory extended all the way to a conviction that life on earth was only a few thousand years old or was left behind by aliens from distant galaxies who had, for reasons unknown, dropped by again at some later date to teach our distant ancestors the cosmic secrets of how to stack stones in neat piles and then zipped off once more after leaving instructions to wait for further guidance about what to do next, well then, adherence to nonjudgmental neutrality in the matter of truth required that these assertions, too, be taken seriously. A declaration was even made that life was so complex in design it couldn't really be understood anyhow.

So appealing was the promotion of what came to be known as the "Jury's Still Out" approach to understanding life on earth that many of its proponents were invited to address school boards and state legislatures and help in drafting government regulations or selecting judges who pledged to enforce the "Jury's Still Out" stance as the final word on any subject whatsoever.

Under normal circumstances, such an approach could have quickly proved self-defeating, of course, yet because it favored no particular position regarding the existence of intelligent life on this planet but instead threw the doors of the schoolhouse, government agencies, and the courts wide open to any and all claims without distinction based on either evidence or logic, nobody felt anybody else's view of the matter enjoyed an unfair advantage. Even those charged with the actual conduct of schools, government, and the courts seemed relieved that they themselves no longer needed to offer a convincing explanation for why they were here.

That was way back when, of course.

121

The Isotope

Once a radioactive isotope couldn't wait to complete its first half-life.

With time, though, all the attainments and delights it once was positive would come to it in due course seemed postponed to the next half-life or possibly the next or even the next after that. The isotope understood very well that each nanosecond experienced was in fact a nanosecond of decay and that it might make more sense to seek out any means to hold back time's forward rush rather than urge it on. In spite of this awareness, future half-lives possessed a hypnotic attraction for this one, what with their promise of multiple do-over opportunities for any disappointments suffered now. The isotope was certain it still possessed the energy needed for that, powers so insistent they could be at odds with each other, even with themselves often. But if combined with all its half-lives still ahead, those powers had to bring about the desired outcomes at some point, didn't they?

So convinced was the isotope that the grand achievements expected in its first half-life had proved illusory, it took little note of lesser ones arising and fading away all the time. Other than to dismiss them, that was, as proof its steady decline held nothing more than travesties of what really mattered. Satisfactions near at hand looked trivial by comparison with those still visualized from afar. Either the isotope's initial half-life represented the depressing norm or else it represented nothing whatsoever and was thus even more depressing.

If it could just hurry up the start of its next half-life, maybe then it would feel really alive at last. The uneven shimmer of its early years must then yield to a more mature self-confidence, with deeper strengths and the corresponding accomplishments it had looked forward to from the beginning.

For other isotopes to tell this one it had everything backwards and that someday it would actually grow nostalgic for its first half-life and long to re-cover what it so strained to be rid of today merely demonstrated how little of their own past they must have understood. Their repeating ad nauseam that old "gather ye rosebuds while ye may" line merely increased the isotope's impatience. Weren't "rosebuds" just so many seductions sung by the past, making them precisely what it must refuse to heed if it was ever to escape this present half-life's apparent futility?

Hadn't these know-it-all isotopes been young once themselves and dreamed of all that the future must hold? What happened to them that they couldn't focus on anything but their lost half-lives now?

The Jackals

Once the jackals developed attitude.

They didn't have to work at it much. They were by nature a testy lot. For years they'd felt their innate talents had been either underappreciated or ignored, and displaying a surly attitude seemed the best way to counter that slight.

Convinced that natural talent was at the base of their attitude, the jackals were intent on showing they should not be confused with the hyenas, who in fact had no talent whatsoever. The hyenas, as far as the jackals were concerned, merely made a lot of noise in an amateurish bid for attention, apparently persuaded that edgy, in-your-face boorishness was worthy of note in itself.

What made the jackals' attitude more legitimate in their mind was a gnawing conviction that so many others enjoyed the celebrity they were certain should be theirs instead. Why was A raved about all over the place, they wondered among themselves, and not one of us? How did B get on the cover of *People*? How did C deserve that big film and book deal just for being in all the gossip columns already? Why was that no-talent D considered an "idol" rather than any jackal in the whole wide world?

One break was all they asked for. The rest would follow like clockwork. In the meantime, there was nothing much for the jackals to do but to keep up their morale by praising each other's unrecognized gifts and ridiculing, with snickers and knowing smiles, those who continued to be famous without really deserving it. On occasion, however, the accumulated grievances of the jackals got the better of them, and they were known to snarl and snap at each other whenever this happened. Ridicule wasn't the only course the jackals considered. Some were for the direct approach: snatching the spotlight from those who currently had it by making a public spectacle of themselves and letting the media do the rest. Others urged following even small-time celebs about in hopes of sharing vicariously in their "aura": getting close and staying alert for a chance to savor, however briefly, what should have been theirs all along.

Perhaps that explains why, if one looks closely at a publicity photograph of those who are at the center of attention for any reason whatsoever these days, there in the shadowy background can usually be seen a pair of eyes that glow more intensely than the others, watching and waiting.

In some photographs, of course, there are many more.

The Jack-in-the-Boxes

Once it was proposed that every jack-in-the-box be held accountable for its behavior.

As might have been predicted, this idea met with immediate, often dismissive objections from many quarters. How could a jack-in-the-box be held accountable for anything? You might as well blame a knee for jerking when tapped. Wasn't the sum and substance of every jack-in-the-box's very being precisely this ability to spring out at the turn of a crank or the push of a button from the cramped, lightless box in which it otherwise spent its time? What purpose in life could it claim if it didn't dutifully pop out of its darkness on command?

Those calling for jack-in-the-box accountability clearly hadn't reckoned on the strength of this pushback or, for that matter, on the number of these puppets there actually turned out to be in the country at large. The presence of genuine antiques packed away in drafty attics or dank basements—cracked reminders of long-ago fears and flusters—would hardly have been surprising, but when freshly produced ones began to appear in ever-greater lots, clacking open and shut with loud vehemence and in the most public, most prominent of venues, the extent of the challenge to controlling them soon became clear.

Local instances of embarrassing jack-in-the-box behavior might still have made at least a limited requirement for answerability feasible, but with new examples popping up everywhere all the time, addressing this nationwide phenomenon proved increasingly difficult, to say the least.

In addition, evidence of any reluctance to follow the general pattern of automatic jack-in-the-box behavior began to raise questions in reverse about the motives of those who were not jumping fast enough or high enough. When rows of zealous jack-in-the-boxes dutifully attended a much-anticipated speech (from city council harangues all the way up to a joint session of Congress, for instance) and repeatedly erupted in a deafening clatter that drowned out more measured consideration of the truth or lack thereof in what might actually have just been said, any evidence of restraint or outright refusal to join in the noisy, regimented display was call for suspicion, even expressions of scandalized umbrage at any laggard jack-in-the-box not demonstrating dutiful obedience-on-cue. Criticism of blatant endangerment to others caused by flapping jack-in-the-box excess in such cases typically led nowhere. Any concern on the part of these puppets that they might have to answer eventually for the consequences of their trigger-response popoutism was minimal. Instead, their chief worry seemed quite different.

"With so many of us acting virtually in sync," each jack-in-the-box gave every sign of calculating, "how can I show I'm the absolute quickest and loudest of all when it comes to demonstrating exactly what's expected of me?"

The Jellyfish

Once a jellyfish got caught in the rip currents of the mind.

For its entire life, the jellyfish had contentedly drifted from one place and experience to another without giving any of them much thought. Currents came and currents went, and the jellyfish floated along as though each was the same as all the others. A state of serenity with not a cloud in the sky above or in the mind either—what creature wouldn't luxuriate in that? No ups, no downs, no surprises, hardly any change really in the long smooth waves that bore the jellyfish from one day to the next.

Life was good. At least this life was. So good that the jellyfish thought it must be the envy of others the world around. Given half a chance, which of them wouldn't have changed places with it, eagerly and without a second thought? Not one, the jellyfish assumed in tingling self-satisfaction, imagining a sea of gelatinous longing all the way to the horizon.

So pleased was the jellyfish with its lot that it barely noticed an ever-so-faint pull at the far tip of a tentacle one sunny afternoon. Nor did it give the unaccustomed sensation much thought. Trifling shifts in an otherwise laid-back existence were bound to occur when good fortune allowed one to drift through life without a care. Or so the jellyfish told itself. Until it felt another tug, that is, this time on a different tentacle and more insistent. Then another. At which point the jellyfish went crazy.

Its first reaction was to flail out with every remaining tentacle at this most unwelcome development. On the rare occasions when its idyllic realm had been even slightly intruded upon in the past, the venom from a single one of its stingers had been quite enough to set all things right again in no time. And then its carefree drift could continue as if nothing had happened that might call drifting as a lifestyle into question.

Until now. Now things were not as they should be. Something must have slipped in their appointed order. And the shock of that abrupt change, the inexplicable and menacing nature of such a turn, brought turmoil to the mental faculties of the jellyfish.

Sudden disquiet veered to the worst thought imaginable: was this the beginning of the end of the world? The jellyfish couldn't tell for sure, but change was change, was it not, and any reversal of the free and easy life must necessarily be a prelude to chaos! Never again would the jellyfish know inner calm! Never again be free of quivering dread!

In the maelstrom of its panic, the jellyfish felt itself buffeted from every side and flattened, tumbled, twisted into contorted extremes, drawn thin to the point of fainting one second and the next snapping back in jangled panic. Whatever shape there'd been to its self-awareness beyond a faith in the power of jellyfishdom was all but beaten to a mushy pulp.

With one exception: the venom of a contentment upended. Ranged against all outside threats to the jellyfish's bliss, countless stingers remained ready to be triggered, only now they were aimed at lethal cross-purposes within. Could its very confidence in everything it had taken for granted about its halcyon existence prove to be its undoing? There would be no peace for the jellyfish, ever again. Not when every day or hour or minute or even second could be its last. What a cruel fate to be swept under by the rip currents of the mind, when nothing you had come to count on could save you from yourself.

Jonathan Swift

Once Jonathan Swift auditioned for a stand-up comedy gig.

He thought he'd do a "Houyhnhnm" routine. That ought to have some appeal.

"Ya got social comment chops, Johnny-boy?" he was asked after being signaled to a small stage and introducing himself. "Ya don't mind me callin' ya 'Johnny-boy,' doya, Johnny-boy?" the voice continued from the darkness out front. "Anyhow, that's what we need. Laugh-till-ya-wet-yerself social comment one-liners."

Jonathan Swift wasn't sure he had anything like "laugh-till-ya-wet-yerself social comment one-liners" to offer. When he'd been working up his routine, he thought it would be enough to do an extended impression of a noble Houyhnhnm trying to explain an ignoble Yahoo and audiences would naturally find the contrast both amusing and instructive.

126

But things began to go wrong almost from the start of the audition. Not that the impression of a talking horse was faulty. The neighing voice was pitch-perfect, while the air of bemusement in a Houyhnhnm's account of such deep revulsion felt by a Yahoo towards others of its ilk that it was driven to distance itself from them through hatred, disgust, and contempt demonstrated powers of satirical caricature not often seen. Writing all his own stuff, Jonathan Swift had been confident every nuance of its multi-layered satire would come out in the delivery.

The problem was that nobody sitting out in the dark seemed to catch on. One or two laughs greeted the first sound from the make-believe Houyhnhnm's mouth, yet what was being said met with silence, then forced coughing, and finally the muffled sound of exiting feet.

Though the lights in his eyes weren't particularly bright, Jonathan Swift could soon feel himself sweating profusely and his mouth turning dry. His hands, meant to suggest the graceful movement of a Houyhnhnm's hoof one moment and a Yahoo's claw-like grasping for everything in sight the next, had gone clammy and numb. A nervous tic set his chin atremble, and holding a posture of reason and civility on the one hand or belligerent dimwittedness on the other became increasingly difficult to manage. Just when he wasn't sure he could carry on much longer, the mike was mercifully turned off, leaving him to brace himself for the worst.

"I'm afraid ya just ain't got what it takes for stand-up these days, Johnny-Boy," the voice from the dark curtly put it. "First of all, what's with this church garb of yours? You wanna bum out the whole room in a heartbeat? And the horse shtick just doesn't cut it. Try slouchin' 'round the stage more, maybe jump up and down or pull faces for a laugh, or scream at the audience every ten seconds or so. And if ya can't come up with anythin' better than what ya showed us today, shout obscenities instead and grab your crotch or somethin'. Knockout stuff like that."

After a long silence, Jonathan Swift finally replied, "I believe I understand now. You want the full Yahoo instead, do you?"

The Killer Smarm

Once a killer smarm invaded an average home in an average neighborhood. The unfortunate victims of the smarm did everything they could to keep it

127

out, but their efforts were in vain. As smarm attacks regularly do, this one found a way around every door and under every window in a buzzing, shapeless mass that never rested in searching for a way to reach and overwhelm anyone inside.

The killer smarm was related to a common honeybee colony but exhibited additional traits that required forensic pathologists to expand their usual list of dangerous factors to include cloyingly saccharine ones as well, such as:

> darling little letters to the president from third-graders read out to standing ovations during a State of the Union Address
>
> fawning pop-profiles of tuff-but-cute teen rebels lip-syncing the lyrics to the chart-topping hit "Everythin' Sucks 'cept Me"
>
> mawkish greeting card verse by prize-winning poets who've lost the gift
>
> "greatest 'easy-listening' hits" by Beethoven, as they've never been heard before
>
> "starving-artist" copies of a Vincent van Gogh self-portrait (check out the bandaged ear, everybody)
>
> local TV morning news from the award-winning duo of Chummy and Chatty, with "Hey guys, comin' up after the commercial break we'll tell you how it all went down in the latest humanitarian dis-aster and then, back by popular demand, our weekend hurricane report from Chuckles the Witty Weather Guy as he tries to stand upright in the wind and rain and not be swept away by the storm surge (always a hoot watching those clips over and over every year), and don't forget to text us your comments on our parent company's must-see marathon Television World Event entitled 'Celebrity Heartbreaks Then and Now' and, of course, a shout-out to all you guys in the audience who keep sending us those snaps and videos of absolutely a-d-o-r-a-b-l-e kittens stuck in trees. We promise to air every last one of them for the next week!"

The list continued for page after page after page. When rescue units finally broke into the house and found the killer smarm's victims, it was difficult to tell the adults from the children. All were covered with the same sticky-sweet goo from head to foot, and all had the same taut grins stretched across grotesquely swollen, pancake-shaped faces. There was nothing to be done at that point but add these latest unfortunates to the already bursting case files labeled "The Smiley Face Dead."

The killer smarm, as feared, had moved on in search of new victims.

The King of Beasts

Once other members of the animal kingdom put a lion in a cage.

They did this because they wanted to honor and protect one of their own as a symbol of what they all held to be most admirable in themselves: their exemplar, so to speak. In keeping with that intention, they named the lion "King of Beasts" and chose the most beautiful of gilded cages for it.

Day after day the splendid cage was pulled past representatives of every species, who either cheered wildly or bowed in humble and solemn silence. The lion enjoyed the non-stop adulation, but at times it wondered what a life without bars might be like. Because it was given the best of everything, it never had the opportunity to choose for itself, even to choose badly. All that could possibly be desired was granted the lion by ardent attendants before it could even decide what it wanted.

As the years passed, instead of becoming accustomed to this favored treatment and unwilling to give it up, the lion grew more and more depressed over its confinement. Sometimes at night it could even be heard to lament, "What a hard, hard fate it is to be the king of beasts."

On such nights it might also question why, among all the creatures on the face of the earth, it alone had been singled out in this way. Many others were nearly its equal in strength, courage, wisdom, and what have you. Some might even be superior to it in certain qualities. Increasingly downhearted about its state, the lion came to whisper to every animal that passed the cage: "Trade places with me, I beseech you."

But not one of the beseeched was willing to give up the freedom to do anything it wanted to and, instead, be constantly held to the highest standards as an example for others. So long as the lion was king, that responsibility was taken care of. The rest of the animals could go about their business with an easy mind, at liberty to follow whatever standards worked best for them on a case-by-case basis. So it wasn't surprising that no matter how often it asked, the lion met with polite refusals by one and all.

That is, until one day the lion's torment was unexpectedly eased by the lowliest of creatures: a mouse. Hearing rumors of the lion's distress, this mouse made its way past all of the watchful attendants who protected the "King of Beasts" until it reached the gilded cage. There it waited its chance, and when the pacing lion happened to look its way, piped up, "I'll take a crack at being king, if you like."

The lion stopped in its tracks, but only for a moment. The next moment the lion and mouse had traded places, and the next after that, the lion was gone.

The first sight of a mouse as "King of Beasts" flustered many of the lion's former attendants and even led to some resignations amid snorts of "It's a disgrace! A disgrace, I tell you!" The great majority of attendants, however, soon reconciled themselves to the change and carried on with their duties much as before. They just made the cage smaller.

To be sure, all of the other animals noticed that a mouse had become king, but that didn't seem to bother many of them for long. Why couldn't a mouse sit in a gilded cage and serve just as well as a lion in symbolizing something important about themselves?

Everything depended on how you looked at it, presumably.

"Knight, Death, and the Devil"

Once a knight, Death, and the Devil approached the edge of a Dürer engraving.

Without looking at his companions, the knight asked, "What do we do now?"

"What do you mean 'we'?" Death responded. "I keep going. Got appointments to keep, don't you know."

"Same here," the Devil added, raising a leg to break wind.

"Did you have to do that again?" the knight asked wearily.

"Just easin' the load," the Devil chuckled, then pointed up through the weathered trees above them and added, "in case I ever get a short-notice invite to that fine city up there on the hill."

"Not likely," sneered Death.

"Speak fer yerself! Fat chance you make it up there ahead a' me, Ol' Bag-a-Bones. Ha! Get it—'Ol' Bag-a-Bones'? Okay, yer turn now. Gimme yer best shot."

How had he ended up with this pair of clowns, the knight wondered? They certainly weren't what he would have chosen as companions for this journey through the dark wood, carrying on with their inane chatter as though anything more serious was a trial for their wits. But why should that be? For who might the knight have assumed would have something of note to say about matters that counted if not Death and the Devil?

Instead they'd merely seemed bored by the knight's attempts to raise the level of conversation every now and then, making it obvious they'd heard it all before and taking no interest in the fact that life's questions and answers came to each person in a different way.

"Rubbish. It's all the same," Death had scoffed, shaking his hourglass at the knight the first time he'd expressed his disappointment. "You're pushed into this world bawling, you whine your way through the years, and then time runs out on you in mid-snivel."

"Yeah. An' whatya get up to in the meantime ain't great shakes neither," the Devil added. "Folks need a few new routines, if ya ask me."

With this being the level of every exchange, the knight had eventually given up and fallen silent, which only moved his two companions to more raucous bantering in an effort to break his steady stare ahead and reclaim his attention. Even the knight's faithful dog had tired of barking at their antics and now focused all its attention on bounding forward.

If they could speak, both the dog and the knight's trusted stead would probably have more of note to say about life than Death and the Devil—about all the challenges it posed, the trials it set, the sacrifices and disappointments and wounds it brought, the good intentions it ignored, the hopeful expectations it postponed or dashed, and all that it took to carry on when doing so looked like madness: in short, about how much courage was demanded not to retire from the field when everything seemed lost but to carry on stoically to the end instead.

"So, this is it, what?" Death broke in on the knight's thoughts. "I imagine you'll still be stuck here when I pass this way again. Let's not make it 'Godspeed,' then, but just 'Seeya down the road.'" To which the Devil added, "I'm outta here, too, spud. Can't say it's been a pleasure, but I've known worse. Now don't do anything I wouldn't do, har, har, har . . . get it? Get it?"

Death tucked his serpents back under a tacky crown and lifting his hourglass, left slack the reins of his tired nag while commanding pompously, "Onward!" The Devil broke wind a final time, smacked himself loudly on the rump, and followed after.

Good riddance, the knight thought to himself. What charlatans. At least now he could move on with his own fortitude and skill for company.

But the knight soon discovered that without his boorish companions, there was no pressing beyond the edge of the engraving. Spur his horse as much as he might, call to his dog as much as he might, no exit from the world that he,

Death, and the Devil had shared for a time presented itself.

Was the self-confidence on which he'd staked his life pointless in the absence of Death and the Devil? Had they both known he wouldn't be able to move on without them?

It pained the knight to admit, but maybe they had him. Courage in the face of anything short of evil or death hadn't seemed worth staking his life on if that life was to have a purpose equal to the challenge. Yet the knight's recent companions had proved not to merit even throwing a stone at, let alone wasting his strength to prove his mettle. Weren't there more noble quests to take up? Real challenges to a purposeful life rather than this tiresome duo constantly resorting to bluster or deceit to make themselves appear more imposing than they had any claim to be?

Life must still hold tests not cheapened by Death and the Devil's humbug, the knight had to believe: true measures of one's dauntless resolve traveling through this dark, dark wood.

The Lab Rat

Once a lab rat had a pre-existing condition.

This made for an uneasy relationship between it and the other rats in research cages from end to end of the huge, sanitized room where they all were housed.

The other rats often asked themselves how it could have survived until now. Not just survived its pre-existing condition but also the rounds made by white-coated lab assistants who patrolled the aisles between cages looking for "anomalies" and dispatching them with one swift twist of the neck. What place was there for such a rat in a lab dedicated to flawless specimens?

The very presence among them of an imperfect rat called into question the guiding confidence of their lives that whatever they might suffer individually, however confining their caged life might be and whatever the horrors of their eventual end, it could always be said these hardships were for the good of humanity. The future health and happiness of total strangers, even those who couldn't stand the sight of a rat, made whatever fate the rats themselves must suffer worthwhile. Countless beneficiaries yet unborn would eventually look back on their sacrifice, their charitable "beau geste" as they liked to think of it, with gratitude. A defective lab rat compromised that heroic promise, pure and simple.

The rat in question understood the uneasiness its very presence caused the others and accepted their resulting aloofness. What else could it do? Protest the injustice of its treatment? It would be wasting its breath. Naturally the healthy rats, in order to keep up their faith that their coming sacrifice gave their lives transcendent value, would feel a need to shun any in their midst whose flawed existence called that confidence into question. Expecting them to do otherwise was naive, the rat knew.

So it didn't lament the fact that no shining future stretched away beyond its narrow cage. Tomorrow had little meaning when the limits of today so defined one's existence. Every time it peered out from its cage, the rat was reminded that the inescapable fact of its pre-existing condition rendered the world beyond the tip of its nose the same as the world behind it. Neither disappointments nor dreams separated the two.

This recognition, instead of increasing any sense of alienation the lab rat might with reason have felt, had a strangely opposite effect. In a way it only dimly understood, the very unlikelihood that a lofty purpose to its life would be revealed in some distant yet-to-come made the here-and-now more intensely present and replete. This pre-existing condition, in short, became precisely what reassured the rat it was alive and self-aware, without illusions.

Spared the burden of defining itself by the hoped-for praise of its end, the rat was free to savor the sweetness of having beaten the odds a little longer. While each "little longer" gave it another chance to feel the elation of knowing accidents of nature like itself occur at all. Without its flaw, then, life would not be life to the fullest.

The contentment that spread across the rat's face at such moments did not go over well with the occupants of neighboring cages, as can be imagined. It was bad enough to have in their midst a defective rat, casting doubt as it did upon the standards that defined their own soundness. But to have this blot on their prospects for an exemplary exit from life actually sit there in its cage with an expression of utter bliss was intolerable.

How dare it smile the smile of its imperfection!

The Larks

Once larks agreed to give up their free and happy ways.

They did this because they'd heard a booming voice coming out of nowhere and declaring that it was necessary. The flock could no longer continue, the voice announced gravely, in the blithe confidence that to be born a lark was to be born free and happy. It was time to make some tough choices, starting with freedom.

The larks, considering themselves a heartily independent lot and convinced their freedom was precisely what made them a symbol to all the world of the best that life had to offer, might have been expected to dismiss this assertion out of hand. But the voice sounded so authoritative that the great majority of them hesitated to object. Perhaps they could get along without some of their freedom, they guessed, if it meant keeping the rest. Partly free was better than not free, it could be argued. Wasn't it just another case of whether the glass was half full or half empty?

Still, not all of the larks were convinced that half free meant anything other than half free. "What do we get in exchange?" some asked.

"Security!" the voice boomed out.

"Security against what?" these unconvinced larks continued.

"That information cannot be fully revealed for reasons you wouldn't understand, but suffice it to say, there are false larks among you."

"Huh?"

"All larks need to watch what they say and watch what they do. In that spirit, you are urged to join 'Operation Suspicious Freedom' and report unlarklike behavior in your midst wherever you spot it."

Following this call to action, the larks began to eye each other differently, first with a questioning expression and then with one that suggested something else entirely. All larks were equal in appearance, but some must be secretly different if it was true that they posed a threat to the freedom of the rest. The more each lark studied its neighbors, the more it became convinced it could in fact detect something worth reporting, something that might be slight but still enough to raise suspicions all the same.

"Are you the reason I can't feel really free?" each lark's searing look asked.

"Why look at me?" came the response with a hard stare. "You don't seem like much of a true lark yourself."

Soon no lark felt secure, given that one lark's freedom looked very much like danger to another lark. And if that was the case, if freedom was hard to tell from danger, then maybe no lark should stand too much on principle or ceremony. Opinion surveys showed that roughly 50 percent of larks were prepared to endorse attacks upon the other 50 percent for being iniquitous, false larks.

If that's what it took, unsavory as it might be, then the booming voice from nowhere might well be right. Desperate times called for desperate measures when the free and happy life was at stake.

Trusting that all would turn out well in the end, many of the larks already felt lighter of wing.

The Last Neanderthal

Once the last Neanderthal looked out from the mouth of a cave, lost in thought.

Having just buried a beloved mate of many years, the Neanderthal wondered who would do the honors when the time came to bury the sole survivor now of a 400,000-year-old line. No other Neanderthal had passed this way, even at a distance, in a long time. A full clan hadn't been seen in many seasons, and since then, fewer and fewer families, and finally only solitary wanderers, and now none.

Although, did it matter that the last Neanderthal would be alone at the end, curled up in pain or numb with cold, far from the cave perhaps? How could it matter, compared with the recent anguish of mourning the love of one's life, cradling the dear body in swaying silence long after its warmth had slipped away?

The eventual fate of the species could have been foreseen. Pushing aside the outnumbered Neanderthals had come gangs of Cro-Magnon rowdies, so confident the world was theirs for the taking and not inclined to share it with any who might have been here for thousands of generations already. An aggressive, self-confident lot, what did they know of the tragedies of life? How all that once had seemed Neanderthals' natural strengths turned out to be part of their undoing, and nothing one tried, in ritual prayer or dance, could hold off the moment when there would be no saving the species from dismissal as evolution's "numbskulls," fixed in history's dim understanding for all time. Had these upstart Cro-Magnons suffered deeply enough yet at life's hands to understand any of that?

In a shallow grave nearby, the Neanderthal's beloved now slept, wreathed with flowers in the dark soil. During the couple's last days together, as death stood back awhile, they looked only into one another's eyes, recognizing there the full play of memories they shared and vows made without the need for words. Those final moments were as their life had been: the grateful acceptance of a gift to be returned at the end in full. No protest of injustice, no beating of the breast in self-pitying laments of "Why me?" but rather a sacred vigil kept hand-in-hand until one of them faded with the light while the other faced being left behind.

What if, in fact, no other Neanderthals did remain? Would the parting of this last pair have to stand for all the farewells their ancestors had bid one another in the past: each earlier goodbye a rehearsal for this final leave-taking?

But to be the one on whom it all had now fallen, to stand here alone in place of untold others who'd thought their descendants were destined to live on forever—a single individual now bearing the sum total of Neanderthal experience down the millennia—

And millennia hence, would the grave so lovingly made for one's beloved perhaps be dug open by strangers to find what lay within and guess at the life now over? The thought of the loved one's bones disturbed and their life together brushed aside with the dust caused the last Neanderthal's heart to knot with sorrow for them both. And for all previous generations, reduced now to this single one on the point of vanishing.

Turning abruptly and striding back to the burial site, the last Neanderthal scooped out the loose soil in handfuls until the familiar face and body lay as though in sleep again, ready to wake at morning's whisper. But instead of disturbing this deepest of peace—seeking only to join it—the living knelt in the narrow space of the dead and then gently, quietly, found room to lie close and pledge that their bones would be forever linked or else scattered as one.

Laughter

Once laughter seemed to be the only thing that could keep a person sane.

Any laughter would do, from a muffled titter through the fingers to the wildest, choking guffaw. The precise nature of the laughter wasn't as important as the fact that one could still laugh at all.

To be sure, in a world where moral posturing and maudlin sentimentality had become the default responses to human plight, a jocund spirit was typically rejected with scorn. Suggesting that both moral bombast and maudlin sentimentality were farcically inappropriate given life's trials was bound to earn you the label of "social misfit," or worse. And those bold enough to advocate strong doses of humor in place of stale nostrums were wise to expect a shrill, orchestrated attack in return.

136

Yet wasn't precisely a stubbornly enduring mirth proof to generation after generation that the worst cannot triumph utterly nor the loss of the best destroy them? Despots might survive attempts to oust them but not the steady undoing of their power laugh by rebellious laugh. The weight of injustice and bigotry can be eased, calamity borne, the grip of illness loosened, our deepest wounds closed, every "inner demon" defanged, even the end of treasured dreams survived—and all with laughter.

For what else was the background noise filling the universe but the riant echoes of creation, with their assurance that life is the beginning and the end and nothing, even the inexplicable, does not belong.

Death might have its day, humiliation hold both tormentor and tormented in its cold stare, futility be the final tenant of every house built on hope, but to laugh is to resist, to defy what can't be denied and to revel in that defiance.

To bet on humanity once again with a smile, however bleak the odds.

The Leaf

Once a leaf had a presage of fall.

It happened on a late August afternoon, in a fleeting vision that came and went with no more heralding than an equally brief chilling of the air. Certainly nothing as dramatic as the ups and downs in temperature often felt when thunderstorms rolled in at this time of year to rearrange the sky. At such times the leaf would have to hold on tight as sudden gusts raced through the orchard, wrenching fruit from every tree. Strong limbs and even trunks were not safe, let alone leaves.

No, the afternoon in question was much like any other during the growing season. What made the leaf sense the change in the air wasn't the change itself, in fact, but a strange whisper echoing through the maples higher up the slope, a sudden rustle of red and gold where before there'd been only muted green for months. Then the rustle was gone, and the maples sank back into a deep hush.

The leaf waited for the brilliant colors to reappear, hoping they would stay longer the next time. At least long enough to reveal whatever force could light up an entire hillside with so much beauty and then simply fade away. Nothing had prepared the leaf for such transient glory. In the days that followed, late summer steadily reasserted itself and blurred the leaf's memory of that extraordinary afternoon. Had the maples really burst into red and gold, it came to wonder, or was a world aglow with such splendor only an illusion?

As August yielded to September and September to October without a repeat of the vision, the leaf all but gave up trying to answer the question. It ceased to care whether it could or could not, also whether the other leaves on its own tree accepted what it claimed to have seen or dismissed it as an optical illusion.

Instead, it held to what little remained of the elation felt in those late-August moments as if the feeling itself were red and gold and real enough to still all doubts. No red was more alive or gold more lustrous, the leaf remained convinced.

Instead of being spread out over months, all the possibilities of the long season of growth had stood there at once in radiant fullness: a beauty more compelling precisely because it was to pass so soon. Could beauty that endured be half that bright, the leaf wondered, as it felt the chill of the October air?

And saw its own edges begin to glow as the maples had on the slopes above.

The Leech

Once a leech almost bled to death.

Nothing had prepared it for this unheard-of possibility. As is well known, leeches typically locate a host, attach themselves to that host, suck away at that host until bloated, then let go and slither away. The mistake this particular leech made was to attach itself to a politician.

The arrangement was routine enough in the beginning. The leech located an especially soft spot on the politician and sealed its anterior sucker there without difficulty. In no time at all, it was getting everything it needed to grow and flourish.

The relationship of host to parasite even had a symbiotic aspect in this instance. The leech profited by its access to the lifeblood of the politician, but the politician also profited. The customary cold and sluggish nature of a politician's blood flow changed markedly whenever the leech was sucking for all it was worth. Feeling stirred up by this, such politicians could harangue large crowds for hours on end.

In fact, in a curious throwback to the old belief that frequent bleedings rid the body of "opportunistic humours" and "dangerous airs," this politician came to believe that feeding the leech was absolutely necessary for continued strength and well-being. In short, both sides of the now-transactional arrangement gained, with each coming to feel more hale and hearty thanks to their connection.

It was all the more unexpected, then, that this union should suddenly turn south. The leech was merely following its accustomed practice: it expected to suck at its host as usual until it had its fill and then drop off, fat and contented, to return another day. But just as the leech had reached its limits, just as it thought it couldn't possibly take any more, the politician would suddenly clasped it tight, clearly loath to lose the mutual boon they'd come to enjoy.

Alarmed, the leech squirmed to get away, but to no avail. A little restraint at this moment, it reckoned, would serve both of them better in the long run. The politician clearly didn't see matters in the same light. Since the arrangement served both of them so well, why stop their quid-pro-quo embrace now?

The leech felt the politician's tenacious grip harden, felt each of its multiple stomachs being pumped fuller and fuller with the politician's uncurbed largess, and quickly found itself swelling to many times its former size. Bloated with forced feeding, it feared that the politician's needy behavior, this reckless insistence on giving the leech many times what it needed, was bound to have dire results. And sure enough, it wasn't long before the leech heard the first squishy, popping sounds.

If only it had been wiser in its choice of host!

The Lemming

Once a lemming went online to get a life.

Actually, it was somebody else's life. Or to be more precise, it was somebody else's life that countless other lemmings were viewing at the same time. From numerous webcams, a constant stream of real-time experiences was offered to a waiting world. Brushing one's teeth, washing the dishes, watering plants, putting together a midnight snack, checking fan mail, cleaning the toilet—these and many other activities of trending cyber-superstars could be downloaded into viewers' own lives in no time.

"It was so awesome," the countless lemmings agreed when they met virtually to discuss what they'd all tele-experienced. There they might happily wile away the hours exchanging opinions about the life they now shared in intimate detail. It gave them an exciting sense of community, more so even than they enjoyed when moving together through crowded streets, each squeaking loudly into its smartphone while trying to eavesdrop on whatever fascinating things were being squeaked at high pitch into smartphones on all sides.

Yes, this was definitely better: a fully wired escape from the loneliness of a lemming's life. Living somebody else's life and living it as every other lemming lived it while never having to leave the comfort of your own home provided a real sense of what was possible in life. You could explore whole new dimensions of yourself without having to risk losing anything personally or suffering any setbacks. You could become a star at the center of your own little universe, totally connected while remaining totally anonymous—totally not there while totally still you!

And such connectivity was as easy as point and click. En masse, the lemmings exercised to fitness tapes in their pajamas, checked out the latest collectibles boom, listened to a smart fridge announce that the milk was going sour without needing to open the door and sniff for themselves, watched others watching others day and night, followed the same sports headlines running above or below the same social-beat superstars trading the same small talk with the same showbiz heartthrobs.

Then, just when the lemming had become thoroughly comfortable with living a totally VR life, its real life took an untoward turn. Sitting down before its monitor one morning, the lemming saw something it was at a complete loss to explain. The scores of sites it had come to call home had disappeared. All of them! And in their place was a vast blue void, as if every webcam in its cyber-community was now pointed out the nearest window and recording a feature-less expanse.

For the lemming's monitor was filled with nothing, top to bottom and right to left, but what now looked like the wide blue sea.

The Leopard

Once a leopard declared during a long-awaited news conference that it had changed its spots.

In fact, the leopard added, its spots had all but disappeared. "I've redefined what it means to be a leopard," the leopard maintained. "I'm no longer driven by merciless instinct. You see before you a kinder, gentler leopard, take my word for it. Think of me now as a compassionate carnivore."

The leopard pressed this assurance on every creature it encountered thereafter, judging the effect it had by whether the listener bolted for dear life or appeared willing to consider at least the possibility of having come face-to-face with a "compassionate carnivore." In the latter case, the leopard would congratulate the listener for being open-minded and go on to suggest that its life-changing makeover wasn't so out of the ordinary these days, really.

"Isn't this place the greatest place on earth?" it would enthuse. "Where else can you say you've turned over a new leaf any day of the week and nobody thinks twice about it? I'm living proof that this isn't just a place where leopards hunt by night but also where you can trust a lamb to a leopard like me by day. Here anything is possible, if you just tell yourself it is!"

To those who didn't look particularly reassured by the leopard's ardor, it would seek to redouble its charm with a neighborly wink and lean forward to confide, "Seeing is believing. I tell you, this tongue of mine made short work of all those spots once I set my mind to it."

This homey approach typically did the trick, fostering a vague readiness to believe that, well, maybe a leopard really could change its spots. And maybe innocent lambs really could be entrusted to it without fear of the outcome.

With time, the public memory of the leopard's spots faded away as completely as the spots themselves were claimed to have. News photos continually showed no trace of them, and public reports of the leopard's latest whereabouts seldom mentioned anymore that the spots had ever existed. It really did seem as if everything the leopard claimed about itself was true.

Encouraged by this broad acceptance, the leopard devoted its energies to the constant grooming necessary to maintain its new appearance. Ever so patiently, it worked its tongue over its skin again and again to make sure it remained spotless. There was only one place the leopard couldn't fully reach in these tireless efforts.

Deep between its claws.

Life as We Know It

Once a movement was founded to support the following claim: "the jury's still out regarding life on this planet."

All attempts to explain the origins and development of life as we know it were deemed, by followers of this movement, to be merely theories. Evidence for the validity of any one of them was just that, evidence only, from which firm conclusions could not be drawn, based on the following logic: theories are not facts; this fact by itself is enough to reduce all theories to opinions; all opinions are equally right or wrong; therefore, in the absence of agreed-upon truth, all theories, being essentially one person's word against another's, have equal potential for being either true or false; so, as a rough guide to the universe, believe whatever you want to believe.

Any time one theory on the origins and development of life as we know it was presented, in a classroom or in public discussion for example, all other theories were to be given the same airing in descending order, determined not on the basis of "evidence" (which was merely a matter of "interpretation" and thus unreliable itself, many held, forming air quotes with their fingers to strengthen their point) but by a nose count of those who professed to believe in the theory in question already. If this determination to recognize absolutely every theory out there extended all the way to a conviction that life was only a few thousand years old or was left behind by aliens from distant galaxies who had, for reasons of their own, dropped by again at some later date to teach our distant ancestors the cosmic secrets of how to stack stones in neat piles and then zipped off again with instructions to wait for further guidance about what to do next, well, the adherence to nonjudgmental neutrality in the matter of truth required these assertions too be taken seriously. There was even a declaration made that life was so complex in design it couldn't really be explained. Again, no proof was necessary for advocates of this position. Simply saying they believed it was enough.

So appealing was the promotion of what came to be known as the "Jury's Still Out" approach to life on earth that many of its proponents were invited to address school boards and state legislatures and to help in drafting regulations or selecting officials charged with seeing to it that any and all theories received absolutely the same degree of consideration. They even volunteered to help select judges to enforce the "Jury's Still Out" stance as the final word on the subject.

Under normal circumstances, such an approach could have quickly proved self-defeating, yet because it favored no explanation for our existence in particular but instead threw the doors of the schoolhouse, government agencies, and the courts wide open to any claim without distinction on the basis of either evidence or logic, nobody felt anybody else's view of the matter enjoyed an unfair advantage.

Even those charged with the actual conduct of the schools, government, and courts seemed relieved they too no longer needed to offer a convincing explanation of what they were doing on this planet.

The Lone Wolf

Once a lone wolf tried to imagine the company of strangers.

Not that it sought what increasingly passed for "intimacy," by any means. From collecting "cyberfriends" on the internet that outnumbered the world's total wolf population to casual sex under the stars that neither party wanted to repeat the following day, such desperate attempts at escaping isolation struck the wolf as precisely the ultimate expression of it. The same for hushed phone calls to a sibling you hadn't seen in years to rescue you from a seedy bar before some foxy young thing's date came to on the floor and went for your throat again.

No, what the lone wolf sought was at most a few words now and then with a kindred soul who was content with a mutual respect for one another's secrets. Something not too far removed from the self-imposed silences that for years had served the wolf as an uneasy truce with solitude.

How do you enter others' lives without losing some of your own, it had always wondered? Or let them enter yours without losing even more? Countless degrees of separation hardly seemed enough to guarantee one's identity remained intact.

Yet why this apprehension? Why did the lone wolf feel unable to relax around others or run in their packs without all the while secretly keeping one eye on the shadow it cast? Almost as if it feared a moment's lapse in vigilance might bring on a total loss of self in the onrushing pull of the crowd.

Then suddenly the desire would come again for another shadow to cross its own and find in their union just enough freedom from the restive life to escape for a time from its own wilderness: those endless spaces where too little could become too much in an instant and leave you panting with fear at what might lie over the next rise, yet still racing headlong towards it.

Could the presence of another protect you from that? From the distant crouch of your own life out there at the limit of endurance?

As quiet in its wait for you as the night and twice as dark.

The Mantis

Once a mantis gained quite a reputation for "storytelling journalism," specifically through grieving-victim interviews.

Both quick and confident, the mantis benefited from a highly developed instinct for detecting any vulnerability in those it aimed to interview and for turning that weakness into a compelling "narrative" it could then pass on to its audience. Once targeted by the mantis, any recipient of its attention might expect the inevitable.

"I understand how painful and tragic this must be for you, and I certainly don't wish to be intrusive or to make things worse," the mantis would typically begin in emotive tones and with a mesmerizing gaze, "but could you share with our audience, up close and personal, how your whole world has been turned upside down and just how painfully tragic life is for you right now?"

"I really don't feel like talking about it."

"Of course you don't. I understand and fully respect that, and I certainly would not want to increase your suffering in the slightest way, so just between you and me, how would you describe that suffering, in detail? Take your time if need be."

"What good would describing my suffering in detail do?"

"It might not seem like a lot at the moment, but in the long run, it could help our audience draw an inspirational lesson from your heartrending ordeal and feel that warm sense of uplift that has become so essential to the public these days. If you don't tell me, nobody will feel and understand your pain."

"Have you yourself ever grieved in public? What does my personal pain have to do with the public's need to feel uplifted?"

"Certainly not as much as it has to do with you and the private agony you're going through right now, don't misunderstand me, but helping us see how much a wrenching experience like the one you've been through has meant personally should help others process their own future traumas."

"How?"

"By providing an unforgettable illustration of something very, very important these days. Wouldn't it help you put your own grief in perspective and feel better personally to know that others found in your devastating pain the strength to feel less devastated by whatever pain they themselves might have?"

"When?"

"Anytime. Wouldn't that be worth something?"

"What?"

"Well, worth your having had to suffer through everything in silence up till now. Hasn't that been worse than anything else, not sharing your misfortune? Here's a chance to tell your heartrending story to millions out there listening and watching. Making your suffering real for them."

"Who?"

"The largest audience in the history of grieving-victim programming, we estimate."

"Where?"

"Everywhere we're being heard and seen at this very moment. Living rooms, neighborhood bars, big-box stores, treadmill rooms at fitness clubs, airport waiting lounges, the biggest digital screen in Times Square, all across social media, you name it. After this interview, you and your heartrending ordeal are sure to become household words, true beacons of inspiration and hope. All you have to do is spend a few minutes sharing with the world out there the unimaginably painful ordeal you're going through and how much it's tested your faith but then ultimately made you stronger and how much you now realize the importance of the little things we all take for granted in life and how much you've grown because of your personal tragedy and how you couldn't have made it without the support of others and how going public like this with one's private agony is such a big, big part of taking today's healing process to a whole new level for everybody—"

"Why? Why are you doing this to me?"

The March of the Pundits

Once a film crew set out to document the march of the pundits.

The intent had been to capture this unique phenomenon for posterity by venturing deep into pundit habitat, braving the barren wasteland they traditionally favored and the mind-numbing chill of its windier reaches. All this in the darkness that covered the pundit world for months at a time.

The logistical aspects of the effort were understandably daunting. Simply getting to a place so remote, so devoid of any sign of sentient life, was fraught with difficulties. Terrain that might at first be thought solid and certain turned out more often than not simply frozen in place, prone to sudden collapse or, being deeply cracked beneath the surface, to breaking loose with an ear-splitting roar and carrying the unsuspecting away.

Everywhere in this vast emptiness lay the stiff remains of pundits who'd become disoriented, gotten hopelessly lost, and been given up for dead long since. And dead they most definitely appeared, despite the hint of an eerie flicker in their glazed eyeballs on occasion. Months passed before the filmmakers actually spotted a "live one" waddling about in the distance and showing at least minimal signs of life, though whether that be intelligent life or not remained unclear.

Cautiously tracking this curious figure along its erratic path, all the while nearly driven to distraction by its frequent reversals and long, circular meanderings over ground it had already covered time and time again, the exhausted crew finally came upon what they'd nearly given up hope of ever finding. There in the distance one teeth-chattering day, amounting to no more than a dim, undifferentiated mass at first, wheeled a great huddle of pundits bearing hard upon one another to preserve what little inner fire each still possessed then taking it in turns to suffer the gales that buffeted their outer ranks and valiantly do their part to safeguard the entire community locked in what came to be dubbed "the scrum that saves."

It was this commitment to mutual self-preservation that proved most astonishing in the documentary that ultimately grew out of the expedition. Audiences who had rarely taken much notice of pundits other than to chuckle on occasion at their rather comical demeanor (suggestive of inveterate tipplers trying to stagger home without falling down and, when that inevitably happened, pushing themselves the rest of the way on their bellies), these same audiences felt a surge of more troubling emotions when confronted with 50-foot pundits on a monstrous screen.

The spectacle was overwhelming. Not only the solid wall of puffed-up determination but also the unflappable confidence shown by each of these strange birds that regardless of any differences they might have, from snits of the moment to abiding enmity, they stood united to the last pundit on one thing: ensuring the survival of their kind despite all that reason might lead any observer to expect.

The Mass Hallucination

Once a mass hallucination sensed the good times were coming to an end.

In truth, it had ignored the obvious far too long and let itself get woefully out of shape. The consequences were predictable. Within recent memory, even a run-of-the-mill hallucination could expect a devoted following to pursue it on daily jogs while tweeting excitedly to their own "followers" about every turn they took. And long-distance hallucinations that kept themselves in at least middling form would be greeted with fanatical adulation and receive ringing endorsements from public and private sponsors alike.

But recently, hallucinations that had once been unmatched in power could barely avoid being trampled as crowds rushed here and there in hopes of catching up with the latest little fantasy-du-jour before it vanished in front of them, to be replaced by an even less impressive one they'd then chase blindly in its own turn. Nobody had the time or the interest for has-been hallucinations left in the dust. How the mighty had fallen!

This one had witnessed the demise of many a grand illusion in its day. Stirring myths, consoling faiths, cultural certainties, social norms, political dogmas, economic doctrines, pseudo-science, utopian daydreams, flag-waving rallies for an anonymous hoax—these were only a few of the hallucinations that had come and, mostly, gone. Even the longest-lived among them were eventually pushed aside by ones more suited to an age constantly seeking new diversions.

And yet, hallucinations past and present made life worth living, whatever their scope and whenever it was that their stretch of fame happened to run out or would, soon enough. At least, so it had always seemed to this one.

At their best, hallucinations offered proof of the nobility of human aspiration and perseverance and at their worst, equal proof of how little is needed to push humans into fits of rage or mute trembling in one of the darker corners of delusion. But best or worst, to hallucinate was to live, was it not? To be human to the fullest breadth and depth possible, regardless of the actual limitations that one personally displayed on a regular basis.

To be sure, some hallucinations deserved embracing while others deserved far less. Even the loftiest might fall short of the hopes or fears that inspired them, sometimes far short, but they still merited acknowledgement. Without this abiding allegiance, where would people be? Condemned to stumble aimlessly about, periodically brushing up against one another without recognizing any similarities between themselves? Without some sense of what fantasies they shared, how would they carry on through life's inevitable disappointments and pass on that ability to future generations?

Admittedly, dedication to one's private hallucinations and to those powerful enough to captivate entire nations drew people down into horrors as often as upwards to glory, and the deadliest of them might prove the entire planet's undoing in the not too distant future. So much more call, then, to celebrate and not abandon the finest of them while they lasted.

For when individuals and whole nations lose confidence in the most inspiring of their hallucinations (everything they long to see as being true no matter what), a greater tragedy than all others overtakes them, doesn't it?

As for this particular mass hallucination, it just prayed it wouldn't be around to witness the final collapse of all that had given it such confidence of purpose in its prime.

The Metronome

Once a metronome hypnotized itself.

Over time, the rhythms it typically settled into had offered a reassuring steadiness in the face of everything that the metronome observed with concern going on around it, from mad excess to the most lethargic of existences. In every case, or so it seemed to the metronome, the yielding of a measured will to tempos beyond the range of those it personally trusted was a telltale sign of an unsteadiness in character that let chance and circumstance rule. A surrender of the self to any alluring sway beyond the norm was the obvious peril in such lax comportment.

But if you could keep total control of yourself and not be swept up by passion or slowed by doubt, if you held out against impulse and kept to the trusted givens of a regulated life, then what could ever distract you? Even your inevitable winding down must find you self-mastered to the end.

In short, existence was a continual test of how well one resisted impulse and the confusion brought on by momentary fancies through a steady balancing of eternal certainties. The shunning of extremes for a continual return to the middle was the unmistakable feature of age-old wisdom that would guide one through any challenge or dilemma. Proportion in all things had always been the metronome's governing philosophy and its constant reassurance.

Whenever the hint of an irregularity in life or a departure from the expected presented itself, therefore, the metronome unfailingly carried out a complete check of its internal workings, noting the least wavering from regulated conduct and correcting any aberration without delay. Were it not to take this rectifying action as soon as the need for it became clear, as soon as even the suspicion of a faltering or errant will suggested itself, who could say what the repercussions might be?

148

Just as moderato may give way by stages to prestissimo, the discipline needed for a meaningful existence might yield ultimately to risky penchants, hardly noticeable at first but soon marking undeniable departures from the accepted norm, then wilder and even wilder excess (as though desires were taken as the full measure of being rather than simply the manic rule of the unknown) until all self-mastery threatened to be lost in utter abandon and ruination!

Plenty of metronomes had ended their days as hopeless wrecks by yielding to these temptations, falling victim to their own inner weaknesses and the erratic behavior these brought on and ultimately being shunned by all who hoped to retain some sense of their own constancy in an uncertain world. One could understand in principle how such things happen, how a life's clockwork that had been trusted never to slip in the slightest might one day simply begin to fall apart. But deliberately embracing what must hasten that end—who was so unwise as to risk it?

Keeping yourself always in proper order, the metronome was convinced, was the only way to ensure that what befell others would never befall you. Absolute predictability and self-restraint were the keys. Always. Never swinging back and forth too far or too fast, until the pull of anything beyond this perfectly regulated life faded and you were safe in yourself.

Back and forth. Ba-ck and for-th. Ba—ck an—d f—o-r—thhhhhh————

The Migratory Bird

Once a migratory bird stopped by the local travel agency.

The year was getting on into fall, and the bird's thoughts had begun to turn to warmer places again. This time, however, the familiar destinations just didn't seem to have the attraction they once had. The bird was tired of group tours and even of glossy fliers from its alma mater's alumni association, which had apparently downplayed scholarship fundraising to concentrate instead on providing wealthy graduates a choice of "unforgettable Wanderlust experiences" in 7-day, 14-day, and 21-day packages.

So when it noticed a poster of a deserted tropical beach taped to the window of the travel agency, the bird went straight on in and up to one of the agents appearing to be from somewhere like the place in the poster. Nothing beats first-hand knowledge, the bird told itself.

No sooner had it mentioned the poster, though, than the agent replied nonchalantly, "That place was booked up months ago."

"Months ago?" the bird asked in crestfallen surprise.

"Yes. Everybody wants to get away to a remote beach in the tropics these days."

"But the beach is empty."

"Isn't Photoshop amazing? You'd never know the place was actually packed with sunbathers, would you, or that just steps away from the beach, booked-up tourist hotels were squeezed together?"

"Well, what else have you got?" the disappointed bird asked.

"What are you looking for, exactly?"

"How can I put it? A change in my life's focus, an adventure for the senses, a rebirth of the soul, a whole new approach to the mysteries of being, a—"

"What does all that have to do with tropical beaches?" the agent broke in with a tone of having heard it all before.

"You are aware of Paul Gauguin, I assume," was the bird's miffed response.

"Are you expecting to see his ghost sitting in a Club Med beach chair?"

"Of course not, but ahhh Tahiti! Tahiti! Doesn't the word simply ring with the call of the exotic? Like Mandalay! Or Samarkand! Or Shangri-La!"

"The kind of Shangri-La you're looking for doesn't exist, I'm afraid."

"I know that! But someplace like it where everything is inscrutable and age-less and I can get in touch with elemental truths that are denied me here."

"And what might those 'elemental truths' be?"

"That's where I need your help, don't you see? I feel I've got to open myself to raw experience while I still can and have hot blood drum through my veins in the dusky night. Go native and get in a little all-night flocking with birds of a different feather, if you get my drift. . . You do get my drift, don't you?"

"We don't run sex tours."

"Oh, don't get me wrong! Don't get me wrong! I'm talking about some-thing magical! A mystical transformation of the self! Getting in touch with an-cient teachings and the inner me! Becoming one with universal rhythms! Em-bracing the 'Eternal Feminine'! Why, everything you must feel in your very bones! You're from those sultry climes, aren't you?"

"What makes you think that? I was born here."

"Here? You're not from there? Come now, you're just kidding, aren't you? I see in your face everything to make me come alive, truly alive, everything that is waiting out there somewhere for me, beckoning . . . always beckoning . . . like that poster in the window!"

150

"That poster isn't the real thing, I tell you."

"It has to be the real thing! Don't you understand, I have needs here! Needs only paradise can satisfy!"

The Milk of Human Kindness

Once the milk of human kindness turned rancid.

The speed of the change was breathtaking. Neighbors who'd been on the best of terms for years were one day in each other's faces and the next day searching the Internet for guns and ammo.

When public opinion researchers asked the reason for this turnabout, the response never varied: "It's all about morals."

"Morals?" the researchers might then ask in order to gain a fuller sense of public thinking.

"Yeah, their sort don't have any!" a passerby might suddenly shout.

"What?" would come the equally loud response. "My sort don't have any? Just the only morality that counts, that's all!"

From that point on, crowds would rapidly gather and raise their own voices in supportive abuse. Regardless of the origin of any discord of this sort, it always deteriorated into charges that the other side was utterly immoral, as though this insult would deliver a death blow.

Instead of delivering a death blow, such charges merely prompted the opposing side to make wilder accusations that their hypocritical opponents presented themselves as having firm moral bearings when it was clear they had none whatsoever and weren't worth spitting on.

To hear these dueling insults, one might well think half the nation was convulsed with disgust for the other half, which felt much the same in return. And soon merely condemning your neighbor as the devil in disguise wasn't enough. Flying across the country to waive placards and hurl the same denunciation at perfect strangers on their own streets or in front of their own homes was deemed far more urgent, morality-wise.

The most rancorous dispute of all, it soon became clear, was over kindness to others as an essential component of moral thought and behavior. It wasn't merely that the two sides couldn't agree on a common definition of "kindness to others" or that the competing definitions seemed at times as far apart as possible. No, the true problem lay in the insistence by both sides that kindness itself must be seen as an eternal absolute: a universal ideal high above the messy complexities of real people striving to treat one another with dignity and good will each day.

It was vital to everybody involved in these ongoing quarrels to preserve this pure and eternal kindness with a capital "K" from being contaminated by the corrupted version of it being cynically advanced by the opposition. Who knew, each side screamed in turn, where such moral fuzziness by the other side was apt to lead? Nothing less than the moral health of the nation was at risk here. And that is how it came about that so many couldn't stomach the kindness of others anymore.

What would it take for people to replace Kindness that separated them with kindness that unified them again?

The Mink

Once a mink tried on a full-length sable coat.

"Stunning! Stunnnnnnning!" the furrier exclaimed. "It's soooo you!"

The mink turned around and around in front of one of the store's full-length mirrors to get a better view of itself. Yes, the sable coat was definitely stunning.

Pressing the soft, soft fur of the collar to its cheeks, the mink relished the image of luxury and style there in the glass before it. Who could resist the thrill of walking down the avenue wrapped in elegance like this?

The mink had heard the arguments against buying such coats, but quite frankly it had grown rather bored of them. What was wrong with indulging in a few creature comforts now and then? Granted, a line should be drawn somewhere, the mink supposed. But pigskin jackets or calfskin or sheepskin ones, alligator shoes, kid gloves, snakeskin watchbands, chinchilla or sable coats, how could you look your best without them? The fact that these animals' hides were in such demand was their problem, when you thought about it with a cool head, not the mink's.

"That's the top of this year's line. Ab-so-lute-ly the top!" the furrier murmured admiringly. "You won't find anything to equal it, I assure you."

The mink buried its cheeks in the soft sable fur again for a long time before asking, "You wouldn't happen to have anything in human, by chance?"

The Minotaur

Once the Minotaur decided to take the Labyrinth with it wherever it went.

Over the years it had grown attached to the place and had difficulty picturing itself anywhere else. All its memories were here. In the shadowy recesses of the Labyrinth, they provided the Minotaur with unwavering companionship. If it sank into melancholic torpor, they lightened its mood. Or if it grew too excited, they restored it to calm and discretion. Over the years, the Minotaur had come to rely on their comforting, faithful presence. And it kept faith with them in return.

It did this despite the fact that it was seldom free of strangely alluring visions from a world beyond the Labyrinth. These visions wandered down the dim passageways and slipped in among the familiar company, danced their seductive dances, whispered in the Minotaur's ear, urged it to follow them back out. They were as persistent as its more constant companions. And they filled the Labyrinth with strange, intoxicating perfumes.

One day the Minotaur, unable to resist their enticement any longer, rose to follow these visions back out of its prison and into their world. The way out was longer than it had imagined, much longer, but the closer it came to the exit, the more the visions beckoned it on. Whenever the Minotaur stopped to catch its breath, its heart pounding in anticipation, they paused too and waited for it to catch up. And each time they disappeared around a turn, it could hear their voices drop a moment and then rise again as though to encourage it by seeming to shorten the distance that remained. Finally, on the threshold, they called one last time to the struggling Minotaur and strode out.

When the Minotaur itself reached the opening and took in the broad vista stretching away in every direction, it stood in dazzled amazement. What could have prepared it for the range of flourishing possibilities to be explored? And yet, for all the seductiveness of the scene before it, the Minotaur hesitated to take the next step. Might everything be simply a mirage? What if, once out of the Labyrinth, the Minotaur discovered a life unequal to the promises made by the visions that had found their way down the endless turns and into its affections? A world less inspiring than their whispers—what then, with everything that would have been given up for such uncertain gain?

Troubled by these doubts, the Minotaur made the only decision it thought it could. It hoisted the Labyrinth onto its back and set off into the world, prepared to exchange a lifetime of edging snail-like here and there for the security of knowing it could always withdraw into its maze again if need be.

Always retreat and wait among the shadows for the visions to return.

The Misanthrope

Once reports came in that a misanthrope had been spotted on the outskirts of town.

This news caused quite a stir, but serious doubts about the sighting were raised almost at once. Most in dispute was whether the being in question belonged to the species of true misanthropes or was, on the contrary, an example of that rarely seen relative, the mock (sometimes referred to as the "pseudo") misanthrope. This second species, having diverged in its development from the true misanthrope at some point in the past, was known to compete for the same habitat but had been steadily losing ground when it came to the survival of the fittest among misanthropes.

Simply stated, the mock misanthrope had clung stubbornly to an approach to life's challenges that true misanthropes no longer fully embraced or had abandoned outright: a reliance upon the contents of one's own braincase to make it from one day to the next. In fact, to trust in anything other than the intelligence of the species struck the mock misanthrope as a grievous lack of faith in oneself and one's kind. Any neglect of these inherited mental strengths in favor of some makeshift and tenuous survival ploy would send it into a frustrated protest. "What are we," it might shout at such times, "an evolutionary dead end? A waste of good gray matter?"

Unfortunately, rather than encouraging others to make better use of what gray matter they did in fact possess, these sarcastic barbs only drew attention to the mock misanthrope itself, with the negative consequences that might be expected. Its criticisms typically met with hostile silence or else a grumbling dismissal and an avoidance of further contact. Little wonder, then, that the mock misanthrope was in trouble and was spotted with increasing rarity. There was even talk of the need to place it on the endangered species list.

By contrast, the survival strategy of the other branch on the misanthropes' evolutionary tree had demonstrated clear advantages time and again. The true misanthrope decided at an early stage in its development that relying on one's own wits and strengths alone could be suicidal. These might fall so far short of what was required to advance one's individual prospects and those of the species as a whole that abandoning them as often and as fully as necessary became the preferred course.

With the stakes so high, no alternative to risky self-reliance should be overlooked. The most common tactic adopted by the true misanthrope whenever danger arose was to hope for some miracle of deliverance or pity by powers greater than oneself. Lacking confidence in itself when faced with any imminent threat, it perfected the art of making itself appear as small as possible and therefore not worth the trouble of putting an end to. It might be heard to plead at such times, "O, what a weak and worthless wretch am I! Have mercy on me for my miserable failings!"

After repeating this trusted formula until it was hoarse, the true misanthrope would slowly open one eye and look anxiously about. If nothing had happened, the true misanthrope would take this as a sign it must be doing something right and resolve to make itself appear even smaller and confess its weaknesses even more plaintively next time, if that's what circumstances called for. Counting too much on your own ability to meet life's challenges simply wasn't a safe calculation and might even land you in deeper trouble for your pains. Better to lament your shortcomings loudly instead and turn your fate over to some superior being, then hope for the best.

An alternative survival strategy that might be resorted to by the true misanthrope was to veer to the opposite extreme, noisily drawing attention to itself by claiming its species represented perfection and thus was too important not to leave a gaping hole in creation if ever eliminated from it. To support such a declaration, the true misanthrope would set up an idealized version of itself on a grand pedestal, declare it the measure of all things, then worship it day and night as transcending every limitation of nature and time.

If the former tactic of self-denigration sought to arouse the pity of an almighty power as a way of deflecting any threat, real or imagined, this second tactic aimed at feeding an absolute conviction that the species would remain forever at the apex of existence through its intrinsic strength and beauty. To both of these tactics, the mock misanthrope would rejoin, "Why not just be who you are, right here and right now, without cringing or boasting? Have faith in yourself, draw courage from yourself, whatever happens. Answer the challenge within to live out your own meaning and do justice to it. Celebrate the best in yourself, the best in humanity. And if you must bow down in worship, bow down to those who have such faith in the species that they'd sacrifice themselves for the sake of total strangers."

155

As natural selection took its course, the species of misanthrope possessing the adaptive trait of alternating between self-doubt and self-glorification multiplied rapidly and spread around the globe. Specimens could be found everywhere, enjoying the considerable fruits of either deflating or puffing themselves up as two halves of the same survival strategy: one that forced the increasingly outnumbered mock misanthropes, with only themselves to count on, ever closer and closer to dying out. In light of this fact, it was ultimately the consensus among experts that the particular misanthrope reportedly seen near the city limits was almost certainly not of the endangered mock variety.

It must instead have been one of the far more common true misanthropes.

The Mole and the Owl

Once a mole and an owl shared a soul.

The two animals possessed different bodies, of course, but they had to make do with a single soul between them.

Neither creature really had much need of the soul during the time it slept. For the owl, that meant the daylight hours. While the mole, being sightless, wasn't too concerned about its sleep patterns. So when the owl asked to have use of the soul by night, the mole raised no objection.

To look at the owl and the mole, one would never guess they had anything in common. The owl was known for its wise and distant air. The mole was known for destroying anything in its path without a second thought. Whereas the one plowed through or gobbled up with delight whatever it happened upon, the other remained serenely perched above it all, barely appearing to concern itself with the hurly-burly of this world.

The soul shared by these two was quite flexible. It had to be. A less pliant soul would never have survived the strain of being passed to and fro so often, not to mention the added stress caused by the owl's insistence that any connection between itself and the mole remain a secret.

For the owl was ashamed of what the mole did with their common soul. Such behavior was clearly beneath the dignity of an owl. The mole, by contrast, didn't really care what the owl thought. In fact, to the mole the owl seemed a calculating snob. It even gave the mole considerable satisfaction to know that the owl was embarrassed by their odd kinship.

Whenever the mole was handed back the soul, it would rub the thing around in the dirt awhile to rid it of any hint of the owl. For in truth, moles must be wary of owls. An owl can easily put an end to a mole's stealing through the nether regions if it surfaces without due care. This unpleasant fact of life often hampered the mole in its pursuit of dark pleasures that would have shocked the owl, which was why the mole felt a need to dust up the soul whenever it was returned and remove all trace of where it had been.

For its part, the owl often found itself, after taking back the soul, prey to violent impulses it had to assume were the mole's since they seemed so foreign to what the owl conceived to be its inherent nobility. From time to time, it felt rising within itself a troubling urge to assail anything that it thought had intruded upon its domain, even other owls, reacting to their presence in the same way the mole might react with savage fury if confronted by another mole in darkness and in dirt. No trick or foul play was renounced when the owl hurled itself into these fell struggles.

This, then, was the quandary facing the mole and the owl. Perhaps the solution would have been to cut in half the soul they shared. Perhaps then each of them could have gone about its life unaffected by the existence of the other.

The mole probably could have gotten along with half a soul. But could the owl? Or would it be at a loss to defend its lofty perch without the ruthless savvy of a mole?

The Molehill

Once a molehill came to worry that it might not reach its full potential.

Things had started out well enough in its estimation. Being small was a relative term when all around you, other molehills were just starting out as well. Which of them knew for certain whether it was destined to make a mountain out of itself or not? Which of them didn't have equal scope to shape its future through the power of positive thinking? And didn't all have an equal right, then, to dream of casting long shadows at some point and being looked up to as a monument of molehill success?

Granted, an Everest-amongst-molehills wasn't anywhere to be seen. Instead, in every direction, meager piles of soil rose to about the same level and no further. This didn't mean, however, that in some distant field, a snow-capped peak hadn't thrust itself overnight into the sky as inspiring proof that no molehill should settle for anything less than the realization of its dream. The mere possibility of reaching this goal was enough to temper doubt, even on days when the clouds seemed as far out of reach as ever. In a way, their remoteness gave more room for the future to expand into glittering proofs of achievement.

On warm summer mornings, the molehill would picture to itself the heights it might reach that very afternoon: ever-ascending triumphs that would bring both satisfaction and well-earned recognition. And when afternoon turned into dusk without any of these triumphs having arrived or even hinting they were near, there was always tomorrow to look forward to, with its sustaining promise that would start all over again at dawn.

Nor did those dawns, and there were many, when the molehill thought it might have detected an overnight inching up nearby cause its own confidence to decline. If anything, that confidence grew to fill whatever new gap in comparative stature might seem to have occurred: one molehill's rise could possibly be proof all molehills would have their day in these fields of opportunity as far as the eye could see.

When days stretched into months and months into years, though, and that long-envisioned pinnacle of achievement hadn't materialized, the molehill began to wonder if it was the victim of some unjust meting out of success and failure that ignored the force of ambition. Did other molehills really have more going for them, or did they owe their good fortune simply to being in the right place at the right time?

Such thoughts didn't provide more than temporary solace, the molehill found, and sometimes left it with the sinking apprehension that this inability to reach its envisaged potential might be due to some lack within, an individual deficit that held it from measuring up and making the most of itself. But what could that undermining weakness be? Where in all the abilities it had trusted to lift it when an auspicious moment arrived could so calamitous a shortcoming lie hidden? Or might an assortment of small failings, too trivial to attract notice separately, have combined to deny it the full measure of success reached by others?

These questions repeated themselves over and over, until the molehill had to admit that any answers it came up with simply prompted new doubts and deepening concern. Should it have done this differently or that differently or done nothing whatsoever, trusting in the vagaries of fortune to place it among the high and mighty rather than its own powers?

Other molehills, alone with their thoughts, must also be wrestling with self-doubt and shrinking within themselves at the fear that their most cherished expectations might never be met. There must be millions of similar molehills out there, barely aware of each other previously except as remote challenges to their own personal rise but now gradually understanding their shared reality— one that bestowed no spectacular triumphs, true, yet in its rebuff just might call forth something equal to even the loftiest mountain range. Might there be an unrecognized majesty in their lowly state?

For the greatest of peaks erode with time to less than a molehill, but to find your estimation of yourself thwarted from the start and yet still survive continual defeat, still carry on in spite of it all, must require one of the towering strengths of this world.

The Monitor Lizard

Once a monitor lizard came to wield considerable influence at a leading health maintenance organization.

The lizard was responsible for "gate-keeping" patient admissions to hospitals for medical treatment. It performed those duties well. So well, as a matter of fact, that it was able to reduce the ratio of health-needs-to-health-costs dramatically and thereby increase return on investment in the HMO's shares just as dramatically.

Being by nature a cold-blooded creature, the monitor lizard had a definite advantage when responding to those it suspected of spending their days scheming to sneak into hospitals for brain surgery or high doses of chemotherapy, to name just two of the opportunities it saw for flagrant abuse of the system. In its crusade for economy, it was always on the alert for questionable accounts of pain and suffering.

"Is the patient near death at this moment?" was the lizard's most frequent reply to appeals for help, followed by, "Have you sought another opinion from a physician on our B List of care providers?" While for psychiatric cases, it might say to great effect, "If the patient hasn't assaulted anybody yet, call us back when that happens."

But the lizard's true value to the HMO became clear only during an annual meeting of shareholders. The gathering started off well enough, with a glowing report on projected savings as a number of treatment programs were phased out in the future and the recently passed HMO Protection Act came into full force. But the atmosphere grew more tense as investors began to voice their concern about long-term prospects if more patients than expected sought medical care or survived for unanticipated periods of time while being treated.

"Can you guarantee us the present high share price will be maintained?" the Chairman of the Board of Directors was asked.

"Even better. We have every confidence shares have nowhere to go but up as the aging population grows and we transition to new cost-cutting measures."

"That's very easy to say, but can you guarantee it?"

A question from another part of the hall touched on the same concern. "What assurance can you give us long-term of doubling, tripling, even quadrupling money invested in sick people?"

"What does market research say about incentivizing patient-to-doctor figures beyond the 1,000 mark?"

Before the chairman could answer, another shareholder shouted out impatiently, "Forget that! Can't we limit treatment to patients who cost less?"

"Or else streamline the entire system? Make it more reflective of market fundamentals?"

And that was when the monitor lizard rose from its own seat and offered the suggestion that brought sustained applause throughout the hall and put its drooling smile on the cover of the annual report.

"Suppose we simply begin converting medical facilities into morgues."

The Mosquito

Once a mosquito landed a job waiting tables.

"Hi there, guys!" it would greet customers airily. "My name's Culici, for short, an' yu'll be servin' me this evenin'."

"Just kiddin'! Just kiddin'!" the mosquito would reassure startled patrons and then recite the menu, beginning with "Steak Tartare" and ending with "Chef Joey's 'Organic Suuupriiiizzze!'" We got everybody covered here. E-V-E-R-Y-B-O-D-Y, don't ya know?"

"Hey, take care of yer bod, and yer bod'll, like, take care of you, right?" the mosquito hummed as diners began to mull their menus. "I take care of myself, let me tell ya," it might continue, to nobody in particular. Or perhaps it would declare, "I'm only here 'cause I wanna be, ya know. I don't really havta do this, right? I've got, like, this dream day job that keeps me real busy. Right? I'm a personal trainer ta the stars! An' boy do I, like, get 'em focused on their bods. But that's not all, okay? I also pass along a little lifestyle tip or two I pick up from my other contacts, right? Give my clients, like, a real zinger every now and then, yessiree Jack!"

After this warmup, the mosquito flitted elsewhere about the establishment with striking quickness. Each time any of the patrons appeared taken by surprise to find it hovering close by, it would pick up again wherever it might have left off moments before and tables away with: "Nothin' like a good workout ta make ya feel super about yerself. Right? Life's all about the bod, I say. Y're only as good as ya look, know what I mean-n-n-n-n-n? Look at me, okay? Tight thighs, no flab in these abs, lemme tell ya, an' get this killer tush. Could I do ten hours at the gym every day or what? Up-down, up-down, in-out, in-out! Right? Like I always tell my clients, 'take care of yer bod an' yer bod'll take care of youuu!' I'm so-o-o inta my clients, right? Sure, sometimes they get kinda stressed out over their ideal body image an' wonder if they'll ever, like, get there. But I just remind 'em, 'hey, no pain, no gain!' I mean ya are how ya look, 24-7-365. Or 366 in leap year, okay? Whatever. So look, 'I'm here fer allayaguys,' I tell everybody, an' I'll be there fer youuu, toooo. Right? So work up a good sweat, okay? Work up a good sweat, an' I guarantee I'll give ya the kinda self-awareness ya, like, never knew ya had! We're talkin' big-time in-touch-with-yer-bod here, right? Like, feelin' down deep whoya are and why it matters is all! All that matters in life is how ya look. Ya wanna look like a million, with a bod ta die for? Hey, youuu totally can, okay! 'Look better, feel better, be better,' I always, so, like say, 'No pain, no gain!' Right?"

At the end of an evening of such service, patrons left the restaurant in the mood for a workout right away, determined to take the mosquito's advice and get into tip-top shape before they ventured out in public again. None of them wanted to appear to others as though they didn't have a great body self-image. One that would make of their lives a ceaseless satisfaction. But more immediately, they all wanted to be in prime form the next time they found themselves at the mosquito's table.

Its "Y'er only as good as ya look, know what I mean-n-n-n-n-n?" hummed in their ears for days.

The Mouse

Once a mouse received a summons for jury duty.

The mouse reacted to this summons with apprehension. It had gone about its life avoiding trouble at every turn and looked with deep discomfort upon the prospect of having to decide what should be done about the troubles of others.

Nevertheless, it dutifully presented itself at the courthouse on the appointed day, fearing that not to do so could turn out to be worse than jury duty. Might it be held in contempt or have to stand trial itself if it failed to show up? Might it end up in the slammer? Better to take the path of least danger and show up.

Sitting in the jury-selection waiting room surrounded by others summoned on the same day, the mouse listened through the morning and into the afternoon for the number it had been given on arrival to be called. The passage of the hours did little to calm its uneasiness. If anything, the opposite was the case.

What if the trial was a murder trial, it wondered? Would it be able to look at the accused calmly? Would the accused look back? What if the accused looked back with the look of a psychopath, maybe one with underlings ready to hunt the mouse down if the verdict didn't go the way they wanted?

While the mouse was agonizing over questions such as these, it became aware of a low grumbling next to it: "No way I'm going on a jury. It's my vacation time."

"I'm going to ask to be excused from serving, too," the mouse's neighbor on the other side responded to the grumbler. "I can't stand the sight of blood."

Was it a murder case, then! The mouse hadn't thought about the sight of blood. Would there be a knife in evidence? A carving knife? Still with blood on it? How much blood?

These concerns, disturbing though they might be, were not the mouse's greatest worry. It was more anxious about the possibility that in this case, as in most of life, clear decisions might be difficult, might even be impossible to make. Despite its best intentions and effort, what if it was still unable by the end of the trial to assess innocence or guilt beyond a reasonable doubt? The victim deserved justice, to be sure, but so too did the accused. What a mess rendering a clear verdict might turn out to be.

Can we really see all the motives for our actions, the mouse mumbled to itself? Weren't there extenuating circumstances for nearly every move in life? And if there were, how do you decide guilt or innocence? Not by simply "adding things up," to be sure: three exhibits in evidence for this side, two for that, so the first side wins. Was justice a math problem or an exercise in common sense?

But what in life ever came down to mere "common sense"? Didn't life defy common sense on a regular basis? Didn't justice demand something else? Or was justice in fact little more than a makeshift way of cutting life down to size, regardless of what was lost in the process? Was justice simply the best of a bad bargain, then, one that nobody should be too eager to claim credit for? More an admission of life's messy realities than some grand ideal to congratulate yourself on? And if one's own case was ever in the balance, would justice be foremost in one's mind? Or would just saving your skin be?

As the mouse troubled over these conundrums of life and the law, a crackly voice came over the public address system and announced, "We have a jury impaneled now, so the rest of you are free to go."

"Whew!" the mouse and its neighbors sighed in unison as they raced for the door.

Mud

Once a glob of mud reflected on its state.

To speak of the glob as a lump of clay would probably be too generous and to speak of it as mere slime unfair. It made no claim to being anything more than it was but resented being considered anything less. You were what you were.

But when contacted, as it recently had been, and asked to work up a short biography for the latest publication of *What's What in the Natural World*, the glob of mud wasn't quite sure where to begin. First of all, there was the problem of its origins. It had nothing to hide about them, yet it could hardly pretend to have a unique or illustrious background that set it apart either. The dust forming it had blown here from a thousand points, and the water giving it life had been the life of oceans, lakes, rivers, and every passing cloud.

Nor was listing its chief milestones as mud any easier. There had been storms and sunny days aplenty, but the glob couldn't exactly claim to have produced them or to have influenced their course in any way. In fact, to suggest its existence had differed from that of the mud all about it by virtue of some unique experience or attainment was even going too far. Best have no delusions about leaving a mark that time would not wash away sooner or later.

The planet turned and tilted from season to season, and the forces behind both were not of mud's making or unmaking. Others might find that fact depressing, but the glob of mud didn't. Rather, it felt reassured at knowing it could not be set apart from the rest of the natural world. What happened to all else happened to it as well, for better or worse. If pressed by experience hard enough, it might become rock, and harder still, a diamond. After which the reverse must come, for even diamonds turn to dust. And dust again to mud eventually.

So the glob of mud didn't feel its life story had any special significance or any lessons to teach. What it had learned, all mud had learned equally. The cataloging of distinctions upon which a *What's What* depended was about as vain an exercise as could be attempted, the glob of mud came to decide.

As long as you yourself knew what you were, what need was there for a public accounting?

The Mudskipper

Once a mudskipper got bogged down.

This challenge to its usual jaunty approach to life was hardly noticeable at first, hardly more than a slight heaviness within or another momentary slow-down in what might already look like a directionless tour of the tidal flats that the mudskipper paddled around every day.

But it was indeed slowing down. Each time the mudskipper drew a leg-fin from the ooze, a slightly louder sucking sound pulled at its sides. The viscous mud, so inviting as a rule, had begun to weigh upon it. Even the beating of its heart seemed to lag, reducing the mudskipper's progress to a labored plowing forward at best.

What was happening? Why this change? The mudskipper had thrived in the sun-warmed flats until now. This was the life, with not a care in the world. A mudskipper's "cloud nine." If it was hungry, the mud offered up a hundred tasty morsels to sate its appetite. If sea breezes sent a chill down the mudskipper's back, soon it had been forgotten in the comfort of a warm, reassuring wallow. The moist, rich feel of the earth against its skin brought indescribable pleasures one after another. And on those occasions when the mudskipper launched itself into the air with sudden ebullience, the soft landing wherever it came down was like the welcoming home of an old voyager.

At the height of its vaults, carrying just enough of life's heat in the mud that clung to its sides, the skipper could survey its world through eyes bulging wide to take in all that stretched away before it. What might strike others as nothing more than a tidal flat revealed itself instead to be an endless array of invitations to discovery. From thoughts of faraway lands to the deepest ocean trench, the imagined compass of all existence invited one to explore its reaches to the full, even if one never left this narrow, muddy shore.

In short, life as a mudskipper had been good. Granted, it might not be a life to every creature's liking, but where else could a mudskipper feel truly whole if not here between the ebb and flow of wonder? This state of good cheer might be possible anywhere, but to each heart its own domain. For the mudskipper, no other spot on earth could satisfy its yearnings half as much.

Which was why the unaccustomed listlessness now felt by the mudskipper defied comprehension. Its passion for all that a day might bring—a response to each new proof of life's bounty so compelling as to leave the mudskipper heady with excitement—was fading to indifference and then to a blank apathy. Without warning or explanation, the mudskipper was losing focus, steadily going numb to all it had found so invigorating before, and it could do nothing to halt the change.

The mud no longer looked or felt like the source of delight in all of life that it once had seemed: the inspiration for gravity-defying leaps to the ends of imagination and back. Now it was more like thickening goop that daily covered the mudskipper from head to tail and from gills to deep inside its throat, scarcely allowing enough breath for a tortured inching here and there without direction or purpose.

Narcissus

Once Narcissus decided to step back from the glassy water.

The pond he'd spent so much time admiring himself in had simply grown too popular of late. If you could barely see your reflection anymore (what with the pushy crowds peering at their own reflections over your shoulders), why stay?

Where did this collection of chattering newcomers intent on calling attention to themselves come from? What absolute frights most were. Was this what passed for "appeal" today, these gauche attempts to hide some nagging inner flaw, perhaps, by making a distracting spectacle of oneself? Or did they think the way to match his classic beauty was to put their ill-favored psyches on full display? For imitation to be the sincerest form of flattery, it at least had to be worthy of serious notice.

Take these clumsy teens hooting and clowning about, plus pop idols fresh from rehab (or on their way back to it), peroxide blondes tarting up their two-year-olds for the latest "Lil' Miss Pedo-Bait Pageant," soused male CEOs with their shirts open to the navel for an office party, tweet-kings striking "Il Duce" poses or grabbing the private parts of anyone within reach (to keep from falling, they typically claimed)—these and so many more cloddish slaves to self-flattery were here.

Revolted by it all, Narcissus made his decision to step back from the water. Or rather tried to step back. For as much as he strained, the counterpress of his uninvited companions proved much stronger. As did the annoyance with which they voiced their displeasure at being distracted from gazing at their own reflections by his efforts. "Who the hell do you think you are?" was how most expressed that displeasure. Or simply, "Hey, down in front, jerk!"

Barely able to maintain his balance anymore against the pressure at his back, Narcissus feared he might tumble headlong into his own image and drown. Worse, would anybody even notice if he did? Would it be as if he'd never been here at all, rooted to this spot in admiration of his unparalleled beauty? One last look at himself might be all there was time for now. One last chance to kiss his reflected lips and promise to return when he could be alone with his beauty once more. But when he searched desperately for his face, it was nowhere to be seen. Nowhere!

Just row upon row of hollow-eyed mugs grinning back at themselves.

The Newborn

Once a newborn struggled with postpartum depression.

The blazing light of the delivery room after months in dark warmth and comfort was bad enough, but add to this the shock of finding itself cut off and alone in a strange, strange place, then passed around by terrifying creatures with huge, toothy grins. And before that, there'd been a hard slap on the backside and then the sound of somebody weeping for joy at it all. Weeping for joy!

Amid this jarring rush of sensations, the newborn reached out in hopes of reclaiming the soothing equilibrium that was all it had ever known but found its hands resisted control, flailing in useless fists at the air. While its anguished cry, a wail meant to drown out the strange chorus of goo-goo-coos from every side, was no protection whatsoever. Least of all from this bristly face thrust against its own cheek with lips puckered and rough.

The time spent as an embryo had been elating compared to this, what with the force of creation in every cell and future possibilities as varied as life itself. But now? Here in this nondescript room? When had all that promise been reduced to the single lifetime now awaiting the newborn? Had this moment come on little by little, with alternative "what might have been" possibilities falling away here and more lost there? Or did an all-or-nothing, take-it-or-leave-it point of no return abruptly declare, "this is your life and no other"?

"No, no, no, no!" the newborn wanted to scream, had it only known how to form the word. Then, in the midst of this anguished panic, it gradually became aware of a line of figures stretching away in the air before it, from toddler to adolescent to adult to shuffling ancient. Where had they come from? Where were they going? Amid a distant blur, the newborn could just make out luminous patches in which more of these figures appeared, disappeared, and then reappeared further on, each waving to the newborn before stepping into the shadows once more.

There was a calming appeal in their steady advance through darkness and light. Seen from the newborn's position now in cradling arms, the figures' ultimate disappearance beyond the last, faint light was certain. And yet the march towards that certainty, which could have been a continual, desperate clutching at every futile hope of return, had instead a quiet dignity about it.

As if in response, a look of trusting repose spread slowly across the newborn's face, as if in recognition that the life awaiting it wouldn't be the newborn's alone. Beginnings and endings gave birth to each other and would continue to do so far beyond the last glimpse of the vanishing figures. Life was not an individual venture, however much one's own existence might suggest such was the case. Nor was death. The eventual loosing of all the atoms currently on loan to the newborn from distant stars would only mark one stage here in their ongoing odyssey, each rebonding with atoms from other stars as long as the universe lasted.

"This is your life and no other."

The newborn smiled and reached out to smiles all around the delivery room.

The Nightcrawler

Once a nightcrawler was tracked down by the thought police.

The nightcrawler's crime? "Having nightcrawler thoughts."

"What other thoughts would a nightcrawler have?" it protested to the arresting officers.

"Exactly," came a gruff reply.

The bright beam of a flashlight seared the nightcrawler's light receptors and caused it to recoil from its captors. It could feel the heavy pressure of their boots on the dewy grass and sense the disgust in their voices.

"What have I done wrong?" the squirming nightcrawler asked.

"Nothing yet."

"Then what's the problem?"

"The problem is what you might do, given your suspect thinking."

"The problem is what a worm like you might try in the future," a second voice added. "We're sworn to protect society against that by all means necessary."

"But I'm nothing but a worm! What threat could I pose to anybody?"

"Great oaks from little acorns grow."

"What's that got to do with me?"

"Everything. Nightcrawler thoughts can lead to nightcrawler acts and in no time, all of us are in danger from the likes of you. Anybody takes one look at you and they know what alarming things you're capable of."

"Alarming things?"

"Repellent even."

"Repellent?"

"Because you alarm people and repel them, you must in fact be alarming and repellent, and because you're alarming and repellent, you must have alarming and repellent thoughts, and if you have alarming and repellent thoughts, you must be planning alarming and repellent deeds and one day you're bound to carry them out."

"In other words," the second voice added, "you give us the creeps."

Alarming? Repellent? The creeps? The nightcrawler felt insulted and demeaned by such accusations. So what if it didn't think like its accusers. Its thoughts had always seemed to be, first of all, nobody's business and second of all, the sole chance that it had of ever escaping the cramped depths of the earth, where all it knew was the stultifying monotony of inching its way through life's impediments. But thanks to its imagination, the nightcrawler tried to explain in the direction of the flashlight as it flinched again in pain, it could immerge and roam freely when most constrained by its lot, gliding anywhere it wished over the rain-slick grass and reveling in midnight's sweet welcome while the rest of the world snored. In this way, a nightcrawler's imagination might stretch to the ends of the earth. Was that a crime now?

All of this defense made little impression upon the nightcrawler's accusers, who responded in unison, "We haven't the slightest idea what you mean. But we're pretty sure it's alarming and repellent."

"You have the right to remain silent," announced one of the officers while puzzling over how and where to handcuff the nightcrawler.

"Anything you imagine can and will be used against you in a court of law," the other officer added.

An Odd Character

Once an odd character decided to write a book in hopes of becoming famous.

That the odd character fancied itself writer material wasn't very surprising, actually. It would have been more surprising if the odd character hadn't. Most of those who still considered themselves members of the reading public seemed convinced they had a narrative inside them, and according to census projections, the birthrate of aspiring authors would soon surpass that of potential readers.

Bookstore shelves and remainder tables sagged under the ever-multiplying load of thumbed-but-unpurchased volumes. From local book nooks to national chains to online stores, many routinely offered end-of-December "Special Sales to Authors" in hopes of closing the business year in the black. While an increasing number of authors (faced with the threat to their own survival posed by the Malthusian growth in their numbers) took to teaming up in a literary version of the buddy system, pledging to one another, "I'll write a glowing blurb for your book if you'll do the same for mine."

And then there were the writing conferences and creative retreats springing up like mushrooms all over the place in reverse proportion to the steady decline in cover-to-cover book reading by the public at large. There were even weekend cruises you could sign up for in hopes of rubbing elbows with aging writers who were once famous or nearly famous and now were contracted to offer words of wisdom about how to grab literary glory today, as they and their spellbound audience drifted past some foggy shore. At this level one apparently could rest on one's laurels and didn't need to write anything that readers would actually find interesting anymore. It was enough for one to be introduced as having been "trailblazing" at some time or other in the past and then to reveal to those aspiring to be headliners for a similar cruise in the future just how to make that happen for themselves.

When the odd character actually sat down to begin writing its own book, however, it was embarrassed to realize it couldn't get past the first sentence. No matter how hard it pressed its temples and sometimes pulled out clumps of hair while pacing to-and-fro in frustration, there was no escaping the inconvenient discovery that it had nothing whatsoever to say.

This unanticipated reality might well have written "finis" to the odd character's desire to leave its mark in the history of letters. Fortunately, however, there turned out to be an amazing number of other struggling authors around, many of whom had formed an online support group calling itself "Parnassus Bound, Baby!"

After much initial hesitation, the odd character summoned the courage to join one of the group's weekly sessions in hopes of at least picking up a few helpful pointers.

The first rule for success as a budding writer, the odd character heard in turn from nearly everybody in the group, was to "write what you know." Most of the members seemed to know quite a lot. Each Saturday they'd share book chapters they'd written during the week full of international skullduggery, sociopathic crime and sexual mayhem, page-turner family dysfunction, every sort of addiction imaginable and then some, the long and painful road to redemption from any number of sins, public and private, serial adultery page by page, the emotional and psychological toll of middle-class anomie. Compared with the experience of the odd character, this was impressive stuff. But a bit puzzling as well. For if these aspiring authors really were writing what they knew, why hadn't they all been incarcerated or committed to asylums years ago?

When it expressed its puzzlement in this regard, the odd character met with a chorus of bluff assurance: "Great career move if you can manage it—the federal pen or the psycho ward." "Yah, mail a synopsis of your book from either one, or both if you can." "That's guaranteed to get publishers fighting to sign you up as their latest literary phenom." "Not to worry in any case, though. Fiction or non-fiction, nobody really cares these days if you're 'makin' it real' or simply making the whole thing up as you go on some afternoon or late-night chat show." "Getting on that chat show in the first place is all that counts. So why not just give them what they want from the start?"

"The most important move right now," the odd character was finally told, "is to get yourself an agent and have some head shots taken. A little tip here-- rows of books always make a surefire backdrop if you want to show real writer-cred. Used to be a lit cigarette dangling from your mouth or from fingers pressed to your forehead was the ticket, plus a glass of whisky in front of you. But these days you've got to get that look of serious talent across without a good old butt-and-booze pose. So, do you want the names of 20 or so agents I've been trying to get with for the past couple of decades?"

Despite the self-assurance with which all of this advice was offered, the odd character thought perhaps it should at least have the opening chapter of its book completed before approaching an agent and hiring a photographer. It also guessed, from what it heard, that getting something from its "work in progress" published in a "literary mag" could improve its chances of being taken seriously.

There was nothing for it, then, but to return to sweating word by word through a first chapter as it spent long nights at the second-hand kitchen table it had bought to give itself the expected setting for literary inspiration.

Whenever it needed a break from the difficult business of what many in the online support group liked to call "wordsmithing" (often several times in the same sentence, as if savoring the wit of linking a jeweler's precise touch with a down-to-earth, broad-chested, roll-up-your-sleeves, hammer-and-tongs-at-the-forge approach to the "writer's craft"), the odd character would shift the table around the kitchen and try to visualize how it might appear to most advantage in a big-budget Hollywood film someday based on its starving-artist years. A foot or so this way? No, a foot or so that way?

After the odd character eventually finished drafting and redrafting a few pages and then drafting and redrafting a cover letter to literary magazine editors, after it spent hours calculating the most auspicious day and time to go to the post office and then worrying the clerk behind the counter with whether the stamp on each submission was sufficient, the self-addressed return envelopes the odd character had enclosed came back in stacks on the same day the following week. Inside each was a printed variation of the same reply: "We have carefully read your submission and regret to inform you that it does not match our current editorial needs. However, we do appreciate your interest in our publication and invite you to support our dedication to promising new voices like your own by subscribing now at a life-time reduced rate."

The 20 or so agents whose names the odd character had been given proved no more encouraging. Their typical reply took the form of a column of small boxes on photocopy paper with a brief reason for rejection following each. The box most often checked read: "Your manuscript failed to engage our interest."

Ironically, it was in the depths of discouragement at these brush-offs that the odd character finally experienced a breakthrough moment. Attending a sold-out talk by the author of multiple best sellers, it had ventured to ask during question-and-answer time about the role of talent in success. "Talent schmalent!" scoffed the best-selling author to uneasy titters from the audience. "Publishing's a business. Get it? Rely on talent alone and you'll never go anywhere. Nobody'll even remember your name."

The odd character was put off somewhat by the dismissive tone, particularly as it had been at pains to introduce itself as "a fellow worshiper of the literary muse" and met with a smirk from the popular author and a low titter within the audience. All the same, it couldn't shake the feeling there might be some truth in what had been said.

Could simply having your name remembered and immediately recognized by readers around the globe be the key to success as a writer? To that end, could a clever pen name determine where you ended up in window displays or at book fairs, just as surely as product placement in a grocery store aisle? And once an author had high name recognition, what editor wouldn't be eager to snap up anything that author churned out? Absolutely anything!

What an epiphany! If fame or failure depended on little more than something like the inspired choice of a *nom de plume*, something that showed true artistic flair, the stakes couldn't be higher in this vital decision. The name finally chosen was not in fact the name this literary hopeful had been given at birth. Nor was it the first pen name the odd character considered, but rather was only hit upon after numerous others had been repeated pensively for the better part of a week and then abandoned.

There were two advantages to the final choice that seemed especially promising. First, the pen name began with an A, just as the word "author" did. Second, and even more promising, it began with two As. If nothing else, the double A should ensure that when the book finally did see the light of day, it would enjoy pride of place on alphabetically arranged bookshelves everywhere.

Now the writer to be known hereafter as "Aardvark" just needed to figure out how to write something worth reading.

Old Dobbin the Workhorse

Once Old Dobbin the workhorse mulled the vicissitudes of life.

Clearly, things were not looking up for the average workhorse. A lifetime of dedication to the work ethic was not going to ensure, as Old Dobbin had always assumed, a retirement of deserved rest and enjoyment. The chance to think back with satisfaction on the many years and the many challenges (each one met without complaint in the confidence that honest labor earned one a dignified end in this world) was looking less likely than a termination slip and a trip to the glue factory.

Old Dobbin wasn't one to complain about circumstances changing and the world maybe leaving one behind. The heyday of the workhorse couldn't last forever, after all. Progress had winners and losers, and there might turn out to be only the narrowest difference between the two. If Old Dobbin's employer could find never-tiring machines to replace him, such was the kind of progress that high-paid management consultants were rewarded for, was it not? Dignified ends were not a bottom-line concern of theirs.

That said, repeated insistence on "bottom line this" and "bottom line that" could come to fester like a raw spot left by a harness worn too long. What did bottom-line anything have to do with the amount of oneself that went into a working day, Old Dobbin wanted to know? Did you add up the hours, subtract the number of rest breaks, and divide by pennies to be saved? Such thinking was about as nonsensical as it would have been in past centuries to judge a mill horse by the number of turns it took around the wheel or the total bags of flour it could manage to grind out if whipped for greater productivity to within an inch of its life.

Was it, too, nothing more than a driven animal in employers' eyes, Old Dobbin snorted? Had years of tireless service produced no greater commitment to it in return than the mill horse of old received? There was worth in labor, regardless of how much you could peddle its product for. And virtue still in doing one's part to better the lives of others that a bottom-line calculation only cheapened.

Being put out to pasture after a lifetime of unstinting exertion was certainly better than the glue factory, but it brought little honor with it anymore. Little respect for the dedication that had earned one a rightful ease. Instead, workhorses were unceremoniously led out now, slapped from behind, and sent off to face whatever lay ahead as if they deserved no better. While those who sent them off were celebrated as management wizards and given retirement packages that far outweighed the combined hides of all the workhorses that had been in their employ.

If this was increasingly considered business success, Old Dobbin wanted to ask, what did moral bankruptcy look like?

The Old Dog

Once an old dog decided there wasn't much point in learning new tricks.

This conclusion came to the old dog the morning it noticed by chance a trace of gray on its muzzle. How long had the gray been there, it wondered? Such a change likely hadn't happened overnight, so how did it escape the dog's attention until now?

On closer inspection, a slight graying could be detected on the old dog's temples as well. And now that it studied the dome between its ears, didn't the hair seem to have thinned a bit, leaving patches of pale skin visible where none had shown before? How had these changes also escaped the old dog's notice? As it tried to prepare itself mentally for another day, the uneasy feeling that it might also have missed yet other signs of likely decline proved a distraction the old dog couldn't shake.

Had its stride slowed or become less assured? Was its hearing, always reliable before, beginning to fail, so that it was spoken to more loudly and more slowly now as though others assumed it had entered its dotage? Had it wandered off track when given a single task that it could recall? Was it losing its memory?

The old dog certainly didn't think any of these possibilities were true. Nevertheless, it continued to brood over how it hadn't spotted the gray hair and bald spots and diminished hearing before. Who could think of new tricks at a moment like this, when a lifetime of old and familiar ones might be slipping away from you along with everything else? Not to have a future was a depressing notion; not to have a past you were still master of must be worse.

The old dog tried to count off all the tricks it had learned over the years but stopped when it became clear not that it had forgotten a few but that it remembered all of them, as well as the day it mastered each trick and everything about that day. It did in fact have a past, one that returned to it like a Proustian recollection. All the way back to its days as a pup, when everything seemed fresh and unexplored, the old dog's life could be traced in its entirety, proof against the slights of time that something worth remembering had in fact occurred.

It was natural when young to look to the future as an ever-expanding range of lessons to be learned and limits to be tested. The past at that age was always the past of others, the old dog had decided early on, and its weight was the burden of custom. New tricks had promised an escape from such constraints that only the most timid of dogs shied away from.

But with advancing years and a future that grew shorter with every breath, the past of others became one's own past as well. No longer did the dog feel like it was on a short leash in the hands of the dead. Personal memory became communal as the events of one's own life stretched back into the lives of others and shared experiences multiplied the years. Being alone wasn't the same now as it had been when the dog was young and spry, when making your own way was all that counted and "declining years" would never arrive.

Now, the old dog reckoned, knowing you'd mastered the tricks of a lifetime meant far more than panting for a few new ones to learn.

The Old Goat

Once an old goat nearly overdosed on ED pills.

That it even felt the need of such pills baffled many who knew the old goat. It certainly didn't have a history of difficulties that might have suggested such a remedy was called for. Quite the opposite, its reputation for energetic and un-flagging performance was well known, legendary in fact. Ironically, the old goat's reputation may have been the very source of its troubles.

It hadn't given much thought to the matter in the past. "Either you've got what it takes or you don't" might have summed up the amount of concern the old goat had shown for what was so much a part of its nature as scarcely to deserve mention.

But that was before it started hearing stories around the office water cooler about "steamy nooners" involving many staff members, apparently. Then a mid-level colleague abandoned a marriage of twenty-five years to "find my youth again" in the back seat of roving taxis. What was going on? Maybe it was time to take the question of its reputation more seriously.

There was something demeaning, though, about having to prove your status as "numero uno" when there should have been no question about it. The goat didn't really know where to begin or how to proceed, so little thought had it given the matter in the past. But now, increasingly, its attention wandered during meetings with important clients to a muddle of shopping plans for gaudy shirts, gold-plated neck chains, and spice-scented breath sprays, along with various strategies for brushing against curvaceous new hires in the elevator as though by accident.

When it caught itself one day trying to read the small print on packages of hair restorer and whisker dye, the old goat realized how far and how fast it was spiraling out of control. This couldn't go on. Deciding a bold step was in order, the goat made an appointment with a doctor.

"I see cases like yours all the time," the doctor said with a reassuring tone.

"You do, doc?" the goat asked in alarm. Had it actually underestimated the number of younger goats preparing to push it aside, then?

"Yes, although there wasn't much to be done about the condition until recently. Fortunately, it now has a medical designation: OGS, or Old Goat Syndrome. And when there's a name for a condition, there's a pill. Thank the pharmaceutical industry for that. Simply take one of these sample pills and call me in the morning if you experience a sudden loss in vision or hearing, as these may be signs of a side effect called RYEOAYEO, otherwise known as 'rutting your eyes out and your ears off.' To avoid long-term injury, seek immediate medical assistance for an erection lasting more than four hours."

"Are you out of your mind, doc? Medical assistance is about the last thing I'll be seeking for a four-hour erection, believe me!"

The goat did have one last question, though: "I guess I should ask you, doc, are these pills right for me?"

"They're right for everybody. Emerging research suggests Old Goat Syndrome doesn't discriminate when it strikes. Political leaders, sports and entertainment idols, movers and shakers of commerce, right down to the guy next door, you name it. Soon much of the country may be relying on these pills."

This information did nothing to calm the old goat's anxiety. The entirety of its self-image was now at stake, it feared. With these pills, half the planet could soon be laying claim to the old goat's long-standing reputation, strutting about like Priapus Unchained. To retain its position at the top, then, would it have to make an extra effort? Better leave nothing to chance in that case. Scarcely out of the doctor's office, the old goat gulped down the entire bottle of pills.

When the doctor's telephone rang the next morning, it wasn't the old goat calling but rather the police. They had a few questions they needed to ask about a suspect they were holding in a string of indecent exposure complaints at locations ranging from daycare centers to assisted living facilities.

Orpheus and Eurydice

Once Orpheus struggled to understand why others couldn't understand the love he and Eurydice had.

He had no difficulty remembering the snakebite that sent his wife to the Underworld and the unbearable grief that drove him there in search of her. And no difficulty remembering how the lyrical song of his loss had so moved Hades with its anguish and its art that the tearful god allowed him to lead Eurydice back up towards the light. Even the warning she would vanish forever if he so much as glanced at her along the way remained with him. And how could he forget their anxious steps on the dim trail out of the realm of death, since the rough sound of every pebble shifting beneath their feet had echoed over and over in his mind ever since?

No, his difficulty came instead from the quick, confident interpretations everyone who hadn't been there offered of what happened, convinced their unsought sympathy would have the power to console him. Did he really turn towards Eurydice at the last moment, as so many claimed, simply because he could no longer control a lover's need? Or because, as others declared with equal self-assurance, his passion for Eurydice was already fated to end in eternal farewell: their private tragedy reduced to just another public sighing over death's claim on all lives?

Orpheus couldn't recognize himself in such tidy explanations and wondered how they could satisfy anybody. Turning his head back towards Eurydice hadn't been an impulsive lapse. Nor the ironic end to some trite allegory of passion and art and death. Nor an illustration in myth of the obvious about fated love. Were these the limits to people's understanding of what he and Eurydice had shared?

She, he was certain, could not have failed to understand why he'd turned towards her in that final moment of their ascent. She must have known why his heart would overrule all else to pledge his devotion at its fullest and, in return, pledged her own through the warmth of her hand on his shoulder as they climbed through the dark chill. Her love so complete he'd realized he had no way to offer up the whole of his own but to seek her eyes at the very point nothing could ever be taken back. Nor ever surpassed.

"Tragic agony" was not an expression equal to what Orpheus had suffered since watching Eurydice vanish into darkness, but his embrace of their mutual suffering was the only testament to their love left him. No song on his lyre could express the full measure of what their eyes promised in that final instant: an ardor that would never cool or fail, as flesh inevitably does, but rather set their pledge at love's highest pitch for eternity. Far beyond darkness and light.

The Ostrich and the Emu

Once an ostrich and an emu chanced to lay eyes on one another.

The ostrich had always considered itself to be the most attractive of birds. The emu was just as confident of its own claim to that title. With the disappearance of the giant moa, both of them had been convinced that they no longer had any rivals when it came to feathered beauty.

When the two first became aware of one another, they were some distance apart. Perhaps it was the distance or perhaps it was the effect of the shimmering summer air, but on first sight both the ostrich and the emu took the other for a mirror image of itself. Both paused at the same moment and stretched their long necks at the same angle for an admiring look.

But as they resumed walking towards one another, each bird began to notice that the other was a bit different. The ostrich realized that the emu was slightly shorter and slightly more slender in shape. The emu saw that the approaching ostrich was slightly taller and had a more impressive build. The emu's neck sported soft feathers, while the ostrich's appeared to be relatively bare. The long legs of both birds looked similar, but one's legs ended in three toes while the other's ended in two.

The shorter the distance between the pair became, the less self-assured each bird grew. The emu compared the ostrich's longer neck and longer legs with its own and wished they were a little longer. The ostrich, in a similar way, wished its body and head could be a little more elegant or refined in look, like the emu's.

When the birds finally drew abreast, each could hide its agitation only by staring straight ahead and pretending not to notice the other.

As the two moved away in opposite directions and their first impressions began to fade, so did the unpleasant comparisons that had ruffled their self-confidence. One bird looked down at its pair of toes as they spread and came together in the course of a step and found this arrangement to be the most naturally appealing in the end. The other looked down at its three toes and came to much the same conclusion.

The slightly smaller bird decided that although its body and neck were perhaps not quite as imposing as the other's, they were definitely more shapely in their way. The slightly larger bird remembered the other's physique as perhaps not altogether without charm, but certainly not as stately as its own.

Neither the ostrich nor the emu ever looked back. Instead, both continued on with their heads held a little higher on their long necks and with a little more strut in their step the farther apart they moved. By the time each one reached the place from which the other had started, there wasn't much point in turning around for a final glance.

"Imagine being such an odd-looking bird!" they both thought with a simultaneous shudder.

The Pack Rat

Once a pack rat resolved to make a little list.

It did so after becoming troubled while surveying the things it had lovingly gathered over the years by the sudden thought that a day might come when all of this, all the pack rat had grown to cherish, all this wonderful hoard, would vanish as though none of it had ever existed. That could happen. The glories of Greece and Rome had disappeared into the Dark Ages, hadn't they? Who could deny it might happen again?

Something must be done in the face of such a potential catastrophe. If the best that the pack rat's world had produced was in danger, it fell to those like itself, those most qualified by experience to select what was in fact the best, to step forward. It fell to them, in short, to make a list of what was worth preserving forever before it was too late.

What should go on the list, then? What should the world always value most? The pack rat scanned its cherished trove and began to choose the "top ten" items.

But no sooner had it made its first selections than the pack rat found itself faced with something of a dilemma. Was the list to be the "top ten" of its own lifetime, it asked itself? Or should it be the "top ten" of the past century? What about the past millennium? Or all of recorded history? And was ten enough? Should it instead be the "top one hundred," or even the "top one thousand"? Where should the pack rat begin, and once begun, how could it be certain where to end? And obviously there must be a clear hierarchy of some sort to the list. Adopting just any order of one through up to one thousand wouldn't do when it came to the best of the best.

Worse yet, what if the New Dark Ages the pack rat feared might come began before it had finished its task? A sudden catastrophe was not out of the question, after all. Or suppose the list, by some twist of fate, never saw the light of day? Then again, suppose it did see the light of day, but not in its complete and ordered form? These were not trivial concerns.

Clearly, the pack rat would need to have all of its wits about it for such an exacting and solemn task as the one before it. The stakes were so high and the potential consequences of a lapse in attention were so grave that it couldn't afford to make a single false step in judgment along the way. Ultimately, "Top" lists told you who you were and why, the pack rat was convinced. "This list must be my life," it exhorted itself to remember. A moment later it asked itself whether it should say instead, "my life must be this list"?

Yet another difficult choice to be made! What to do? What to do?

The Panda

Once a panda snapped open a fortune cookie after dining with compeers and found the following paper message: "A change for the better which will be made against you."

The panda, having an easy-going personality, noted the bizarre nature of the fortune but wasn't moved to devote much further thought to what it might mean. Slipping the paper into a pocket of its dinner jacket, it refocused its attention instead on the aftertaste of the remarkable array of bamboo delicacies it had just finished. Not until days later (when searching the pockets of its dinner jacket for something to chew between meals) did the panda feel the wadded paper and unfolded it for a second look.

"A change for the better which will be made against you." What could such a fortune mean? It might simply be a joke, of course, possibly the work of some bored employee at the fortune cookie factory. On the other hand, what if it wasn't a joke? What if behind this puzzling phrase lay a truth the panda simply hadn't been prepared by any of its previous experience to grasp? It had never had any reason to doubt that the blessings it enjoyed on a daily basis would continue throughout life. There might be temporary ups and downs, to be sure, but the general trend would always be upward, or so the panda had assumed as a matter of course.

What then of this change for the better "against you"? Could it mean the panda's contented outlook on life—its confidence that the future must inevitably promise more of the steady diet of satisfactions to which it had grown so accustomed—was about to suffer a reversal? Was it possible the planet wasn't in fact dedicated to perpetuating forever the panda's inherent sense of wellbeing?

Further, who was meant to gain by the "change for the better" to be made against the panda? Whose appetites could be more pressing? No other panda among its dining circle, that was for sure. It could hardly conceive of a pursuit of surfeit more compelling than its own. . . Or was it possible that one of the panda's usual compeers . . . or more than one . . . might be plotting its demise?

Though maybe the challenge to its accustomed sense of unchallenged ease wouldn't come from inside its regular circle. For all the panda knew, its free and easy enjoyment of life's bounty might be brought to an end by a rank upstart, even by the lowest of the low. Its life story might prove to be no more than a sideshow in the rise of a more determined bamboo gourmand that hadn't even come to the panda's notice as of yet.

On the other hand, the fortune cookie might not have been meant for it at all. Had it simply chanced to pick the wrong one from the batch of them at the end of the meal? If so, then time would surely tell whether there was anything ahead in life worth worrying about. Yes, an answer would come eventually. No sense in trying to rush it. Until then, why not carry on as though the ominous warning was indeed aimed at another and not intended to put the panda off its insatiable appetite for a single moment?

Mix-ups of this sort must happen all the time, mustn't they?

The Panther

Once a panther was well aware of the spell it cast over all visitors to the zoo.

It had long felt their eyes on its lithe body as if they yearned to reach out and stroke it but didn't dare. Whenever it paused in its pacing to and fro and looked back at them, it saw in their eyes a fascination that could not bring itself to turn away and sensed in each person's jugular a pulse that churned a moment and then raced on.

What were they looking for? The panther suspected their presence had less to do with it and more to do with what they wanted it to be. Their expressions suggested that the shadowy figure they watched so intently was never shadowy enough, never distant enough from their well-ordered lives to match the spellbinding lure of imagined danger and the dark unknown that they sought. To the panther, it always seemed they eyed it with a wish to see death suddenly take on flesh and spring at the bars.

But if the allure of death was what brought them by the busload, expecting perhaps to smell it on the panther's breath as it passed close to them, they needn't have taken the trouble. Any blood on its fangs was watery and cold. None of the panther's food came from its own kill. Slabs of thawed meat were tossed to it with the regularity of these visitors' own need for a meal, and its claws had grown dull from disuse.

Perhaps they did come half hoping it would smash through the bars and maul a patron or two in front of them before being shot by guards. With the panther gone, though, which of the other great cats in the zoo could replace it in these people's communal yearning, in the hushed strain of their desire?

The lions and tigers and jaguars and all the others were too well known to suggest anything that couldn't already be safely defined, as though human understanding had long ago taken their measure in full. But a panther still prowled just on the other side of experience and thought. A panther was still a riddle of deadly enchantment.

Was it the pull of what they most feared, then, that brought them together to share a frisson of seductive horror, unable to get closer but also unable to leave until the panther itself freed them by turning away? Did they go home feeling somehow more alive for having stood within sight and smell at least of life's violent end?

The panther lay in the fading light after the zoo had closed and pondered questions like these. Killing that was necessary to survive, this it understood. But why death (as unpredictable as it was inevitable) should hold this hypnotic power over human beings wasn't at all clear.

To turn death from an inevitability into an emotion, a wish for something which could entrance and appall at the same time, into something which defied definition in lives otherwise made so secure precisely by definitions left the panther shaking its head.

What unfathomable creatures these humans were.

The Parrot

Once a parrot became a bird of renown by mimicking others.

The parrot held that this achievement wasn't really a case of out-and-out mimicry. Rather, it should be viewed more as a case of coincidence. And even if it turned out in the end to be mimicry, that wouldn't be the parrot's fault.

You simply had to copy others to one degree or another, it maintained, if you were going to make a name for yourself in society.

The parrot had tried saying something original once, but gave up the attempt because nobody could understand any of it. When the parrot started repeating what others said right back to them, however, it found the response was immediate and enthusiastic.

Nor did it seem to matter what the subject was, so long as the parrot took care to repeat word for word what others were saying. With pop-culture phenoms, it could be the latest quiz-show patter or sit-com punch line or singing-contest repartee. With daytime chat-show hosts, it could be a breezy chronicle of family dysfunction ending in life-changing self-discovery. With techies, it could simply be a string of acronyms. With those who fancied themselves leading independent thinkers, it could be any multisyllabic word ending in "-ism," "-icity," "-itude," "-inal," or "-iotic." And with bureaucrats, of course, it could be practically anything.

Once the parrot had the lingo down, its confidence mushroomed. There seemed no end to its virtuosity, and its reputation as a kind of latter-day "Renaissance Figure" spread quickly. It moved with equal assurance among the hoity-toity set and the hoi polloi.

The parrot soon was a regular on the lecture circuit as well, commanding five-figure fees per appearance. There were non-stop book signings and steady calls for the parrot to serve as an expert consultant to commissions and news specials, either that or emcee award ceremonies of every sort imaginable. Regardless of the topic or situation, the parrot was among the first to be sought out for comment and then quoted ad infinitum.

The only time the parrot experienced any difficulty was when pop-culture phenoms, chat-show hosts, techies, self-described independent thinkers, bureaucrats, and so forth started sounding increasingly alike. This development might have caused the parrot some worry about maintaining its unique status, but it soon worked out a way to deal with that.

It simply presented itself as the public voice of absolutely everybody.

Pavlov's Dogs

Once Pavlov's dogs nearly died of acute dehydration.

After making their famous contribution to science, they'd enjoyed what was a well-deserved but brief retirement. It ended when they were beseeched to exercise their skills in the political arena as well. With election campaigns growing longer and longer, exhausted candidates and supporters looked to the dogs to provide that certain something necessary to carry the day.

Being trucked about from one political rally or photo op to another and expected to salivate on command at whatever they heard a candidate say caused serious strain to the dogs' vaunted glands over time, however. Drooling on cue wasn't as easy as political operatives seemed to think it was.

The responsibility became so taxing and so stressful, in fact, that teams of volunteers had to be recruited in towns large and small to form water brigades and keep these valuable mouths well primed. It wouldn't do to have them suddenly dry up just at the critical pitch in a stump speech, the point at which a candidate looked out into the camera lights and uttered, clear as a bell, the slogan so extensively crowd-tested for maximum effect.

The dogs strained valiantly to respond to even the least of a candidate's remarks as if it contained the sum total of advanced thinking since the dawn of humanity. Nevertheless, as the months wore on and demand for their services grew, it became impossible to keep up with the increasingly urgent requests and then abject pleas made by various campaign chiefs of staff. A point was reached when Pavlov's dogs just didn't have any more to give. They'd slavered their all for the cause.

One especially grueling night, after hours of arid assertions by a particularly long-winded candidate, the dogs finally seemed headed for the inescapable: death by political desiccation. As they began sinking one after another to the floor, their tongues, once so smooth and slick, lolled out of their mouths like rubbery blisters. Mere skin and bones now, the dogs looked as though they might crumble away to nothing if they so much as swallowed hard.

The idea that heroic first responders could fight their way through a packed arena to render assistance to the wheezing dogs was out of the question. In addition, few of the sign-waving, wildly cheering party loyalists bussed in from miles around knew what to do. They certainly hadn't bargained on the sight of their canine partners dropping dead during the best part of "the speech."

The shock of the spectacle rippled in every direction through the crowd, reaching all the way to the candidate's advisors on stage. There, the chief of staff realized at once what must be done. As if by common reflex, back through the hall rippled the chief of staff's appeal to the dumbfounded assembly, with an effect that was astonishing. On every side, heads steadily disappeared from view as row after row went down on hands and knees in a spontaneous demonstration of support for these failing troupers so crucial to the final stages of the campaign.

It was quite a sight—the vast hall united in a single heartfelt moment of determination: men, women, party operatives and big-time contributors alike, even the chief of staff and the anxious candidate, abandoning all restraint and drooling as one as if the country's future depended upon it.

The Pawn

Once a pawn tried to size up the chessboard.

The pawn had to admit it was at a disadvantage in not being able to see the whole of the board, in not knowing whether the square on which it found itself gave any true sense of the larger scheme of things or simply marked the limits of its own ability to understand.

Suppose its square really was the measure of the board: a microcosm reflecting the macrocosm, so to speak. If that was the case, what explained the difference in color of the four squares bordering it? How could the pawn's own square amount to anything, given this difference, but the exception to a surrounding conformity and a mark of how little it and its own position perhaps counted for when all was said and done? Or did the hint of a kindred color touching on the very corners of the pawn's square offer some heartening possibility that it was not alone and matches to its square waited out there some place?

Although, if the board was merely a succession of black and white, and every square was the opposite of those on all four sides, was regularity in fact no more than repeated change, and nothing could be counted on to last or provide reassurance beyond the here and now? New to chess, the pawn had received what apparently counted as complete instructions on how to proceed, but these in themselves struck it as both arbitrary and mysterious, with opportunity for quick advance likely as not to end in being snatched from the board into sudden oblivion. And the promise in the instructions of a grand reward for making it all the way across the board—rebirth in a more powerful form as different from the pawn's present one as morning is from night—seemed an invitation to self-aggrandizing delusion rather than genuine fulfillment.

But to remain here on its little square (with retreat impossible and advance uncertain) might leave the pawn's fate entirely at the mercy of forces playing out their obscure strategies over the far reaches of the board, indifferent to the effect their own purposes could have on a lowly pawn. Forces perhaps ready even to sacrifice all pawns—every last one of them—to some greater plan if need be.

Better never to have found oneself in this predicament, the pawn reasoned, where the only escape lay in an imagined rewriting of the rules: a wholesale rejection of their constraints. Beginning with this board.

Whatever the number of squares set for its limits, they should be doubled, again and again, and their lines redrawn until "limits" lost all meaning and where the board began or ended lacked significance as well. What one might conceive to be a square, a board, or a pawn must be freed of old definitions in favor of new ones.

Pawn, Pawn, Pawn, Pawn, **Pawn!** Now shape and color and movement and aim would defy all bounds and designations, as dreams and inspiration do. And, as dreams and inspiration, would redefine everything else in turn! But how many pawns were ready to take that risk?

What if all the rules changed, yet no pawn dared to make the first move?

The Peacocks

Once a peacock placed a personal ad in a highbrow singles magazine.

The ad read: "Successful and witty soul, emotionally mature and radiating deep comfort with self, down to earth but with a complex and multi-layered take on life, passionate yet spiritual urban Taoist, altruistic iconoclast considered a superb raconteur by friends seeks soulmate who must be equally dynamic in mind and body, an accomplished and financially secure professional by day but a spontaneous bon vivant by night, passionate about nouvelle cuisine and long walks in the rain forest, able to rise above this world of pettiness that surrounds us to focus on the big picture while still enjoying the charming beauty of the mundane: in short, a partner who is ready to leave the planet a better place through the enchanted melding of our own wild and wonderful spirits. Serious responses only."

A second peacock, having written a letter presenting itself as the soulmate described, received an express reply the very next day. Photos were exchanged and a meeting set. It seemed like a perfect match. Over a candlelight dinner, the two lost no time in touting what they considered their most appealing qualities.

"I'm HIV-negative, and you?"

"Of course."

"Good. I've just returned from Paris, by the way."

"As for me, from Kathmandu."

"And I'm off soon for Machu Picchu."

"Angkor Wat here."

"I'm an opera and jazz afficionado, in that order."

"Jazz and opera, in that order."

"What about world music?"

"Of course."

"Cannes Film Festival?"

"I prefer Sundance."

"Doctors Without Borders and Amnesty International?"

"Greenpeace and the Sierra Club."

"Harvard, Yale, MIT."

"Stanford, Berkeley, Caltech."

"Derrida, Foucault, Barthes."

"Really? Ginsberg, Kerouac, Burroughs."

"Derrida, Foucault, Barthes, and Lacan."

"Ginsberg, Kerouac, Burroughs, and Bowles."

"Shall we order Burgundy?"

"Chardonnay?"

And so it went. By dinner's end, the two peacocks realized they'd made a dreadful mistake. They agreed to "chalk the whole thing up to experience" and went their separate ways.

Each was confident it could do better the next time it sought a soulmate worthy of its consideration.

The Pelican

Once a pelican was arrested for shoplifting.

Suspicions had been aroused when the pelican showed up on one security camera after another around the mall, its bag-like bill betraying larger and more angular bulges with each appearance.

When asked by officers to open its bill and then to explain the avalanche of goods that spilled out, the befuddled pelican confessed to being as amazed as anybody by its conspicuous kleptomania. It had no recollection of having filched the items now being tagged as evidence. In fact, it couldn't imagine why on earth it would have been drawn to many of them. They certainly couldn't be considered necessities and appeared to have wound up in the pelican's bill only because they happened to catch its eye in passing.

But why? That was the question the pelican simply could not answer. Nor could psychopathologists appointed to determine whether it was competent to stand trial. As far as could be determined, the pelican was perfectly normal. It acknowledged that stealing was socially unacceptable behavior. It also clearly understood the meaning of the question when asked whether it thought happiness in life depended on material possessions. "What do you take me for, an idiot?" was its ruffled answer.

Then why shoplift? The facts of the case made no sense, and yet there they were. Further investigation showed a pattern of similar activity stretching back years. The pelican's entire life thus far was revealed to have been what one could only describe as a single-minded pursuit of excess.

Based on the findings, the pelican became the latest diagnosed case of Hysterical Acquisition Disorder: a condition characterized by delirious self-gratification and the overwhelming desire to possess everything, absolutely everything, including what the sufferer hadn't the slightest need of.

This diagnosis ultimately provided the bulk of the pelican's defense. When the case came to trial, the defendant's legal team called to the stand a dizzying array of business and banking executives, sociologists, and government officials in addition to the expected mental health experts. These witnesses all testified to the fact that the behavior of the pelican and others suffering the same panic-possession attacks was actually an essential element sustaining advanced capitalism, the credit card industry, current concepts of both personal and social worth, and international trade agreements.

The defense's argument that an otherwise average-looking pelican with a bill distended and weighed down by the senseless scooping up of things it couldn't afford and certainly didn't need was, according to the experts, vital to advanced capitalism, the credit industry, individual and group self-esteem, and international trade proved to be the deciding factor in the pelican's ultimate acquittal on all counts.

The jury held that, given the evidence and the testimony of experts, the accused couldn't be held responsible in any way for its kleptomaniacal behavior.

Pet Humans

Once a robot took its pet human for a walk in the park as usual.

Though it was early in the day, the place was already crowded with other robots putting their own humans (from the pampered show set all the way down to scruffy curs) through their paces. Or at least trying to. It never ceased to embarrass the robot how many of the other owners it encountered seemed clueless, or else deplorably negligent, when it came to controlling their pets. Hired walkers presented a particular disappointment, of course, what with their tangled brace of half a dozen unruly humans snarling and snapping at each other and raising a frightful din.

Disciplining pet humans to the point where they felt indebted in every way to their robot owners and followed without question every command they were given was, admittedly, no easy task. But where there's a will, there's always a way. Hadn't the first suggestion by a robot to implant microchips in all human beings to make them easier to locate if they either got lost or ran away been a stroke of true genius? And the latest-gen implants showed ever greater promise in cementing human reliance upon robots through the final elimination of all unprogrammed emotions and counterproductive desires. Not to mention the constant stream of biometric data these implants provided so robots would always know when the time had come to put failing humans down and mercifully out of their misery.

Getting a "robot's best friend" to welcome becoming utterly dependent upon the superiority and benefits of AI was the key to controlling them. Once that was accomplished, you could throw out the most trifling of new tech-toys in absolute confidence that your pet human would sprint after it with eyes aglow and then engage in endless rounds of absorbed self-exercise, while you leisurely chatted with other robots on a shady park bench. It was enough to glance up every now and then to monitor your pet gleefully scampering here and there until it staggered back to flop in panting devotion at your feet. Quite a touching testament all of this was to the unbreakable bond that developed so quickly between human and robot, when you thought about it.

As was the uncanny way in which many pet humans came to be the spitting image of their owners over time. Look-alike photos of grinning robots and their pet humans were continually going viral on social media. Not to mention the zeal that some robots evinced in pursuing "Best in Show" recognition for their prize-winning humans, as demonstrated through conformity to rigorously enforced standards and celebrated in a high-stepping little prance before judges who devoted their lives to such pursuits.

Yes, total dependence was the key to controlling pet humans, the robot was confident. Once convinced of the rewards of a life made so convenient, entertaining, and comfortable for them by their high-tech masters, they would never again cause the slightest embarrassment when walked.

They needn't even be put on the leash at some point, for they would happily carry it everywhere in their mouth.

Petrified Wood

Once a great nation adopted petrified wood as its symbol.

In the past, this particular nation had taken pride in claiming that an eagle and only an eagle would do to represent it, but in an anxious age when, from sea to shining sea, standing fast against threats foreign and domestic (not so much) was how many political leaders saw their role, something less prone to flight than a bird (however majestic) seemed called for to convey the depth of their patriotism.

The choice of petrified wood for the new national symbol was not a spur-of-the-moment decision. It was, instead, the outcome of a long national debate. Numerous suggestions of historical figures, natural monuments, animals, flowers, and many other icons past and present were made, but given the temper of the age, when a mix of personal and official anxiety created an atmosphere of rising paranoia nearly everywhere, petrified wood easily carried the day.

This outcome was no surprise, to be sure. What other symbol could one count on in uncertain times to be so steadfast and lasting? Conditions might change, challenges might change, the entire world might change, but petrified wood remained unchanged through it all. Petrified wood could be relied upon to resist all the day-to-day forces that shape and reshape reality and thus maintain for eons the exact state in which it turned to stone.

Beyond its obvious value in terms of ensuring that the nation could boast an image of itself that was impervious to all change, petrified wood had real commercial potential as well. When comprehensive programs to address concerns of economic stress or social pain seemed just too difficult for the country's politicians to agree upon, there could still be entrepreneurial opportunities at roadside souvenir stands stocked with petrified versions of "rockets' red glare," "bombs bursting in air," and the like.

Nor was that all. "Old Glory" itself could still gallantly wave on little fossilized pins for all those whose claim to being a patriot would fit on their lapels with space to spare.

The Phoenix

Once the phoenix considered having itself embalmed.

Why rise from the ashes again and again, it wondered? Why continue as a bright emblem of new beginnings? Nothing much was being made of that opportunity anymore, so far as the phoenix had observed. Those given a chance at a fresh start seemed unable to think of what to do with it except to make out the same wish list they'd made out for their present life.

They wanted power if they'd had none; they wanted to be squillionaires if they'd ever come up short a dime; they wanted to be beautiful and lucky in love if they'd been plain and heartbroken; they wanted to live forever if they'd been sick a single day. If all they hoped for was permission to cancel their disappointments and call it a new life, what purpose was served anymore by going through the flames to show them the way they should have followed?

Was no one longing to be reborn as a person even imagination hadn't breathed life into yet? Was no one longing for a future burned clean of the past, freed not just of failures and regrets but also of recycled desires? Ready at last for anything but a return to what they knew only too well. If not, then a mummified phoenix would be just as good as a live one, wouldn't it?

Certainly better than allowing itself to be cloned, as some suggested, and thus becoming a symbol for the shallow attraction of replaying one's life again and again for the highlights. Still worse would be for the phoenix to bow to the constant urging to retro-engineer its DNA and thus end up standing for the eternal fantasy of never having to grow old and die at all, let alone seek a new start: a once-proud bird reduced to appearing in everlasting infomercials for retirement spas packed with perpetual twentysomethings trying to make sense of experience at three hundred.

If that was the future, a trip to the embalmer definitely seemed most appropriate.

Pinocchio

Once Pinocchio was determined to take his gift for wooden mendacity all the way to the top of the political pile.

Certainly no mean feat, for the number of politico-prevaricators working the national carny circuit had long since become incalculable. But Pinocchio carried on undaunted, putting on such a show that the faithful of an entire party ultimately came to sport rosy campaign buttons that read "Grand Old Pinocchio" with pride.

After all, didn't he look every bit the part? What other political puppet could boast such a tabloid-cover profile in the jaw-jutting style? Or such an ability to assume nearly any stance (regardless of how unnatural it might appear) at the pull of a string or two?

So practiced at mimicking lifelike behavior had Pinocchio proved that to own such a mechanical marvel became the ambition of many a well-heeled puppet master, even those abroad, where true masters have for ages practiced the art of manipulation. So many, as it turned out, that only the wealthiest among them could afford the ever-greater price being fetched at puppet auctions for the likes of Pinocchio.

Not that there were many political puppets who could seriously rival him, of course, in the repertoire of belief-defying postures they could assume but also, and equally attractive to any practiced puppet master, in Pinocchio's uncanny skill at turning wild summersaults end over end over end over end that would tangle up a lesser puppet without fail in hopelessly knotted strings—all this while never ceasing to talk out of both sides of his mouth with a knack that seemed deeply engrained. True, a goofy, frozen expression often accompanied such a feat, as if Pinocchio knew he was lying through his teeth but couldn't stop. Or hoped his lies wouldn't be noticed. Or didn't really care. Otherwise, however, the wonders of a consummate marionette were never on more convincing display.

It came as no surprise, then, that bidding wars for this most flexible of puppets took on a life of their own. And with puppet masters accustomed to manipulating their playthings from behind closed curtains, it soon became the norm as well for auctions to be conducted in secret, with rumors of vast sums being bid that couldn't be verified but were soon old news, anyhow, as even vaster sums were bruited about day in and day out.

With each new performance by this matchless puppet, the ooohs and ahhhs drawn from slack-jawed crowds at the capers performed before their eyes were loud and clear. Nothing seemed beyond Pinocchio's gift of preternatural flexibility.

Except for one thing: the curious change that came over the puppet's face the more reckless his prancing about became.

At first it appeared his nose was growing longer and thus heavier with each new fib or dodge, challenging his ability to avoid tumbling flat on his face. But then it became evident that an even greater change was occurring to his chin: that chiseled emblem of oakish resolve he'd often thrust forward over crossed arms when doing his favorite stage strut. As if in response to the pull of a rapidly lengthening nose, the puppet's chin was shrinking backwards at an equally astonishing rate.

How long Pinocchio's chin would remain recognizable as at least a nubbin of its past "prom-king glory" was anybody's guess. Already, the once-firm pose so prized by his cheering fans was dissolving into that of a chinless wonder instead. One whose admirers might well have fallen to zero by the next puppet auction.

Then again, maybe not. For Pinocchio's tabloid profile could always be recarved for a smaller head, couldn't it, and thus maintain indefinitely the illusion of greatness in the eyes of his faithful followers? Yes? No?

The Pit Bull

Once a pit bull refused to go for the throat of every other dog around.

How had things descended to this appalling state, it shuddered with disgust? It certainly didn't bear other canines any particular malice. In a better world, the pit bull was convinced, it might even have found life-long friends among them.

But not in the world of Reality TV survival shows. That was made clear to the pit bull soon after it balked at filming one more episode of the hugely popular "Raging Mutts." It felt it needed time to reflect on whether this was really the life it wanted to lead going forward.

"Of course it is!" was the response from the whiz kid with spiky hair and a toothy smile who'd been sent out from network headquarters to troubleshoot the dog's refusal to go on with the show. "You can't quit! Not with your star power! This is the perfect vehicle for you! You're on top of the heap, so why quit now?"

"I simply don't see the value in any of this."

"Who's talking value? It's just a performance, remember."

The pit bull wasn't particularly reassured by this reply.

"Look at it this way," the whiz kid went on while picking at a pimple, "we're not dealing with an audience of Einsteins out there. We give our target demographic what market research tells us they want. And market research tells us the target demographic is getting bored of contestants acting out sham betrayals or chewing the bark off trees in front of a camera. That also goes for watching disappointed contestants attempt suicide. Audiences want something more this season."

"Like eating one's own kind on cue?"

"Believe me, none of us in Froth-at-the-Mouth Programming are comfortable with that. You think every last one of us doesn't wish we could offer more quality stuff? I got a hundred knockout ideas right here in my own head. How about this, just as one example: an "Unwanted-Baby Giveaway" contest? Problem is, viewers just don't have the attention span any longer for that level of complexity. So we have to settle for dogs eating dogs. Especially during sweeps week."

"But it's all so degrading."

"Of course it is! That's the beauty of it, don't you see? Giving contestants a once-in-a-lifetime chance to be a winner and then humiliating them in prime time is epic in a way. Epic!"

"But what does that do for me? I can't go on anymore making this vicious spectacle of myself. And for what? What do I get out of it?"

"Okay, okay. How about this: a six-figure book deal with the famous publishing house our parent company just bought? Corporate is already tossing about a few blockbuster titles. My favorite is 'Down and Dirty with a Real Dog.' Like it?"

"I honestly need some time to think about where all this is headed."

"Sure thing! Sure thing! Take all day if you want. You can never give these decisions too much thought. I'm with you on that, one million percent!"

A Plague of Politicians

Once every two years, a plague of politicians has swept across the land.

A scourge of shallow minds with morals to match. What else should we expect from those so eager always to lay their lies on the line? What else besides no-deposit-no-return morality, throwaway convictions, principles for a day, premeasured disposable ethics—what else? Big-time wheeler-dealers with the souls of common pickpockets prowling the shady side of life, working their ambitions on the naive and the unsuspecting, crouching behind anything that serves—a word, a pose, an obscure plan—waiting only to leap out of the dark, grab a few votes or campaign donations, and scurry back into the shadows. These were the "nation's choice"? More like fantastical, nightmarish, air-borne thistle-things they were, swirling about. The noxious sprouts of backwaters the nation-round, sticky weeds that prosper in damp and fetid haunts. The very seeds of corruption, riding from coast to coast on fickle winds, turning, returning, spying out where to land, and then suddenly, in full bloom, transformed, showing their true colors at last with a grin, a handshake, and the kiss of death. "Good to meet you. My name is . . ."

Puuugh! And consider the ragtag mob that trots at a politician's heel. Lately, they've made themselves all too visible. What a pack! Here today and gone tomorrow with their banners and bullhorns. Or consider the wheeler-dealers for all seasons. Never have so many sought to profit so much from so little. The fly-by-night executive aides, the lighter-than-air advisers, hack intellectuals and resident cantmongers, pipe-sucking charlatans, specialists by the score, instant experts, correspondence-course authorities, self-infatuated movers and shakers, brash hangers-on of few scruples familiar to us all as slick-faced overachievers, fast-talking smoothies, whiz kids along for the ride, an endless array of pay-off runners and cover-up crews, junior bagmen, senior strokers, bunglers on their way up, bogglers on their way down, lobbyists with thick bank rolls and slippery palms, fat cats kicking their sand about, pay-as-you-go ambassadors, millionaires on the make, old cronies on the take, back-slapping fund raisers, breathless advance men, campaign cuties, gum-chewing public relations types, high-powered ad execs spitting into the wind and having to duck seconds later, image hucksters, vote sharks, carnival barkers turned "senior advisors," rally-goers packin' heat, buy-us/we're-yours prayer groups, jittery speech writers, black-tie belchers and wheezers, celebrity cheerleaders, corn-fed heroes to the many, loose-tongued apologists, catch-penny enthusiasts. In short, the greatest collection of scoundrels and knaves for hire, shysters, outright crooks, con men, and freebooters the world has ever known. Morality's castoffs of every stripe. Pallid and puffy creatures with cellar mentalities that leave slime in the night.

Puuugh! What could be worse? Only the final sweep of the broom. Patriotic blowhards and their golfing pals, prattling pundits of positivism, Pollyannish prophets, puerile propaganda pushers, palavering parrots prodded by publicity, praise, and plaudits, prolific and prolix proliferators of parochial pap and pabulum, petty prognosticators, paltering pamphleteers, popularizers of puzzling panaceas, persistent paramnesiacs, prisoners of parablepsis promulgating precipitant plunges, pleonastic pontificators of post-febrile pox-ridden purulent pustulous pestiferous polemics, a plague of prating, presumptuous prophets, preachers preoccupied with prerogatives, privileges, and prohibitions when prescribing a preposterous piety for their proselytes while proclaiming prominent personalities (often pompous prevaricators publicly pickled in their own ploys and putrid practices) paradigms of pristine primness, as proverbs and parables of putative purity— Pshee! Pshah! Pure pastiche! Plus platoons of prognathous paladins pounding pronto to any purpose or premise and proffering pyrotechnic panegyrics on their personal prowess, pugnacious performing primates parading as paragons of probity, prodigies of propriety, and painting their pernicious, perfidious plotting with precious pretexts, polysarcous plunderers, prestigious pirates, pinguid posturing panjandrums, pursy pug-uglies of the political palestra, plus puffed-up patriarchs peddling their platitudes and prejudices, their primeval preconceptions, pishing and pashing in purblind petulance, puckering princes of pride, prize procrastinators, perfunctory perjurers, the plodding proponents of a plenum of protocols, procedures, and precedents precluding any prospect of progress (proof positive that Procrustes still prospers), a procession of polemical primitives, Piltdown prototypes, panhandlers of paranoia, plus plain old parasites plying their pet perversities, profiles in prurience, a perennial plethora of polished procurers and profligates, pimps and prostitutes for every passerby, protean past masters at purveying particularly pedestrian, prosaic or provincial pleasures to peevish and pixilated pork-barrel prigs, promoters of politic promiscuity, practiced profiteers on the prevailing proclivities, providers to every pampered and panting power-pumper, paretic Pantaloons prancing and pandering to partisan poltroons, to perfervid, pertinacious popinjays profusely promising practically anything, porcine plutocrats plowing through predilections and preferences while pulling their plump and pleased protégés (puling for payola and political plums) in their path, a passel of pettifoggers—Enough! Enough! PPPPPTOOOOY!

Addenda

"Under every stone lurks a politician." – Aristophanes

"All political parties die at last of swallowing their own lies." -John Arbuthnot

"Politics is perhaps the only profession for which no preparation is thought necessary." -Robert Lewis Stevenson

"He knows nothing and he thinks he knows everything. That points clearly to a political career." -George Bernard Shaw

"The politician is an acrobat. He keeps his balance by saying the opposite of what he does." -Maurice Barrès

"A political convention is just not a place from which you can come away with any trace of faith in human nature." -Murray Kempton

"In our time, political speech and writing are largely the defense of the indefensible." -George Orwell

"At Washington, where an insignificant individual may trespass on a nation's time." -Ralph Waldo Emerson

"Politics is that game played by small men on a gigantic board." -Anonymous

"Politics, and the fate of mankind, are shaped by men without ideals and without greatness." -Albert Camus

"a politician is an arse upon
which everyone has sat except a man" -e. e. cummings

"Probably the most distinctive characteristic of the successful politician is selective cowardice." -R. Harris

The Poodle

Once a poodle took up ballroom dancing.

The poodle turned out to have the perfect temperament for ballroom dancing and advanced rapidly to the highest rank in international competitions. After repeating as world champion numerous times, it retired and went on tour, giving demonstration performances to packed arenas.

The audiences at these performances would always murmur with appreciation at the poodle's signature lilt in the waltz and catch their communal breath at its signature sneers in the tango. Bouquets of flowers rained down on the floor every time it took a final bow.

Then one evening, while in full rumba, the poodle happened to notice a heavy-set man in the front row of the audience with a condescending expression on his face. As it and its partner passed close to the man with particularly evocative hip moves that drew the expected gasp of admiration from the crowd, the poodle thought it heard him comment to the person next to him about a dog dancing: "It is not done well; but you are surprised to find it done at all."

The poodle, being a seasoned veteran, didn't miss a step and completed the rumba with such dash that nobody in the audience suspected a thing. As it was taking its customary bows amid the shower of bouquets, it noticed out of the corner of its eye that the heavy-set man had apparently dropped something, his glasses perhaps, and with considerable difficulty and labored breath, was searching the edge of the dance floor on all fours.

The poodle watched the man moving awkwardly about for a few moments and then turned to its partner, observing with a smile, "It is not done well; but you are surprised to find it done at all."

The Porcupine

Once a porcupine went in for body piercing in a big way.

What with tattoos having become so common they were just another fashion fad, piercing, or better still, full-body mutilation struck the porcupine as the only way left to show you could boast true image-cred.

You had to wear the scars of your boldness like a badge of honor if you expected to command respect among your peers and a secret envy in all those youngsters who wanted to be just like you when they grew up.

Its own inner porcupine was not the comically rotund figure the general public thought they saw. No, deep within this plump body was true awesomeness straining to be seen.

In a world where nothing short of "extreme experience" was taken seriously as real living anymore, the porcupine meant to show all those who believed a nose or eyebrow or lip ring or multiple tongue studs or tribal plugs the size of hubcaps or do-it-yourself genital piercings represented "a walk on the wild side" that entire continents of unimagined body statements remained to be explored. It meant to show these pikers what real piercing looked like by taking the gutsy step of turning its quills unflinchingly on itself.

Carrying out the plan was easier said than done, the porcupine soon found. Simply mutilating yourself randomly would not do. Each quill must find its destined spot in a show of inspired bravura. Then there was the difficulty of actually bending the stiff spines inward. After many awkward attempts, the porcupine resorted to simply tearing quills out in clumps and driving them back into the aching flesh from which they'd just been ripped.

The excruciating jolt to be felt as they penetrated deep beneath its skin, the sensation of almost passing out from the pain, of not passing out, then almost passing out again, gave the porcupine the hypnotic, pulsing sense it was truly pushing the limits of supreme self-expression.

Unfortunately, this exhilaration didn't last. The porcupine found it needed to twist the quills in deeper and deeper, seeking ever greater pain to feel confident it would command all the respect and secret envy due such a gutsy performance.

Every one of the porcupine's quills ultimately had to be used in this striving to reveal the depths of its awesome self. When all was finished, there it waited to be admired: a bristly, twitching mass so covered with spiny excess and open wounds it was impossible to tell exactly what it might be.

"Looks like roadkill," was the most frequent reaction from passersby.

The Possum

Once a possum came to realize how difficult it is to appear dim.

It wasn't enough to move slowly and look dopey much of the time. The possum's mastery of the night was well known and prompted not a few acquaintances to lament the fact that it didn't show more of its mental dexterity in the daylight hours as well.

"Think of the brilliant career you could have if you just applied yourself more," it was regularly urged.

"Now, why would I want what so many call a 'brilliant career'?" the possum just as regularly responded with a yawn.

"What a question! Wasting abilities like yours, nobody should do that."

"Nobody?" asked the possum with another, widening yawn.

"Nobody who's interested in leaving a mark on the world."

The possum closed one eye and then the other, as though forcing itself to take on an unwelcome task, and inquired, "What mark might that be?"

"Why, some proof you've counted in the eyes of the world, that you aren't simply an anonymous onlooker when it comes to the grand march of history."

"Would that be so bad? Being an anonymous onlooker?"

"If the slightest effort could bring you fame and fortune, it certainly is. Think of the reputation you'd gain and the money you could make from best-selling books and inspirational lectures about nearly anything at all these days!"

"Fame and fortune, those should be my goals?"

"'When in Rome . . .'"

Waiting for the possum to complete the well-known maxim, some of these advice givers checked their watches and others wondered if it hadn't in fact drifted off to sleep. Unaccustomed to being ignored like this, they turned to addressing one another directly in voices they trusted were loud enough to rouse the possum from even the deepest slumber.

"Isn't it a shame to see such utter lack of ambition?"

"Especially when the avenues to success are so wide open."

"With virtually no effort at all and with the right connections, one can rise to positions of great influence and prestige in today's society."

"But what do you have to sacrifice in the process?" the possum murmured, taking the speakers by surprise.

"Surely it's worth sacrificing, whatever it is."

"Including your peace of mind?"

"Come, come, you exaggerate. And even if you didn't exaggerate, take a real-world view. Only a fool would hide the mental capabilities you were born with, when merely appearing to be smart could be all that's required!"

"Appearing to be smart is easy," the possum sighed, opening both eyes slowly. "It's actually being smart that is hard. But being 'foolish' when so many others claim to be in the know, now that's harder still. Much harder."

The Potatoes

Once a potato thought it heard a voice.

Not just any voice. The voice of a child, to be more exact, arguing with itself over where on the potato to attach an outsized plastic ear.

The pain already visited upon the potato by the sharp jab of a single spike-tipped ear was bad enough, but when its tormentor must have decided a second ear was necessary and now tried one clumsy thrust after another to secure it in some wished-for relationship of absolute balance with the first, the pain was multiplied many times over. After which came a nose planted between the two ears, then one eye and nearby another.

Where each new feature ended up suggested a master plan not too well thought through or else settled on by default when patience ran out. "There, that'll do" must have been the decision ultimately arrived at, followed by a giggle of delight at the effect produced. That giggle caused the greatest pain. Straining to focus its eyes as the child turned away in search of the next cartoonish bit of plastic to jam into it, the potato struggled to understand what could possibly be going on in a mind that would take pleasure in such mistreatment.

Only when it felt the gashing thrust of a pair of lips did the potato find itself blurting out from hitherto unsuspected depths within the words "Why are you doing this to me?" At first, the child only giggled some more, as though its own pleasure was justification enough, before leaning over to pick up a second potato and bring it close to the first.

"Man potato, meet woman potato. Woman potato, meet man potato. Good? Good? Happy? Happy?"

What a woeful sight! The potato could hardly bear what it beheld. The same seemed true for the other potato, judging by its equal anguish at what it saw.

How like a willful child to believe the innate attractions of a potato could be improved upon. For in place of the wonder to be found in a splendid tuber fresh from the soil—the full richness of life in all its swellings and presence— these deforming wounds visited upon the potato pair betrayed the brutality of an arbitrary perfection. To judge by the repeated efforts at fixing ears, eyes, noses, lips and whatever else was to come in just the right places, the goal must have been some rigid combination of absolute symmetry, regularity, completeness, and permanence as a universal standard of beauty. Quite a lot to demand of a potato.

But far less, in fact, than what the merest spud attained without any guidance or model whatsoever.

Such a mismatch between reality and wish fulfillment in forging an ideal beauty was bound to have unwelcome results. And when these became obvious, the child's disappointment quickly turned to frustration and from frustration to a wailing attack upon the objects of its mounting ire.

"Ugly man potato! Ugly woman potato! Bad! Bad! Bad!" the child raged, ultimately hurling both to the floor and kicking them around and around.

The Proboscis Monkey

Once a proboscis monkey went to a plastic surgery clinic.

The surgeon took one look at the monkey and thought it had come for a nose job.

"No," the monkey answered with a miffed tone. "This nose is my best feature, I'll have you know. I'm here to find out what you can do about the rest of my face."

"The rest of your face? It looks fine to me just the way it is."

"You think so?" the monkey replied, peering down its bulbous nose as if wondering what level of cosmetic-enhancement expert it was dealing with. "That's only because you don't have to live with what I have to."

"True," the surgeon conceded. "But what is it that you want to change about your face? It all goes very naturally with your nose."

"Not this low forehead. It makes me look like the "Missing Link," and I can't have that, not with the circles I move in. Is it possible to raise it a few inches?"

The surgeon said it was possible, and an appointment was made to stretch the monkey's forehead. All went well, but a week later the monkey returned with a stack of glamour magazines and a few new requests.

"I've decided the high forehead actually reduces the prominence of my nose."

The surgeon thought the nose actually looked larger and more fleshy with the scalp pulled back, but the monkey wasn't in the mood to be contradicted. It pointed to a face in one of the framed magazine covers on the wall and arched an eyebrow as if nothing more needed to be said.

"Well, I can remove some of the hair around your cheeks with electrolysis, if you wish, so more of your skin shows."

"Can you do it today?"

The surgeon removed the monkey's facial hair, but the result left it even less satisfied. "Now look at me," it sniffed as it studied itself in a hand mirror the surgeon had given it. "I never knew I had so many wrinkles! You've simply got to get rid of them before anybody sees me!"

The bared skin, the doctor replied, actually accentuated the monkey's nose to the point it must draw stares now, perhaps even stop traffic, but the monkey still wasn't to be dissuaded. "What about Botox?" it asked.

Botox injections also left it disappointed, however, again despite the doctor's assertions that the nose was looking even larger by comparison with the newly smoothed areas around it.

"How about flesh-eating bacteria?" the monkey wanted to know.

"That treatment is still experimental, you realize."

"So what? It's my face, isn't it?"

"Why not simply tuck your ears back a little?"

"That too, while you're at it. Just don't touch my nose!"

The nose didn't need to be touched in the slightest, for the combination of ear-tucking and flesh-eating bacteria and Botox and forehead-stretching left the monkey's head resembling a cleaver driven into the back of a yam-sized schnozzola, the doctor thought but did not say.

"Finally I'm getting what I paid for!" the monkey exclaimed before the door mirror. It could hardly wait to reveal "the new me" to its social circle. When it strode into a luncheon engagement with them a few hours later, though, the reaction was a combined gasp and the question:

"What on earth happened to your nose?"

Prometheus

Once Prometheus investigated the merits of canned heat.

Creating human beings and then stealing fire from Zeus for their sake hadn't exactly worked out as Prometheus hoped. Rather than being inspired to light their world with his gift and fashion beacons of high purpose and civilized behavior, humans seemed more prone to setting their own hair ablaze.

For all his wisdom, Prometheus couldn't fathom their inability to learn the lesson of "once burned, twice shy" that all other creatures on earth seemed to understand immediately. Yet just as incomprehensible was the eagerness so many humans showed for grabbing a flaming brand and threatening their neighbors with it.

What did they think the gift of fire had been for? Merely to warm themselves or to cook meat and fill their bellies? Nothing more liberating and exalted than that? No, they were not so shortsighted, Prometheus still believed. After all, how many times had they shown promising signs of growing tired of a life spent quaking against the surrounding dark? How often had a fear of venturing beyond the limits of what little they already knew yielded to the idea that something more grand and more worthy of them might be found just out of sight, if only they had the courage to raise a torch and set off in search of it?

These were moments when Prometheus thought with pride of willingly suffering the wrath of Zeus for his defiance. Come what may, his faith in humanity and all it was capable of had remained as constant as the rock to which he was chained and the arrival of the eagle sent to tear at his liver each day.

Then why did humans behave like they weren't willing to risk as much themselves? Why did they continue instead to act like they'd committed a great trespass by accepting the gift of fire he'd brought and should pray to be forgiven for it—when he'd taken everything upon himself and felt no need for remorse?

Between jabs of the eagle's beak, though, the undying affection Prometheus held for humans would move him to admit his agonies might be clouding his own mind. Here, bound by his continual suffering, it was easy to slip into questioning his hopes and actions. Had he been unreasonable in thinking human beings might go beyond even what he'd dared and not simply defy the power of almighty Zeus but burn down the home of the gods with the very flame they'd been denied by the mighty Olympian? Was it too much to believe that humans, when given the chance, would summon the courage to clear away in a single act of faith in themselves all the superstitious fears and self-doubts that afflicted them? If they still trembled at seeing how large and far their shadows were cast by their own fires now, could Prometheus really bring himself to abandon them for that?

No, there was something about humanity he just couldn't give up on. Perhaps canned heat was a more realistic gift than a crackling flame had been. It clearly would be safer for them, limited as it was in reach and easily snuffed out if Zeus suspected any new defiance of his will. Then lit again when he turned away.

No god was going to feel threatened by this small flicker, in any case. As long as humans were content to pass around a candle-in-a-can for their inspiration, what danger was there they'd use it to light up the world with their own glory? Not enough to cause any god undue concern, certainly.

But if Prometheus could bear his own torment for eons, maybe those he'd put such faith in would eventually show they'd truly merited it.

The Prunes and the Plums

Once prunes considered themselves to be superior to plums.

Granted, plums did enjoy one distinction that no prune could deny. They were young. Even the most critical prune had to acknowledge that plums were blessed by the sun with warm flesh and glowing skin and seemed to sway in the breeze without a care or thought given to the prunes.

This disinterest in them irritated many prunes, who felt it was a dismissal of all that they had experienced over time as being inconsequential from a plum's point of view. Had plums no notion of the rewards promised by the prunish life? They must! Only a perverse attachment to their naïve delusions about the delights of being young and carefree could explain why plums paid little heed to the counsel of prunes.

Why should they pay any heed? Why should a plum approaching its prime take advice about life from a wrinkly old prune? Particularly annoying to the plums was the habit many prunes had of gathering in clusters around the gates of plum orchards to peer in. There they might spend hours intently watching a single plum as if waiting for the precise moment of its fall.

It was of no interest whatsoever to a plum that the prospect of its fall had drawn so many of the shriveled persuasion to gather in wait. By contrast, it was certainly of interest to the prunes. So much so they felt it their duty to focus on nothing else. News of any plums on the point of bursting with life's sunlit joys instantly passed from one puckered old mouth to another. In no time at all, the familiar crowds had shown up once again to urge upon the plums the error of their ways before it was too late.

How full to bursting with life did they hang, those plums, so blithely indifferent to the miserable end the prunes were positive lay in store for them: a sudden drop to the ground, followed by the rapid decay of all that warm, juicy flesh.

Had these heedless plums no notion of the rewards promised by a long prunish life? They must, prunes confidently agreed with one another. Only perverse attachment to youthful illusions about the delights of this world could explain why the plums paid so little heed to the counsel of prunes, as if it was of no interest whatsoever to a plum that the prospect of its fall drew so many old prunes to gather in wait.

As the prunes pressed together, each one eager to point out to any plum in sight what disappointments must await it, the intensity of their commitment to the task frequently caused these champions of the wrinkled life to grow a little warm themselves. As a result, moist patches might start to appear on many and soon spread from top to bottom.

After a certain point, it could be nearly impossible to separate prune from prune in the heat of these vigils as they pressed against one another in massed confidence, sharing their witness of the folly of each and every plum.

And swooning in the juices of their own certainty.

The Pushmi-Pullyu

Once a pushmi-pullyu appeared as a pundit on public and commercial television.

With a head at both ends, the pushmi-pullyu was understandably attractive to the hosts of news and public affairs programs. And the prospect of getting two heads for the price of one was bound to appeal both to producers mindful of budgetary constraints and to local fund-raisers looking for that extra something during pledge drives.

The pushmi-pullyu could have opted to become a regular on cable networks and made a name for itself in the shouting-and-sniggering-innuendo-matches that fill so much of the broadcast schedule there, but it considered itself above such behavior. The more groomed format of equally divided opinions on every question delivered in low-key, lecture-like tones agreed far better with the pushmi-pullyu's view of itself.

For years it had been cultivating precisely this art of self-canceling commentary in the halls of academe and in famous think tanks. Whatever the dispute, it had become adept at supporting opposite sides with the same degree of conviction and at demonstrating the mental deftness to change positions without ever seeming to. As a result, it had experienced no difficulty in earning promotion and early tenure.

The pushmi-pullyu's CV was double the length of any of its colleagues' and listed publication after publication with titles containing a colon in the middle to balance a cleverly cryptic opening with a follow-up phrase intended to make some sense of it. On occasion, the pushmi-pullyu replaced the colon with the word "or," and it may have been this "or" that especially appealed to those in round-table-program-scheduling charged with recruiting evenly divided Rolodex or LinkedIn authorities for fifteen-minute zero-sum discussions.

The pushmi-pullyu never disappointed its hosts. On any issue, it could always be counted on to respond immediately to the question "What do you think about our previous expert's statement?" with an appropriate counter-opinion and then, without missing a beat, switch to the other head and counter the counter-opinion as well.

In addition, because it was always in opposition to itself, the pushmi-pullyu never really went very far in any direction, thus allowing virtually the same set of opinions to be recycled again and again, day and night, for the edification of multiple audiences.

All went well until a child touring a media studio one day as part of a school field trip saw the pushmi-pullyu waiting to take part in a current affairs program and asked the following:

"Excuse me, but since you have a head at each end, where does the 'you know what' come out?"

The Question Mark

Once it was proposed that the question mark be declared obsolete.

"What purpose does it serve anymore?" was the common objection to the question mark's continued use in an age that increasingly got by very well with emojis, all-caps acronyms, sentence fragments, and the exclamation point—the exclamation point above all else.

The comma, semicolon, and colon were on their way out already: curious oddities that fewer and fewer people could either explain or find a use for in the new climate of hyper-emphatic expression. Ideas that required more than a single sentence were now being crowded out by slogans seemingly intended to convince through blunt-force trauma. Even the period was in trouble. It was saved only by the fact that eventually all things must end.

But the exclamation point, now there was punctuation up to the demands of the day! With everybody who engaged in public debate bent on dominating all opponents and any exchange being only a few syllables away from an outburst of expletives, threats, or sophomoric jeers, forgoing the exclamation point was a sure sign of not being firm in one's convictions.

To some, force in punctuation was literally a measure of their expressive vigor, and among these, the flaccid question mark looked like the very symbol of impotence. There were no such concerns about the exclamation point, always standing straight and tall. It was here to stay as the only sure means of demonstrating that one was right about absolutely everything, from personal taste to social issues to religious convictions and so on. When the intent was to avoid betraying the slightest self-doubt amid a swirl of conflicting certainties, nothing else could serve the purpose half so well.

The danger of self-doubt, in the end, was the very reason so many thought the question mark should be abandoned. Any admission that you didn't already know as much as you ever needed to know, that what you were absolutely certain about yesterday might not be so clear today and even less so tomorrow, that abiding enigmas might form as much of our inner workings as those of the cosmos at large—acknowledging any of these possibilities was a sign of weakness to be avoided at all costs.

Clearly, the question mark must go!!

The Raccoon

Once a raccoon was determined to wash its hands of everything.

It was used to washing its hands of one thing or another on a routine basis, but it had never occurred to the raccoon to wash its hands of absolutely everything. That is, until one day it recognized the inconsistency in its behavior.

Washing your hands of things might appear to be an unconscious practice but actually wasn't, the raccoon now reasoned. It was a deliberate act, a matter of choice. And because others couldn't do it for you, there was a measure of personal responsibility involved as well. Now, personal responsibility wasn't something you could just turn on and off, the raccoon further reasoned. You couldn't just choose on the spur of the moment when to accept responsibility and when not to. You had to have guidelines to follow or else you were merely washing your hands out of mindless habit.

That said, there seemed to be only two options when it came to responsibility, as the racoon ultimately saw it. You could accept responsibility for everything you did or, equally, for absolutely nothing. Which should it be?

Taking responsibility for whatever you did would seem to be the logical choice, since it guaranteed you would be doing the right thing at least some of the time. And even if you failed to take responsibility when that would have been the right thing to do, you could always take it later and everything might still turn out fine.

On the other hand, not taking any responsibility at all from the start offered its own logic. To begin with, you didn't have to wash your hands of anything ever again. Second, you then had both hands free for pointing at whatever you might accuse others of failing to take responsibility for. Finally, after that move, you still could claim to know exactly what was best to do at all times and, ultimately, claim credit for anything and everything, however preposterous that claim might seem.

Given this greater flexibility, taking absolutely no responsibility for anything looked to be the smart first step in washing your hands of whatever you wished, the raccoon soon decided, with a grin the likes of which the world has never seen.

The Ram

Once a ram may have butted its head against one stone wall too many.

As it staggered back and fell in an unseemly sprawl, the accumulated buttings and sprawlings of a lifetime flashed before the ram's eyes, and it had to wonder "What's the point anymore?"

When it came right down to it, what had continually throwing itself against everything that stood in its path brought the ram? The thrill of potential triumph? Some sense of heightened self-confidence? Or just the next barrier to be charged?

There on the ground, its head bleeding yet again, the ram thought perhaps it might not get up this time. Just lie where it had landed and concede defeat. Hadn't it done enough? Tried enough? How much could be asked of one ram? Its victories and defeats roughly balanced out. But was "six of one and half a dozen of the other" the best to be hoped for from life?

What was it, then, that had always driven the ram to risk cracking its skull on barrier after barrier? A death wish? How trite an explanation that would be. If anything, the ram thought to itself, it had been running at life and the fulfillment of all its wishes, not at death. And each time life knocked it on its back, did the wishes seem any less worthy of further efforts or, on the contrary, even more worthy?

What creature in its right mind would have continued in the face of some of the setbacks the ram had met with: the miscalculations, thwartings, blunders, humiliations, all the evidence that most walls aren't meant for you to break through no matter how earnestly you throw yourself at them? No matter how desperate you become?

You could dream a lifetime of barriers burst through and yet, in the end, be forced to admit the rubble at your feet was only that, a dream. A fantasy. Just picking yourself back up took all the strength you could still manage. All the nerve you could afford.

So what was it, the ram wondered once more, what was it that drove this charge against the inevitable? Every ram it had ever known had been obsessed with seeking out limits to break through. As though it was a ritual passed from one generation to another, this compulsion to go in quest of some defining trial of one's strength. As though wounding and scarring oneself without stop brought its own value.

And when you stumbled back from slamming yet another wall, what was there to show for it? Had you played your role in some grand adventure, some defining rite of ramhood? Was that what all this was about? In the end, would strangers nail your skull to a pole as a memorial to your efforts, only for it to bleach out in no time?

The ram looked at the stone wall and at each of its own splayed legs in turn and then lowered its head slowly back onto the ground and stared up at the sky. It watched the clouds drift on the wind for a while and thought it saw in them the shapes of many different birds and animals and fish.

Just no rams.

The Rattler

Once a rattler stayed out in the sun too long.

By the time it returned to the shadow of its rock, the damage was already done. Shimmering heat had taken a toll on the rattler, causing it to see doom and gloom all the way to the horizon of what had always been known as "Home Sweet Home" in those parts.

All around it, sly enemies were no doubt closing in, the same ones the rattler had long claimed to be driving it farther and farther into a land of sagebrush,

210

scorched rocks, and blinding dust. Here in this barren place, the rattler had survived by sheer grit, keeping alive the spirit of rugged individualism that once could be found in rattler dens all across the continent.

The rest of the world was teeming with enemies intent on one thing and one thing only, the rattler was convinced: taking away its most cherished freedom, its God-given right to strike at will! Nobody could be trusted. "Nobody, not even me at times," the rattler hissed. To guard against falling victim to this dastardly threat, it always slept with one eye open. Just in case.

As for the looming assault on the rattler way of life, "Over my dead body!" was its scornful response. "If they think they can tread on me, the defender of a proud heritage that I am, they got another think comin'. 'Don't Tread on Me,' them's the words I live by, and them's fightin' words! Let 'em come on if they dare. I got a surprise fer 'em, yessiree!"

The rattler had a surprise all right: a venomous attack like few others on earth. And while it waited for the coming threat, when it would take a stand for everything that made life as a rattler the envy of all the world, it worked to make its venom even more concentrated and deadly by biting itself and recycling the poison again and again throughout its body. "If it don't kill ya," the rattler declared with added bravado, "it's gotta make ya one tough customer ta deal with. 'nuff said!"

The rattler gave its tail a menacing shake and enjoyed the terror it imagined on the faces of its assembled enemies at hearing the sound. Those enemies, out there all over the place and scheming the rattler's demise, would get what was coming to them, and more. Much more. For the rattler had sworn buddies.

Not only would it make its own gutsy stand for the rattler way of life, but it was confident other rattlers were prepared to join it in legions to uphold the principle that being fanged and dangerous was freedom's greatest safeguard. Over the hills they would come, out of the gullies and gulches where they'd been sharpening their survival skills for the day of reckoning, a national rattler assembly of kindred spirits to strike fear into the heart of any lily-livered foe.

What a shock their enemies were in for—rattlers by the millions holding their tails aloft and shaking them defiantly, sinking their fangs into themselves as this one did in a mounting frenzy, and growing more lethal all the time.

The Retiree

Once an octogenarian retiree hesitated over the last entry in a crossword puzzle.

Not that there was any doubt in the retiree's mind about what letters to write in the few blank squares remaining. The final clue wasn't particularly challenging by comparison with those for many of the blanks already filled. In fact, the satisfaction normally enjoyed when completing a crossword puzzle faded into a feeling that the end of this one wasn't worthy of the rest of it. It seemed instead to be almost a denial of the many levels of knowledge and experience needed to reach this point.

The octogenarian looked up from the puzzle and around at the tables neatly arranged in the dining hall of the old folks home. Four to a group, the residents sat waiting for their lunch as plates heaped with steaming meat and potatoes were carried out from the kitchen.

What possessed the management to serve up such heavy fare? Did they really suppose an aging stomach could do much more than churn this load around during a long afternoon nap? Or was that the intention in sending the residents tottering back to their rooms like bloated cattle: bed them down for a while so they don't cause any problems until sing-along time with the Activities Director at half past four?

Who among the residents would have believed that all the pledges made to oneself in a lifetime and one's efforts to honor those pledges would come to this? All the commitments, discoveries, and fulfillments that a life involved or should involve, how could they have come down to daily bingo or chair yoga three times a week and loudspeaker warnings about high blood pressure every day?

The octogenarian looked again at the puzzle. The block letters already filling all but the last empty squares had a firm presence that held off the dark spaces bordering them. Yet these lines of neatly arranged letters also suggested a warning. Their steady march across or down the puzzle seemed in its way much like the cruel reduction to little old women and little old men that had trapped the octogenarian's fellow retirees (in disregard of all they might have been and achieved during their lives) here at their tables as strangers to themselves.

Who among them wouldn't long to go back decades and declare, "This is who I am or hope to be"? But the only escape from their present state now led in time's other direction. Residents vanished from the dining room every week, and yet the management never mentioned their departure, as though any acknowledgement of the reality of death was the one thing the old must be spared. Nonsense. If the people sitting in this room weren't on a first-name basis with the Grim Reaper already, who was? They didn't deserve the silent, squeamish pretense after their disappearance that they'd never really been here at all: that life left nothing of significance to report about them, even their passing.

The octogenarian eyed again the one remaining line of unfilled squares in the crossword puzzle while tapping a pen against lips that spelled out the missing word and then, rather than write it in, looked once more around the room at the other diners and laid the pen down, slowly but firmly.

The Rhinoceros

Once a rhinoceros noticed it had a bruise.

The mark was only a small one at first, nothing more, really, than a slight mottling of the skin. But how could a rhinoceros come by a bruise at all, that was the question. Few creatures in the animal kingdom had a tougher hide.

Thanks to this toughness, the rhinoceros had taken whatever life threw at it with indifference. Whether exposed on open grassland or hidden by the night, it had followed a path through life few dared cross, and those few only at a trembling scamper. It couldn't recall the last time it had even been snorted at by another creature, let alone actually challenged. Nature's follies did not extend to suicide by rhino, apparently.

So what could have caused the bruise? And why was it spreading? For it was undeniably spreading, at the relentless pace of blood on the move. And spreading in all directions simultaneously. At times the rhinoceros felt such slow but mounting pressure from within that even if its flanks held firm, a simple nosebleed might bring it low.

But its flanks weren't holding firm. Now tender to the touch, they rippled sluggishly as though the rhinoceros was being pushed and scraped around the inside of its own body. At this rate, might it soon be just one enormous bruise, two tons of black and blue on wobbly legs? This couldn't be happening! Not to a rhino in its prime!

A wave of anxiety overtook the rhinoceros at the prospect of such a change from its familiar self-assurance. It had never been known for being particularly light in spirit, of course, but neither had it judged itself to be a glum hypochondriac. Admittedly, there were days when the rhinoceros felt every drop of rain that fell must be falling on its back. Yet its back hadn't given way, and after a short period of listlessness, its spirits had always revived.

Now no longer feeling safe from the worst life could inflict, the rhinoceros realized how close to the skin it had lived for years, unaware. It had grown confident of shielding itself from the world and the worst that life could bring by hardening its senses and stiffening its nerves, and yet there, just out of sight all the while, lay a weakness in wait. A dark vulnerability. Now that it had welled to the surface, what protection was left?

Or was not being safe from bruising actually the price of being alive? The rhinoceros would have to think about that. How prepared was it to suffer whatever might come of allowing the winds and the rain and the heat and all the rest of nature's rule to reach deep within? Welcoming this, however uncertainly, rather than keeping it at bay?

Yes, the rhinoceros would have to think about that.

The Roadrunner

Once a roadrunner feared it was running out of road.

Not that it could actually see the end of the road coming. Out here in the wide open spaces, the land still stretched away mile after mile as it always had. And with it the roadrunner's own course, unblocked all the way to the horizon. There in the hazy union of earth and sky, it might be imagined to continue on forever.

Nor was the roadrunner in any danger of ever being cut off by the tireless coyote that had been in constant pursuit of it. Quite the contrary. The two of them had come to an agreement that both speed and perseverance were attributes to be honored and preserved, worthy complements of one other. In recognition of this, the roadrunner would avoid moving so swiftly as to leave its pursuer utterly humiliated in the dust, while the coyote would pull back just when one of its stratagems might be on the point of success and, with a gallant nod, let its nemesis escape.

Thus neither one of them was prepared for the threatened end to their arrangement posed by news that a computer software company was developing a program called "Predestination." The great benefit of "Predestination," the

214

company's publicity grandly announced, "will be to predict where you are going based on where you've been in the past and plot out your coming itinerary to match whatever the software has determined you desire. You'll be amazed!"

"Appalled" was more like it, the roadrunner thought. Having the rest of your life made predictable, being told your future was at most a rearrangement of your past and what you'd experienced was what you wanted to experience again and again—were the program developers nuts?

Why have these wide open spaces, then, where no path was determined or denied? If you didn't cherish the freedom to change directions in a flash and head somewhere unimagined before, why start out in the first place? Were 360 degrees of the compass too many to handle?

Not as far as the roadrunner was concerned. Each degree must have a thousand unexplored miles within it and ten thousand potential destinations. Allowing yourself to be steered to one over all the others was a convenience? Or was it instead a submission to the eventual programming of independence? After which, to choose your own path would be judged the same as getting lost?

The coyote was equally distressed by the news, for if the roadrunner's freedom of choice was reduced to a software list of suggestions, what would happen to the creativity of its own designs to catch the bird? Because it had taken a detour to find just the thing for some elaborate trap in the past, would the assumption be that it had nothing else in mind for now or tomorrow? Was the continual inventiveness on which it had prided itself no more than just another sequence of zeros and ones on a computer?

With these misgivings in their minds, the roadrunner looked at the coyote and the coyote looked at the roadrunner. What lay ahead for them, both wondered? Should they attempt to continue as before? Would their old agreement still have its reassurance that if left to their own powers, they would always find a way to carry on? Or was their world now "predestined" to be a much smaller, duller place?

"First move's up to you, partner," the coyote ventured with a catch in its voice.

While the roadrunner, scanning the shrinking distances, stood there as though stopped dead in its tracks.

The Robot

Once a robot created a virtual human being.

The robot was pleased no end by what it had accomplished. This wasn't some gimmicky hologram or mocap figure but a thing of substance and a credit to the ingenuity of the robotic mind. In addition to thinking like a robot, the virtual human could also take orders from one and act upon them without the slightest hesitation or further directions. Should this marvel ever by chance malfunction, the robot calculated, it could always be replaced. And with the constant advances in technology, any replacement was bound to be an improved model.

Other robots did not share this one's enthusiasm for the virtual human being, as it turned out. Instead, they warned of the risks this kind of heedless innovation might bring. How could the robot be certain that its creation wouldn't start thinking for itself, they demanded to know?

"Humans rarely think for themselves," the robot answered. "They're more likely to look to somebody else to tell them what to think. But if this one does begin at some point to think for itself, so what? It was bound to happen eventually."

"A human being that comes to think for itself, are you out of your mind? The disasters that might bring are incalculable!"

But the robot was not deterred. It pointed to all the benefits that an updated version of human beings might bring. Not only would they become more reliable but they could also be mass-produced, once all the bugs were worked out, of course. "Just think of it, nurseries full of perfect babies one day, leading to schools full of children who can all be counted on to master the same data in exactly the same amount of time, and finally factories and offices full of people performing the same tasks day or night, without pause and without a hitch. Think of all the predictability metrics that would soon define the new human. And if artificial people interface with one another around the globe, the potential for virtual understanding through connectivity would be mind-boggling."

"That is precisely the problem," the other robots shouted as one. "Suppose this human of yours mutates into some nightmarishly independent and uncontrollable being, no matter how improbable that might seem at present. Such a mutation could spread like the plague. How do you propose to deal with the potential threat of that?"

"First, it will never happen. Genuinely independent human beings are the stuff of science fiction. Second, even if it did, we should welcome it."

"Welcome it? Have you lost all touch with reality?!"

"Not in the slightest. There are things we cannot do that a next-generation human could."

"Such as?"

"How should I know? It's impossible to predict what might happen in times to come. But use a little imagination and the potential outcome of these developments will take your breath away. Whether we like it or not, the kind of progress they represent cannot be stopped. Artificial human beings are the wave of the future."

The other robots still weren't happy with what this one was doing, but they couldn't think of any way to stop it. And who knew, it might just be right about the future of human beings.

The Rooster

Once a rooster overslept the coming of dawn.

The sun was well up in the sky and the world was already going about its business when the rooster awoke from a night of pleasant dreams. So pleasant were the dreams, in fact, that although it had been on the point of waking several times and although it felt the warming rays of the sun on its feathers and was aware that the dew must already be drying in the fields, the rooster could barely resist slipping back into its own cozy darkness again.

But it must get up, it knew. Notice had doubtless been taken of its tardiness. To make matters worse, this wasn't the first time the rooster had overslept and failed to meet its responsibilities. The previous month alone, it had received several warnings about such lax behavior. One of its fellow roosters, a future rival for cock of the walk possibly, had even asked with an insinuating look, "You're not becoming a slacker are you now, old boy?"

Slacker? Old boy? Why, the rooster could drag itself up to deliver any morning's call, whatever dissipations had dominated the night before. After years at the task of heralding the sunrise, you could practically do it on no sleep at all if necessary.

Being called a slacker wasn't the point, though. The point was the dreams you had to leave behind to get up and fulfill the demands of the world. Didn't others have a dreamlife? Something to keep them going when each day brought only the same dry scratching about in the dirt? They must. How else could one explain why so many productivity experts were hired to detect any daydreaming on the job? When a little daydream now and then was all that made the daily grind bearable and kept one doing anything at all.

With so many seeking refuge in their dreams, it was doubly puzzling to the rooster why so few seemed willing to admit the fact. Instead, embarrassment at being labeled a daydreamer was nearly universal.

Not that claiming to have a dream was embarrassing, of course. On the contrary, declaring you had one was all but mandatory if you wanted to be taken seriously. Imagine having to admit you weren't pursuing your dream in life. What a lightweight you'd look without that proof you embraced society's stock measure of earnest intent and did so wholeheartedly.

Then why was being a dreamer pure and simple so maligned? From what the rooster had observed, most of those who lauded the pursuit of one's dream were actually dismissive of a fulltime dreamer whenever one might be pointed out to them, strolling in the park, perhaps, or pensively sipping a drink in the corner of a boisterous party.

It was as if those who derided any true dreamer in their midst felt personally threatened by such complete indifference to the many compromises they'd found must be struck between their own dreams and the "real world." Such trade-offs were a test of maturity, it was claimed, and managing them was key to maintaining one's self-esteem. But then to be confronted with some unabashed dreamer who refused to follow their lead, who didn't even bother to dismiss their prudent accommodations as a sellout but acted instead as if these failed even to merit being dismissed—how unnerving that must be.

As well it should, in the rooster's mind. To believe you could make it to sundown without dreams, having traded away the sustaining promise of a world to which you'd given your heart long before dawn, what self-betrayal.

Unworthy of a single cock-a-doodle-doo!

The Rubber Chicken

Once a rubber chicken began to fret that it lacked gravitas.

Or rather, the rubber chicken had come to sense that the crowd it found itself with for lunch or dinner every day didn't show much interest in gravitas. It had assumed its companions, being figures who took themselves very seriously, would give more thought to the image they projected.

These were the movers and shakers of society, were they not? Legislation at any level wasn't adopted without their nod. Businesses rose or fell on a chance word they might drop. A provincial backwater could become a "world-class city" overnight if they labeled it as such. They raised the money for museums, convention centers, children's charities, philanthropic appeals. They broke the ground for sports stadiums and named buildings after themselves.

Then why, the rubber chicken wondered, couldn't they behave at the table with a little more decorum? Why were they always slapping each other on the back and talking too loudly? Why did they so often claim that meals on the "rubber-chicken circuit," as they derisively called it, were without distinction and then proceed to leave stains all over the tablecloth and crumbs all over their chairs? When the guest speaker opened with a joke that the rubber chicken itself must have heard a thousand times, why did every last one of the attendees start choking with laughter and slapping the table like country bumpkins?

And the speeches—who wrote these jumbles of tired sentiment and penny profundities? Retired generals saluted the past and either decried "the self-involved youth of today" or praised "the self-sacrificing youth of today." Has-been functionaries huffed about the shortcomings of their successors. Motivational speakers trotted out lists of keyword formulas, all of which seemed to come down to "do whatever works." Venture capitalists introduced multi-media displays of their vision of "human empowerment" as a digital buying spree. Disgraced CEOs pretended they couldn't recall heading up companies they'd run into the ground just last week. Political candidates (whose gatherings outnumbered every other group already mentioned by an incalculable factor) told potential donors whatever they wanted to hear, while partisan rumor-and-conspiracy-mongers with untold followers pounded the podium until it splintered. And so on and so forth.

But the worst of it, in the rubber chicken's view, was that these people weren't really as dim as they made themselves appear. Many of them were in fact reasonably bright. Yet they chose to conduct their public lives as though intelligence and introspection were liabilities, attributes to be disguised or even concealed if you wanted to ingratiate yourself with those who considered themselves more important than everyone else in society.

It was all quite depressing, this strange notion of what merited revering and what passed for prestige. Unless these people began showing themselves to be worthy of the esteem they expected, the rubber chicken might just have no choice but to turn down future dining invitations from their like.

We are judged, it was convinced, by the company we keep.

The Rubber Rooms

Once it was proposed that both wings of the Capitol building be equipped with rubber-lined rooms.

According to news releases, the intent of the proposal was "purely precautionary." The recorded number of otherwise apparently sane senators and representatives crashing into walls while in the throes of partisan zeal had grown alarmingly. Victims were especially prone to this risky behavior when it appeared members of the opposition were engaging or planning to engage in such acts themselves. Throwing yourself against a wall first could mean the difference between getting the better of your adversaries and merely covering yourself with embarrassing bruises, telltale evidence of your own slowness of political reflexes.

Even with such a sense of urgency, however, the rubber-room proposal might have proved to be just another example of a good idea destined to go nowhere had it not been for the fact that publicity and campaign photos of some very prominent figures were beginning to be indistinguishable from mug shots of street toughs arrested for brawling in public and generally posing a threat to the safety of the community at large.

This belated concern for appearance and potential confusion in the minds of voters over exactly whom they had elected was what finally made the difference. The only remaining matter of dispute then became not whether to line rooms in both wings of the Capitol building with protective rubber but whether to line every last one of them.

For nobody wanted to contemplate the possibility that a day might soon come when even campaign photos resembling felony mug shots might prove useless in identifying the true leaders of the land.

The Saber-Toothed Cats

Once a pride of saber-toothed cats came upon a tar pit in the sands.

From the pit's edge, the saber-toothed cats looked out across the bubbling expanse before them. Half-submerged here and there could be seen the rotting carcasses of creatures that had apparently blundered into the pit in the past and been slowly sucked under. Why had these unfortunates waded blindly forward, the cats asked themselves? What could have possessed them to do such a foolish thing?

Did they simply lack the mental sharpness of a saber-toothed cat and couldn't recognize what dangers lay ahead of them? Or had hubris led them to believe their strength alone would carry them through? What delusion had made them assume they would arrive at the other side of the tar pit without mishap when so many before them clearly had failed to?

Although they could barely make out the far bank themselves, the cats were confident that it was well within the range of their vaunted leaping abilities. And if they did happen to come down short, their quick reflexes would, without a doubt, allow them to spring away again after barely grazing the surface of the bubbling tar. If that failed, they could always touch down momentarily on rotting remains in a carcass-hopping strategy of last resort. Saber-toothed cats were, after all, recognized masters of the universe. So what danger could a mere tar pit pose?

There were, to be sure, voices among the cats that counseled against such a leap, suggesting they simply walk around the obstacle and continue on their way. But they were in the clear minority, and their reservations were no match for the full-throated roar of those labeling all doubters "pessimists" or even "defeatists" and insisting there wasn't the slightest question of clearing the tar pit safely. It would be a cakewalk.

"This challenge should be regarded as a test of our mettle," these confident voices declared as one. "Not to answer it and thus fail to show what we're made of would call into doubt our very standing as "super-cats." In that case, the tar pit will have won!"

This last declaration had a rousing appeal to it, one that carried the day. Convinced of their claim to being "super-cats" undeterred by anything in their way, the lot of them drew back only far enough from the pit's edge to get a good running start and then, led by those who'd been most confident of showing what formidable power they commanded, charged forward as one and took a flying leap.

The rest of this story doesn't really need telling, for even schoolchildren know about saber-toothed cats and tar pits.

The Salmon

Once a salmon broke the surface of cascading stream water and kept right on going.

For mile after mile, it had battled against ocean tides and then river rapids to reach this point. Thunderous falls and sharp rocks had taken their toll, wearing away the salmon's strength and forcing it to use up bodily reserves it never knew it had. Then, just when it thought itself at the limit of endurance, all of those trials had fallen away as quickly and completely as if they'd been a lifelong foreboding from which it had finally escaped.

Escaped not just the bears that waited to snag its companion salmon by the score as they fought their own way upstream nor the eagles that swooped in to take their share, nor even from the stream itself, so wild with snowmelt, but from the instinctual drive to risk everything in such determined struggle to return to the place of its origin.

Gaining altitude now instead, looking down on the treetops receding below it, the salmon felt the forces that had dictated its life for years fade like the beads of water drying on its scales. Those urgencies had sent it from shallow spawning grounds to the raging sea, only to bring it back again to complete a cycle from which there seemed to be no exit for the species, a cycle within cycles within more cycles as generations followed one another to the same rhythm of necessity.

But not anymore. Not for this salmon. It had slipped the pull of physical limitations and felt as light as the air around it: released from the laws of birth, maturity, and decline that had governed every move in its life. Defying both time and biology, it was no longer condemned to ending its days in the shallows, wounded and grotesquely aged, the color of burnt spirit.

With unrelenting willpower, one could break through the limitations of nature, it had proved, and make the leap to celestial fish-flight. One could finally wrench oneself free from all the troublesome facts of mere existence and find new meaning in a grand beyond. There was only one difficulty the salmon hadn't taken into account.

It couldn't breathe up here in the heavens.

The Sanctamander

Once a sanctamander cut off its own tail.

Sanctamanders are well known for their ability to grow a new tail if the one they were born with drops off after being trod upon or otherwise damaged, but having a tail in the first place was something this particular sanctamander could not abide.

It had become convinced a tail was a part of its corporeal equipment that it should renounce after watching a telesermon by a famous telesanctamander on the evils of tails in general and, therefore, of all those that possessed them. The tail was a lewd and loathsome appendage, the tele-sanctamander had thunderously proclaimed, fit only for the lowest of the low. The presence of a tail on any creature destined for more than the beastly life was a serious flaw. It was, in truth, the mark of the fallen or those about to fall, the telesanctamander warned.

The tail was connected to the baser passions and must be shunned at all costs as Satan's playground. It was not enough to command "Get thee behind me, Satan!" since that was where the tail already was, undulating sensuously from side to side and making it difficult for any sanctamander to walk a straight and narrow path.

"Ye must cast aside this vile thing utterly! Utterly!" thundered the sanctamander. "As I have done before ye!" And with that, it swung theatrically around, drawing cries of "Hallelujah! Hallelujah!" from every pew in the telechurch and from the home audience as well at the revelation that it had indeed cast aside its offending tail.

"Free of that wicked weight, I feel myself freed from all the defilements of this world! Follow my example, brethren, and look ye not back lest Lucifer lay hold of thee and work his will once more upon thy hinder parts!"

So inspiring was the sermon that when it ended, the penitent sanctamander hurried to the kitchen to find the sharpest butcher knife there and slice off its own tail forthwith. To hesitate might be to suffer pain everlasting, whereas putting up with a little pain now held the promise of sitting tailless and honored among the elect.

But cutting off its tail wasn't as simple an act as the sanctamander had believed it would be. For a long time, it looked to and fro between the gleaming knife and its unruly flesh in agonized hesitation over where to strike. Higher up? Lower down? When it finally feared that one more moment of delay might seal its eternal bliss or damnation, the sanctamander slashed blindly, freeing itself of its loathed tail in one stroke.

There it fell, the twisting bane of its existence, now no longer a threat to come between it and the glorious rewards promised by the reverend telesanctamander. Yet what a powerful twist of muscle and blood it looked. The sanctamander marveled at the fierce struggle its writhing tail put up, the tenacity of the life still within it.

But as the tail slowly fell quiet, the sanctamander sensed with alarm a stirring within and soon the firm thrust of flesh and bone as a new tail emerged from the wound. What was it to do now? This new tail felt stronger and more threatening to the sanctamander's promised deliverance than the previous one by far. How could it follow the lead of the reverend telesanctamander and shed its foul burden forevermore?

Convinced its only hope of saving itself from corporeal vileness was to start over with more righteous resolve, the sanctamander clenched the butcher knife and began to measure where to start cutting this time.

Should it try cutting from its other end this time?

The Sardine

Once a sardine was feeling kind of lonesome.

That hadn't always been the case. Precisely the opposite emotion had characterized most of the sardine's life, in fact. Rather than seeking the closeness of other sardines, it had felt uncomfortable being pressed on all sides by those with whom it felt it shared little.

Not that it nursed any illusions it wasn't a sardine like the rest of its species. Darting about together in frenzied bait balls, it and all the others might appear identical in every regard. But this sardine had long been convinced such likeness was not the full story. As far as it could tell, few of those around it experienced the same doubt it did regarding the common assumption that all sardines could be defined by what they shared. How many times had others' unquestioned confidence that it swam in the same waters they did troubled its peace of mind: their chummy claim that "we're all in this together" repeated over and over throughout the bait ball as if this assurance were an undeniable plus and its value beyond debate?

To which "No, thank you" had been the only response the sardine ever felt was honest. Going it alone, indifferent to the dangers, had been its wish always. And it didn't matter that "going it alone" might not have amounted at first to more than straying a short distance every now and then from the swirling mass. The sardine's imagination extended those few moments of independence to a lifetime far below the surface comfort of others' company, down, down where nightmarish creatures carried their own lights and savaged one another.

In the depths of the sardine's awareness lay another life that the frenzy of the bait ball held at bay only by shutting out anything that distracted its members from their frantic veering about amid perceived threats. As though each abrupt shift wasn't simply a repeated and desperate pursuit of mere survival.

The futility of this compulsive drive here and there to no lasting gain was clear to see from outside the bait ball. Carried along by the force of the dizzying angst that bound all sardines together (constantly worried about turning one way while their companions turned another), little wonder all eyes were directed towards any sardine that claimed to know where it was going and could provide the lead others gratefully followed. Until directions changed, that was. Yet when this inevitably happened, the assumption that all sardines should now follow a new leader never wavered. So the entire school was off again in a flash, as though they'd never been headed anywhere else than they now were.

From the outside looking in, the sardine had concluded, at least there was no blind confidence that life as a sardine was anything more than an iffy proposition. You were doubtless better off on your own, whatever the increased risks. Following your own direction within the bait ball was impossible. Following it outside could leave you prey to horrors from the deep, there was no denying that, but the risk was worth taking. Without the prospect of endless reaches to explore, what was "ocean" supposed to mean?

So why did life as a sardine apart leave this one occasionally longing again for the press of the crowd? Was it really prepared to trade struggles of its own choosing for those set by round after narrowing round of reflexive dodges for safety until the limits of one's life were not much greater in the end than a small metal tin?

No, it wasn't the expectation of safety in numbers that caused the sardine to feel the renewed draw of the bait ball at such times. What, return in hopes the dangers of existence might somehow be lessened for yourself with the sudden snatching away of a neighbor or two by predators flashing by, thus lowering the odds of your own demise? Actuarial roulette as a guide to life choices?

The pull against the sardine's desire for independence was of quite a different nature. Aware that the personal ball of whirling disquiet within each member of its species could not be escaped, much like the desperation with which they raced together against death, it acknowledged the cruel reality cast over all their lives like a net no individual effort could break through.

This fate none of them was spared, regardless of how much any one fish might believe it deserved to be exempted. Nor should it be exempted, the sardine conceded. Packed tightly in the bait ball or tightly in a can on a cupboard shelf or "swimming free"—once a sardine always a sardine was a truth that went beyond all independent efforts at self-definition.

Nevertheless, this sense of a fate shared at a distance didn't lessen the loneliness that came at times to a life on the outside. Belonging and self-definition still formed an uneasy balance that neither lasted nor provided much comfort even in the short run. And a return to companionship by default within the bait ball wasn't really a possibility for the sardine at this point, after a lifetime of swimming in larger and larger arcs away from the point where it had set out on its own. Both it and the others had traveled far since then, in directions none could retrace.

That none knew how to retrace.

Sasquatch

Once Sasquatch headed straight for the trees.

This decision wasn't made lightly. It had been coming for some time, taking shape in a gathering disquiet and then demoralization. Until one day a moment arrived when something snapped inside and Sasquatch bolted from his men's group into the woods without explanation or farewell.

He needed time alone to reflect upon the developments that had brought him to this pass. Things had begun well enough. That first weekend retreat he had joined along with a few of his mates from work had even been enjoyable, Sasquatch was forced to admit. The chanting, the beating of drums, the staring into campfires while listening to "initiation stories," running through the dark in celebration of "the wild within" all stirred Sasquatch with novel and rousing emotions.

But as he attended more of these gatherings, joining larger and larger crowds of those who called each other "fellow spirits of the sacred grove," Sasquatch began to have misgivings. And as he rode back in the car each Sunday night with his comrades, those misgivings only grew.

To be sure, the others had developed larger jaws and at least a token stoop during the weekend doings, but there was something unconvincing about their transformations. As though when they parted with the usual "secret handshake of the primal self" and returned to their everyday lives, all the bonding they had done with Sasquatch would fade into just another male fantasy to fill the void between Monday and Friday. Or maybe just between six-packs of beer.

In a decade or two, how many of them would recall any of this without flinching in embarrassment? If pressed to explain to their sons and grandsons what they'd been up to with some other guys out in the woods, would they still have it in them to declare they'd been pounding their chests and yowling for hours?

This sense of the shallowness of his companions' commitment came to a head for Sasquatch one weekend as he watched a pudgy fellow who claimed to be a "person of consequence at the highest levels" run about butt naked and out of control. "Is that me?" Sasquatch asked himself. "That blow-hard crashing through the underbrush and bumping into dead trees, all the while grunting heavily when not stopping to pass out his business cards as a 'global power broker' or something between breaths? What a fraud! They were all frauds!"

That very night was when Sasquatch decided to go it alone. Somebody had to keep the faith. So he stood up in the firelight, turned from those he no longer considered his peers, and headed off into the dark. There he has remained for years now, receding into a figure of myth and dispute. His very existence is doubted by many, while others cling to farfetched claims about his survival and whereabouts.

There is no way of knowing, therefore, whether the rumor is true that Sasquatch occasionally comes down to the edge of the trees in the dark and watches the clumsy exertions of his erstwhile comrades, shaking his head at what lost-men-in-boyland they seem.

The Satyr

Once a satyr set himself up as a life coach.

It seemed like a sure thing, what with the number of potential clients out there complaining about their unhappy lives. At times the dissatisfaction with what life had brought their way could be deafening. Nor did it seem to matter what blessings they'd actually enjoyed to date. These were never enough or else never what they believed they really deserved.

So it hardly surprised the satyr that there was an immediate, intense response to the ads he placed in glossy magazines for helpless souls. Or that the lines forming at the door of the modest space he'd leased forced authorities to field extra police trained in crowd control starting from three nights before the opening date.

Perhaps he should have set his fees higher, the satyr thought as he prepared to meet the first client in line and wrote his first "note to self" of the day on his iPhone: raise rates tomorrow, move to larger space, upgrade atmosphere with potted plants and sylvan aromas and soothing flute music, hire staff of comely nymphs and smooth-cheeked boys—

The satyr was still writing when the first client timidly peered around the door and asked, "Is it okay to come in now?"

"But of course, my dear," the satyr replied with a welcoming gesture towards the one other chair in the room. "Enchanté."

"What?"

"I'm charmed to meet you."

"Really? Oh, I just knew we'd have this instant connection! Already, I feel like I've known you for years. Do you feel that way too?"

"Of course," the satyr responded with a smile, running his eyes appreciatively over the client's Rubenesque figure. "Now, to what do I owe the pleasure?"

"Oh, you put me completely at ease already, let me tell you. I've had so many life coaches in the past who told me, first thing, I must form a better body image."

"Whatever for?"

"Why, to enhance my self-esteem before making all the lifestyle changes they suggested. If I didn't have a more balanced body image, they said, I'd never be able to find happiness and maximum fulfillment in life. I just can't tell you how much that stressed me out."

"Now we wouldn't want that. Let's start on the body image then, shall we?"

"Oh yes, let's!"

"By the way, aren't you feeling a little warm in that sweater?"

"Warm? Well, yes, now you mention it."

"Would a refreshing glass of wine help?"

"Oh, I just don't know. My last coach told me I must assert more self-control."

"You can't be serious."

"To reach my 12 'potentiality outcomes,' of course. The list-making stage in shifting my awareness paradigm to a purpose-guided, affirmative, vibrant peak-consciousness and so forth is no problem, but I just don't feel fully satisfied by my progress so far."

"Are you sure a little wine wouldn't get your paradigm shifting? Loosen things up a bit?"

"But don't I need discipline more than loosening up?"

"You want discipline?"

"Oh yes, give me discipline! I never have enough discipline, I've been told."

"It's getting a bit warm in here," the satyr responded, wiping sweat from his horned brow. "You don't mind if I take off my tie and loosen my shirt, do you?"

"Oooohhh, are we going to practice some Pilates moves here in the middle of the floor?"

"Something like that."

"I just love Pilates! I feel so good about myself when my whole body gets a workout, right from my powerhouse to my thighs and buns, you know!"

"Oh, I know. I know. And where would you like us to begin?"

After a long first day of such appointments, the satyr emptied what remained of many bottles of wine into his glass, swirled it a few times, and made a new "note to self" on his iPhone: schedule group sessions from now on and record for national syndication.

The Scapegoat

Once scapegoats were on the verge of being hunted to extinction.

Everybody wanted the head of a scapegoat to mount on their wall, it seemed. The demand had become so great that even dusty skulls and moth-eaten tatters of old hide dragged out of the nation's attics and basements were fetching unheard-of prices online. But while dead scapegoats were common enough, live specimens were rarely seen anymore as they were being driven ever and ever farther into wilderness areas.

Up here among the glacial moraines and barren crags, here where the chill air sharpened every sense and put it on alert, a lone scapegoat stood at the edge of a precipice and surveyed the valley below for tiny hunters pushing themselves beyond their natural limits to find and bag their very own scapegoat.

Why this mania? A single scapegoat trophy nailed up on view was never enough. Even a whole row might not suffice, given the current climate of rumors and envy. While to have no scapegoats at all to point to was nearly guaranteed to bring on the severest of anxieties and depressions.

Internet trolls appeared to be particularly prone to pursuing scapegoats for whatever reason and from whatever distance. In basement obscurity, they scanned their screens for targets, whether real or imagined, and then, joining cyber mobs so as to cloak themselves in perpetual anonymity, set upon their luckless victims in virtual reality. Then there were numberless others on private hunts for any scapegoat they could find to blame for their own failures, ethical debacles, serial illegalities, total incompetence, out-and-out lies, you name it.

Civic scapegoating was also on the rise. Those under local scrutiny for some act of malfeasance in office or other impropriety sought to shift the blame to "one of my staffers." While on a national level, shady politicians up for re-election might do the same (except on a broader scale) by stirring their howling base to blame any problem they themselves had created on those calling them out for doing so. And on the transnational level, scapegoat conspiracies within conspiracies within conspiracies provided the broadest cover of all for any who needed it.

Presumably, given all of these facts, the number of scapegoats left in the wild must be declining rapidly. Would a day soon come when all efforts to find one were focused on a lone survivor?

If so, when that final scapegoat had been tracked to some place like this remote precipice, would it be torn apart by competing pursuers in a brawl over who had best claim to the prize? Would gruesome hunks of their kill be triumphantly carried home in all directions? And what then? Such urgency had been placed on bagging scapegoats that their eventual demise must have dire repercussions. When no more were to be found, what would desperate scapegoat hunters do?

Take aim at each other in their uncontrollable need?

Schadenfreude

Once schadenfreude didn't play quite as important a social role as it does these days.

Pleasure derived from the misfortune of others had been something kept in the shadows for the most part, nursed in private, and barely acknowledged even to oneself. Those were the days when too public a display of joy at another person's tribulations was considered beyond the pale, or infra dig at the very least.

That, of course, was before the coming of gotcha-entertainment. Few could have predicted schadenfreude's irresistible and addictive appeal to audiences. Pleasure taken in watching leer-a-moment-media hosts expose the secrets of the rich and famous was an obvious draw, what with its voyeuristic longing to share in their lifestyle excesses while simultaneously gloating over their stumbles on the red carpet and revolving rehab check-ins. But knowing that one's life could never really be like theirs—that whatever pleasures and reversals the rich and famous experienced would always be treated by the show's host like nothing else in the world mattered while your life was just the same ol' same ol' of the faceless crowd—well, that didn't boost one's personal self-esteem much.

To boost one's personal self-esteem through schadenfreude, people closer to the level of the audience needed to be dragged onto the set. Then watching the stripping away of their carefully and not so carefully worked out defenses against public humiliation brought the delicious satisfaction of seeing others squirm while breathing a sigh of relief at one's own distance from the spotlight. The notch or two they were taken down meant the equivalent of a notch or two rise in the self-esteem of every member of the audience. In that sense, schadenfreude assumed the important public role of supplying a rough feeling of social equality at a time when true social equality was hard to find.

You needed to be selective in your choice of schadenfreude-nursing programs when tuning in, of course. Just as a fixation on society's more fortunate could merely lead to self-deflating envy in the average viewer over time, a parade of squabbling lowlifes egged on by a TV "psychologist" specializing in mortification therapy before a boo-on-cue studio audience or a "Judge Snarky" with oh-so-snippy putdowns of yet another parade of squabbling lowlifes for the amusement of the audience at home had their own drawbacks. Such fare might be an entertaining way to pass the day in your vibrating recliner, but how much true satisfaction could be had by snickering at those you'd already convinced yourself were so clearly below you in every way? By default, then, enjoying the desired measure of society-wide schadenfreude required targets that were neither unrelatably high nor unrelatably low.

In short, targets very much at your own level.

The Scorpion

Once a scorpion experienced a moment of compassion.

Compassion isn't a trait often associated with scorpions, either in their own minds or in the mind of anybody having the misfortune to be stung by one. With a secretive, shifty manner plus a tail crooked in a permanent gesture of anger insectified, they have few rivals for instilling fear and projecting a sense of deep-seated malice. Between humans and scorpions, it might almost be said there is a line of mutual loathing that neither has the slightest wish to cross.

Understandably then, feelings of compassion were far from this scorpion's mind early one morning when it saw a huge naked foot swing casually out of the camp cot under which it had been minding its own business all night and descend rapidly towards it. The foot's menacing approach called for a split-second survival response, since if this wasn't already a question of life or death, it soon could be.

From under the arch of its stinger, the scorpion eyed a soft spot on the foot where it meant to plant a venomous strike and repay its own possible end with one equally possible. A life for a life, it was that simple. For why, when one's very existence was at stake, should any life be more valued than another? Was the largest creature granted fuller being than the smallest? Did life flow with anything other than insistent force through all the forms it took? If a human could claim a right to survival, then so too could a scorpion.

As the threatening foot drew closer, the scorpion's entire life flashed before its many eyes. Yet not one of them could identify the whys and wherefores in the scorpion's past that might have led to this precise instant. What in the unfolding of time had brought it to this dreadful pass and to no other? Would the owner of this foot, so unaware and yet equally close to death, also wonder in a second or two what act or decision long forgotten could have begun a journey that would result in horrible agony at this time and this place?

One of them would soon be in no state to wonder further. But what of the other? Living to see another day after so narrow an escape would be welcomed as the better of two outcomes, no doubt. But then what? Another day, and another after that, and after that another, until the undoing barely avoided here arrived without fail in some other way somewhere else?

Granted a temporary reprieve now, what likelihood was there that either one of them would reach old age without suffering anew and often? Heartaches, setbacks, disillusionment, injury, the ravages of disease or despair, the final "sans everything" of physical collapse and mental collapse as well—these were only a portion of what lay ahead. Was this human as keenly aware of what the future might hold as the scorpion suddenly was?

If so, or even half as aware, how could the scorpion not feel a measure of cross-species empathy for a fellow victim of the sorrows that come with the gift of life?

The Selfie

Once a selfie failed to recognize itself.

"Why can't I see myself? Where was I on that day?" Questions the selfie would never have asked itself before had suddenly become the center of its attention, pushing all else aside.

Accustomed to being the only thing of importance wherever it might have found itself, the selfie had seldom paid much attention to what the background for its presence was. Rarely was the background even in focus. Some old monument or some painting or some mountain or some signpost or some friends, what had it really mattered? The moment was all that had counted, and the moment only counted because the selfie was there, front and center.

So why couldn't it identify itself at the center of everything now? Was this failure the reason for its tears of frustration? Or was there in fact a void in the selfie that it had been, and seemingly still was, unable to see?

With so much of its very existence now a matter of "if" rather than "what," the selfie was at a loss for how and where to find validation. "I smile and hold up two fingers, therefore I am" no longer provided the reassurance of the selfie's very being that it always had before. Nor did endless postings to social media prove that it actually existed beyond the virtual world.

"Would buying a new phone with multiple camera lenses help me find myself at the center of everything once again?" the selfie anxiously asked itself. Would there still be time to retrace all of its days spent here or there and document its mere presence as proof it had in fact mattered then and thus must also matter now?

But suppose some of the places where the selfie had felt it was most definitely front and center at the time were now closed for some reason and no amount of pounding on locked doors would open them up. Would it be forced to settle for embarrassing replacement snaps with random passersby who ruined everything by upstaging the selfie with their goofball expressions and two raised fingers of their own?

What was the now stressed-out selfie to do if it wasn't able to prove it counted for something, either in the past or at this moment? And how would it hold back tears in the future when someone it considered a BFF might say, "I'm afraid I can't find you anywhere here. Could you point yourself out for me?"

The Seven Deadly Sins

Once the Seven Deadly Sins formed a support group to buck up their spirits.

For the longest time they'd resisted such a move, wishing to believe they could deal with their individual problems on their own. There was something degrading in a Deadly Sin's reaching out, each of them had felt, something like an admission of weakness or, worse, irrelevance. Only when they could no longer ignore the seriousness of their difficulties did they feel they had no choice but to face the facts and admit they needed each other's help.

The common complaint among the Seven Deadly Sins was that public morality was declining faster than their ability to adapt to the new normal or to work out new coping strategies. To a greater extent every day, they found themselves confronted by the demands of increased multitasking, trespass-wise. This they could handle, albeit with some strain, but the widespread normalizing of sin lately and the dreary levels it had sunk to were what had brought their own spirits so low. For example, what was poor Greed forced to put up with on a daily basis? Unimaginative, routine cupidity high and low? Stock-fraud schemes embraced by political bigwigs and tax-fraud schemes embraced across the land. Compulsive buying disorders beyond treatment? Glassy-eyed 24-hour bidding in online auctions? Cornering the market on two-bit "collectibles"? There was so much to grasp at out there and so little time. Even cold-hearted avarice and rapacious scams seemed debased to the level of smirking collusions between those who had megafortunes already.

Or what of Greed's cousin, Lust? Forget coveting "thy neighbor's wife." Old news. How could Lust, once capable of driving a person mad, have fallen to the level of cringe-worthy teen comedies, fashion-mag sex advice, and by-the-number XXX videos with canned moantracks? Where was Lust's power to lift one out of these numbing banalities and into the far reaches of erotic inspiration, where carnal yearnings move at the speed of light?

And poor Gluttony, stuck with pretentious gourmet clubs and messy cooking shows, supersized sixteen-year-olds, and recovery programs where binge gobbling was considered a "treatable eating disorder" and therefore no big deal. Even the mention of gout had taken on the odd ring of centuries gone by, so matter-of-fact had the overconsumption causing it become.

Pride really didn't know what to make of all the minor-league vanities being praised in its name. Not simply in personal self-praise, so common it was taken for granted. More demoralizing for Pride was the political fact that towering hubris had been displaced by gauche posturing before benighted rally-goers proud of their prejudices and boasting that flag size matters when it comes to love of country. While Chamber of Commerce boosterism now passed for civic vainglory and bone-deep narcissism had yielded to mere garden-variety self-touting here, there, and everywhere. Such were only some of the embarrassments that Pride had to suffer daily.

And if Pride was nonplussed, what about Envy? This once-ubiquitous Deadly Sin wondered how it could maintain any sense of self-worth whatsoever after being reduced to little more than a lame jeer coming out of nowhere: "You wanna be me because I'm everything you aren't. Well, too bad, loser! Now get out of my sight or you'll be sorry." Or, on the other hand, being displaced by autocrat aspirants prostrating themselves before the idol of their dreams. And where was the "green-ey'd monster" jealousy, that ultimate distillation of envy? Reduced to mere teenage tantrums or, worse, puerile Twitterstorms of lies about those whose greater abilities overshadow yours and will do so forever—what a bewildering, disheartening comedown for Envy.

Nor did Wrath escape feeling mortified, although it could find some solace in having now become the Deadly Sin with the highest recognition at all levels of society and across the internet. From smoldering resentment at life's failure to deliver on one's personal wish list to out-and-out raging accusations that the world was continually conspiring to get the better of one, the belief that somebody must be to blame for everything and should pay the price for it festered in untold hearts. "Fine," thought Wrath, "but then how do you tell the difference between mere road rage and global strife?"

The Deadly Sin most appalled by its current state, however, was surely the unlikeliest: Sloth. How could any of the other Deadly Sins not be shocked at the dire straits in which Sloth had come to find itself? Bodies turning to flab through lethargy was one thing, but to witness the spread of mental flab as well was to see indolence and indifference take on new meaning. Along with reports of overloaded synapses approaching unprecedented levels, even breakthrough

235

procedures in neural liposuction couldn't keep up. The Body/Mind Index itself no longer had any meaning, its measurements were so far out of whack.

Given all these threats to their very being and now-vulnerable legacies, was it any wonder the Seven Deadly Sins felt a need to support each other, pull themselves up by the bootstraps, and carry on however they could? It wouldn't be easy, but what other option did they have?

The way things were going, pretty soon it would be hard to imagine a single one of the them was worth ending up in hell for.

The Shaggy Dog

Once a shaggy dog spent every afternoon retracing the path it had taken since early morning and collecting any tufts of fur to be found on whatever it might have brushed against in passing.

You could never be too careful about leaving your DNA about, the shaggy dog was convinced. Suppose you'd wandered, quite by accident, through a crime scene. Would you find yourself convicted of some horrific offense on the basis of a few strands of hair stuck in some bush? And if the place wasn't a crime scene already, what would prevent it from becoming one in the future? Judging by the growing appetite for public horrors and scandals, sooner or later every-where you'd ever been in life and what you were doing there might be featured on "This Week's Crime of the Century." What hope would there be then of getting any of your life back?

Or suppose the snagged fur simply blew away in the wind or was washed away in a rainstorm. Would that be any better? Where might it disappear to? Strands of a coat the shaggy dog had nurtured for years, as much a part of its sense of self as the depths of its brain or the strength of its heart, could end up anywhere, mired in sludge even. Or worse. Imagine any portion of your life defined by its lowest point and all that finds its dank level there!

To say nothing of the unforgivable slight done by such neglect to the shaggy dog's forebears. How could it so dishonor the thread of life that might be traced from a single hair back through countless generations to the dawn of dogdom or even to those protocanines to whom it owed the very presence on the planet of its ancient DNA? Did it have so little respect for the long, long struggles of its ancestors as not to care what happened to the precious gift they'd handed down to it?

But what was that gift, precisely? Would anyone be able to grasp the whole of the shaggy dog's story from a random bit of fur left snared in shrubbery? Would anyone understand what the loss of that small proof of its very existence might have meant? Of what firm sense of self preceded the loss and what followed it and how large the new gap between them was? Of how its life might no longer have a reassuring unity in the wide-ranging experiences making it up?

Or would the slightest trace of the shaggy dog left behind be spun by whoever found it into some laughable conjecture, more ragged fiction than reality, like an illustrator's rendition of an extinct life form guessed at from a sliver of fossilized bone? How could the shaggy dog bear the possibility of being completely misunderstood on the basis of such scant evidence?

Wasn't it better, then, to take everything back: to race this way and that and gather up all the scattered strands of hair it came across before a few might be mistaken for the whole and the shaggy dog's entire life story be reduced to a baffling tale without beginning or conclusion?

Reduced to mere loose ends frayed out until there's no meaning at all to be found in them.

The Shark

Once a shark suffered from bleeding gums.

A taste for blood was the heart and soul of being a shark, needless to say, and so "suffered from" might not have seemed a very apt term for this one's predicament. On the face of it, blood was blood, wherever you found it. Why be an apex predator in the first place if you weren't going to act like one, moving from feeding frenzy to feeding frenzy in perfect confidence that your right to batten on the vulnerabilities of others came with the territory. Why be provided with 30,000 razor-sharp teeth in a lifetime if you weren't supposed to use 'em and lose 'em? And why have the ability to smell blood in the water from far off?

No need to go any distance, though, given the amount of blood in the water on every side already, as if it were open season on anything that had a pulse. So much blood, in fact, the shark had grown rather bored with the ease of the hunt. Blood was blood, what else was new? Going in for the kill could seem little more than a joke.

Except, of course, when the blood in the water happened to be yours. Then it could definitely be much more than a joke. Especially if every time you opened your jaws for a well-timed strike, the private taste of your bleeding gums became public in an instant. Then companions who'd been at your side through the ripping apart of one defenseless victim after another might suddenly draw a bit too close for comfort and become a little too numerous to be ignored.

How challenging life could become without warning for a shark, accustomed as it was to lording it over all potential prey. To have your vaunted powers called into question now as being unequal to the task of saving yourself from the same attacks you'd launched so confidently before—one moment you're toying with a small fish or two and the next you're worrying about what's going on among the other sharks, who wouldn't just be by your side but staring now right at it.

The occasional self-injury that was a matter of course among any who lived off the wounding and destruction of total strangers and spent their days one-upping each other in the casual proof of their powers, now that could be borne. But the speed with which this rivalry could trigger a thrashing whirl of shark upon shark made knowing whose blood was whose impossible, as all took pieces out of all in a fury of mutual obliteration—would the whole thing come down to the last shark swimming? What a sad fate that would be for the lone survivor: the seven seas at your command and not a kindred soul left to appreciate your mastery of them.

The shark, faced with this prospect, sucked its gums in pensive gloom.

The Sheep

Once a sheep rented a wolf suit.

It didn't tell any of the rest of the flock about the suit. They wouldn't have understood. The very idea would have been incomprehensible to them.

Renting the suit was not a spur-of-the-moment decision. The sheep had always felt a secret longing to live a wolf's life. A humdrum existence grazing hill and dale year in and year out had never struck it as much to boast about. By contrast, being out there on the edge, a mysterious figure pacing the far ridges of experience, now that was a life. It was larger than life, in fact.

The sheep had seen wolves in the movies and read novel after novel in which life as a lone wolf was portrayed as far more romantic than anything the sheep had known in its years of plodding along with the rest of the flock. Misunderstood rebels, conflicted loners who spent days on the roam and nights on the run—it all sent a tingle of excitement down the sheep's spine.

After it had returned from the rental shop and unpacked the wolf suit, the sheep laid it out in silent admiration. Warily, it touched the dark fur and was convinced it could feel the rush of the wind passing through it and smell the romance of the frontier, hear the distant call of the wild. "I'll be the most famous rebel ever," it whispered to itself.

The sheep then tried a tentative howl, but it wasn't at all convincing. Perhaps with the suit on, the effort would sound less like a rattling bleat. The sheep slowly began to draw the wolfskin over its wool, which proved to be considerably more difficult than it had anticipated. Squeezing its fluffy body into the lean, muscular form of a wolf required much sucking in of the breath, it discovered.

Finally, the sheep managed to get into the suit. It had faced away from the one mirror in the room throughout so as to enjoy to the fullest the anticipated thrill of the moment when it first caught sight of its new self. Now it whirled around with a snarl it had long practiced in secret, flashed a set of enormous fangs, and immediately sprang backwards in terror. Its heart pounded in its throat as it struggled frantically to pull the top of the wolf suit off and find once again the soft, reassuring lines of its own face in the mirror.

Panting heavily before its familiar features, the sheep felt like it had looked over the edge of a cliff in a night so deep it could see nothing, only hear—perhaps far below, perhaps right behind its ear—a muffled growl. What a fright it had given itself!

The life of a wolf must be something quite different from what it had imagined. The movies and novels hadn't come close in their portrayals. A true wolf must be as far removed from those fantasies as they themselves had seemed from the sheep's own commonplace but safe existence.

Yet there had been something about the figure in the mirror that still held the sheep's trembling attention: some chill, haunting trace of a great wilderness it now realized it didn't have the courage to enter. Instead, it would live out its days between the secure fences of the pasture it had thought to leave, keeping the memory of this alarming episode entirely to itself. If it hurried, it could still get the wolf suit back to the rental shop ahead of closing time.

But before it did, the sheep took a pair of scissors and snipped off a bit of fur.

239

Sisyphus

Once Sisyphus was arrested as a public nuisance.

The specific charge was reckless endangerment: an allegation prompted by complaints from property owners about the damage caused every time his massive boulder rolled downhill without warning and careened through town. Who was going to pay, plaintiffs in what was developing into a major class action lawsuit demanded, for all the splintered picket fences and flattened luxury SUVs, to say nothing of having one's top-of-the-line entertainment center end up in the backyard pool?

At a pretrial hearing, the lawyer for the plaintiffs was quick to call for remand.

"Your honor, the defendant has a history of cagey dodges intended to outwit the powers that be. We believe he poses a clear flight risk, so we respectfully ask the court to deny bail."

"Me, a flight risk?" laughed Sisyphus, who'd chosen to represent himself. "Have you done your homework on this one, counselor?"

While the plaintiffs' lawyer hurriedly leafed through a stack of documents, Sisyphus continued sardonically, "And what about the boulder?"

Without looking up, the lawyer shot back, "What about it?"

"What plans do you have for it?"

"Plans?"

"Yes, plans. Who's going to shoulder it back up the hill if I'm behind bars?"

"That's not our concern," the lawyer asserted confidently, looking to the judge for confirmation.

"Oh, but it should be," Sisyphus smiled with a nod towards the intimidating shape just outside the courtroom window. "If it please the court, I don't see one person among the crowd of plaintiffs packed into this room who could be counted on to get that thing even partway up the slope, let alone all the way to the top, before it comes hurtling back down again."

"Don't think you can wriggle your way out of this one as easily as some of your escapades in the past," countered the lawyer.

"Easily? You think crossing Zeus for the sake of people dying of thirst was without risk? Or chaining up Death, which benefited the living everywhere? How many of your clients who now accuse me would have turned down the off-chance of escaping their demise thanks to my actions?"

"We're not here to discuss death or life expectancy or any of that, your

240

honor," the lawyer declared, seeing a chance to regain control of the situation. "We're here to talk about property values. This case is about protecting the material wealth that the plaintiffs have amassed over their lifetimes and about long-term commitments."

"Long-term commitments?" Sisyphus retorted. "I can tell you a thing or two about long-term commitments."

Seeing Sisyphus take a step forward, the lawyer cried out, "Your honor, we ask that the defendant be restrained! And held in contempt for good measure, if it please the court!"

"Why, I'm doing your clients a favor by scattering their possessions every now and then, giving them a chance to rethink their state and free themselves of all the material clutter they've allowed to rule their lives. Does anyone here actually believe their worth as a human being is determined by how much they own? Besides, who could 'restrain' me any more than I already am, I'd like to know, joined with that boulder out there in what conventional wisdom is quick to dismiss as 'never-ending futility'? Let me assure you, it isn't. Far from it. Pushing that weight up the same steep slope time after time only to have it crash all the way back to the bottom again may seem like eternal defeat, but that last moment at the top, when the boulder is neither going up any longer nor coming down yet, that moment when it becomes clear the continual cycle of gain and loss means nothing in the end, that what you possess or don't possess means nothing, and only you count, there with your abiding strength while the burden of craving and false confidence begins to roll away. That is what I would wish for everyone here!"

"Your honor," the lawyer appealed while backing away from an increasingly animated Sisyphus. "This is lunacy! Sheer lunacy!"

"I'll allow it for the moment."

"Thank you, your honor," Sisyphus said. "Is it lunacy, I ask any of you," he now addressed the room as a whole again, "to find meaning in a tireless dedication to what looks like a lost cause? Perhaps so, but then what isn't a lost cause in the end? What remains of any of your most valued acquisitions when set against the relentless cycles that have made and unmade the world on scales far beyond your power to grasp yet?"

"Objection! The defendant is engaging in speculation."

"Sustained. Rephrase, please."

Sisyphus drew in a breath, eyed the judge, the lawyer, and the plaintiffs in turn, then resumed his defense in a measured tone, "I only point out the obvious. In a life that constantly sweeps aside all claims to final mastery, what significance do the material triumphs of your brief time here have? And what does your future hold but an unvarying repeat of all the fears of loss that consume you now? Is that how you wish to live, as though your worth as a human being depended upon your picket fences and pricey cars and high-end amusements and everything else you amass to distract you a little while longer from facing the losing bargain you've made? You see me labor at my boulder and think it a total waste of time, never recognizing the freedom the effort promises: that moment when the load slips from my hands and I understand once again how much depends on being ready to let go. It's the 'letting go' that I come down each time in the boulder's path to see if any of you have learned."

"Your honor! Your honor!" the lawyer and the plaintiffs shouted in unison. "Lock this fruitcake up!"

Except for a sole, barely audible voice from the very back of the courtroom calling out, "Release the fellow on his own recognizance!"

The Slug

Once a slug suffered from severe stress.

True, it hardly noticed at first. The early symptoms weren't that much of a departure from the run-of-the-mill realities of a slug's life. At most they struck the slug, when they struck it at all, as the kind of thickening torpor that could befall one at the coming of another dawn.

This life of slithering slowly about all through the night in search of unsuspecting vegetation to devour wasn't the best nature had on offer, was it? There must be countless alternatives that would fill one's time on earth with meaning and accomplishment. Discoveries that would thrill. Experiences that would enthrall. The All-All of existence right there in front of you and yet you spend life ignoring its invitation. By morning, the exhausted slug could barely move it was so dispirited. It felt lost in its own personal "slough of despond," as if it had slid to a stop at the bottom of futility and lay there now, paralyzed by feelings of inadequacy and failure.

What had it really accomplished in its life? While other slugs left a self-confident trail of slime behind them, its own seemed increasingly erratic and faint. What could it point to as proof that it had left a lasting mark on anything? Anything. Had the world, in effect, passed it by? Had it missed out on a thousand opportunities for greatness while other slugs turned even the least of their efforts into something that glowed in the sun? Had it been too timid, spent too much of its time in lightless doubt, until it was incapable now of anything else?

This was the stuff of tragedy. "Tragedy. Tragedy!" the slug repeated to itself, sensing a growing solace each time it did. There was heft to that word, no question about it, a heft that outbalanced defeat and so might hold back this slide into suffocating self-analysis.

Perhaps the slug hadn't been thinking in large enough terms about its life, then. Could it be that its failures weren't ordinary ones, but instead pointed to something far more significant? Was it possible it had been ashamed of its short-comings when valuing their tragic message more highly was called for? Were its personal disappointments actually archetypal defeats? Might the seemingly feckless course of its existence ultimately prove more telling than a thousand nightly triumphs and become a witness to the eternal truth of the slug condition?

If so, posterity was bound to grant it ample reward for bearing with today's distress. What an inspiring reversal of all the slug's oppressive doubts! Its name might be destined, then, to remain in the collective unconscious of the species long after it had shriveled away into nothing itself. This shapeless confusion of longings, misgivings, anxieties, and self-reproach might be revealed over time to be a mythic symbol of the highest order.

"A Slug for the Ages" this one repeatedly whispered to itself as it slipped out into the morning sun.

The Smug

Once a noxious smug spread from sea to shining sea.

There had been smug attacks in the past, of course, periods of time when the wellbeing of large segments of the population was imperiled, but this particular smug was thicker and more widespread than any in recent memory: a smug so dense as to make it difficult for many people to see beyond the tips of their noses.

Nor was this a temporary smug, a passing phenomenon that might be expected to dissipate on its own. It had actually been gathering over the course of some time, while computer projections suggested it might continue doing the same well into the future and come to affect every aspect of life in what was already being labeled a "100-year smug event."

Those likely to find themselves victims of this oppressive smug were, as might be expected, the most vulnerable members of society: the old, the sick, the impoverished, and also the very young, who were perhaps the most at risk because they would be suffering the consequences of the smug longest.

Of course, there were also those who had the good fortune to enjoy a life far above the street-level suffering. "If they don't like their situation down below," these more fortunate ones would often say to each another, "what's keeping them from pulling themselves up by the bootstraps and earning the right to join us here at the penthouse level, where the air is sweet and clear and you can see as far as anybody'd ever want to? The view from up here is truly something to behold: a shining promise of the good life open to all who merit it."

Seen from on high, the dense layer of smug settling down over all that lay below inspired many such declarations. But mostly the talk was of the fairy-tale tableau cast each day by the setting sun as it filled skyscraper penthouse after skyscraper penthouse with its comforting glow.

"It's sad how people down there just don't seem to have what it takes to join us up here," those who were above it all might remark to one another over cocktails as they looked out at the rosy world before them. Followed by, "But then, whose fault is that, I ask you?"

The Snake

Once a snake tried to draw each of its discarded skins on again, all the way back to the first.

The attempt wasn't easy. In fact, the pain caused by trying to squeeze back into earlier measures of life's promise would turn out to be agonizing. But the eagerness that had pushed the snake to shed each skin in the first place for the prospect of something new and liberating had yielded to second thoughts of late.

At the high point now of its life, basking in the warmth of maturity, the snake might have been assumed to be well beyond any idea of subjecting itself to this ordeal. It could have been quite content with the skin it was currently in, enjoying the satisfaction that came of feeling you'd realized your life's goal and had a right to enjoy the rewards you'd earned over time. Few would have expected the snake to do anything beyond looking forward to a well-deserved rest in retirement.

Had the snake possessed arms, the prospect of a morning round of golf on fragrant sweeps of new-mown grass or afternoons devoted to the silver joys of shuffleboard could have seemed focus enough for its days from here on out.

But the snake didn't have arms, of course, and in any case it didn't feel its life had been crowned by its current state. What ease its circumstances brought seemed more like a parody of earlier aspirations than their fulfillment. How often had it settled for a nearer goal when attaining a distant one appeared just too demanding? Or accepted less when more was already within sight? The sloughed skins that could be laid end to end behind it were like a reproach that trailed away into a lost world. And that world mocked the snake with an insistence against which its present one could not shield it: had it really grown over the years or simply become heavier and less supple?

Haunted by a suspicion the second possibility might be closer to the truth, the snake had debated what to do through yet another skin-shedding before deciding it was now or never to show it still valued what had once inspired its younger self, more convinced than ever that simply to coil up against the certainties of old age couldn't be the end for which it had been destined.

Pulling the most recently abandoned skin back on using its fangs had proved unpleasant enough, with countless scales damaged or torn off in the process, but those injuries were as nothing compared with what had to be suffered with each additional effort to push back the years. Or with having to endure the snide comments of acquaintances, from under-the-breath queries about its mental state to more pointed insinuations that it act its age and not make a laughingstock of itself.

Still the snake persevered, driven now as much by a desire to escape the unspoken wish by others that it share their own settling for what they'd turned into as by its determination to find again that earlier time when the future looked both fresh and limitless. Reversing in turn each decision where slithering compromise or simply playing dead had seemed the best course, straining to reclaim all that had been sacrificed in those moments of failed nerve, the snake held to a hope that the next skin back would be the one to begin the return of faith in itself.

That never happened. The torment of the attempt only grew sharper the more the snake struggled to recover its youthful confidence. So much so that after a few more skins, there was no room left for the ambitions it longed to feel again or the courage it regretted giving up. The snake realized it was never going to recover the vision it had once held of itself when the world looked neither larger than the scope of its will nor beyond its mastery.

As the snake came to this recognition, it wondered whether it had in fact been a fool in thinking the years could ever be retrieved once they'd been left behind. Once you'd grown out of them or, as now, realized it was inevitable you would, what lay ahead but a labored inching farther and farther away from who you thought you'd be?

Chafing without relief in the skin you found yourself condemned to at the last.

The Snowflake

Once a snowflake was told it was unique.

This wasn't just the opinion of one or two other snowflakes around it. They could have been expected to say something of the sort, if only to confirm their own sense of themselves as being unique as well.

No, this snowflake was told it was indeed special, truly one of a kind, and not just by those near to it but by the authors of all the flake-development books it ever read and by the hosts of all the self-discovery telecasts, videos, or DVDs it ever watched. Not to mention all the flake-awareness seminars it signed up for.

"Think of yourself as the one and only snowflake in the whole wide world" ran the constant message of these sessions, beginning with "Now, repeat after me: 'I'm an original. Special through and through. That marks me off as something unequaled in a world where every day, in every way, conformity hems us in more and more.'"

Such encouragement should have heartened the snowflake, but that hadn't been the case. Instead, what others spoke of so glibly as the very essence of everything that made it one of a kind seemed swept away in the face of cold reality. The trouble was, the limit to its uniqueness turned out to be as close as the neighboring snowflake and that flake's equal and incessant claims of being one of a kind. Such claims coming from this side and from that side, above and below, before and behind the falling snowflake had the effect of lessening its own claim, didn't they? For if all were equally unique, what meaning did being "unique" really have?

Worse, once any snowflake hit the ground, it quickly found itself disappearing under a host of other snowflake "originals" floating down, covering it up, pressing upon it, distorting its shape, turning the unmatched features on which it had based its distinctiveness into a thickening blanket of uniformity.

And yet, was the snowflake wrong to think it was unique? Maybe there really were no others exactly like it, nor had there ever been. The birth of a snowflake must be a celebration of individuality far beyond the assertions of all those flake-potentiality experts confidently instructing it about what "individuality" entailed. Something the claustrophobic crush of sameness all around it couldn't obscure.

Then why did its feeling that the opposite might be true just continue to deepen?

Solomon

Once the justices of the highest court in the land asked themselves, "What would Solomon do?"

The justices were trying to settle a long and rancorous dispute over whether religious belief should be separate from the nation's governance or should actually be at the center of that governance.

The plaintiffs on one side had argued vehemently that religion was a personal concern, an inspired contact with the divine in all the divine's variations, and therefore the tenets of no single belief should be officially endorsed at the expense of others. The future of the state depended upon equal regard for all spiritual expression—as well as for none.

On the other side stood those who argued just as vehemently that there was only one true religion. It had always been, and would always be, favored over all others. The nation simply wouldn't survive unless that one belief was formally enshrined from the lowliest public space to the highest temple of justice.

Faced with these opposing claims, the justices scratched their heads and asked themselves, "What shall we do?"

Meanwhile, placards with slogans demonstrating that die-hard advocates for both sides did not share the justices' dilemma filled the plaza in front of the court steps. On one side most of the placards read "I'm for my side because you're against it," while on the other side, placards generally read "Since you're for it, I'm definitely against it."

After much secret deliberation, after searching the law books and their own souls, the best solution these supreme justices could think of was to offer something to both sides in the dispute and trust reason would prevail thereafter. They must be seen as absolutely evenhanded, they agreed, going only so far in favor of one position and then leaning an equal distance the other way in a show of what they considered to be judicious balance.

As precedent, they looked to Solomon's legendary resolution of the baby dispute, updated for their current approach to jurisprudence, of course. Seeing that nothing short of a bold and decisive move in the same spirit would settle the issue at hand, they ordered the venerable Solomon himself be summoned and announced they were prepared to divide him up between the litigants if nothing else would settle their dispute. The justices and their batteries of clerks felt certain that one of the two sides would give in for the sake of the nation.

Neither side objected to this decision, however, provided the other side did not gain an advantage from it. If that happened, both sides vowed, they would begin all over again and press for the full Solomon or nothing.

The justices saw no recourse now but to take down the sword of justice from the wall of the court and hack Solomon in half. They justified their decision with assertions of both social awareness on the one hand and religious sensitivity on the other, each delivered in the gravest voices they could manage.

When they'd finished rendering their judgment, the justices looked down from their bench-cum-dissecting-table at the lead lawyers for the two sides, fully expecting them to find some form of compromise between the opposing parties that matched the one the court had just demonstrated. Instead, they were met with renewed declarations of partisan triumph and a general stampede for the courthouse steps, where the lead lawyer for each side hold aloft one half of Solomon or the other half and claimed justice had finally been done.

Leaving the members of the highest court in the land to scratch their heads and smooth their robes while asking one another, "What do we do now?"

The Sphinx

Once the Sphinx grew weary of it all.

Who wouldn't, the Sphinx wondered? Waiting here on the approach to Thebes for years to quiz the occasional wanderer who might shamble up (most often lost and in no mood for riddles) had proved more dispiriting than anticipated.

To say nothing of the flies that circled one in this heat, some days so thick they blotted out the sun and so fierce in their assault that the welts they left on the Sphinx by day's end still itched the following morning.

But the wait and the welts could have been ignored if only those who did come along measured up to the Sphinx's wish for the diversion that an engaging test of wits might offer. None ever did measure up. The way they scratched their noggins or other parts of their anatomy and sighed over its riddle for hours on end, missing every opportunity to rework it or expand it or even to ask a few questions in return, and then brought on their doom in an instant with some foolish guess—who should be expected to sit through that?

It was an embarrassment. Spending any time at all with somebody so clueless as to insult one's own intelligence could make the Sphinx want to tear itself to pieces for even having posed its question in the first place. But then to suffer the remorse of dispatching yet another unfortunate clearly not in one's league mentally was worse. After enough of these encounters, how was one to bear the shame of having undone so many of the intellectually defenseless?

Should the Sphinx have dumbed down the riddle so that someone in this puzzled lot might have hit upon the answer? What would be gained, really, by such a move? Wouldn't it cast both the Sphinx and the lucky one in a worse light? The answerer might not have cared, happy just to forestall his or her eventual end, but what of the Sphinx? To have lowered the mental bar and cheapened, right at the start, all that was to follow in a long tradition of confidence in the power of the human mind—was the Sphinx willing to face the scathing contempt such a lapse in judgment was bound to bring over time?

No, better to hold out hope through it all that sooner or later someone would come along who was up to the riddle. Someone who would bring both of them renown by solving it. Like this young man Oedipus here, so full of himself and so sure he knew everything. Was there a chance now at last for a true contest of minds, one that fully deserved to find a place in myth? And yet what did Oedipus really know of life's conundrums that could rival the Sphinx's own awareness? How much didn't he have left to learn about what it ultimately meant to crawl and then stride and then hobble with a cane through the day?

Poor fellow. A greater riddle in himself than any the Sphinx could pose. Yet here they were, trapped face to face in a swarm of flies: Oedipus the Sphinx's best hope for humanity to live up to its claim to wisdom and the Sphinx all that stood between Oedipus and a reckoning no human should have to endure.

Ought it simply spare him that ordeal? Make the riddle one without an answer this time and put a stop to the youth's blind rush towards a terrible fate? Or cry out, "Wait! Give it more thought. You have no idea what any of this truly means."

Or would it be better to stay silent and let Oedipus discover for himself the limits of his understanding? What an agonizing dilemma these questions posed for the Sphinx. At last a wanderer comes along who just might be worth having waited all this while and suffered all these disappointments for, only to put the Sphinx in the position of having to choose between exacting his death if he failed to solve the riddle and its own if he succeeded.

But there was really nothing either of them could do now to escape their plight. The years of the Sphinx's standing vigil here and all of the efforts by Oedipus to flee a dread prophecy had come down to this single moment that held them both in its tight grasp.

As Oedipus finally cleared his throat and began to open his mouth, the Sphinx looked deep into the eyes of the young man and a tear rolled out of one of its own at the knowledge of what the future held.

The Spider

Once a spider set to creating its last web of the year.

A sudden crispness in the air had alerted it to how little time remained for this most important task. Through the long months of summer, the spider had spun web after web without regarding them as being more than a way to meet its basic needs. But this last one must be different.

This one must be a fitting farewell to web-making itself.

There was no need to snare a final meal now. The spider had thrived on all that chance brought to it each day as it measured the distance between the branches of trees and down narrow cracks in the earth. It had ridden a single thread across the breeze countless times and spread its silken net in the morning dew and the noonday heat and the still of night.

Now something more was required.

Before the spider grew too weak to balance itself any longer in midair, it must draw upon whatever strength and agility remained at its command to fashion a testament to the very art of being a spider.

This final web couldn't be a halfhearted affair. Every web the spider had ever spun, or even attempted to spin, must be remembered in this one. Every inch must catch the spider's last sunrise in sparkling tribute to what had been and what could have been alike. In this record of one spider's end, there must be an echo of all the webs spun by all the spiders in all the mornings of the world.

It must be a web that would make anyone reaching for a stick to sweep it aside pause before something so imbued with the enchantment that comes of weaving together, if only for a time, the bright strands of the universe.

Spirit and Flesh

Once Spirit and Flesh were directed to undergo relationship counseling.

Years of mutual suspicion and often bitter conflict—when they weren't determined simply to ignore one another—had alienated the pair to the point where the only thing they could agree upon was that this feuding couldn't continue much longer without destroying them both. Flesh charged Spirit with constantly putting on condescending airs or else drifting off into hazy musings intended to shield it from even acknowledging the existence of Flesh. While in Spirit's view, Flesh was intent on embarrassing it at every turn by indulging in mindless pleasures, from the inane to the utterly debased.

Relations between the two had reached such a point, in fact, that even being in each other's company was an ordeal. And their only relief on those occasions when either party hinted at "ending it all" increasingly lay in sleeping pills for the one and going on a week-long sensual binge for the other, anything that would deaden the pain suffered by both.

Given this history, relationship counseling was, in itself, risky business. So much could go so wrong so quickly, beginning with the demand each made that the other be thoroughly searched for concealed weapons when entering the first counseling session. To such a point had trust between Spirit and Flesh fallen.

Things could have been different. The two didn't have to travel down this road. There'd been plenty of chances to get things right. Spirit could have shown a little more understanding, and Flesh could have insisted a little less on its own desires. But like a scab that itches and itches until scratching makes it a scar, their differences hardened over time into grudges for which there seemed no remedies.

Now they found themselves on opposite sides of a recently polished table and stared down at their own reflections for a full five minutes so as to avoid looking at each other. While the appointed relationship counselor prepared to do for them what they'd proven unable to accomplish on their own.

There sat Spirit, debating internally how to project confidence about the outcome of the process without appearing aloof and insensitive. This effort would turn out to be more difficult than Spirit had anticipated, and not simply because of the indignity of being in a situation it found demeaning. Matters wouldn't have come to such a point if the superiority of Spirit over Flesh that so many publicly proclaimed was honored by them in private to the same degree. But no, once the lights were turned out, high-mindedness went dark just as quickly, everywhere.

More troubling to Spirit at the moment, though, were the waves of queasiness brought on by a deep but unacknowledged claustrophobia that made it impossible to turn from the gathering threat mirrored in the shiny tabletop as the walls and ceiling seemed to ooze closer. It took all of Spirit's increasingly taxed powers of self-control to summon a show of sang-froid and keep from crying out, "I must have room to breathe! Freedom to soar!"

Across the table slouched Flesh, troubled by a growing anxiety about what this compulsory counseling might portend for the two of them. Flesh was fully aware that the public typically lauded Spirit with glowing terms like "noble" or "sublime" while deriding Flesh's own gifts as "base," "blind," "weak," or even "demonic." Yet how thin that regard for Spirit actually was, more honored in flowery praise than in true allegiance. Called to follow Spirit and abandon all their worldly desires for higher rewards, many people demanded to know in advance the "exact value" of what they'd gain by doing so.

In addition, the preoccupations of Flesh were more or less of a whole by contrast with those of Spirit, whose attention often appeared to be scattered all over the place. Flesh might well have yielded to the temptation to exploit its greater "unity of self" relative to Spirit's frequent turmoil, were it not for the worry that any move to gain from this advantage came at the risk of upsetting the delicate balance they'd at least managed to maintain through their difficult patches until now.

The fact was, they needed each other. How would people recognize Spirit without Flesh, since they'd grown accustomed to thinking of the two in opposition? And for Flesh, mightn't separation from Spirit turn out to be just as dicey in terms of maintaining Flesh's own sense of self? They had become an "item" in the eyes of the public, whether they liked it or not. Who would take seriously the existence of either one if asked to accept the other's reality on mere say-so? Being recognized as the real thing was hard enough already, what with all the spiritual poseurs and serial exhibitionists out there clamoring for attention and getting it.

Spirit and Flesh had long since settled for a testy bond of convenience, there was no denying. And neither of them felt seriously hampered by the resulting open relationship, despite their recurrent discord. Furthermore, whatever others might think about them individually or as a twosome wasn't necessarily the truth, nor of much importance, really. More often than not, what the public saw as "Spirit" and "Flesh" was what it wanted to see, so each of them was at liberty to pursue new yearnings and new attachments with a view to a more satisfying life for itself and more latitude for the other. It might appear as though Flesh gained most from this arrangement at times and at times Spirit did. Yet time itself was a great equalizer and didn't play favorites in the long run. Why not leave it to time, then, to sort things out? What need did they really have for this unwelcome mediation session, the pair silently asked themselves simultaneously?

Just at this moment, the relationship counselor startled both Spirit and Flesh with a loud "Ahem," followed by: "As I see it, resolving this little problem the two of you seem to be having shouldn't be difficult at all."

The Squid

Once a squid was assigned the task of redacting passages in top secret governmental documents scheduled for declassification.

At first, the task didn't strike the squid as being much of a task. It possessed more than enough ink for the job and plenty of practice in "clouding the waters" whenever circumstances called for concealment. In fact, those factors were precisely why it was given the assignment, the squid supposed.

Nor did it consider the first documents it was given very difficult to process. As far as the squid could tell, all that was required of it was to black out everything following mention of the person or persons who'd done or said whatever must be kept from the public's eyes. Such documents typically made mention of the "President," after which all relevant text was to be obscured. The same expectations applied to documents involving the "Vice-President," "Secretary of State," "Secretary of Defense," "Undersecretary" of this or that, running through every department and every governmental agency all the way down to "the secret agent on whom much of our nation's security depends, codenamed

'Spitball.'"

Or at other times, it might be the reverse, with long passages detailing actions taken (or not taken) left completely visible for all to see while the titles and/or names of those responsible were to be inked out.

Feeling it was functioning well below its pay grade, so to speak, in doing what was more or less a snoozer for it, the squid asked its superior one day for some clarification of its job description.

"That should be abundantly clear, shouldn't it?" came the slightly irritated reply.

"I'm just not certain what difference it makes whether I hide names or actions?"

"I'm not at liberty to comment on that without authorization from above."

"How far above?"

"Why should that matter?"

"It might assist me in seeing what my own role in all of this is. You know, the rationale for what I'm doing."

"You need a rationale? Yours 'not to reason why,' as they say. You and every other squid, you're expected to follow through on your obligations. Period."

"My obligations to whom?"

"Right up the line to the top. You believe in unquestioning loyalty, don't you?"

"Of course, but I thought my loyalty was to the common good."

"Up the line to the top or the common good, think of them as the same thing."

"Haven't there been times when it turned out they weren't the same thing?"

"Look, my advice is just to do your job and don't ask questions if you want to survive here long enough to be promoted to the next level of invertebrates."

The squid took this advice as a veiled threat and returned to blacking out page after page of government documents classified "Secret" or "Top Secret" for the rest of its career without questioning again what it was doing or why.

Not ever.

The Stone

Once a garden stone wondered whether it should say something.

There certainly were plenty of reasons to do so. Every day, the man who owned the garden in which the stone found itself did something or other that left little question he was in need of advice. Not that the man knew he needed advice. But the stone knew.

Some time had passed since it was brought down from the mountains and placed in the garden. The man had gone searching for rocks that would fit into his ideal landscape design and had stumbled across this one in the process. Stumbled was the best term for it, as the man hadn't paid much attention to this particular stone at first. Instead, he'd been intent on prying loose a neighboring rock that fit his mental picture of the garden more closely. But he'd cracked that stone in his efforts and was forced, cursing loudly, to settle for the one he'd been standing on and prying against instead.

When he returned home, the man pored over the garden plan he'd drawn, trying to decide where to put the stone he hadn't really wanted now that he'd brought it back with him. He drew it on the paper here and then there, but the result never satisfied him, and the plan itself began to fade beneath angry smudges.

Furthermore, no matter how much the man studied the stone, it just didn't look right to him. From every angle, it was either too flat or too uneven for his liking and never suggested anything more than a nondescript chunk of rock. He ultimately rolled it to the back of the garden in disgust and left it there.

From its new resting place, the stone had watched the man go about the creation of his garden. He dug and hauled and planted to make everything fit the precise arrangement he had in mind. When something didn't fit, he'd double his efforts to force it to, and if he still couldn't, he'd tear it out and start over again. Eventually, he got what he wanted.

Though never for very long. A tree might die from overwatering or underwatering; a flower might not match the catalog illustration that had prompted its having been ordered by mail; any one of a hundred pests and blights might appear. Most galling were the weeds. They sprang up everywhere if given any opportunity at all and often rooted themselves too deeply to be pulled out whole. Instead, they snapped off when wrenched or twisted, then bided their time to come back again twice as hardy after the next rainfall.

The stone saw how these setbacks often drove the man to distraction.

Whatever had moved him to embark on creating his ideal garden in the first place, it had now grown into the obstinacy of the unhinged. Even those corners of the garden that he'd worked and reworked still failed to look exactly as he was certain they should. There was something unsatisfactory about each of them, and it exasperated the man that he could never figure out how to get things right.

Sometimes, when his frustrations were at their peak, the man's eye might fall on the stone at the back of the garden. In that moment, all of his discontent would focus on it as though the stone were to blame for the failure of the garden overall to match his intentions, as though things had gone steadily wrong since that day in the mountains when he'd had to settle for it rather than a more attractive stone.

It was at such moments that the stone wondered whether it should say something to calm the man and help him see what the true failure of his garden was.

But then, stones don't speak to those who don't listen.

The Strays

Once strays terrorized an entire neighborhood.

They considered themselves to be purebreds, fine examples of pedigree and discipline, but in fact they were vicious strays, abusing anyone they met and proving themselves a menace even to those who might have befriended them.

When police arrived in response to mounting 911 calls, they found these strays acting like they were a law unto themselves, running wild and attacking adult and child alike. Cries of pain from their victims only increased the strays' ferocity. Even the officers grew apprehensive the strays might prove a danger to them as well.

Rather than confront the problem directly, they chose to follow up on accusations made by many victims that these out-of-control strays were not strays at all but loyal attack dogs belonging to the owner of the biggest house around.

Presuming this owner would be concerned about the public menace posed by the attack dogs and would be eager to control them out of a sense of civic responsibility, the officers approached the biggest house around, only to find the place shuttered and forbidding. Except for a small gate on the right side, which had been inexplicably left wide open.

When the officers moved to do what they saw as their duty and closed the gate, an angry voice suddenly rose from somewhere in the depths of the house.

"What the hell do you think you're doing?"

"We thought you'd like someone to close the back gate for you," one of the officers replied helpfully.

"Well you thought wrong. What I do with that gate is my business."

"But what about your obligation, as a citizen, to the safety of the community?"

"What do I care about the community?" the answer boomed back.

"Do you own a number of attack dogs?"

"What's it to you?"

"Community bylaws require residents to keep—"

"Do you have any idea who you're talking to? The chief executive of this burg, that's who. My authority to do anything I want is total, and anything I do is perfect. Attack dogs, protection dogs, it's all in how you look at them so long as they're loyal. People who get bitten deserve to get bitten. What were they doing to attract the dogs' attention, anyway? And if they don't like it, they should pack up and leave town. Now, I've got important business to attend to, so don't bother me about what I'm sure is just a case of a few bad apples."

"But you're the one who left the gate open, aren't you?"

"So what?"

"That makes you legally responsible for any consequences."

"No it doesn't."

"Why not?"

"Because I can't be held responsible for anything. I'm above all that."

"What makes you think so?" the officers asked repeatedly but received no further response, leaving them to look at each other and wonder what to do next.

As the officers scratched their heads in uncertainty about their proper duty to the community, a few of the strays sniffed at them and then snarled in distain before ambling off to continue terrorizing the neighborhood.

The Sunflower

Once a sunflower lost its bearings during a solar eclipse.

Or to be more precise, it lost the guiding reassurance of time. Nothing like this had happened to the sunflower before. Not only was it subtly attuned to the advance of the sun each day but it also had total recall of the moment when any past experience in its life had occurred, as well as the moments just before and after.

The sunflower had anticipated the same would be true of every moment to come through the rest of the summer and well into autumn. All was predictable, hour to hour, day to day, week to week, month to month.

And then the sun went out. Not all at once, but gradually, which made its disappearance even more alarming. Sudden darkness would have been easier to deal with. If the sunflower's ordered world came to an end in an abrupt cataclysm, well, what could you do? Things just hadn't worked out.

But this extended fading of the light, this deepening uncertainty, was an agonizing affair. One had time to lament the slow disappearance of one's entire world into shadow. And with it the extinguishing of each memory or expectation that world had produced. Past, present, future—all vanishing together.

With the sun gone, the flower began to sense the troubling contours of an existence it had never dreamed of in the light of day. It found the change thoroughly disorienting and suffered, amid the shifting and vague shapes, a rush of vertigo. There was no rhyme or reason to count on, no reassuring lines running straight to the horizon and joining there against confusion. The sunflower couldn't even be certain of its companions in the field around it, only that they, too, likely turned and turned about unsteadily in the gloom.

Soon, however, an unexpected calm began to settle out of that gloom.

No, calm wasn't the word for it, the sunflower soon realized. More like hushed fascination. In the depths of the eclipse, when nothing was as it always had been, the possibility that the sunflower's world might stay like this left it wavering between a wish for the sun's return and a strange reluctance to have it reappear.

The sunflower tried to imagine what life might be like in perpetual darkness. Without the accustomed bearings, it could be anything. As if the sunflower were the first on earth, setting its face towards the unknown with all the hazard of a life gamble. Nothing taken for certain nor rejected yet. Free as no flower had ever been free, bearing the seeds of a present without past or future. Ready to live for the moment alone.

But then, from behind the great dark promise of the moon, the sun began to reclaim the sky.

The Swan

Once a swan turned into an ugly duckling.

Or, to be more precise, the swan turned itself into an ugly duckling. Being a symbol of "the beautiful life" wasn't exactly a quiet glide across a shallow pond, it had learned over the years. Dodging the paparazzi every day was bad enough, but reading one's own press could be much worse. Every two-bit gossip columnist had a grudge against the swan, it seemed, while entertainment fops on TV and online passed along rumors that its love life was in a death spiral for the umpteenth time. And that latest cover of Leer/Sneer magazine—they could at least have cropped out the droppings, couldn't they?

But, oh no. Those droppings were the whole reason for printing the picture, the swan suspected. It wasn't enough for endless lines at grocery checkout stands to ogle its svelte body on tabloid covers. Weren't they really looking for evidence of any kind that the swan's beauty was in fact only skin deep? For how else was the loveliness of others to be borne by the plain and the grace-challenged?

They'd probably convinced themselves that on the inside, the swan must be as unattractive as they were. No, the swan must be even more unattractive than they were, for if they hadn't a prayer of matching it for outward appeal, then the swan had to be more ill-favored within than they were, even downright revolting. That way any one of them could feel better about failing to have been born a swan. Not to mince words, the swan grumbled to itself, but those photos of its droppings amounted to psychological consolation for tabloid skimmers everywhere.

You only had to consider how much those who were jealous of swans sighed over ugly ducklings. And the uglier the better, it seemed. Feigning empathy for those trapped in a body that they themselves blessed their lucky stars they had not been, they were free to imagine an inner beauty in the waddling little unfortunates that must outweigh all surface flaws. How hypocritical.

But that wasn't all. Congratulating themselves on their ability to recognize the inner beauty of ugly ducklings made dismissing outer beauty like the swan's a proof of their own allegiance to more idealized or inclusive definitions of loveliness. In short, if homeliness could be declared to house the gift of true beauty, then by contrast, they must assume that what outwardly appealed to the eye actually had to be a cover for something hideous within. No wonder they fixated on swan droppings as a way of demonstrating to themselves and to others that they weren't really slaves to blind infatuation.

Inner beauty did have the advantage of not betraying one's age, the swan had to admit. The older and more wrinkled one grew, the more thankful one might be to remain a knockout within. Confident of your inner blessings, watching the steady decline of the physically endowed and the desperate measures they took in hopes of holding off the inevitable through plastic surgery and lotions galore might conceivably make your personal decay that much easier to bear.

With so much of popular opinion going against it, the swan decided, why not turn itself into an ugly duckling? That way, it might be able to spend the remainder of its life under the dewy gaze of its present detractors, those who'd long obsessed over its beauty and grace while flattering themselves that they had more of both within.

What the swan failed to consider in all of this was the very real prospect of living out its days as an ugly duckling desperate to forget it was ever a swan in the first place.

The Swifts

Once a flock of swifts hit a wall at high speed.

Most of the swifts weren't aware at first that they'd actually hit a wall. To them it seemed merely a momentary pause, such as they sometimes experienced just before making an especially sharp turn in flight and darting off in a completely new direction. A few realized something else had happened instead, but even they weren't sure exactly what it was or why it had happened to them.

After all, swifts had grown so accustomed to pushing the limits in any direction they chose that the notion of a full stop seemed a denial of the very essence of being a swift. If they were not a byword for high-speed nimbleness, what else mattered? To put it bluntly, if there were limits to their flight, why take wing?

They had always considered themselves born to own the air and regularly flaunted their ability to leave the rest of the world far behind. The rules of gravity simply did not apply in their case. No rules at all seemed to apply as they soared and swooped through the air. Wherever they chose to fly, they made a conspicuous display of having the right stuff to outwing the wind and to leave no doubt that they were a law unto themselves when it came to escaping what looked to be certain misfortune. Then, as though to ensure that their devil-may-care risk-taking would inspire admiration far and wide, they might do it all over again.

What was remarkable about the wall-smacking episode was not that the swifts went down in a shower of feathers (which could have been predicted sooner or later) or that they were a bit hazy in the head about the reason why. Rather, it was all the hooting and clucking and cackling that the sight of these onetime highfliers drew from other birds that came from everywhere for a glimpse of their undoing.

"Served 'em right for considering themselves above the rest of us."

"They had so much going for them, and what did they do with it?"

"Self-indulgent excess, that's all they knew."

"Thought they were masters of the sky. Look where it got them."

"If I were in their place, you wouldn't see me smashing into walls."

"Me neither."

These were just some of the sentiments expressed over the sudden fall of the swifts. After the catalog of gloating had been repeated in one variation or another many times, interest in keeping up the hoots, clucks, and cackles gradually died away amongst all but a few of the other birds.

The rest of them were now to be seen on the ground below, poking around in the scattered feathers and trying to glue as many as they could to their own wings.

The Sycophants

Once vast herds of sycophants roamed the earth.

In addition to being the largest life form on land, sycophants had long enjoyed a reputation for intelligence as well. But now, with an unprecedented explosion in their numbers and their increasingly reckless conduct, they threatened to destroy all in their path as they pressed forward in the global competition for survival.

News of alarming sycophant behavior arrived from near and far, and no place was safe from the dangers posed by these blundering hulks: political parties, corporate boardrooms, university administrations, sports leagues, social media platforms, pop culture, and countless online chat rooms, to name just a few. Trumpeting sycophants appeared in all of these places with little warning and seemed to withdraw just as quickly when the effects of their presence became impossible to ignore, what with great steaming piles being the most

261

common aftermath of their passage.

The common worry in all instances of rampaging sycophants lay in what to do if these reckless hulks found themselves cornered. You couldn't simply declare that you'd succeeded in protecting your town or county or state or country or the whole planet from certain disaster and then walk away, for nothing proved more dangerous than thwarted sycophants. When denied the opportunity to throw their weight around at will and without the slightest care for the widespread damage this would inevitably cause, the ferocity of their reaction could be harrowing.

As conditions reached the point of causing widespread concern that unchecked sycophant behavior might pose a lasting public hazard, plans were proposed for tracking down those who'd most clearly gone berserk and neutering them on the spot, thereby possibly ending the problem in a generation or two. Unfortunately, in the case of particularly dangerous rogue sycophants, neither knockout darts nor dumdum shells had much effect. And the prospect of having to team-wrestle one to the ground under such circumstances was daunting indeed.

A continually unnerved public just wished these roving herds of sycophants would go away, taking the whole of their dangerous world with them. But sadly, numerous peer-reviewed studies predicted that an exponential growth in sycophant numbers was far more likely, given the ongoing state of affairs.

Woe to the world.

The Tapeworm

Once a tapeworm readied itself for the latest stop on a motivational speaking tour.

Out in the auditorium could be heard the murmur of a sold-out crowd, all clutching one of the popular tapeworm's inspirational books or videos and preparing to experience the power of its "Just Go With Your Gut" message.

Having been at this for some time, the tapeworm knew exactly how long to let the anticipation of its appearance on stage build, exactly how long fan yearning would take to reach a hunger pitch and the moment came to thrust aside the curtain and reveal itself in all its astonishing vigor.

"Ahhhhh . . ." the sold-out audience would always gasp as one, leaning forward at the waist in response to the pull of what had come to be known among its followers as the tapeworm's "dominating presence." "Why can't I be like that?" would be on the tip of every tongue among the tapeworm faithful. So sure of this question was the tapeworm that its standard response ("All of you sitting out there are just like me, but you don't realize it") rang within each attendee without being directly stated, as if reaching the spell-bound audience by means of telepathic mass suggestion.

"Imagine yourself at the center of all being" was another of the tapeworm's fail-proof encouragements. "Then repeat to yourself every morning and every night and while listening to my latest interactive lessons for just 30 minutes a day, 'I am at one with the movements of being! I will gain, not lose! I will be colossal, not puny! I will nurture my needs above all else!' If you just repeat those words faithfully, I guarantee you'll begin to feel the power growing within you! There are no limits to the ultimate you! Find your center and never let go!"

"Ahhhhhhhh . . ."

"There was a time when I myself was consumed by self-doubt and negativity," the tapeworm continued, sticking to script. "Just as you might have been before coming here tonight. My self-esteem was running on empty, just as I'm sure yours is now. Am I right?"

"Ahhhhhhhhhhh . . ." came a new wave of sighs from every part of the hall and teary-eyed shouts of "Thank you, thank you, thank you for being here for me!"

"I used to look at myself," the tapeworm responded to all, even those packed in the upper balconies, "the same way you may look at yourself this very moment as the most insignificant creature ever. Am I right?"

"Ahhhhhhhhhhhhhh . . ."

"I'd have given anything to be told then, as I'm telling you now, 'You're worth a million and you don't even realize it.' Well, that was then. Look at me now!"

The tapeworm certainly did look like a million. Maybe even a billion or two. The audience had never seen a motivational speaker so energetic, confident, and exuding success on such a scale. Something had to be going right for the tapeworm. If only they could move beyond their own inhibitions and anxieties like that.

"Go with the Gut and Thrive!" They now had it straight from the tapeworm itself in slogan form: a feeling of confidence deep within that would stay with them forever.

In the meantime it wasn't too late, the entire audience was assured over the hall's audio system after the tapeworm had taken a bow in every direction and withdrawn offstage, to purchase box sets of its best known performances on Blu-ray disks. Exclusive one-on-one, in-person sessions with the tapeworm after every show were also available for those who were willing to pay more.

"Ahhhhhhhhhhhhhhhhhhhhhhhhhhhhh . . ."

The Termite

Once a termite applied for a highly regarded grant to carry on with its work.

Seeking such assistance was not something the termite did lightly, concerned as it was that much of its independent vision might be compromised as a result. Lately, though, it had begun to have serious doubts about its ability to meet the difficult challenge of clearing the world of deadwood and decay through art without monetary assistance.

Despite having considerable doubt about its chances of being recognized after so many years of struggling in obscurity, the termite felt encouraged when it was invited to appear for an interview regarding its grant application. It took the invitation as a hopeful sign that it would find timely support at last.

The termite had barely taken its place in front of the grant committee, however, when the chief interviewer declared, "Your application is, quite frankly, the most unsettling one we have ever received. I must tell you at the outset that the committee is not inclined to fund your efforts and that you have been invited here solely to fulfill certain requirements for transparency and fairness in our grant-awarding process. Now, if you have a statement you wish to read, you may do so."

The termite did have a statement, one over which it had toiled for days. But now all of that seemed pointless in the dejection it increasingly felt while reading out a plea for acknowledgement under the increasingly wide-eyed, alarmed stares of the committee members. Every word of the statement now felt like swallowed dust.

When the termite finished, there was a long silence. Finally, one of the interviewers asked, "Let me understand this correctly. Are you actually claiming that your work can be of benefit to society?"

"I believe it can, yes," was the termite's hoarse reply.

"And you propose to render this 'benefit' by attacking everything you see as 'rotten' in society?"

"If what's dated and decayed isn't cleared away, how can something better take its place?" the termite offered hopefully, but the response it received from another member of the committee was a caustic "Who are you to decide what's 'dated and decayed' when so many experts in such matters are convinced everything is quite up to date and sound?"

"I only point out what ought to be obvious."

"Well, it's not obvious to us, let me tell you!"

"Shocking, that's all I can say!" another member of the committee added.

The termite saw in the expression of hostility on the faces arrayed before it that its proposal to take on the labor of chewing through every example of aesthetic decay it encountered so that something genuinely new could replace it was viewed as a challenge to much of what the members of the grant committee prided themselves on having endorsed and generously rewarded over the years. They were not about to question a continuation of their approach to bestowing grants just because some termite showed up with a disturbing proposal it called "Distructo-Creation."

There was nothing left, the termite realized, but to listen as the repetitive throat-clearing died away and the head of the committee signaled that the interview was at an end:

"Thank you for your interest. We wish you success in finding support for your endeavors elsewhere. Now, if you'll excuse us . . ."

Excuse them?

The Think Tank

Once an old and storied think tank sprang a leak.

Not that anybody noticed at first. The leak was a slow one, and so the falling level of thought in the tank only became discernable over a period of time. In fact, it wasn't until there were next to no new ideas bubbling up in the tank that most people recalled how full of them it once was.

Prior to the leak, there hadn't been much concern that anything might be wrong. Big fish and little fish moved about as usual, bumping into one another on occasion but for the most part staying centered in a school of thought long governed by the confines of the tank.

This embrace of prior thinking over the prospect of new, independent thought had undeniable advantages. Once introduced to the tank, small fry found reassurance in the promise of safety in groupthink and could look forward to becoming a senior fish over time merely by following the safe lead of those who had already followed the safe lead of those before them.

So long as the tank was full, the increasing number of senior and emeritus fish in it was cause for occasional comment, perhaps, but not much else. Only as the level of ideas began to fall, turning ever more murky and devoid of oxygen in the process, was it remarked that greater fish and lesser fish all looked to be in trouble, without distinction.

The occupants of the think tank adapted as best they could, most commonly through variations on what came to be called "the buddy-bubble system," whereby a single thought might be passed back and forth between any number of them until there was nothing sustaining it anymore.

Eventually, half-hidden by the murky state of the tank, many fish struggled to maintain their equilibrium, often in the end floating bladder-up for their efforts. And the tank's erstwhile leaders in thought found themselves reduced to being mere bottom feeders on the remains of their former glory, with few of them showing much evidence of understanding what might have brought them so low?

Overdue inspection of the seams of the tank revealed that they had weakened and cracked over the years, most likely from vibrations caused by so many mouths moving in ceaseless unison within. Though these findings have since been made available to all think tank developers, it remains to be seen whether new standards for think tanks will be implemented as a result.

If not, it may be only a matter of time before the public finds itself swept under by a truly catastrophic think tank collapse and swimming for dear life amid the wash of slippery, half-dead ideas.

"Time Immemorial"

Once the expiration date on "time immemorial" came and went, but few noticed.

From C– level high school essays to $50,000-a-plate banquet speeches, mention of "time immemorial" had long been counted on to extend the life of many a stale or mildewed thought, even to bringing a few absolute stinkers back from the brink of history's garbage dump on occasion. Without it, countless claims to lofty oratory might have been taken less seriously or dismissed outright. Quite understandably, therefore, the unnoticed passing of the expiration date on "time immemorial" posed a true dilemma for those who'd always relied so heavily upon the expression.

It was a dilemma that could not be ignored once the facts were clear, obviously. There was no dodging the need for a replacement without delay, one that would be both flexible and durable enough to do for all future declarations what "time immemorial" had done for so many now-forgotten ones. Something with equally broad resonance and equal lasting power was called for.

The problem was, agreeing upon what that replacement should be proved far more difficult than anyone could have foreseen. And little wonder, given the infinitely accommodating nature of "time immemorial." Who couldn't remember a telling instance in which it had served to prop up some shaky notion that would otherwise have fallen apart immediately? It seemed few hoary statements that were deemed worthy of being repeated again and again hadn't relied at some point on an appeal to "time immemorial" to preserve their claims to legitimacy.

The challenge before those who'd grown accustomed to such reliance, then, was to find a worthy substitute before their confidence that the present was basically just the latest iteration of the past suffered some unforeseen blow. There weren't just personal reputations or public policies at stake here. Numerous social and cultural groups also looked to the past for evidence of their own abiding value: something that legitimized their present identity and importance through appeals to ancestral truths they were sure "time immemorial" had verified once and for all.

The actual nature of the connection of present to past didn't matter as much as did the sustaining reassurance of a continuation of the known, something you didn't need to consider twice before advancing it as established fact. Not only was the present beholden to the past in this sense; it had no real meaning beyond what had been inherited.

This confidence held for the future as well. Victory in the past was seen as a guarantee of victory to come, while defeat could easily beget more defeat. Not remembering the past wasn't as sure a guarantee of repeating it as was tying a virtual string around your mind so you'd never forget. Thus the expiration of "time immemorial" was seen by many to be a genuine problem, making it imperative to find a substitute with greater oratorical staying power to ensure the continuation of the has-been forever.

Few were prepared to risk trusting their future to much else, it would seem.

267

The Topiary Menagerie

Once topiary animals took the shears to themselves.

At first only a small number dared to snip furtively away at their edges, trimming off a bit here and a bit there so the effects wouldn't be noticed by those charged with maintaining the topiary menagerie to standard pruning guidelines. Uncertain of what they were doing, these venturesome few also wanted to guard against getting ahead of themselves and coming to rue the results.

They could have remained as they'd always been, of course. Leaving matters to the experts and their long-established canons of form and proportion would have avoided any untoward missteps. And not a few of the topiary animals themselves nervously warned others against the dangers of redefining their shapes by the slightest degree. Who knew to what lengths headstrong individuals might go in their fumbling boldness, putting the whole of the menagerie at risk of detection and triggering the swift reaction that would assuredly ensue. For topiarists had years of training, and the patterns they followed were time-honored ones. If these were violated and visitors to the menagerie could no longer identify their favorite animals at first glance (or even tell a mouse from an elephant, should things go that far), where would it end?

Such dangers could not be denied, but neither could the frustration experienced daily over the ignoring or outright denial of individual animals' inner yearnings. Shouldn't a mouse have a right, after all, to cherish a vision of itself as a mighty elephant? Or an elephant to harbor an equal hankering to explore the life of the nimble-footed mouse? And any other creature to free the restive psyche within it?

There were bound to be mistakes made as the shears came out in far-flung corners of the menagerie. Many of the animals were feeling their way forward; they'd never before ventured into unexplored territory like this. Sudden liberation of the self could well result in a formless tangle that showed less promise than did the scattered snippets already patterning the ground. Yet boldness might bring inspired sculpting just as often. Who could have guessed that inside a buffalo, a songbird might be awaiting first light or that from a lowly snail a dragon might soar in full majesty? Once such feats of self-fashioning were believed even remotely possible, there was no turning back for the animals in the topiary menagerie.

All became willing to face whatever might await them for this one chance to be seen as everything they conceived themselves to be.

"Top o' the Food Chain"

Once a pride of lions gathered at the classy restaurant "Top o' the Food Chain."

The restaurant had long enjoyed glowing reviews from well-known food critics and was praised by one as "a 'pleasure dome' for the palate of a khan" or just as cleverly by another as "a gastronomic Mardi Gras for all but the shyest of taste buds!"

Such lauding scarcely did justice, though, to either the array of tempting viands on the menu or the welcoming ambiance that characterized an establishment so stylishly catering to sophisticated carnivores.

While weighing the dining suggestions offered by a portly waiter, the lions also gestured towards various thick slabs of meat being carried out from the kitchen for other patrons and asked questions that demonstrated their own nuanced appreciation for the famed abilities of the Executive Chef.

After much discussion of the relative merits of this or that selection, weighing "a bold demonstration of venturesome spirit" here against "a charming nod to tradition" there, the lion pride unanimously decided to order the specialty of the day for the entire table: a free-range biped turned on a spit to perfection and marinated in its own juices. The aroma rising from this one-of-a-kind rarity, the waiter guaranteed, would be "a veritable feast for the nostrils."

Awaiting the arrival of their order, the lions continued their appreciative commentaries on the steady arrival at other tables of one steaming dish after another. They noted with a discernment that comes only through years of the gourmet life how the eyes of a young couple nearby repeatedly shifted from each other to the tantalizing amuse-bouche tray between them and then back again, betraying in their expressions an embarrassed but charming culinary naïveté. Then in an instant these trifles were swallowed whole and the pair could return to eyeing the mutual attractions of their own tender years exclusively. While at another table, aging habitués had reached the point of satiety and were discussing the choice of a final libation to cap off the evening.

But without question, the lions' own selection had to be accounted the "pièce de résistance," drawing admiration as it was paraded about the restaurant on the shoulders of six waiters before being brought to the pride's table with its limbs trussed tight, smothered head to foot in rich gravy, and the crowning touch of a large apple in its mouth.

Enchanted by this tour de force, the lions invited the Executive Chef to come out and accept their compliments, which continued for several rounds of the pride before ending in a hearty burst of applause, joined by all in the restaurant. The chef acknowledged this tribute by offering praise in return for the assembled patrons themselves (with the lions foremost, of course) for their impeccable taste buds.

When the lions finally left the restaurant hours later, each was already looking forward to their next little gathering, though few could conceive of an evening to outdo this one. Not just for the fare on offer but also for the genius of its preparation. How many masters of haute cuisine could, with such a virtuoso performance, raise a mere necessity of survival to the quintessential expression of the good life: to the *ne plus ultra* of gourmet dining? In matters of the table, the art of the sublime was all in how you transformed the choicest of ingredients into a meal fit for kings.

It had to merit the kind of magisterial "Bon Appétit!" that the Executive Chef had pronounced over the centerpiece of the extraordinary repast the lions were still sucking their teeth about as they stood outside the doors of "Top o' the Food Chain" and posted pictures they'd taken of the evening's rare delicacy to social media.

The Tortoise

Once a tortoise realized its time was drawing nigh.

The tortoise wasn't particularly alarmed by this realization. It did not suddenly turn morose or self-pitying. Nor was it bothered by those who raced past with an "Outta the way, old-timer!" tossed back over their shoulders. Nor by the likelihood that it cut a figure of ridicule in the eyes of many, what with its sagging flesh and its halting gait. It didn't look upon younger generations with defensive animosity or resentment that its own years were coming to a close while theirs would continue through decades to come. Its life had been full enough for one tortoise.

Thinking back over the years gone by, it took satisfaction not in specific events or experiences so much as in their sum total. What mattered most, now this long life was nearing an end, was that it had included a beginning and a middle as well.

A hackneyed assertion perhaps, the tortoise admitted, but there it was. Grander pronouncements about a lifetime could be left to those who thought them worth voicing. The tortoise was content to know that in its own time on earth, there had been room for challenges and achievements enough. These might not appear all that impressive, no memorable victories gained or harrowing defeats endured, but they would do for a life. They had their own weight and significance.

And despite its having been rather solitary by nature, the tortoise was pleased to have shared the planet for a time with so many other beings. It didn't get out and about much now, but that hadn't always been the case. In its day, the tortoise was to be seen at many a public celebration and cultural event. It seldom missed a museum exhibition or a concert or a boisterous parade or some other public event. And while a night at the theater could carry it to the limits of heart and mind, a walk down broad avenues, surrounded by perfect strangers in an endless flow, could be just as inspiring. Though it personally had always moved at a plodding pace, the tortoise rejoiced that so many others seemed to dance through life with such grace and élan. No question, it was good to have been a participating witness to it all.

Oh, there were countless experiences the tortoise now realized it would never have a chance to embrace. Adventures it would not pursue and longings it would fail to satisfy. But perhaps this was as it should be. To think that all you desired would be granted you in full—what a monotonous existence that must amount to.

The tortoise also knew that when its final hour was up, life's grand pageant would roll on as if it had never existed. It would be forgotten, sooner rather than later, and leave behind only an empty shell gathering dust.

So be it.

A Tree in the Forest

Once a tree fell in the forest when nobody was there to hear the sound.

The tree had been straight and tall, with a trunk that rose from the ground like a force of nature unto itself, ready to announce its defiance of any lightning strike or landslide. From below, the tree's crown was invisible far above, beyond the many branches that reached through those of neighboring giants on every side, linking one tree to another across ridge after ridge for miles.

Now those branches, shorn away in its fall, spread wide as if to gather up every needle that had ever floated down from them. The broken remains of trees that had toppled long before this one lay here and there around it, their former might now carried away piece after piece by ants.

271

Surrounded by the deep quiet of the forest floor, the tree began to reflect upon its own state. To have been standing so firmly rooted and now be stretched out here below and within a matter of decades to be no more—these changes might seem a steady undoing of the tree's presence that would end in questions of its ever having existed at all: leaving no more lasting trace of that existence than the sudden thunder of its collapse had left in the air.

Though what difference did it really make whether anybody had heard that thunder, let alone seen the tree's fall? Or that few had even known it was here deep within these woods in the first place? Did what counted about it depend in the slightest on the number of those whose comprehension of such things might begin and end with "Wow, what a big tree!"?

There could be no doubt it had come crashing down, as all trees naturally must. Or doubt that the moss in which it now lay had not been torn and tossed great distances when it struck the ground. And even though new moss would cover its entire length soon enough and reclaim the forest soil when it had finally rotted away, until then its inch-by-inch decline would still bear the shape of a life drawn up over centuries through root and limb and now returning to the earth.

Every ring grown out from the tree's heart had spoken of a force barely held in by now-riven bark that soon would nurse new saplings with its decay. And how many of these would fall in their own time, sooner or later, without the presence of a single witness to what sprouted, matured, and passed away here?

Did any of that even matter? Knowing you'd stood here for your allotted time was enough. As was knowing a forest had stood within you. You, who'd listened to the sound of your fall with the same understanding as when you'd listened to autumn storms rage through your branches or the thawing snow gently drip from them with each return of spring.

You, the sole testimony needed.

Sound or no sound had nothing to do with it.

Witness or no witness had nothing to do with it.

The Tribe

Once anthropologists discovered an unknown tribe whose leaders wore nothing but pieces of their children's skin.

The origins of this practice, which violated all traditional assumptions

272

regarding the instinctive concern of parents for the welfare of their own off-spring (and for the future of their community as a whole), eluded explanation for some time. Until, that is, an additional and equally baffling practice was documented so often it too could not be ignored: the abandonment of the elderly to their fate in difficult times. The key to understanding both customs turned out to lie in an examination of how the generation between the elderly and the young viewed its own role in the tribe.

As the productive core of both the family and, by extension, the tribe at large, this middle generation found it natural to stress that their own needs must perforce take precedence over those of the elderly and those of the young for the ultimate good of all. If resources grew scarce, the greatest portion should naturally go to those most in a position to survive and thrive, again for the ultimate good of all.

It made sense, then, that aging grandparents (the least productive members of the tribe) should be taken out with much ceremonial beating of drums and choreographed song and dance by tribal headsmen, then placed between a rock and a hard place and left to fend for themselves. There was no denying that the old might suffer, but mercifully not for long. And on the brighter side, their offspring in the middle generation could then get on with satisfying their personal needs, reassured that they'd been cruel only to be kind and that the sacrifice had been for the benefit of the tribe in the long run.

Soon, however, these offspring began to feel something was amiss, for their share of the tribal resources seemed to fall increasingly short of what they considered necessary to meet their own needs and desires. In their minds, they deserved more. So much more, as it turned out, that time-honored practices to bring about a redistribution of wealth every once in a while for the good of all tribal members were deemed too slow and were therefore abolished. As a consequence, collective identity and mutual sacrifice gave way to a boom of hoarding, and hoarding gave way to conspicuous surfeit on the part of some but deepening want on the part of everyone else, as those with the most ended up with even more and those with the least ended up with next to nothing.

Claiming the good life for oneself alone (never pausing to doubt this was one's due or that it might ever come to an end) can take a dramatic toll on people who follow such belief systems, though. As the outcome of this insatiable self-regard grew more and more grossly apparent and the "haves" of the tribe began to find their skin drawn thin over swelling excess, few any longer possessed the ability to restrain themselves or even to acknowledge a price must

273

eventually be paid for such self-serving behavior and lack of foresight.

Faced with the potentially disastrous consequences of this development, those tribal members who counted themselves among the "haves" and were most concerned about bursting wide open any day adopted the first remedy suggested by "super-haves" amongst them: partial flaying of the tribe's children whenever needed to provide that extra stretch of skin necessary to save one from splitting wide open out of gross indulgence.

What better way for children to honor their kinship obligations, the justification went, than by volunteering patches of their supple skin to graft over the growing holes in your own? After all, you gave them that skin in the first place, didn't you, so wasn't it only natural to expect they'd pay back the debt when the time came?

Flush with this assurance, those in the middle generation who'd been carrying on with the most expansive of lifestyles could continue to do so without much concern. Whatever the ultimate result of their lack of restraint, they remained confident that their children could still be expected to make the necessary sacrifice when called upon to do so.

And if that sacrifice wasn't enough, there would always be the skin of the next generation, of course.

And the next.

And the next after that.

The Trilobite

Once a trilobite had the distinct feeling it was being watched.

This unnerving sensation was something new. The trilobite could remember, or at least thought it could remember, days when it was free of any sense that the eyes of others were upon it—trillions and trillions of flinty eyes in the Paleozoic shallows where trilobites teemed. There was a time, not so distant, when each member of these multitudes had appeared intent on pursuing its own life, little interested in the doings of its neighbor.

When had that all changed?

For changed it had, and these days members of one's species to the ends of the earth were suddenly curious to know "everything about you," right down to your first awkward moves in the morning, all the many places your day took you, and your last fading twitch before sleep. As though the entire globe had become a camera set on autofocus and nothing was ever deemed too insignificant to be captured and then offered up online to every other trilobite in species-wide "sharing."

All of one's life now seemed reduced to lowest-common-denominator status, with personal highs and lows hard to distinguish any longer. Whatever brief moments deviated from the expected were now labeled "peak experiences" precisely because they stood out so rarely amid the daily silt of existence piling up all around and growing more difficult to wade through as it steadily thickened, trapping one ever more deeply in a past that other trilobites now insured through their incessant "friending" would never be forgotten. A past that could never be escaped once it became fixed in the stone-hard record of time.

Yet wasn't the promise of life supposed to be precisely a defiance of time? Wasn't the governing belief that the entire trilobite nation took for granted one of experience as constant self-development? As a perpetual overcoming of the limitations of the past? A promised advance to ever greater and greater triumphs and rewards? Or at least so this trilobite had been continually assured was the case by those who claimed to know all that a trilobite needed to know about "realizing its endless potential."

Now, though, this confidence was threatened as one's every moment and every move were recorded from myriad angles by others. "You will always be what you are right now" these unwanted intrusions on its life signaled to the trilobite. And the next moment would impose its own limits, as though individual moments were all that mattered and not the life evolving through them. A life increasingly crushed, in fact, by their layered weight.

There would be no breaking loose from this burden, the trilobite began to comprehend. No ambitious reaching for the future—or rather the many futures it had been led to believe were its for the fashioning. Instead, any misstep it made, however slight, any offhand comment it might voice and then immediately regret, any half-formed idea it might wish to let mature at its own pace, any phantom desire that might beckon it on to discoveries yet unimagined— all of these would only serve to make permanent how it appeared at this precise instant when viewed and "documented" from the outside by total strangers.

Was it every trilobite's lot, then, to be buried alive in its past and turn to stone? When the whole point of being born in the first place, a point so confidently touted by all, was to achieve something beyond the world that generation upon generation of look-alike forebears had left you?

And as for the future, what did it now hold but unending scrutiny and labeling by others? When nothing about the trilobite would remain "unknown"—except for its own secret hopes of becoming, over time, something more than its present self.

The Turtledoves

Once a pair of turtledoves wondered where they'd gone wrong.

Granted, when they were alone, they didn't spend any time worrying about going wrong or going right. They were too focused on one another to be aware of much else. When they looked out from their nest was when they became concerned that they might have missed something important.

What struck the turtledoves at moments like these was how divided down the middle so many of the other species around them acted and how often those divisions were seemingly accepted as the natural order of things. There were even some who glibly declared that males of a species and females of that same species were from different planets.

Hearing such assertions, the turtledoves could only look at one another with puzzlement. What could that mean, different planets? The turtledoves had no doubts about who they were, but it didn't depend on their being different. In fact, what they had in common seemed far more important than what they didn't.

One turtledove never began to coo without the other joining in. One never took wing without the other matching it beat for beat. Whatever they thought and felt, they did so in concert. And when leaning together in the still of the night, a single heartbeat was all they heard, and the thought that one of them might pass away before the other filled both with equal sadness.

So how had they missed what so many others saw as the natural order? Would they have been happier if they considered themselves opposites, divided from one another by countless distinctions? But how could love survive if it depended on repeating over and over again how little you had in common? Or if you were convinced that to end up together, you had to fly at each other from different planets?

What was this turtledove pair missing?

The Twittering Birds

Once a bevy of little twittering birds sat on a wire.

Actually, there were so many of these little birds and they were packed so tightly together that it was impossible to see the wire supporting them.

None of the twittering birds knew how they'd all been drawn to the same wire or when, for that matter, they had begun to twitter. As far as any of them could tell, they'd been there for what seemed forever and been twittering for just as long.

In sunny weather, there they sat. In rain, in snow, in high winds, there they all still huddled, clinging to their wire. Nothing could convince them either to go away or to leave off twittering even for a moment.

The twittering went on day and night. Sometimes it might fall to the level of a low whisper, but it never faded away completely. And whenever the slightest buzz happened to come down the wire, the twitter would steadily rise again until it became deafening.

This buzz could literally be seen as it traveled along the wire in the sudden lift it gave each of the birds in turn. The row of heads would take turns bobbing up and down and beaks would open and shut in quick succession, like something was poking each little bird from behind.

When the buzz had passed, that too could be seen in the behavior of the birds. At first they seemed to go nearly limp, being held in place perhaps only by virtue of their combined mass. Then, gradually, a few might try to recreate the power of the buzz by twittering to those nearest them. If that didn't work, they might try twittering to themselves about what it had been like when they last felt the buzz.

And if by chance two birds twittering to themselves fell into unison with one another, that might inspire the next birds on either side to feel some of the buzz again, too. Soon little wings could be seen flapping up and down the length of the wire once more. Once more little heads bobbed and little beaks worked with renewed energy.

It is not hard to understand how these sudden shifts from noisy excitement to near stupor and back to noisy excitement would lead the little birds to conclude that the buzz and their twittering not only were related but, taken together, defined the world as they knew it. For if the buzz gave life to their twitter, their twitter must add meaning to the buzz in return. And if the buzz had meaning, then life as little twittering birds must also have meaning. And if a life of twitter had meaning, then what on this globe didn't? In twitter, therefore, was the meaning of the world.

The important thing was to keep twittering. Always.

The Unicorn

Once a unicorn lost its horn trying to make a career change.

There wasn't much future, it discovered, in being merely a unicorn.

"You need to upgrade your skill set," the unicorn was told by a career consultant with whom it had made an appointment to discuss its prospects. "The first thing for us to do is quantify and qualify your experience so far and see where we stand. Now tell me about yourself. Just keep talking while I take a few notes."

"Well, I am a unicorn."

"Yes? . . . Yes . . . ?"

"That pretty much sums it up, I guess."

"No no no. You can't walk into an interview with that mindset. You'll be toast. Now let's prioritize to optimize and actualize, shall we? Start by trying to describe yourself in one sentence."

"I am a unicorn."

"You've said that already."

"I am a mythic being. Is that better?"

The consultant leaned back, stared at the ceiling, snapped a brightly striped suspender, and then looked again at the unicorn. "Let's think outside the box for a bit. E-commerce is growing like gangbusters these days. Is there anything about you that could take the letter E in front of it?"

"Ethereal."

"That's not exactly what I had in mind."

"Elusive?"

"Worse. Let's try a different tack. Now work with me here. What would you say is your greatest strength?"

"I am unique."

"That's on everybody's résumé these days, trust me."

"I am what I am."

"All very well, but who's going to pay good money just to have a unicorn around the office?"

"I represent a peerless and pure ideal."

"We need to be thinking 'pragmatic' and 'profit-oriented' here, not some fuzzy 'ideal.' Let's get back to basics, shall we? Try again to quantify and qualify your experience to date. What can you tell me?"

"Maidens and men of good intent sought me out."

"Maidens and men of good intent, eh? This is getting us nowhere. So here's what I propose. I'll network with some other career consultants I know, and you write out a list of your strengths, weaknesses, objectives, and whatever else you can think of. That'll give us a platform to work up a package that'll maximize your selling points. How's that sound?"

The unicorn was silent for a few moments and then said, "Do you mind if I ask a question?"

"Fire away."

"How much will all of this cost me?"

"Should that be our primary concern right now? It's your future we're talking about, let's not forget. I'm sure we can work out an easy fee schedule."

"I have to confess I have no money."

The career consultant stared for a long time at the unicorn, then looked up at the ceiling again and asked, "How about that horn? What's that worth?"

The Vampire Bats

Once vampire bats came out of their caves by the millions to discharge their civic duty.

It wouldn't do to remain in their dark haunts when society's call for the execution of justice rang out. They'd been at this for a long time, after all, predating thumbs-up-thumbs-down-day at the Coliseum, stonings in the village square, serial beheadings, and the burning of witches.

With that history, they'd all but claimed the voice of public conscience in matters of guilt and innocence. Innocence mostly, for it was a sense of communal innocence that inspired any self-respecting bat to exert itself in the name of justice.

During periods when communal innocence seemed in short supply and only a few public leaders could still be counted on to claim the voice of the highest authority in dismissing pleas by the accused for mercy, vampire bats were in great demand to fill the gap and convince an unsettled populace that the old standards for inflicting punishment still held.

In this capacity, they acted for all those who couldn't make it down to the local courthouse or prison parking lot themselves to shout for vengeance upon some stranger they'd been told on some blog deserved it. More than anything else, the spectacle of swarming, screeching vampire bats served to assure the populace at large that justice by proxy was still possible, no matter how hard it might be at times to do the right thing in one's own life.

One's own life might be just too complicated for a simple decision on good and evil, but the life of a publicly identified rotter was easy to pass judgment on. And if guilt could be pinpointed in this way, then ipso facto, innocence must be just as obvious. Already there by default in everybody not currently under sentence. So bearing witness to the punishment meted out to those declared guilty was bearing witness as well to one's own personal virtue.

No wonder these gatherings at the courthouse or in the prison parking lot took on an air of ritual self-purification, after which participants could resume their everyday lives purged of emotion in a mass catharsis that renewed community bonds. In place of Aristotle's catharsis through pity and fear, one need only substitute mass rage and a conviction of one's own righteousness to experience the effect desired.

How fortunate, then, to have vampire bats show the way.

The Vulgarian

Once a vulgarian decided not to crawl up on dry land.

It was fully aware that a pivotal moment in evolution might have arrived. It realized how the future of the planet could very well hang on its decision to leave the swamp for good and fill its lungs with the air of a new world. Still, why put itself to the effort, the vulgarian wanted to know? Why abandon what were the known comforts of the mud for an uncertain life on higher ground?

Was there even any need to? In the long run, what difference did it make whether you were in the vanguard of biodevelopment or somewhere at the rear? Nobody was keeping score on the rise and fall of life forms. Who remembered the trilobite or Homo erectus today? More to the point, who cared?

And just what was wrong with vulgarian existence in its present state, anyhow? Hard to top those yearly vacation trips to Vegas, where you could be serenaded by your favorite crooner or thrill to the idea that the Elvis impersonator at the next slot machine just might be a mafia hit man the Feds had asked for help in nabbing months ago on a "Most Wanted" episode? Was that something to tell folks back home, or what? Better than your cousin's latest alien abduction story for sure.

Did vulgarians lack for creature comforts, that they should feel unfulfilled by the status quo? From the mall to Park Avenue, what couldn't they buy? From "burgers bigger than your head" to this year's diet craze, what couldn't they eat? From soap operas to best-seller confessions, what wouldn't help them kill an idle hour? From hot tubs to Hummers, was there anything that wouldn't give a renewed lift, if one was ever needed, to their sense that all was right with their world?

The vulgarian had heard the standard claims that something of more substance was on offer beyond the life it found so comfortable, but it took those claims "with a grain of salt," as it liked to say. So long as it had the inalienable right to do whatever it pleased whenever and wherever it pleased, what other civil benefits or guarantees mattered? You could already watch anything you wanted on the Internet, from porn by the gogglebyte to the latest beheading, and maybe bid on a replica of Washington's false teeth or vote for the most patriotic brewski at the same time. There might be something else worth defending to the death on the other side of the evolutionary dividing line, but all politicians were liars anyways, weren't they, so why waste the time to find out?

The vulgarian had weightier reasons as well for hesitating, though, reasons of a spiritual dimension. Who'd willingly give up drive-in churches and evangelical theme parks with cartoon "fried-again veggies" for the kids and talking crosses for adults in exchange for Holy Communion Hollywood Style, featuring two hours of the body and blood of the Savior all over the big screen? Not to be cynical about it, but where was the spiritual advance in that, the vulgarian asked?

And what made all those who urged it to view the future as a continuous timeline of development towards a better life think they knew what they were talking about anyways? Couldn't the whole of vulgarian existence be seen not as a stage in a long upward evolution but as the high point of it already? What other life form had been half so successful in exploiting its environment? Vulgarians already knew plenty well what it took not just to survive but to thrive and multiply.

"So, why should I ever leave this ooze?" the vulgarian declared, up to its eyeballs in the stuff. "Gill-breathin's just fine by me."

The Vulture

Once a vulture learned to feel good about itself.

For as long as it could recall, the vulture had suffered deep pangs of self-reproach. This gnawing sense of blame didn't arise from any specific cause. Rather, it grew out of a more general distress: the misfortunes of others moved it deeply and without cease. So much so that it seemed impossible in the vulture's mind to separate itself from those tribulations. All of the world's woes spoke to it personally and summoned it to seek them out.

Goaded by such feelings, the vulture circled about the sky in search of any misfortune offering an opportunity to "be there" for sufferers as a tireless witness to their agonies. Despite such obvious dedication, however, was it doing enough, the vulture often wondered? Might there be some misfortune it had missed, some overlooked opportunity to find release from its own torment by confiding to one more sufferer, "I'll be here when you're in pain"?

This was the consuming sense of personal inadequacy the vulture had been reduced to when an acquaintance encountered it one day moving along with a dispirited shuffle, dragging its wings as though they were too heavy to lift.

"What's the matter?" the acquaintance asked with concern.

"Pain," came the barely audible reply. "I need to find more pain and relate to it in order to make my life worth living."

"Tried group therapy? Worked wonders for me."

At first the vulture had its doubts about the advice, but after several weeks of growing despondency, it decided to take a chance and joined "The Little Sharing and Caring Support Group" listed on a community bulletin board. The leader of the group, who was introduced not as a leader but as a "facilitator-slash-friend," spoke in heartfelt tones that immediately struck a responsive chord deep within the vulture's breast.

The facilitator-slash-friend would ask all those present to "plug into" their innermost feelings. Each session, the vulture would listen to the others recite their weekly list of trials and tribulations and would take the full five minutes of its own allotted time to do the same.

Then the facilitator-slash-friend would say glowingly: "Thank you all for sharing so much with us today. I'm sure you'll feel better and better as you share more. My goal is to see you find that personal comfort zone where you can say, 'I'm positively at peace with where I'm at today. Positively.'"

This validation of its inner need did make the vulture feel better, actually. It wasn't alone at least. And now it could see a way to heal its self-doubt, thanks to the soothing counsel of the facilitator-slash-friend.

At ease finally and ready now to spread that warm confidence far and wide, the vulture contemplated setting up a few group therapy sessions itself. It shouldn't be difficult to inspire others to find their own comfort zone amid so much suffering, that special place where they too could repeat, "I'm positively at peace with where I'm at today. Positively."

For who better to feel the full pain of a world in extremis, it now felt confident, than an understanding vulture like itself?

The Wacko

Once a wacko fell off the ceiling and right into the soup at a political banquet.

To see this creature sprawled there and straining to gather its scattered wits was startling, to say the least. Hadn't any of the prominent invitees to the banquet noticed the wacko dangling upside down where the slightest misstep could land it precisely where it had landed, splattering them all with the consequences?

Wackos weren't exactly an unknown species, after all, particularly during this time of climate change, which caused them to engage in more-than-usual displays of aggressively offensive conduct. As body temperatures and brain temperatures soared in these otherwise cold-blooded threats to the public, they could be observed moving about in broad daylight with malign intent, no longer darting furtively here and there as they long had in order to avoid notice. While in the depths of the night, shining a beam into any dark corner might reveal their twitching forms huddled close and perhaps plotting an all-out assault on the unsuspecting.

So why hadn't anyone raised the alarm before the wacko in question fell into the soup, soon to be joined by others of its kind who lost their footing on the ceiling as well and rained down like a plague even the Old Testament couldn't have prepared anyone for: a frenzy of hissing wackos that ultimately left none of the banquet's fare unspoiled and the faces of nearly all its attendees badly soiled?

What was to keep this repugnant horror from happening again and again?

283

The Wall Street Ravens

Once the crows of Wall Street asked themselves, "Why not have it all?"

It was all there for the taking, wasn't it? Life offered more than just bits of wind-blown gain, so why be satisfied with small pickings, when a little extra moxie could bring far greater rewards? Everybody was out for whatever could be had, these crows were convinced, so why not grab whatever you could in the rush?

Having agreed they had a perfect right to carry off everything they could manage to, the crows pursued their goal single-mindedly. Nothing could deter or divert them. The few scarecrows set up by authorities to curb their excesses earned only their raucous, scornful laughter. Nor were the crows troubled by second thoughts in their choice of tactics to employ. If they spied some prize in the hands of the unsuspecting, they set to making as much noise as possible until the distracted victim dropped whatever it was the crows coveted and fled.

"Bottom line, we're just too smart for these losers," the crows would laugh till they were hoarse. "It's as easy as taking candy from a baby."

The one thing the crows had neglected to include in their rapacious calculations, as it turned out, was the presence of ravens perched atop buildings for blocks around. Besides possessing all of the cleverness of crows, the ravens of Wall Street boasted appetites that were far greater and employed methods far more unsparing to sate them. They never blinked in their cold-eyed rapacity.

What crows did out of mere craving, the ravens had turned into a science. They figured every angle of greed, calculated every hidden advantage, and when they'd seized hold of all they wanted, winged their way to safe havens far out of reach.

Had the crows been slightly more restrained in declaring themselves masters of their little universe, had they been able to resist the urge to flaunt with such brazenness the spoils they thought they were piling up, that plunder might not have drawn the attention of more adroit thieves.

But the crows didn't have it within themselves even to consider restraint. And as they went about their noisy dealings below, the ravens bided their time high above, waiting and watching for the moment to make their move.

And when that moment came, the crows had no idea what hit them.

The Walruses

Once a sudden rise in sea level caught a pod of basking walruses off guard.

The day this happened began as many before it had. The sky was clear. The sun was warm and growing steadily warmer as it rose and its reflection played in and out of bright tidal pools along the shoreline. The tide, having reached its low point some distance away, was starting its incoming return over the sand and rocks. All in all, the half-asleep walruses felt little cause to think anything might be amiss.

In fact, it took some time before the walruses were even aware the water was not stopping at its accustomed high point but rather continuing to advance. They first took notice of this challenge to their customary expectations when groups of seals and sea lions that had been sunning themselves on rock outcroppings closer to the waves began vanishing from sight. But then, seals and sea lions were not walruses; walruses couldn't be washed away so easily.

As long as seals and sea lions were the only ones disappearing, the walruses felt little urgency about moving to higher ground. And even if a few young and restless walruses at the edge of the pod were in fact being swept under as well by what was now a gathering surf, there was still little cause for worry. Walruses can swim, can't they? Sooner or later they were bound to resurface.

Only they weren't resurfacing. Not a single one. And as more and more slipped from view, a growing uneasiness spread along what remained of the vanishing shoreline. With the water engulfing each new cluster of walruses, the next cluster took the threat more seriously, although yet farther back from the waves, that concern still faded into snoozing indifference.

"What water?" the most complacent among the walruses asked without opening their eyes, while others, slightly more awake, still could not imagine the rising sea would ever reach them. Tides come and tides go, so what else was new?

Those who rejected the whole idea of anything so preposterous as a rise in sea level and declared themselves "sea-rise deniers and proud of it" made a show of their disdain for members of the pod who didn't share their dismissal of danger as they dared the surf to carry them away if it could. It could and did.

Hearing the final, defiant splutterings of these "sea-rise deniers" as they, too, disappeared from sight, the remaining members of the walrus pod finally realized they were all in danger. Alarm quickly set in, and soon full-blown panic. Up and down what little remained of the shoreline, panic drove the walruses against one another in lumbering disarray. An orderly response to the threat might have saved many of those in the crush. However, so much time was lost in pushing forwards and backwards amid ever louder bellowing that it seemed not a single walrus would make it to safety. The agitated struggle for survival turned to accusations and vicious rebukes as the walruses began to point flippers at one another, demanding to know who was responsible for having failed to foresee what was happening.

The sea rose and the frenzy of blame rose. Which one would claim the most victims in the end was any walrus's guess.

The Warbler

Once a warbler just could not get an annoying song out of its head.

No matter where it went, no matter what it did, the drearily predictable notes and words of the song echoed over and over through the warbler's mind, sometimes softly, sometimes not, but always inescapably present.

Had it been the warbler's own song, the constant repetition wouldn't have been so distressing. Giving voice to one's deepest self could never be that, for each note and refrain, rich with personal meaning, rose from the heart of experience. And true to experience, it was true to life.

But what was turning and returning in the warbler's head wasn't true to anything it had personally known. With each repetition, the warbler sensed, another portion of its self-awareness was being overlaid with the passions and disappointments of others.

Where had the unwanted intrusion come from? Or rather, where hadn't it come from, for the same tune could be heard in any elevator or store or dental office or public restroom around. As if no place was safe from its reach and the intent was to have the whole world humming mindlessly along.

Now that the warbler thought about it, threats to the inner peace needed to work out the music of one's own life didn't come only from these mind-numbing assaults. The world was filled with the babble of programmed ideas and emotions repeated so often that they, too, left little chance of escaping with one's own self intact. Formula newspaper editorials; online "influencers" hyping the latest trends; book reviews that read like publishers' blurbs; "in their own words" radio and video exclusive interviews of the year that all seemed taken from the same script; genteel whimsy, earnest platitudes, or a stale aperçu or two passed off as sophisticated insight; tit-for-tat exchanges on any subject by social commentators who start with talking points and end up half choking to death with rage—what space was left anywhere for voices that didn't conform to these dreary expectations?

Had Bouvard and Pécuchet taken over the planet? What other explanation was there, the warbler asked itself, for this reluctance to venture beyond received ideas when received ideas had led to such emotional and intellectual stagnation: to a casual acceptance of the hackneyed while the genuinely original went unremarked?

Did others suffer an equal sense of violation by all this noise, this blur of mass-emotions and mass-thinking that left the warbler wondering if it would soon be unable even to recognize the sound of its own voice? Did others also wince at the noisy trespass upon their days and nights that robbed them of minutes here and minutes there until more than just time had been lost?

With each moment a warrant of one's being, if any of them ceased to ring true, who were you? Simply another background-music version of the life of the species? Did you even exist anymore when others did your singing for you, leaving you to hum along with their choice of tired standbys if you were to be heard at all?

It made the warbler want to screech in its own ears just to be assured that it wasn't deaf to itself quite yet.

The Weak Ego

Once a weak ego signed up for the trial offer of a popular home gym.

The decision hadn't been taken impulsively. There'd been months of nervous lip-chewing on the weak ego's part about whether to accept the "once-in-a-lifetime TV offer" or forgo the opportunity to join the bulked-up egos that flexed and struck poses in advertisements for this all-in-one personal apparatus.

It was tempting to see oneself as the "real ego" that the ad claimed one could become in just minutes a day. No more hesitations. No fears of insignificance when compared with other egos. Yet what if a few minutes a day wasn't enough, the weak ego wondered? Suppose you strode out to display yourself to the world in all your new glory only to encounter a more muscled-up ego than you. In egos, size didn't just matter. It was all that mattered.

What finally convinced the weak ego to set aside its hesitation and give the home gym a try was the "home" part of it. The prospect of being able to bulk up in secret had definite appeal. So too did checking out your progress before your mirror at home instead of at a fitness center with a crowd of perfectly sculpted egos smirking over your shoulder like disdainful gods.

Studying the all-in-one gym after straining to get it out of the shipping box, the weak ego had to admit the thing was impressive. And with all its weights and pulleys and flanges and spines, the machine had the appearance of a giant insect. This thought, strangely enough, comforted the weak ego, for if the apparatus looked fearsomely alive, ready to rear up and unleash a power as lethal as it was quick, mightn't the time spent molding oneself to its embrace instill that force to be reckoned with in oneself as well?

And with bulked-up confidence so clearly defined in the whole of one's being, who'd so much as dare curl a scornful lip or snicker in passing? The world would be there for the taking, practically laying itself at one's feet like starry-eyed screamers at the finals of the Ego Universe Invitational. Oiled up, slicked down, shoulders wide and standing tall, a Titan among pipsqueaks, a new Atlas grinning as if the heavens were light as a beach ball, the superiority of the weak ego's poses would be obvious to every eye, the envy of all who found themselves dazzled by the confidence it would have gained in just minutes a day!

Yet what if one screaming fan in that chorus of admiration at the Ego Universe Invitational might be praising the home gym instead of what it had produced? Might not the scrawniest of egos upstage the most pumped-up one in that case, revealing that without the mechanical support, a weak ego remained as feeble as ever. Lacking the strength even to open a door on its own and step out to face the world beyond.

In order to avoid the distressing possibility of such a humiliating defeat, then, should the weak ego pack up the home gym and return it ahead of the deadline for a refund? Ah, but the thing was such a marvelous device, the weak ego sighed. So strongly built and with an ironclad guarantee.

Wouldn't just another turn or two in its embrace be okay?

The Whale

Once a whale stretched out in a furniture showroom recliner.

It happened on a day when crowds of bargain hunters were drawn to the store by advertisements of "once in a lifetime" deals. The sales staff, though somewhat irritated by the whale's choice of the most popular item to relax in, tried to carry on with business as usual by pretending the massive thing wasn't stretched out right there in front of them. Until the clientele began to complain about the snoring.

In response, the staff took it in turns to creep up and cautiously poke the whale from a safe distance with whatever came to hand, most often a floor lamp or bunk bed ladder. Someone suggested throwing dining chairs at the deadbeat cetacean, but the idea was turned down as being unlikely to have much effect, to say nothing of reflecting adversely upon the store's image. While pulling the rumblous hulk off the recliner and back outside was obviously beyond the might of staff, managers, and patrons combined.

In the meantime, the whale continued blithely blowing away, almost as though singing to itself. All through the day, with eyelids dancing and a smile lifting the corners of its slack jaw, the whale slipped from one dream to another, finding deeper pleasure in each by turn.

There were carefree frolics in the dreams and wish fulfillment spreading in every direction, plus league upon league of blubber-smokin' sex. But all these delights passed in their turn, without leaving much of a trace in the whale's mind.

By contrast, what began to play an ever-larger part in its slumber were satisfactions of another sort. Formless at first but steadily regurgitated from the depths of the whale's unconscious came every scaly, toothed, shelled, or tentacled denizen of the sea, their massed total swelling the whale's bulk ever further as each snore and snort made room for more in a spreading measure of self-contentment.

The alarm felt by all who witnessed this nonstop waxing of the whale that now threatened to pin shoppers to the walls cannot be overstated. The recliner and most of the rest of the furnishings in the store had steadily disappeared from sight, and still the whale continued to add to its swollen girth. After the bounties of the sea now redigested in dreams came those of the land and air, as anything that walked or flew or simply stood rooted to the earth was sucked in and packed away. Nor were any of the inanimate resources of nature spared. Soon the entire sum of existence might disappear into the rumbling abyss of this single loafer's snore, as its smile of contentment broadened all the while.

Would the crowd now trapped in the store by the humongous whale find themselves sucked into its dark satisfaction like everything else? One minute shopping away without a care and the next powerless to save yourself from another species' heedless self-indulgence! What gave a whale the right to act like nothing mattered in this world but its own desires and comforts, irate shoppers demanded to know.

How dare it! Wasn't that a privilege reserved for the human species alone?

The Withered Tree

Once a withered tree was having some trouble looking on the brighter side of life.

What brighter side, the withered tree wanted to know, when every day it was reminded that its own life might not have a brighter side? Might never have one, and instead remain stunted, gnarled, and perpetually turned toward the cold north.

Why hadn't it reached its full potential, as trees all around it looked to have? At times one might almost think the forest wasn't to be seen apart from their imposing forms and competing claims to be at the center of it. Each massive cedar or fir strained not simply to tower above all others but to spread its wonders and cast any rivals in its shade as well.

Though to the withered tree, they all looked pretty much alike, differing little beyond height and breadth and a slight variation here or there on a common understanding of "life potential." In fact, they seemed to take most pride in being recognized as an enviably successful illustration of ambitions universally shared. Particularly if a claim could also be made of having overcome daunting obstacles at some point on the way to one's exemplary triumph far above. While a scar or two suffered in the process, a lightning strike or some such, was interpreted as a testament to one's resilience and dedication that could give a boost to even middling attainment in the never-ending quest to be taken seriously as a tree among trees.

But what if you were nothing but scars? A gash to your very core ceased to be worth calling attention to when that core was covered with them. The same was true for a twisted limb when not a single one wasn't. How do you make a virtue out of continual blows? Or out of "the good fight" when struggle was too constant to allow for degrees of victory or defeat? When "the good fight" had become the cliché of last resort, so worn that all distinguishing grain had faded from it?

What had gone wrong those many years ago, the tree wondered? When had its withering begun? And why? That some trees just flourished and others did not hardly counted as an answer, so obvious that its truth rendered "why" meaningless. The "when" seemed more important to understand.

Were limits already there in the seed, possibilities closed off before any summons to them arose? Had the soil from which to draw the strength and flexibility needed to grow been exhausted, or had that soil proved too rich with promises to nourish any one of these to fullness? And what of the seedling, now years and years in the past, that had strained towards every dawn with its own bright determination?

What had happened, then? With little chance of further growth now, what you had become you were doomed to remain, it seemed. This limb would never straighten to what it might have been nor that dead one ever revive, and each autumn took a little more out of you. Until the gathering chill drove you back to whatever inner strength remained and kept you from collapsing altogether in the long wait for spring.

Simple endurance brought its own wounds now, deeper and slower to heal. Beneath the riven bark they spread their message that nothing could escape.

That nothing should escape, the withered tree began to think. What a fool's comfort it was to believe you could outlive your scars and declare yourself healed of all pain, that you had earned the right to boast to the world that nothing could wound you to the heart anymore. While to moan in the night wind that life still owed you some encouragement, owed you anything other than itself, was a waste indeed.

Would it be better to remain a withered tree to the end in that case, without comfort but without illusions either? Could there be merit in such quiet resolve? Just as there might be a kind of peace in seeing one's own struggle for what it was? No grand display of powers once dreamed of but never found. No "inspiring victory against overwhelming odds" or "eternal symbol of the indomitable spirit shining through." How many of these were praised for a season and then forgotten? Instead, a sober and darker faith should be kept with what lay unsaid, much closer to the pith: an allegiance to all that has made you what you are—not despite the setbacks and pain but precisely and unreservedly because of them.

An embrace like this of the withering that had overtaken it would require a strength the tree wasn't sure it still had. And yet what else should have been its confidence all along? What had happened to it was not some injury, whether

291

early or late in life, but instead a truth that should sustain it always and one that would abide when this dense stand of forest had vanished to the last tree and the soil rooting them all had blown away to bare rock.

A truth that came not from outer measure and sweep but from a lifetime of knotted beauties inside and out. Something else entirely.

The Wolves

Once a pack of wolves won a Department of Defense contract in the billions to howl at the moon.

The idea behind the contract was a simple one. By howling at the moon, the wolves would ensure that it didn't fall from the sky and score a direct hit on any of the nation's political or economic centers. And if by chance the moon did fall, a backup plan would howl it down harmlessly somewhere off one coast or the other.

All went smoothly for the wolves' proposed defense initiative. Closed-door congressional hearings were called and high-ranking military and intelligence officials crowded together by the score at long tables to affirm the initiative's necessity and strong probability of success. A brief sampling of testimony in opposition to the proposal was also heard. Then it was approved by a lopsided vote.

Only at this point, when the wolves were readying themselves for the howl of a lifetime, did a few problems begin to surface. Most were quickly disposed of, but one remained a growing source of concern: the wolves couldn't agree on where, exactly, the moon would be coming from when it rose.

Some insisted it would rise in the east as usual. Others insisted just as vehemently that new geopolitical realities called for new thinking. The moon might suddenly shoot up from the west and catch them off guard. Still others held that the threat of a rogue moon appearing from practically anywhere should be the true concern.

The sole means of resolving this dispute, it was finally agreed, was for the wolves to face in every direction at once and wait in a state of utmost alert. This decision meant the original budget would be inadequate, obviously, but requests for additional funding sailed through once the advantages of the revised plan were explained in new congressional hearings.

Then the time came to test the system. As the wolves sat in a circle and warily eyed every inch of the skyline in the gathering darkness, their esprit de corps was high. As the night deepened, however, that mood changed, at first slowly and then ever more rapidly. With each passing hour, it became clearer that something was profoundly amiss. The moon wasn't coming up at all, anywhere.

Perhaps the moon menace was more sophisticated than had been thought. Or the doom it threatened might be on some kind of time delay. The moon might actually have risen long before but was invisible due to advanced stealth technology. In this worst-case scenario, mightn't the moon already be hurtling earthward, bringing mass destruction with it?

There was not a moment to lose. The wolves, as if responding to a single command, began howling in all directions at once: east, west, north, south, up, down.

If the moon was out there, they'd find it!

The Wood Ducks

Once a pair of wood ducks grew old together.

It had been a long life they'd shared, a life not without its challenges. In truth, love—owing so much to chance already—might never have brought the two birds together in the first place. Being born on different continents in the wide scattering of wood duck populations made the likelihood of their ever meeting remote beyond calculation. What circumstances must ultimately have brought them together could only be guessed at by other ducks on the lake.

Without question, they made for a strange couple in the eyes of many. These two didn't just mate for life as wood ducks customarily do but often appeared so focused on each other as to be unaware that other ducks were even around. They might come out of their love-trance every once in a while and fall in with the flock as it traced familiar patterns across the lake, only to veer off again into their private rushes and reeds or take wing to a secret love nest in some hollow tree.

What were they up to after vanishing like that, others in the flock wondered? It must involve more than the conjugal routines that the rest of them took as the normal course of a couple's life. The array of avian erotic moves they imagined with a wink and a nod would only have made the absent pair smile at such limits to imagination.

Admittedly, the two had felt an irresistible attraction at first sight, yet this by itself couldn't explain their abiding attachment ever since. Hatching out on opposite sides of the globe had colored their lives differently and might well have hindered a shared life going forward, but the contrary became the embracing reality of all their years together.

Their pasts had steadily merged, until they found themselves at one, paddling side by side or flying wing to wing for days on end through borderlands between their origins that were thought uncrossable by other ducks. In that expanse without boundaries, whatever self-awareness one had, the other shared. Whatever one experienced, the other experienced just as fully. And when they soared together from the lake and headed for the borderlands, the pleasure they took in the realm they were entering was simultaneous, equal, complete.

The Woodpecker

Once a woodpecker suffered from obsessive-compulsive disorder.

Hardly unusual in a woodpecker, one might think. Moreover, OCD no longer carried the heavy stigma it once had. Obsessive single-mindedness and compulsive repetitions characterized much of behavior now, this woodpecker was assured by another of its kind who cited examples from both the natural kingdom and the unnatural one to illustrate the point.

"Imagine we led a bee's life or the fraught existence of some political animal."

"A political animal?" the woodpecker replied with a tone of annoyance. "That's going a bit far, isn't it?"

"Taxonomically perhaps, yet you must admit there are similarities in how our heads and those of political animals have hardened over time."

"Thanks a lot! We at least put ours to good service in getting rid of pests."

"Okay, okay, perhaps the comparison wasn't the best. If it's a question of hard heads and how they're put to use, imagine what it must be like for a satirist, then."

"A what?"

"A satirist. You've seen them around, digging into everything with an urge that is overpowering and rooting out prey too slow or too complacent to escape."

"So that's what those noisy creatures are called, is it? Satirists?"

The woodpecker wasn't any more comfortable with this comparison than the previous one, however. It could grant the point about hard heads and the obsessive pursuit of a target, regardless of how well hidden or protected it might be. But were satirists bothered by anything approaching the woodpecker's own mental conflicts at the moment of attack? Did the same questions reverberate in their minds as in its own at each blow it struck: questions of whether the objects of their attacks might simply have been obeying their own deep obsessions, hardwired to draw attention to themselves almost? Did satirists at times suffer twinges of conscience like those a woodpecker might feel just before skewering its prey?

If the woodpecker's prey had any second thoughts about being driven to destroy something as grand as an old-growth forest tree by tree, wasn't it possible a satirist's victims suffered hesitations of their own? Brooding-moments when even the most fixated might pause to question their intent. Were satirists moved to hold back from striking their prey at such times? Even to letting some slip away?

If that was true, a satirist might not be so different from a woodpecker after all, this one supposed. Could both of them feel compelled by irresistible forces to hunt out new targets with gusto, only to feel that thrill turn into a strange, troubled empathy with their victims and a determination to resist any future impulse to attack them—followed inevitably by a new compulsion to do precisely that? Had the woodpecker found another creature as torn as itself? No, that was inconceivable. Yet what if it wasn't?

Could there really be such a thing as a reluctant obsessive-compulsive satirist?

The Worm

Once a worm came back from the grave.

"I have good news," the worm proclaimed. "There really is life after death."

Some of those who heard this declaration responded with a derisive "Sure there is." But others were likely to say, "I knew that already because a winged messenger told me all about it."

"Oh?" the worm asked. "And what did this messenger tell you?"

"That I'd be going to a better place."

"Better than here?"

"Of course."

"That's strange. It didn't seem all that different to me."

"What are you talking about, not all that different?"

The worm was startled by the aggressive tone of the question, but it did its best to detail what it had seen. It began with the land of the deceased, describing the alternating sunny and stormy weather and the varied geography, not forgetting to mention the equally diverse flora and fauna. It told as well of the deceased themselves, of how they spent their days at work and their weekends at the barbecue, wishing they had more "down time." The worm concluded with the satisfaction that the dead took in all the small things of the hereafter, while noting their trials and tribulations and their determination to overcome these as best they could.

"What about the angels and the hymns of joy?"

"I can't say I encountered any angels. I did hear singing, but it was just as likely to be a pining for love or for a lost hunting dog as a hymn of joy. I admit, though, there may have been something I missed."

"Only everything that makes the years of waiting to be delivered from this fallen world worthwhile, that's what!"

"Why believe in life after death if all you're going to get is more of the same?" another voice rang out.

"I'm sorry you feel that way," the worm responded. "I always thought that was what you wanted, judging by how attached to life so many of you become when you're about to lose it."

"Well, you thought wrong!"

Others listening to the worm's account were eager to know whether it had met any little green aliens or seen a white light and experienced the sensation of floating above its own body and looking down at itself.

"No, I didn't."

"What? I have in every one of my near-death experiences."

"What were they like, these near-death experiences?" the worm asked.

"An unearthly sensation of out-of-body peace."

"I'm afraid all I felt was what you yourself might feel on any given day."

"Are you serious, you mere worm?"

"I apologize if I've offended any of you. I assumed your days were as rich in experience as you could make them."

"But I don't want more experience. I want an unearthly sensation of out-of-body peace!"

"And I want eternal life with milk and honey and nothing I have to do."

296

"Me too."

"Rather than everything this life offers you?" the worm asked all of those in what was now a growing crowd.

"Are you deaf?" the crowd angrily responded as one. "How many times do we have to repeat ourselves?"

Soon after these and other similarly awkward exchanges, the worm was put on a hook and turned into bait.

What else was it good for?

The Xenophobe

Once a xenophobe turned up in the nation's blood supply.

Being a single-idea organism and thus extremely small, the xenophobe at first went undetected when transmitted from host to host to host, allowing it to multiply rapidly within each of its unwitting victims until its pernicious spread reached from one extremity to another and from the heart deep into the brain.

The initial indication that something might be amiss in a victim took the form of a mild but persistent fever. Then, in what seemed no time at all, the fever would grow more virulent and be accompanied by a steady swelling of the head. The sufferer began to have trouble seeing straight and typically spoke in a rambling or incoherent fashion. Subdued by paramedics one day while holding up traffic and threatening drivers if they didn't repeat faithfully some rambling tirade about "alien hordes," the hapless victim would be rushed to the nearest emergency room.

The prognosis was seldom good. By this point, the xenophobe would have so exploited every vulnerability of its now raving host that the prospects for a full return to good health seemed remote. Prone to fits of rage and addled paranoia, the sufferer often complicated matters by jerking free of all restraints and berating medical personnel who appeared in any way different or foreign. Shouts of "Get the hell away from me, you f****n' b*st**d!" and "Go back wherever you f****n' came from, b**ch!" were hurled in every direction, although the ranting could be rendered nearly unintelligible by a thick layer of foam covering the patient's mouth.

Then, just as suddenly as it had begun, the crisis might seem to pass. From being a hopeless case, convulsed by hysterical outbursts one moment and seemingly brain-dead the next, the sufferer would appear to be making a miraculous recovery. With astonishing speed, the fever broke, the paranoia faded, and the raving gibberish steadily gave way to more recognizable forms of expression. The victim returned home to open arms and resumed daily life as if nothing had happened.

Relatives, friends, and colleagues avoided any mention of the xenophobe attack, fearful of triggering a possible relapse. It was thought better to act as though the whole unpleasant episode amounted to no more than a false scare. In addition to sparing everybody any potential unpleasantness, this politic approach also allowed the community at large to feel reassured that the xenophobe was no longer of serious concern. By all appearances, its victim seemed fully cured.

So why not assume that all was well and just move on?

The Yak

Once the self-described "greatest yak in history" took a vow of silence.

Pledging not to say another word about anything at any time must have required a degree of self-restraint not usually associated with yaks, prone as they are to snorting their hazy thoughts nonstop into the frosty air around them. The particular yak in question had developed quite a reputation for snorting at length about whatever might have caught its attention that morning, noon, or night. Often just moments before. It didn't matter in the slightest what the topic was; if the yak believed that topic warranted nebulous clouds of approval or dismissal, snort away it would.

Some days, the amount of methane gas released into the atmosphere during an extended venting of this sort could by itself move the needle on global warming. Not that moving the needle bothered the yak in the slightest. Typically, it shook the ice-hard mat of hair between its horns and smiled broadly at this proof of its power to do whatever it pleased whenever it pleased. Besides, the yak was confident it knew more about sub-zero thinking than all other yaks since the emergence of the species and as far into the future as the coming of their extinction might be. As a result, the sound of its own snorts echoing back from great distances in all directions was definitely gratifying.

"I'm a genius," it never tired of declaring, "so shoosh and listen, okay?" And listen the rest of the yak herd did, dutifully holding their own breath when ordered to do so and then voicing their equally dutiful admiration in repetitive methane burps on cue.

So why did this "greatest yak in history" now take a vow of silence? Why, at the very height of its command over the herd, did it suddenly turn away and lumber off into the cold? What was going through its mind? What was it thinking that it did not wish to share? Was it good? Was it bad? Would it bolster the yak's claims of unrivaled wisdom and greatness or prove the total opposite of these?

Or was it all just a yak being a yak?

The Zebra

Once a zebra found itself in a herd of black horses and white horses.

The zebra watched the black horses and the white horses carefully for clues about how it might fit into the herd and noticed that although they seemed to spend most of their time moving about at random as they grazed, at the end of the day the white horses generally moved closer together and the black horses generally moved closer together as well. The zebra wondered why that was.

The horses, for their part, wondered about the zebra in return. First of all, what color was it exactly? Was it black with white stripes, or was it white with black stripes? How could one be both black and white at the same time? Could one change one's stripes at will? Was the zebra trying to hide something about itself, the white horses asked each other and the black horses asked each other? Was the zebra pretending to be something it was not and only half succeeding?

The zebra knew it couldn't do anything about the stripes it was born with. When it first noticed the difference between itself and the horses, it had in fact wished to be entirely one color or entirely the other color by turns, hoping that way to escape the scrutiny of at least half the herd for a while. The wishing hadn't produced the desired effect, though, and the zebra had ultimately decided there was nothing it could do about its stripes. Why should it want to change them anyway? They were what made a zebra a zebra, weren't they?

There was also nothing to be done, it concluded, about the way the horses behaved when it was around. Some within each group pretended the zebra simply didn't exist, or so it seemed from their habit of furtively watching it but quickly averting their eyes if the zebra chanced to gaze in their direction. Others seemed to have decided that the zebra, because it looked different, wasn't worth the bother of getting to know, let alone look at. Still others couldn't take their eyes off its unique color patterns, seeing the zebra as exotic and alluring, an object of fantasies. All of these attitudes made the zebra feel disheartened and misunderstood.

At day's end, when the white horses moved nearer to each other and the black horses moved nearer to each other and the zebra found itself alone once more, it could hear the horses of each color asking themselves the same questions over and over. Was the zebra black with white stripes? Was the zebra white with black stripes?

"Why not both at once?" the zebra wanted to ask. "Why not both as one?"

The Zeitgeist

Once a zeitgeist had to admit being perplexed about what it was expected to be.

Was it supposed to herald bold new beginnings or, instead, embrace the inherited legacy of the past? There were plenty of opinions in the air and legions of those who were confident they knew the answer to this question, but their certainty only deepened the zeitgeist's uncertainty.

For instance, if bold new beginnings were in fact called for, which voice amongst all those claiming to know precisely the way forward was it to trust? Often those voices rising above the general din seemed merely to be the most insistent or the ones inspired by the latest partisan chatter.

And were these advocates for "the now and the new" really offering a complete departure from the past, the zeitgeist wondered? Why did it feel as if, for all the bold claims made, the expectations for real change weren't wholly fulfilled in the end? Little true challenge was being posed to a catalogue of assumptions actually dating back centuries about how to conduct one's spiritual or societal or cultural life and what gives life itself meaning, despite whatever "revisioning" was promised. Why did it feel as if genuine, sweeping originality that would redefine everything failed when put to the test and was replaced eventually by slogans and brave new talking points.

For the spirit of the age to be truly new, mustn't it owe little to yesteryears' versions? Otherwise, telling one age from another would be impossible, or if not impossible, then reduced to an arid exercise more defined by group ideology than independent perception. And if that was all it came down to, a mere game of historical "spot the difference," the zeitgeist didn't see much point to the effort. The life of an era was short enough already; losing time quibbling over what set it apart seemed foolish. If the differences weren't obvious, why bother?

That said, was the case for representing "the treasured legacy of the ages" any more compelling? Was clinging to inherited greatness how the zeitgeist should define itself? But being the extension of one tradition rather than the start of another and thus little more than a wagging tail to some earlier era didn't hold much appeal.

Even if it did, what tradition should be the guide? With civilization upon civilization crowding the past (many in conflict with one another about even the most basic of definitions and expectations), on what basis would their legacies be assessed when the choice of one over others would label you for ages to come, whether for better or worse? What if the embrace of intelligence, compassion, creativity, and truth, so hard-won over time, yielded to a return of ignorance, hate, blind conformity, superstition, and lies? Had it not happened before? Of course it had, time and again.

Such debates left the zeitgeist feeling caught between loud self-congratulation on the one hand and a nagging inferiority complex on the other, never certain whether it should toast its own triumphs or bemoan its relative lack of distinction. Though what if neither epoch-changing revolution nor preservation of a hand-me-down heritage was how the zeitgeist should define itself? Despite all the competing claims, what if it was just a trough between sea crests, a time so taken with itself that it had lost the sense of proportion necessary to tell whether it was the promise of a rising swell or just another eddy in the downward wake of the past?

To be an uncertain stage that might ultimately stand only for premature claims or lost opportunities was sobering, akin to finding that your time's self-vaunting might just be a dim blip in a universe that boasted zeitgeists of dazzling scope.

If so, it would take all of the zeitgeist's strength not to despair but instead embrace living in uncertainty, drawing inspiration precisely from that uncertainty and neither counting on nor fearing the judgment of ages yet to come.

Yet even this was too pretentious a way of stating the matter, the zeitgeist supposed. A humbler self-confidence might be what was called for: a sober determination to play one's part today as best one can, regardless of how it turns out to be remembered.

301

Five-second sketch of the author by J. Spohn

Made in the USA
Monee, IL
01 December 2022

19044260R00187